D0848155

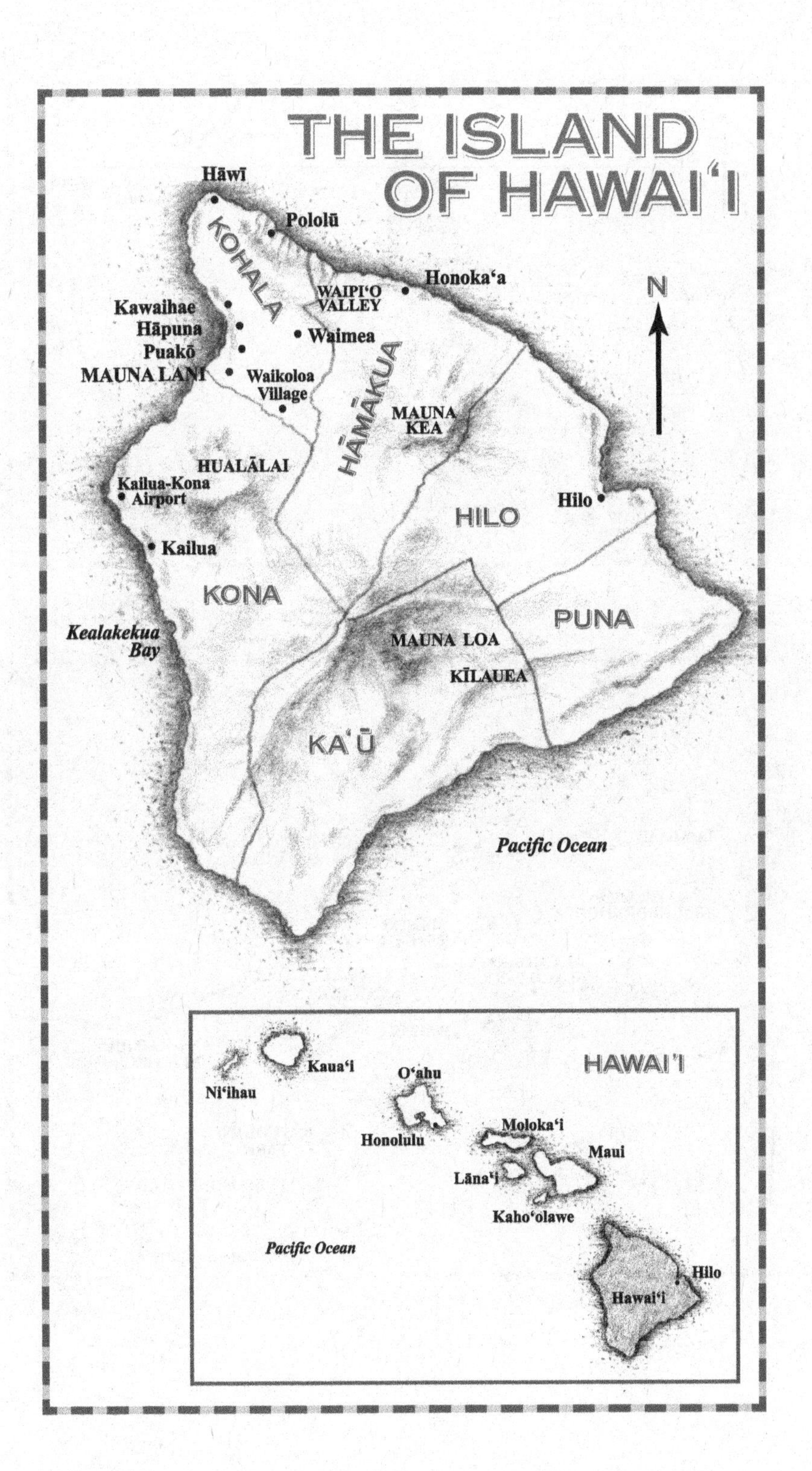
THE ISLAND OF HAWAI'I
Hāwī
Pololū
KOHALA
Honoka'a
WAIPI'O VALLEY
N
Kawaihae
Hāpuna
Puakō
MAUNA LANI
Waimea
Waikoloa Village
HĀMĀKUA
MAUNA KEA
HUALĀLAI
Kailua-Kona Airport
Hilo
HILO
Kailua
KONA
PUNA
Kealakekua Bay
MAUNA LOA
KĪLAUEA
KA'Ū
Pacific Ocean
Kaua'i
Ni'ihau
O'ahu
HAWAI'I
Honolulu
Moloka'i
Maui
Lāna'i
Kaho'olawe
Pacific Ocean
Hilo
Hawai'i

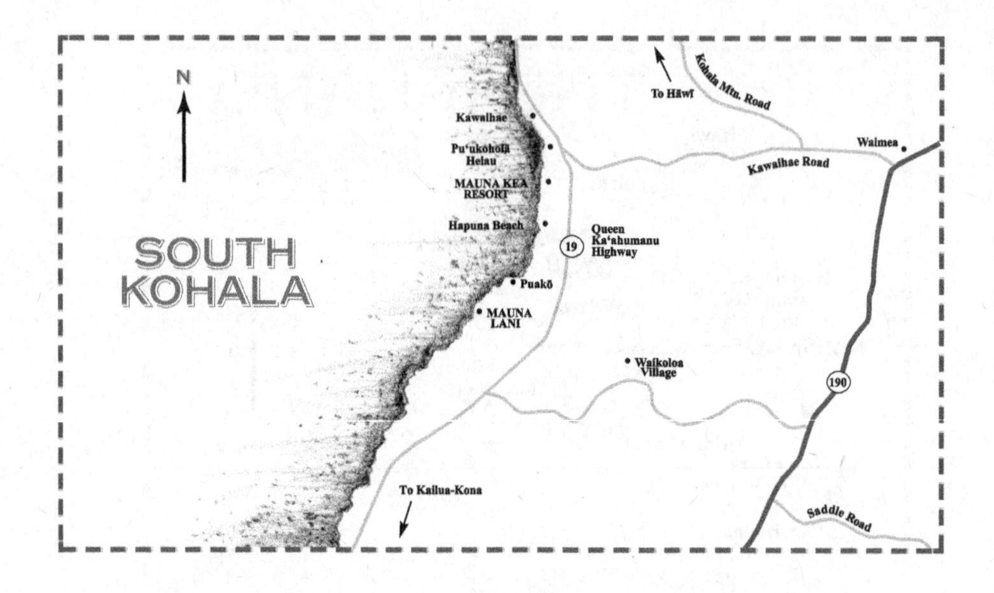
N
SOUTH KOHALA
To Hāwī
Kohala Mtn. Road
Kawaihae
Pu'ukoholā Heiau
MAUNA KEA RESORT
Hapuna Beach
Queen Ka'ahumanu Highway
19
Puakō
MAUNA LANI
Waimea
Kawaihae Road
Waikoloa Village
190
To Kailua-Kona
Saddle Road

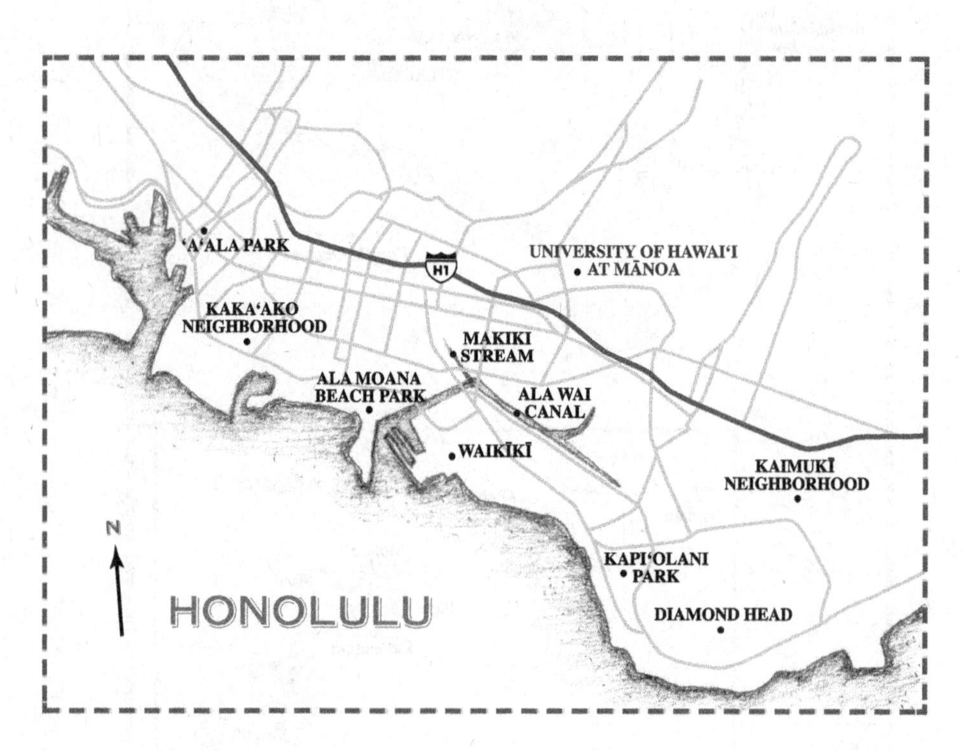
'A'ALA PARK
H1
UNIVERSITY OF HAWAI'I AT MĀNOA
KAKA'AKO NEIGHBORHOOD
MAKIKI STREAM
ALA MOANA BEACH PARK
ALA WAI CANAL
WAIKĪKĪ
KAIMUKĪ NEIGHBORHOOD
N
KAPI'OLANI PARK
HONOLULU
DIAMOND HEAD

DEATH
IN
HILO

ALSO AVAILABLE BY ERIC REDMAN

Bones of Hilo

The Dance of Legislation

DEATH IN HILO

A NOVEL

Eric Redman

NEW YORK

Published in the United States by Crooked Lane Books, an imprint of The Quick Brown Fox & Company LLC.

Crooked Lane Books and its logo are trademarks of The Quick Brown Fox & Company LLC.

Library of Congress Catalog-in-Publication data available upon request.

ISBN (hardcover): 978-1-63910-286-0
ISBN (ebook): 978-1-63910-287-7

Cover design by Kara Klontz

Printed in the United States.

www.crookedlanebooks.com

Crooked Lane Books
34 West 27th St., 10th Floor
New York, NY 10001

First Edition: February 2024

10 9 8 7 6 5 4 3 2 1

For Heather, the love of my life

Deborah and James Fallows,
my lifelong friends

and Gail Mililani Makuakāne-Lundin,
my muse for this one

Like other Hawaiians, he stressed the violence of his ancestors as if it were the only racial trait that could offer him an identity. "We Hawaiians are really a very violent race. There is this profound need in the Hawaiian to shed blood. The blood is not flowing these days."

—Francine du Plessix Gray,
Hawaii: The Sugar-Coated Fortress (1972)

A Note on Hawaiian Language

In keeping with convention, the few Hawaiian words that appear in this book are italicized the first time they appear. Hawaiian words end in vowels and are usually accented on the next-to-last syllable. In Hawaiian, *e* is almost always pronounced *ay* as in *say*. Thus, the *Kea* in Mauna Kea is pronounced *KAY-a*.

Kawika, a Hawaiian transliteration of David, is pronounced *kuh-VEE-kuh*. Hilo, a Hawaiian word, is pronounced *HEE-lo*, not *HIGH-lo*.

The ʻokina, an inverted comma, indicates a glottal stop before a vowel (as in *uh-oh* or *Hawai-i*). The kahakō, or macron, signifies that the vowel sound is prolonged rather than short, as in *Waikīkī*.

The ʻokina is absent when referring to the official State of Hawaii. Otherwise, the ʻokina is always used with the name Hawaiʻi.

Apart from these matters of language, little in this book should be relied on as factually or historically accurate. This is a work of fiction, for which history and contemporary Hawaiʻi simply provide points of departure before imagination and invention take over. The characters are fictional, apart from such historical figures as Kamehameha the Great and Prince Jonah Kūhiō Kalanianaʻole. No resemblance to any person, living or dead, is intended.

In particular, although the Thirty Meter Telescope Project actually is an observatory proposed for the summit of Mauna Kea, and although the TMT has long been debated along the (oversimplified) lines suggested here, no individual or organization, either TMT opponent or supporter, is a model for any character or organization in this book.

The book is set in 2014. Since then, the TMT controversy has transformed, intensified, and become more complex. This is not a contemporary account of the TMT controversy as of 2023. It's more like an origin story—TMT 101.

PROLOGUE

Walla Walla, 2014

The taxi dropped Zoë Akona at the penitentiary a little before eight AM. The morning was still dark and very cold. Daylight Saving Time had returned to the mainland just two days earlier and the sun hadn't yet caught up. By the time Zoë walked from the main gate to the front door—never having imagined how glad she'd be to step from the open air into a prison—she'd covered a substantial distance on foot and gotten seriously chilled. A guard, the third she'd had to pass, asked who she'd come to see.

"Michael Cushing," she replied, her lips so numb she had difficulty forming the words. "He's an inmate," she added. "From Hawai'i."

No one offered her a cup of coffee to warm her hands, but the guard allowed her to remain indoors while he consulted his clipboard and called to check that her visitor's application had been approved. She rubbed her hands vigorously while she waited and quietly stamped her feet in a restrained little tap dance, hoping to warm up. She hadn't thought to bring gloves, wasn't sure she even owned a pair back in Hawai'i; she'd certainly never needed any there. Eventually another guard arrived, bringing her visitor's badge, and took her down a hall through more locked doors to an unexpectedly spacious room. There, through a large window of thick glass embedded with chicken wire, a spectacular sunrise pushed away the night and began to stretch itself across the eastern sky. A prisoner in a blue jumpsuit awaited her as well.

"And the dawn comes up like thunder out of Idaho across the way," the prisoner quipped, jerking his head toward the window while raising his arms slightly so the guard who'd brought him to the room could remove his cuffs. "*You're* the reporter they sent?" he asked, rubbing his freed wrists. "A teenager? I would've thought it's a lot bigger story than that. The Fortunato murder is the most famous homicide in Hawai'i for, what, at least a quarter century? Your editor should've sent Scully."

Zoë remained unruffled. "Yes, I'm the one they sent. I'm not a teenager." She handed him her card. "Zoë Akona of the *Honolulu Star-Advertiser.* Thank you for contacting us, Mr. Cushing. And you may have missed it, but it's safe to say the Slasher murders are a bit more newsworthy in Honolulu right now than the Fortunato case. That's why they sent me and not Mr. Scully. So, shall we sit?"

Michael Cushing smirked, but he sat.

* * *

"So, I'm finally getting out of prison," Cushing said with a laugh. "For a crime I didn't commit. That's the big story. It's why I wrote to your paper." Looking pleased with himself, he leaned his narrow metal chair back and clasped his hands behind his balding head. The guard had told Zoë that Cushing's blue jumpsuit signified "low threat," even though he'd been convicted of two murders and an attempted third. Low threat because he hadn't killed anyone with his own hands—he'd hired a hit man.

Cushing looked much older than Zoë had expected. But he'd been incarcerated for twelve years since the mug shot the Hawai'i police had provided her. Now he also sported a neatly trimmed beard, flecked with gray. Zoë hadn't brought a photographer; she'd planned to take his picture with her cell phone, if he'd agree. Her editor had said they might use it alongside the 2002 police photo if she could get it.

Sitting across from him at the metal table, the young journalist tried to suppress a smile of satisfaction. Zoë was only twenty-three, a novice reporter and jet-lagged after the long flight from Honolulu to Seattle. The tightly enclosed prison room smelled of stale sweat, which made her faintly nauseous. She'd been wearied by the prior day's bumpy ride in a small plane across the Cascades from Seattle, and now she was sleep-deprived as well, having set her alarm for six AM local time, meaning three AM back in Hawai'i. But she recognized a good quote when she heard it.

"Wait a minute," she pressed the prisoner. "You pleaded guilty, didn't you?"

"Yeah, I hired a guy to kill a woman with a baseball bat—Melanie Munu. He was supposed to kill a detective too—Kawika Wong. But he only batted five hundred. Anyway, I've paid my debt to society and all that." Cushing tilted his chair forward again, banging the front legs on the floor—startling the guards—and leaned his bare forearms on the table, speaking earnestly now. "What matters is that the hit man I hired, that unlucky bastard Rocco Preston, did *not* kill Ralph Fortunato. Despite my being convicted for it."

Even better quotes, she thought.

"But you pleaded guilty to all three crimes," she prompted, sounding skeptical, although she already knew the explanation. She'd interviewed Cushing's two prosecutors, both now retired, before she'd left Hawai'i.

"Yes, because I had no choice. The prosecutors wouldn't budge, those assholes. All three or no deal. But you know the Bob Marley song: 'I shot the sheriff, but I did not shoot the deputy.'"

Zoë checked some notes on her spiral-bound pad. "Yet the prosecutors tell me your sentence was the same as it would've been for just the two you admit, the murder of Melanie Munu and the attempted murder of Kawika Wong," she said, continuing to prod him.

The prosecutors had explained the sentencing anomaly to Zoë: they hadn't been sure they could prove beyond a reasonable doubt that Cushing's hit man had killed Fortunato. The hit man himself had been killed—"unlucky bastard," as Cushing had said—and couldn't testify. The part of the hit man's recorded confession dealing with Fortunato, in contrast to the sections detailing his two other crimes, seemed arguably ambiguous. And although the murder weapon, an ancient Hawaiian spear, admittedly belonged to Cushing, he claimed that someone had stolen it from him. So the prosecutors hadn't gambled on taking the Fortunato murder charge to trial. But Cushing really was guilty of it, they'd assured Zoë.

"That was the *plea bargain*," Cushing insisted. "Plead guilty to all three crimes, get fifteen years—three for the price of two—with time off for good behavior. They just wanted to boost their conviction rate, didn't care what I told 'em. Didn't care who really killed Ralph Fortunato. And look, I'm getting out three years early. So I'm not complaining. I'm trying to make a different point entirely."

"Which is?"

"Which is, the person who actually killed Ralph Fortunato is still out there."

Better and better, she thought.

"Okay. If your hired hit man didn't do it, who's the killer?"

"Zoë," Cushing said, leaning his chair back again. "For that you've gotta interview the guy who knows: Kawika Wong. And I wish you would. *I'd* like to know who killed Fortunato—and I'm the guy who went to prison for it."

It would have been a good idea, interviewing Kawika Wong, Zoë knew. But she had a scoop, she had Cushing and the prosecutors on the record, and she wanted the story to run right away. She didn't need to mention Kawika in this first article. Interviewing him later might help propel a second.

So after Zoë snapped several pictures of Cushing, who readily consented and sat there looking smug, she returned to her room at Walla Walla's Motel 6, typed her story on the wobbly desk, and used the hot spot on her cell phone to file it and send the photos by nine AM Hawai'i time. Then she checked out, right at noon Pacific, and began the long trip home.

PART ONE

2014

The most common type of relationship, however, was one in which the victim and offender knew one another but were not directly related.

—Paul A. Perrone and James B. Richmond
"Murder in Hawaii 1992—1997," *Crime Trend Series* 6:2 (1998)

1

Honolulu

On this day, a Saturday, Major Kawika Wong of the Honolulu Police Department stood with a new detective trainee beside a naked and decapitated corpse in Kapiʻolani Park. Although it was still early morning, the air was already warm and heavy and thick with the smells of tropical vegetation and humus. There weren't any maggots on the body yet, and hardly any flies.

In addition to the victim's head, crudely severed at the neck, the hands were also missing. Kawika wondered briefly if the killer had kept the hands and stuffed them with salt to preserve them, as Captain Cook's Hawaiian killers had done centuries before. Probably not, he guessed. Such ancient rituals had disappeared long ago. Anyway, he figured this killer was unlikely to be a Native Hawaiian, at least statistically. He knew that military personnel in Hawaiʻi, including veterans, outnumbered self-identified Hawaiians, and that the armed forces periodically produced killers in uniform. In addition, each year's tsunami of tourists exceeded actual Hawaiians by two orders of magnitude, and sometimes the tourists also included a murderer.

Kawika guessed the killer would turn out to be a non-Hawaiian local, or perhaps military, but not a tourist. The millions of tourists who came to Honolulu every year rarely ventured into the "Lei of Parks" in which city residents took pride. Even Kapiʻolani Park, the dumping spot of this particular corpse and five other naked corpses in the past two months, almost never saw a tourist outside its zoo or aquarium, despite adjoining the beach at Waikīkī.

The dark-haired detective trainee at Kawika's side, dressed in street clothes like Kawika, was young, fresh from the academy. Unlike Kawika, she wasn't Hawaiian. Her name was Yvonne Ivanovna, but she wasn't Russian, just a newly arrived, well-educated Mainlander. She pronounced her surname the Russian way: *Ee-VAHN-uhv-nuh*, accent on the second syllable, just like her first name.

As the chief of Honolulu's homicide detectives, Kawika ordinarily wouldn't mentor a trainee himself. Those days were far behind him. At his age, forty-one, and at this stage of his career, he rarely led homicide investigations personally, just supervised teams of other detectives. But in the department's gender awareness training, he'd been told that a woman's professional success could be powerfully influenced by a favorable experience with her first boss. So he'd plucked Yvonne from the otherwise all-male incoming class of trainees to help her succeed.

The department's culture of racial diversity was excellent—probably the best in the nation. But on matters of gender, HPD was no better than others, despite having Maureen Fremont as chief of police and, earlier, Ana Carvalho, Kawika's original HPD detective partner, as deputy chief. Ana Carvalho had brought about impressive changes, so many that she'd attracted favorable attention and recently been hired away to become chief of police for Hawai'i County—the Big Island. She'd moved to Hilo, where in his twenties Kawika had been a homicide detective trainee himself.

Kawika was aware of how his new trainee would see him: visibly *hapa haole*—literally, half-white—from his Hawaiian father and haole mother; solidly built without being heavy or tall; brown haired instead of black, thanks to his mixed race; and endowed with startling hazel eyes. With his maturity and authority—and a few extra pounds he regretted—he guessed he might seem imposing to her. He'd try to soften his manner.

In Kapi'olani Park this morning, with the air becoming more dense and sticky as the sun rose higher, Kawika wasn't surprised when Yvonne Ivanovna rushed to some nearby bushes to throw up. Then, wiping her mouth, she walked a bit unsteadily back toward Kawika, who'd moved to the shade of a palm tree and waited.

"Good," he said. "You didn't spoil the crime scene. Or your shoes." She nodded, attempting a smile while still looking pale, and wiped her mouth again with the back of her hand. The body wasn't the most gruesome Kawika had ever seen. Apart from the missing pieces, it seemed intact. But the missing pieces were significant, and Yvonne Ivanovna hadn't had much experience.

Before transferring from Hilo more than a decade earlier, Kawika had seen only five murder victims himself—including a murder-suicide. Four of the victims had been shot. The fifth, Ralph Fortunato, had died with an ancient Hawaiian spear plunged through his chest; pretty awful, but not this awful. Dismembered victims had been new to Kawika, too, when he'd come to the big city and joined the Honolulu PD. But until recently he'd never seen a victim in Kapi'olani Park. Now he'd seen altogether too many.

"So, what's your first impression?" Kawika asked. He knew focusing would settle Yvonne a bit. Gamely, she craned her neck to see better as Kawika's veteran detectives and the rest of the crime scene investigators knelt by the body, working carefully as the police photographer moved in for close-ups.

"The victim's male," she began. "Mixed race. And given what body parts he's lacking, it wasn't suicide."

Kawika smiled to encourage her. "Yes," he agreed. "A safe assumption. Hard to cut off your own head, much less both hands. So, what about cause of death?"

"Impossible to know yet," Yvonne ventured, seeming to regain a bit of composure. "He might've been shot in the head. Or bled out, if his hands were cut off first. There's almost no blood here. He was killed somewhere else, just like the others. No obvious entry wounds on the front. Shot in the head or blunt-force trauma—I'd guess that's what happened, or maybe throat slashed before his head was cut off? Depending, of course, on what we find on his back."

"*Iiko, iiko,*" Kawika said. *Good child.* A parent's praise in Japanese. Something he'd first heard long ago, at her age. He liked her quick recovery from nausea and her logical thinking, rudimentary as it might seem. "Can you guess anything about motive?" he asked, testing her a bit more. "If you had to guess, I mean?"

She looked up wryly, then smiled—not what he'd expected. "If I *had* to guess," she said, "I'd guess the motive wasn't robbery. The work's a bit extreme for a stickup artist."

Kawika chuckled appreciatively.

"But seriously," Yvonne continued. "Why does someone dismember a body like this? To slow down identification, sure. Killer and victim may be close enough that the victim's ID would point us toward a suspect. But what else might it be? Jealousy? Anger over something? Revenge? Sex? Or just another random victim of our serial killer?"

Kawika shrugged, but it made him wonder. The rampage of the Kapi'olani Park Slasher, as the media had dubbed the recent serial killer, mystified and frustrated Kawika and his detectives. The park itself, at three hundred acres, was large but not huge, and not remote or forested. It shouldn't have been easy for the Slasher to dump five bodies—his count before this one—while remaining unobserved. The park hosted a zoo and a dozen athletic fields and courts: soccer, baseball, rugby, lacrosse, tennis, basketball, and even an archery range. Joggers circled its two-kilometer perimeter in large numbers, including many at night. It was a busy place, used by locals who could be counted on to report anything strange. Yet still the Slasher had managed to deposit bodies at night whenever he chose.

The Slasher's modus operandi, his MO, was careful and unrevealing. He apparently chose his victims at random, without regard to age, race, or sex. Despite his nickname, he'd slashed the throat of only one, his first. Others had been stabbed or strangled. One had been shot with a 9mm pistol, a Saturday night special impossible to trace. What was consistent was that the killer drained and stripped the bodies and left them near the park's perimeter, where they'd be discovered in the first light of morning. It appeared none of the victims had been sexually molested. Apparently, they'd all just been murdered. It was hard to imagine revenge as a motive, given the number and varied demographics of the five prior victims, who seemed to lack any connection with one another.

The department had assembled a Slasher Task Force of some forty professionals. Besides detectives, there were other HPD personnel, including civilians, who compiled data, performed computer analyses, handled calls on a hotline, and offered assistance to the victims' families. But the detectives were in charge.

Kawika had assigned two detectives to run the Slasher investigation day to day: Jerry Sakamoto and Jerry Rhodes. He called them the "Two Jerrys," but Sakamoto's nickname, Kyu, prevented confusion. Kyu Sakamoto, short with a fireplug build, was a veteran homicide detective whose service at HPD predated Kawika's by a decade. Sakamoto was celebrated within the department for having solved two baffling homicides, one a classic "locked room" mystery and the other involving a car crash that had looked like an accident at first.

Jerry Rhodes, tall and thin, was a recent addition, having arrived from the mainland at the same time as Yvonne Ivanovna. Kawika had added Rhodes to the Slasher investigation a few weeks later, right after the first killing—that of the slashed-throat victim—and before HPD knew they faced a serial killer situation.

Rhodes had come from the Los Angeles Police Department and been briefly famous for catching the prolific Griffith Park Serial Killer in the act of depositing yet another body. Confronted by Rhodes, the killer had tried to flee, but Rhodes had shot him dead. An internal LAPD investigation quietly concluded that Rhodes might have used deadly force unnecessarily. His marksmanship should have allowed him to wound the suspect without killing him; perhaps his adrenaline had gotten the better of him? It had seemed in Rhodes's interest and that of the LAPD for him to move on, once he'd been duly lauded for stopping LA's worst killing spree. Like a pro football coach snaring a top player released by a rival team, Kawika had been happy to offer Rhodes a job. "You'll still have the palm trees," Kawika had said in recruiting him. "But more drinks with paper umbrellas."

Sakamoto and Rhodes, the Two Jerrys, were too busy this morning with the headless body in Kapi'olani Park for Kawika to introduce them to Yvonne. They squatted by the corpse and examined it while Kawika and Yvonne observed their work.

Just then, with an *'ukulele* ring tone, the name of the man who'd taught Kawika *iiko, iiko* popped up on his iPhone: Major Teruo Tanaka, his former boss, the chief of detectives for Hawai'i County, calling from Hilo. The two still talked frequently—once a month at least. Getting a call from Tanaka didn't surprise Kawika.

"What's up, Terry?" Kawika answered. "Big news on the Big Island?"

"Not here," Tanaka replied. "In Walla Walla. Michael Cushing gave an interview to a reporter two days ago. It's in today's *Star-Advertiser*."

"Haven't seen it yet," Kawika said. "We're out in Kapi'olani Park this morning with a new John Doe."

"Ugh, another one?"

"Yeah, unfortunately. Seems the Slasher's ambitious."

"Just broke the Hawai'i serial killer record?"

Kawika understood Tanaka's reference: the Honolulu Strangler had killed five victims in 1985 and 1986. This corpse would bring the Kapi'olani Park Slasher's total to six.

"Looks that way." But even as Kawika said it, something struck him as wrong. Something he couldn't quite articulate.

"I won't keep you," Tanaka said. "Just check the paper later. Cushing got time knocked off his sentence. I should've been told. I'm the one who put him away, after all. Paper says he'll be out next month."

"Yeah, you should've been told," Kawika agreed. "But why's his release a news story? He's just another ex-con. He's not dangerous. He isn't going to reoffend. He might not even come back to Hawai'i."

"No, in fact, the paper says he's going to resettle on the East Coast—as far from Hawai'i as possible," said Tanaka. "But get this, Kawika: the headline is *Big Island Killer Recants Confession on Eve of Release.* Because Cushing still claims his hit man Rocco didn't kill Ralph Fortunato. Same as he originally insisted back in 2002. Same as you told me yourself."

This caught Kawika by surprise. Instantly, he felt as if someone had just opened a forgotten crypt, the one in which Tanaka had sealed the now-moldering body of the Fortunato murder investigation years ago. "I didn't *tell* you," Kawika cautiously corrected his former boss. "I just hinted. I was trying to warn you, Terry. I could have done a better job of it."

Tanaka didn't respond to that. "The paper printed what Cushing said," he went on. "*Ralph Fortunato's killer is still out there.*"

Kawika paused only momentarily. "We both know that's not true," he said confidently. Back in 2002, Kawika and Tanaka had differed on the identity of Fortunato's killer. But neither Tanaka's candidate—Cushing's hired hit man Rocco—nor Kawika's, who had escaped notice and whose name Kawika had never mentioned to Tanaka as a suspect, was still alive. Tanaka's version had been the official one, and it remained so.

"The real killer was dead before Cushing went to prison," Kawika assured Tanaka. That was true regardless of whether Kawika's candidate or Tanaka's was the guilty one—both men had died by then. "No one will believe Cushing. No one will even care."

"Hope you're right. Otherwise, this could be a real can of worms."

A real shit show, actually, Kawika thought. But he didn't say it, because Tanaka hated swearing. Besides, Yvonne Ivanovna was looking up at him as if waiting for further instruction, averting her eyes from the apparent sixth victim of the Kapi'olani Park Slasher lying mutilated at their feet.

Apparent, Kawika thought, as the incongruity struck him. The Slasher's MO included taking the lives of his victims. But not their heads or hands.

2

Honolulu

That night, Professor Elianna Azevado da Silva—"Elle" to her family and friends—awoke around two AM to find her husband staring at the ceiling fan in the bedroom of their condominium high above Ala Moana Beach Park.

"Kawika," she asked sleepily, "what are you thinking about? The Slasher?"

He sighed and turned to face her in the dark, with only the lights of cars on Ala Moana Boulevard playing off the bedroom's surfaces. A few palm fronds, illuminated by display lighting from below, rustled against the window in a breeze from the ocean just beyond the park. He moved closer and reached out to her.

Kawika and Elle could never have afforded the condo in which they were now lying awake. It was a luxury condo in a building whose homeowners' association had enough influence with the city that no tents of homeless people in Ala Moana Beach Park could be seen from its windows. The tents and tarpaulins and crates and cardboard boxes were out of sight, relocated a hundred yards away, behind the trees.

Kawika and Elle were house-sitting. An astronomy professor from UH Mānoa who'd gotten rich designing guidance systems for commercial spacecraft had bought the condo as an investment, like most owners in the building. Now the professor had taken a two-year leave to work on a project with the astronomy department at the University of Washington in Seattle, where Lily, Kawika's mom, remained a professor emerita. Lily had made the connection for her son and daughter-in-law. It provided them, for a time, a respite from Honolulu's pricey housing market.

"Yes," Kawika answered, his arm draped over Elle. "I'm thinking about the Slasher." In the dim light, his tanned Hawaiian skin seemed very dark against hers, with her olive complexion. "But something else too. The Fortunato murder, back at the Mauna Lani."

Kawika knew who'd killed Ralph Fortunato. Elle did too. He'd told her—and only her—long ago. If he hadn't, she wouldn't be lying beside him now. The unlikely romantic relationship and cautious courtship between Elle, a journalism professor who wrote crime fiction under a pen name, and Kawika, a handsome homicide detective who'd come to Honolulu from the Big Island, had been based on honesty from the start. Fortunato's murder would've been too significant for Kawika to omit. It had actually been a relief to confide in someone. Someone he liked and trusted. Someone he'd begun to love.

They'd been married for seven years now.

To his surprise, instead of repelling Elle, the Fortunato murder story and Kawika's decisions at the time—his recognizing some higher moral value than merely catching criminals—had helped endear him to her. She admired what he'd done, given the strange and complex circumstances of that case. She'd even borrowed and fictionalized large chunks of it for her popular mystery *Murder at the Mauna Lani*, the third book in her Detective Malia Maikalani series, written under her pen name Ellen Silver.

Tonight, with her hand resting against his smooth bare chest, Elle asked Kawika, "You're thinking about the article in the paper? The one Zoë wrote about Michael Cushing?" Zoë Akona had been one of Elle's journalism students at UH Mānoa two years earlier, before Zoë had graduated and gotten her job with the *Star-Advertiser.*

"Yeah, that one," he replied.

"She never should've written that without interviewing you," Elle said with irritation. "Never. Who's her editor, I wonder? That was sloppy and unprofessional. Can't believe I gave her an A in my class. I even wrote her a job recommendation."

"She probably couldn't restrain herself," Kawika reasoned. "She thought she had a hot story. She's young; I get it. And she did have the prosecutors on the record, so she had enough to balance what Cushing told her. I wouldn't have told her much anyway. But I bet no one will pay attention to her story. It's really not news. Still, I'll have to talk with Terry Tanaka, and probably Ana Carvalho. If there's an investigation into how we handled the Fortunato case, it'll be Ana's responsibility, now that she's the chief over on the Big Island."

"Ana adores you, Kawika," Elle responded. "All those years as your partner in Honolulu PD. She's my friend too; we *Portuguesas* stick together, you know."

"I do know," he agreed.

"She's not going to investigate you or Terry based on something Cushing says," Elle asserted. "He's a liar and a murderer. The prosecutors say that right in the article. And anyway, his claims are old news in Hilo, correct?"

"Yeah, for sure. But still, I think Terry and I better come clean with each other about the Fortunato case. That won't be easy. Not after so many years. We've never talked about it. Just locked it away and tried to forget. Then I left Hilo and came here."

"No, it won't be easy," Elle agreed. She turned to lie on her back, looking at the ceiling fan herself now with its play of light from the softly flowing traffic on the boulevard below. "I hadn't thought of that. If there's an investigation, Terry will be in more trouble than you, won't he?"

"Afraid so," said Kawika. "*If* there's an investigation. And not just because he's still in Hilo—because of what he did back then. And what the two of us covered up."

* * *

To his relief, though, the next few days seemed to prove Kawika right. No one cared what soon-to-be-ex-convict Michael Cushing had to say. Despite the newspaper story, no one asked Kawika about it. Not even his colleagues at the Honolulu PD, although some certainly knew he'd led the Fortunato murder investigation on the Big Island more than a decade earlier. It had been a particularly notorious case.

Kawika checked—apparently no surviving relatives from the Fortunato murder case still lived in Hawai'i. After Fortunato's death, his widow, Corazon, had moved to California with her infant son. She'd remarried and turned her back on the Big Island, where she'd lived for only three years.

In Honolulu the hunt for the Kapi'olani Park Slasher was the big story: front page, above the fold in the *Star-Advertiser.* Multiple victims. A mysterious serial killer. And given the randomness of the victims, a whiff of panic was beginning to show up in Honolulu homes and workplaces and citizen-in-the-street interviews.

"If it bleeds, it leads," Kawika told Tanaka by phone after a few days passed. "That's what the news is all about—the Slasher. Although he never leaves much blood. We haven't even found this last guy's head or hands."

A few mornings later, however, Kawika did find something: a plain white envelope on his desk. He opened it to find a pencil-written note in block capitals: THAT ONE WASN'T MINE. KPS. The message itself didn't entirely surprise him; someone else dropping an unclad corpse in Kapi'olani Park, infringing on the Slasher's territory, apparently offended his sense of propriety. But how the message reached Kawika was a puzzle.

Kawika rose from his chair and shouted into the squad room, waving the envelope. "Hey! Anyone know how this got to my desk?" But half his detectives hadn't come to work yet, and the others shook their heads.

"No, boss," a few answered, and turned back to their work.

Could this brief note really be from the Kapi'olani Park Slasher? Kawika wondered. Or might it be a tasteless prank? And if the latest victim wasn't the Slasher's, as Kawika had come to suspect, then whose was it? Kawika's team hadn't yet established the dead man's identity; no help there.

Kawika's misgivings remained: Why would the Slasher take the victim's head and hands when he never had before? As souvenirs? Didn't sound like the Slasher. To prevent identification, or at least delay it? That would make sense, but the Slasher had never concealed his victims' identities before. His five previous victims had been ID'd within hours.

Though Kawika had already touched the paper, he slipped on gloves to prevent further contamination, then bagged the note and envelope and walked them to the lab himself. They'd be checked for whatever clues they might provide. Kawika doubted there'd be any. The Slasher was too careful for that; he'd have worn gloves when writing that note and used tap water to seal it.

Perplexed about the note and the newest body—and with the newspaper story on Cushing's accusations having prompted no follow-up, just as he'd hoped and predicted—Kawika decided to stop worrying about whatever Cushing had to say. Although Kawika knew very well that part of it—only part of it—was true.

3

Honolulu

"Why did the Slasher have to pick Kapi'olani Park?" complained Dr. Noriko Yoshida, the chief medical examiner for the City and County of Honolulu. She looked across her desk at her visitors, Kawika Wong and Yvonne Ivanovna. "Kapi'olani Park's way across town, Kawika. And we got that rush-hour traffic. The Slasher's responsible for half our homicides this year. Why couldn't he pick 'A'ala Park, next door to our building here? Much more convenient."

"Probably couldn't pronounce 'A'ala," Kawika deadpanned. "Didn't have a way to ask directions."

Dr. Yoshida laughed. "Well," she said, "I don't think this one's the work of the Slasher anyway. For reasons I'll explain."

The medical examiner raised her half-frame glasses from the lanyard dangling around her neck and glanced at some notes she held in her hand. "I wish I could tell you more about your headless guy," she said. "I can't remember many corpses that provided this little information. But since he's missing his head, at least we've got a nickname for him: Robespierre."

Kawika hadn't expected allusions to the French Revolution, but he and Yvonne smiled politely. "Just tell us what you can, Noriko," Kawika requested. He nodded to Yvonne, who began taking notes on a department iPad. Kawika realized he should have warned her that Dr. Yoshida considered herself very witty. The police considered her just plain quirky, if not downright strange. Too much time with dead people, they said; not enough time with live ones.

"Okay," Dr. Yoshida began in a didactic tone. "Robespierre's male, of course. Almost certainly very dark haired, though without his head, that's not completely certain. Not much body hair, apart from that trimmed strip of pubic hair, and pubic hair doesn't always tell the whole story. We can guess his age, of course—late thirties, give or take a few years."

"Time of death?" Kawika asked.

"Probably within an hour or so of midnight," she replied. "That's based on body temperature and rigor mortis, the weather conditions that night. It's complicated, though. He was killed somewhere else, right? Don't know anything about conditions there. For what it's worth, he died with a reasonably full stomach. Some shrimp and Chinese peppers not fully digested yet, although most of the noodles are gone. So if he died around midnight, he probably had a late dinner."

"Ethnicity? Race?"

"Hapa haole, obviously," Dr. Yoshida said. "Have to guess about the non-haole part. Hawaiian, probably, or other Pacific Islander? Maybe even Japanese or Filipino. Hard to tell. Have to guess a bit about his height too—it would help if we had his head. Five eight, maybe five nine. We know his shoe size would be nine and a half, so his feet are consistent with that height. If you had an ID, Kawika, we'd have ways to confirm it from his feet. But no one has much of a database of footprints, not even the FBI."

"How about his weight?"

"We can guess that pretty well, even without his head. We've got him at one forty-nine on the scale. Head would add eleven pounds or so, so you're at one sixty. Figure the missing blood at six-point-five percent of body weight—I'd say seven percent if he were missing all of it—and that's another eleven pounds, more or less. So you come out about one seventy, one seventy-one, something like that. Not a big guy. Montgomery Clift sized, I'd say. You know Montgomery Clift, Kawika? Old movie star?"

Kawika shook his head and looked at Yvonne, who shook her head too. Dr. Yoshida beamed and leaned forward, about to speak.

"Blood type? DNA samples?" Kawika responded, not wanting to learn about Montgomery Clift just then.

"Yes," replied Dr. Yoshida, disappointment in her voice. "As I mentioned, there was still some blood; he wasn't drained or washed off entirely. It's Type A, nothing unusual in the Rh factor or otherwise; we'll give you details in the report. We took some for DNA samples. They can be run against the database. But unless he's got a record, or unless we have some idea who he is, the DNA won't do you much good, will it?"

"Not yet, but it's good to have," Kawika agreed. "What can you tell us about the mutilations?"

"Not done by a professional," Dr. Yoshida replied. "This Robespierre didn't die on the guillotine." She paused to smile at her joke. "But his head wasn't just hacked off either, although that might be your first impression. The killer used a rough-toothed saw. I'm thinking a pruning saw, maybe. Handsaw, not a power tool. Which is interesting—a tool of opportunity, maybe? Smaller teeth than a crosscut saw but bigger than a hacksaw or carpenter's saw, for example."

Dr. Yoshida seemed pleased with that recitation. Kawika decided to indulge her. "You've got all those saw blades here?" he asked, as if it were remarkable for a medical examiner's office to have an assortment of saw blades handy.

"Oh yes," she boasted. "All those and lots of others too. Surgical saws, chainsaws, table saws, marine saws, bandsaws, jigsaws—got 'em all."

"Lotta bodies get cut up on jigsaws?" Kawika asked.

She responded with a smile, then continued. "Anyway, for Robespierre here, the wrist cuts are decently well done, but the ones on the neck are a mess. Probably the killer turned the body a couple of times, working from different angles. Tore an awful lot of skin and flesh. As I say, not the work of a professional. But whoever cut up the body was almost certainly right-handed, if that helps at all. When you're sawing something, you keep the blade in a straight line with your arm. In this case, the direction of all the cuts is that of a right-hander."

"Great," Kawika said sarcastically. "That really narrows the field."

Dr. Yoshida raised a cautionary finger. "The Slasher is right-handed too," she pointed out. "We know that from his first victim—the one whose throat he actually slashed. But still, I don't think the Slasher did this."

"Why not?" Kawika didn't think this was a Slasher victim either, but he wanted to hear the doctor's reasons.

"You're the detective, you and this young lady here." Dr. Yoshida tilted her head toward Yvonne. "But Robespierre's just too far from the Slasher's MO. All the others the Slasher just killed, stripped, and dumped. No mutilations, apart from the fatal slash or stab or crushed throat or whatever else he did to kill them, depending on the victim. No dirt on those corpses either, hardly any blood, and the Slasher wrapped them in something very nearly sterile before dropping them off. Almost antiseptic, the Slasher's murders. This one, the blood's been cleaned up a bit, but not thoroughly, and some of the dirt on the body isn't from Kapi'olani Park. Some came from the trunk of a car, it seems—pretty typical car trunk bits. Robespierre hadn't been wrapped up, or at least not very well."

"Cause of death?" Yvonne inquired, looking up from her note-taking and asking a question for the first time. "Any idea?"

Dr. Yoshida swiveled her chair to face the trainee. "Find the head," she said, "and you'll probably find a bullet hole, Ms. Ivanova." She pronounced the name—the wrong name, even though she was reading from Yvonne's card—*ee-vuh-NO-vuh*. She sounded as if she considered the bullet hole an almost foregone conclusion, something too obvious to have to say.

"Thank you," Yvonne said politely. "But it's Detective, not Ms. And the name's *Ivanovna*, not Ivanova. Two *n*'s, accent on the second syllable."

Dr. Yoshida looked surprised. She seemed to bristle at being corrected. "Oh, sorry," she said, almost mockingly. "*Ivanovna*, then."

"What about tattoos or scars?" Kawika interjected, trying to keep things professional. "And piercings? Any of those?"

"I was coming to that," Dr. Yoshida said. She looked at Yvonne and smirked. *She's preparing something*, Kawika thought. He'd learned long ago that Dr. Yoshida took pleasure in unsettling visitors. One of her quirks. Kawika again realized he should have warned Yvonne. Especially since this smirk seemed somewhat hostile.

"No tattoos or scars at all," the doctor replied. "But he's got a genital piercing. A penis head piercing, to be specific. Goes through the ridge of the glans, from front to back, or back to front, depending on how you look at it. Most people would look at it from the front, of course, except for Robespierre himself. Parallel to the penile shaft, in any event. Guys who go in for this type of thing call it a dydoe piercing. That's spelled D-Y-D-O-E, *Detective* Ivanovna. It's for genital jewelry. Probably a D ring or a little silver barbell, in this case. Not wearing either when he arrived here, of course. But it's a piercing he kept in active use, not one that's healing up."

Dr. Yoshida looked at Yvonne. "I hope you're not shocked, Detective Ivanovna," she said with mock solicitude. "I wouldn't want to make you uncomfortable. But you missed this at the crime scene, didn't you? So I wonder: Do you avoid looking at penises in general, or just this one, for some reason?"

Kawika hadn't expected *that*; it was outside Dr. Yoshida's normal repertoire. He started to object. "C'mon, Noriko. You can't just—" But Yvonne Ivanovna interrupted him.

"Not shocked at all, Doctor," she responded cheerfully. "My last boyfriend had two of those piercings. He was going to get a third, so I had to ditch him. Damned uncomfortable for the woman, those things. Well, the D ring wasn't so bad, actually. You could lead him around with it. But that little barbell—ouch. And yeah, given my experience, I should have spotted the piercing at the crime scene. But I'm used to seeing dydoe piercings with jewelry in them, not empty."

Dr. Yoshida gave Yvonne a wide-eyed, jaw-dropping stare. Kawika's jaw almost dropped too, but he recovered quickly. "Thanks, Noriko," he said smoothly, standing up to end the interview before things got worse—this was just a training exercise for Yvonne, after all. "Unless there's more, we'll leave you to it. Really appreciate your time. Team Robespierre will look forward to your report. As always."

"Great to meet you," Yvonne added pleasantly, reaching out to shake the limp hand of the medical examiner.

As they walked from the building, Kawika turned to Yvonne. "That was pretty clever," he said, with a tone of grudging admiration. "Noriko was hoping to shock you. She does that a lot. I should've warned you. But you shocked her instead."

"I had to try," Yvonne said, smiling. "Making up stuff like that is one of my specialties."

"Wait, what?" Kawika exclaimed. "You didn't really have a boyfriend like that?"

"Ew! Of *course* not! What kind of woman do you take me for, Officer?" she teased, pretending indignation. She stopped walking and faced him with arms akimbo, tapping one foot.

Kawika shook his head and laughed. "*Iiko, iiko*," he said, and stuck out a fist; she bumped it with hers. "You got me that time, Yvonne."

All at once he experienced a pleasant sensation, like a memory, one that flowed in and suffused him. He recognized it from years before, from when he'd been Yvonne's age. He'd first felt it with Terry Tanaka in a bonding moment like this. He tried to remember just when and where that moment had occurred; there had been so many with Tanaka.

"But seriously," Yvonne resumed. "What does Dr. Yoshida think we study at the academy these days? How to write a parking ticket? We had a whole course on human genitals, for gosh sake. Men, women, children. Pretty detailed. You can't believe what people do with genitals, their own and ones that aren't theirs at all. After that course I swore I'd stay away from other people's genitals forever. And I actually did, for a while."

4

Honolulu and Hilo

When Zoë Akona returned to the *Star-Advertiser* after her trip to Walla Walla, she was surprised to find Bernard Scully, the paper's senior crime reporter, wanting to talk with her. Zoë knew Scully was immersed in the Kapi'olani Park Slasher case; she found herself curious and a little awed that he'd seek her out.

"Congratulations," he began. "Your piece on Michael Cushing was terrific, Zoë. A really fine bit of work. You got good quotes from Cushing and the prosecutors. You're also a talented writer; I'm impressed. The managing editor agrees. She asked me to give you some suggestions for a follow-up. You know, ways to keep the story going."

Zoë felt flattered. In the past, Scully had never even said hello when they passed in the hall—probably never known her name, she suspected. Yet here he was, a legend of Honolulu journalism, a guy who'd won a Pulitzer, practically the only *Star-Advertiser* reporter with a corner office, going out of his way to mentor her a bit.

Silver-haired with a ruddy complexion and well into his sixties, Bernard Scully was someone Zoë had always thought and spoken of as Mr. Scully, never as just plain Scully, which his more senior colleagues called him. He always wore a starched white shirt with an aloha-print bow tie, making him a distinctive figure in the newsroom. Outdoors he wore a straw boater, making him distinctive on the street as well. All in all, she thought, as unlike her as anyone could be. Yet here he was, offering to help her.

"The thing is," Scully resumed, "as it stands, you've just got a one-day story. A convict about to be released denies he killed someone; the prosecutors insist he did. And the guy's moving to the East Coast, not back to Hawai'i. Not a lot of zing there, right? I mean, it *was* a spectacular murder—I covered it myself—but that was twelve years ago, and worse, it happened on the Big Island, where we don't have a lot of circulation. So how can you turn it into something folks in Honolulu will want to read today? A story that could lead to bigger things—maybe even a Pulitzer—if it goes somewhere. Especially if there's a scandal involved."

Zoë tried to stay calm, but she was fascinated. She felt her pulse quicken.

"Seriously," Scully went on. "I was about your age when I won my Pulitzer for a series on the Honolulu Strangler, back in 1986. What if you can turn this Cushing-Fortunato murder thing into a series yourself, something big? It's too early to know if the facts will support that. But the boss is willing for you to pursue it."

Now Zoë felt flustered. "How *should* I pursue it?" she asked. "I'd love your advice, Mr. Scully."

"Well," he replied, smiling. "I *have* got a few ideas for you. And please, call me Scully."

* * *

Zoë was too young to remember Fortunato's murder or Cushing's arrest. But Zoë's journalism class at UH Mānoa and her professor's fictionalized tale, *Murder at the Mauna Lani*, had piqued her interest in the case once she got to college. Now, with her editor's support and Bernard Scully's suggestions, she was free to dig into it.

Although she worked in Honolulu, Zoë had grown up in Hilo. Before interviewing Cushing, she'd read everything about the case in the newspaper archives of both cities and pieced together the official story of the murder, said to have been committed by Cushing's hit man stabbing Fortunato on a South Kohala golf course with an ancient Hawaiian spear. Zoë felt certain that renewed coverage of the Fortunato case would appeal to *Star-Advertiser* readers; true crime always did. But she needed a fresh news hook to revive it—something beyond Cushing's assertions of having been wrongly convicted. That had been Scully's first bit of advice.

"You covered what Cushing and the prosecutors say," he'd told her. "Now you're looking for something more. Where's the next place to look?"

"Victim's family?" she ventured hopefully.

"Well, they probably don't know more than the prosecutors. And even if you can find them, disturbing the family might be tricky."

"Okay," Zoë responded. "Then how about the cops? Kawika Wong, like Cushing suggested?" She felt a qualm as she said it; Kawika Wong was married to Professor da Silva, Zoë's first journalism mentor—in fact, her only one before Scully. What if there *was* a police scandal, as Cushing asserted, and Kawika was implicated?

"Yes, the cops, certainly. But don't start with Kawika," Scully had advised. "He's high-ranking at HPD now; he'll just blow you off unless there's something new to ask him. If and when it becomes time to interview him, I can help you. I see him every week on the Slasher case."

"So, who should I start with?"

"Talk to his Big Island colleagues first, or ex-colleagues. You've got to be subtle; cops stick together. You go to the Big Island—go visit your parents, let's say. Kawika isn't there, so you're asking other cops what they remember, what they think about Cushing's claim. Get them talking, see what they say; maybe you'll find a discrepancy with the official account, maybe not. But you might get something worth asking Kawika, something you can use for the next story."

Zoë knew just how to put Scully's advice to work. After an additional day of research, she flew home to Hilo to interview Detective Sammy Kā'ai of the Hawai'i County Police. Sammy hadn't worked on the Fortunato case, as far as Zoë knew. But he was part of her family's *'ohana*, their circle of relatives and close friends, and he was a homicide detective about to retire. Zoë knew Sammy was divorced, drank too much, and resented his Hilo police career stalling out. She also knew he tended to talk a lot.

"So, what'd you want to know?" Sammy asked with amusement when she'd found him at his modest—and, she couldn't help noticing, distinctly messy—home on Hilo's outskirts. It was a working-class dwelling from an earlier era, with a red metal roof, green board-and-batten sides, and white trim—"charming" in realtor-speak. There was no one but Sammy on the premises. Sammy's motorcycle, a metallic green Harley, stood under the disintegrating roof of an open shed, looking dusty and disused. Zoë noticed the chrome had begun to discolor.

Sammy, off duty, was dressed in cargo shorts and a faded aloha shirt that failed to cover his belly. His brown arms and legs sported tattoos. One forearm was large enough for the classic image of Pele, goddess of fire, her head encircled with a floral ring, a *lei po'o*, and her hair and robe streaming out behind her.

Zoë had a tattoo herself, a garland of hibiscus flowers above her ankle. Like Sammy, she wore shorts, and she crossed her brown legs to display the tattoo more prominently, propping her ankle conspicuously on her opposite knee, hoping it might evoke a Hawaiian bond and make the interview easier.

"You on duty, or just dropping by to say aloha?" Sammy inquired further. "Here to talk story? Or are we on the record?"

Zoë knew why he asked. Off the record, two Hawaiians chatting would normally speak their mutually intelligible pidgin. On the record, Sammy would speak everyday English. "Yes, Sammy, I'm on duty and we're on the record." Zoë started her recorder and put it on his discolored koa-wood coffee table. "You've had a long career. A colorful one. I think our readers would enjoy reading the reflections of a retiring homicide detective. Especially your most exciting cases. True crime is big these days. So yeah, let's talk, but not talk story."

That was the ruse Zoë had decided upon; a useful one, she thought, since it might yield material for a weekend magazine story even if Sammy failed to help her on the Fortunato case.

Sammy leaned back and smiled. He held a bottle of Kona lager, half-finished, and gestured with it as he spoke. Zoë noted circular stains on his table from previous bottles—countless ones. Zoë's armchair had holes in the seat cover, and the arm of Sammy's couch appeared well used as a scratching post. Zoë thought the house smelled faintly of cat, but no cat appeared.

"I didn't start out in homicide," Sammy began. "In fact, my first case was about a champagne cork."

"What?" This wasn't where Zoë wanted Sammy to begin.

"Yeah," Sammy laughed. "First day at work was New Year's Day. Guy put another guy's eye out the night before, popping a bottle of champagne. Didn't take the metal off. Wire cut through the pupil, ripped up the retina. Pretty awful. Boss sent me to investigate. Did the guy do it on purpose? The victim said yes, wanted to press charges. The cork-popping dude denied it, of course. Difference between an accident and a felony. Insurance versus prison."

"Interesting," Zoë said, not meaning it and not caring how the case had turned out. "So, what happened when you got to homicide, Sammy?"

"Well," he said. "Let's see."

For an hour, Sammy regaled her with incidental tales, obviously enjoying himself. He began with the guy in Puna who'd pushed his wife into a stream of molten lava. One leg hadn't burned completely before the lava cooled. A charred foot had stuck out. The DNA matched the wife's.

"Yeah," Sammy said. "Hawai'i leads the nation in murder by magma. Technically it's lava, but murder by magma sounds better."

Sammy next told her about Harriet, who'd rented a meat grinder on one side of the Big Island and ground up her husband at their home on the other. She'd flushed him down the toilet in small batches. She'd told neighbors and his boss he'd gone to Denmark to visit relatives. Someone had finally reported suspicions to the police. Harriet hadn't realized her house didn't connect to a sewer line. Sammy had found a thousand bits of human flesh in her septic tank.

"Gross," Zoë said. "Still, it *is* kinda funny."

Partway through Sammy's reminiscences, the skies burst and Hilo's midafternoon tropical downpour began. As the deluge grew in intensity, the metal cottage roof resonated at first with the intermittent sound of a few distant tambourines, then the staccato chorus of a dozen angry castanets, and finally the overlapping booms of kettledrums, swelling into a continuous pounding. Sammy spoke in a booming voice himself, adding to the decibel count, but Zoë could still follow him even if, she suspected, her recorder could not. She wondered, though, if the roar of rain pounding on that roof might help explain Sammy's lack of a live-in partner; it rained a lot in Hilo.

Deftly, Zoë nudged Sammy's storytelling around to the case that interested her: the murder of Ralph Fortunato on a golf course in South Kohala in 2002.

"What about cases that got solved wrong?" she asked, trying for subtlety, as Scully had coached her. "Or never got solved at all? There must've been some."

"There always are," Sammy acknowledged. "Well, there was Shark Cliff."

"Ooh. I remember that one!" she exclaimed, even though it wasn't the case she wanted to hear about. "It gave me the creeps. I was only in fifth grade. But I thought you solved it?"

"Part of it. This is probably what you remember: someone dropped some druggies off the cliff at Waipi'o Lookout. The victims were Hawaiians. But there was also another victim, one who'd been handcuffed earlier.

Before we ID'd him, I called him the Handcuffed Haole. Eventually I did ID him as a guy named D. K. Parkes, from Waimea. But we never found where he fit in."

"You caught the killers, though?"

"Only the killers of the druggies."

Zoë wrote quick notes on her spiral-bound pad. For interviews she didn't rely on the recording alone, certainly not with a metal roof amplifying a downpour.

"But what about this D. K. Parkes guy? He didn't fit with the other Shark Cliff victims?"

"No. You wanted to hear about unsolved cases. That one was unsolved—maybe, maybe not."

"Maybe not?"

"Not solved by me, okay?"

"By someone else, you're saying?"

Sammy sipped some beer and resumed. "D. K. Parkes, he was an operator for other people's sportfishing boats. A skipper for hire on the Kona and Kohala coasts. He worked out of Kawaihae mainly. Didn't do drugs, far as we could tell. We had a handcuffed victim in a different case too—another haole, but we couldn't link the two."

"The other case being . . . ?" Zoë asked, sounding innocent. *Now we're getting somewhere*, she thought.

"The murder of a resort developer over in South Kohala. Ralph Fortunato. You heard of that one?"

"Oh, yeah. I read about it in the morgue—the newspaper's morgue, that is," she replied. "We've still got one, for old issues. I read a novel based on it too—*Murder at the Mauna Lani*. Did you read it?"

"Yeah." Sammy waved his beer bottle dismissively. "Murder mysteries, they're nothing like real murders. Not like actual homicide investigations."

"But the Fortunato case got solved, right?" Zoë asked, pressing on. "The guy who pleaded guilty—you know, Michael Cushing—he's over in Walla Walla. I just interviewed him. Did you see my story in the paper?"

"No. Don't see the Honolulu paper much. You interviewed Cushing in Walla Walla? That's a long trip—hope your boss picked up the tab. I thought newspapers were all broke?"

"Discount fare on Alaska," she said. "Motel 6."

"Ah. Well, anyway, what'd Cushing tell you?"

"He insists he didn't do it—his hit man didn't do it, I mean. He says whoever killed Fortunato is still out there."

"He's probably right. I never bought Cushing for that one," Sammy volunteered.

Pay dirt, Zoë thought. "Really? Why not?" she asked.

Sammy frowned and paused briefly. "It wasn't my case," he finally responded. "But put it this way: the murder weapon was an old wooden spear. You know, an *ihe* in Hawaiian. Cushing admitted he owned it; he was a collector. The thing is, that spear actually belonged to Kamehameha the Great once. Two hundred years old, yeah? Never made sense that Cushing would have his hit man use that particular spear instead of some other one. Cushing claimed someone stole it from him. That makes more sense."

"And if someone stole it from him . . . ?"

"Then someone else probably killed Fortunato. Just like Cushing says. And the killer framed Cushing by using that spear. Successfully, yeah? So the killer got away with it."

This is on the record! Zoë thought, silently congratulating herself that she hadn't agreed to a casual conversation in pidgin.

"Wow," she said aloud. "Who else can I ask about this?"

"Well," replied Sammy. "You could start with Kawika Wong. You must have read about him. That was his case. His wife's the one who wrote the book."

"Oh, yes," she said. "I'm planning to interview him." *Good thing I didn't do it earlier*, she told herself. *Asking him now will be much better.* Yet her qualms about cornering Kawika, the husband of her mentor Elle da Silva, stirred again. She'd need Scully's advice, and maybe the help he'd offered, for this particular situation.

"Ask him about D. K. Parkes, the Handcuffed Haole at Shark Cliff, while you're at it," Sammy said. "Ask Major Tanaka too, for that matter. Teruo Tanaka, that is. Everyone calls him Terry. Chief of detectives for Hawai'i County—my boss, for another week or two. He's here in Hilo; Kawika's over with Honolulu PD these days. Terry and Kawika knew more about Fortunato's real killer than they let on, that's for sure. More about D. K. Parkes too."

"I'll ask 'em," she said, making a note and suppressing her excitement. "Thanks." Now she had two detectives to interview, not just one, and two murders to ask about. At least one follow-up article for sure. She could hardly wait to tell Scully; *came for the Fortunato case, stayed for D. K. Parkes.*

"By the way," Sammy added. "Someone called me a month ago with questions about D. K. Parkes."

"A reporter?" Startled, Zoë felt an unpleasant sensation: the sudden fear of being scooped.

"No, a state tax lady from O'ahu. Trying to track down D. K. Parkes and his family, she said. Claimed she didn't know he was dead. Didn't care about that. Just wanted to know if he had kids, where they might be."

"Kids?"

"Yeah. Guess you still gotta pay taxes, even if Daddy gets murdered."

5

Honolulu

Now on the verge of retirement, Honolulu's police chief, Maureen Fremont, had worked her way up through patrol and narcotics and vice and eventually to homicide, from her initial position as a twenty-five-year-old typist, the best starting job she could get in 1974. The news media and family and friends called her Mo. Her two thousand HPD officers and civilian employees, on the other hand, often called her Mighty Mo, a nod to her toughness. The borrowed nickname came from the *U.S.S. Missouri*, the World War II battleship moored at Pearl Harbor and standing watch over the *U.S.S. Arizona*, her sunken sister, and the remains of the eleven hundred men entombed there.

Chief Fremont had asked Kawika to brief her about the latest corpse in Kapiʻolani Park, the headless one. Kawika took the opportunity to let his two lead detectives on the Slasher case, those who'd examined the body, have some time with the chief. And he'd brought along Yvonne Ivanovna for the experience. In the waiting area, while the four waited to be admitted to the chief's inner office, Kawika introduced Yvonne to the two detectives.

"These guys are in charge of catching the Slasher," Kawika explained. "Both named Jerry, inconveniently. You saw them at the crime scene. This tall guy is Jerry Rhodes. Like you, he joined us from the mainland recently—LAPD, where he put an end to the Griffith Park Serial Killer. This other Jerry, the one who's not so tall, who's compact and condensed, he's Jerry Sakamoto, and he's been with Honolulu PD since statehood."

"Ha! That's what Major Wong says about anyone who got here before him," Sakamoto responded, extending a hand to Yvonne. "My nickname's Kyu. A joke by my parents. Before I was born, a guy named Kyu Sakamoto, a Japanese singer, had a silly hit song—'Sukiyaki.' Made him famous for a while. Anyway, call me Kyu."

"Joking parents," said Yvonne Ivanovna. "We've got that in common." Sakamoto looked puzzled. "*Ee-VAHN ee-VAHN-uhv-nuh*," she demonstrated. "Apparently 'Denise' or 'Margo' or 'Valerie' wouldn't do." She shook hands with Sakamoto, then turned to shake hands with Jerry Rhodes.

"I think we were on the same plane together," she told him. "We were sitting next to each other at LAX, right? While we were waiting to board. I thought I recognized you at the crime scene, but I was a bit distracted. It was my first homicide."

"I don't remember seeing *you* at LAX," Rhodes responded, with what struck Kawika as a lascivious smile. Rhodes looked Yvonne up and down, a visual body search. "I can't *imagine* how I missed you," he added.

"Hey!" Kawika snapped. "Watch it, Jerry. This is Honolulu, not LAPD."

"Sorry." Rhodes, reproved, did sound genuinely contrite. "Forgive me."

Kawika still scowled, but Yvonne smiled at Rhodes tactfully. "No worries," she said. In that moment, disconcertingly, Kawika realized that Yvonne, an attractive young woman, probably endured comments and looks of that type all too often.

Just then an officer emerged from the chief's office and invited them in. The chief rose from her desk to shake hands. She was dressed in what Kawika, out of uniform as usual, considered her full battle regalia: four gold stars on each of her dark epaulets, eight stars sewn in two rows above her right chest pocket, and her chief's badge—with a large number *1*—above her left. Her hat with its double gold braid, however, hung on a clothes tree behind her desk. She had her hair pulled back in a twist.

The chief already knew the Two Jerrys. She seemed pleased to meet Yvonne. "You can't go wrong learning from Kawika and Kyu," she told the trainee. "About Jerry, I'm not so sure. He's not a *kama'āina* yet." In other words, not a longtime Hawai'i resident. She was teasing, they could tell, and the detectives shared a polite laugh before taking their seats.

"Okay," Chief Fremont said, turning to business. "Is this new victim the Slasher's sixth? Or someone else's? A copycat, maybe?"

"We're thinking he may be someone else's," Kawika responded. "I'll let Kyu and Jerry explain. By the way, for now we're calling him Robespierre."

"Robespierre?" The chief sounded astonished. "We're using French history now? Who's next, Napoleon?"

"Noriko Yoshida came up with the name," Kawika said.

"Oh, Noriko!" Chief Fremont sighed comically and rolled her eyes.

The detectives smiled knowingly. Kawika motioned to Sakamoto to proceed.

Kyu nodded and began. "This victim is missing his head and hands, and we can't identify him yet. That's something new, Chief. All the others have been intact and easily identified. So, on first impression, this doesn't look like the Slasher. On the other hand, it's not unheard of for serial killers to deviate from their standard MO for some reason. That means we can't draw the copycat conclusion quite yet."

"Jerry," the chief said, turning to Rhodes. "You agree?"

But then she stopped. "Sorry," she said, holding up her hand. "Let me go back and explain to Yvonne. We've had only one other serial killer in Honolulu, Yvonne—one real one, I mean. The Honolulu Strangler back in 1985 and '86. I'm not counting Eugene Barrett, the guy who murdered his three wives, one after the other, over three decades. The Strangler, on the other hand, raped and murdered five young women—five we know of, anyway—all within a year. We never caught him. And he never deviated from his MO."

Kawika cleared his throat. "Of course," he added, "there may've been some confirmation bias there, Chief. I mean, the only murders the department credited to the Strangler were ones that fit his MO, right? So if he murdered others without following that MO, he was never a suspect in those."

"True," the chief conceded. "We did wonder a bit about that at the time. But regardless of how many victims the Strangler murdered, he got away with it. So let's focus on the Slasher now and not let *him* get away with it. I don't want any of his victims ending up on our cold case website, Kawika. So go ahead, Jerry."

Jerry Rhodes moved forward to sit on the edge of his chair. "This decapitated one wasn't the work of the Slasher," he stated flatly. "It's probably a copycat, just as you say, Chief. These serial killers don't deviate that much from their MO—unless they have to kill someone unexpected, that is."

"Like the Griffith Park guy who might've killed you?" the chief asked. "You surprised him in the act, didn't you?"

Rhodes smiled. "Well, fortunately for me, he turned and ran. But you know, Chief, generally these serial killers had something wrong with them as children—cruelty to animals, pyromania, long-term bed-wetting. That used to be called the Macdonald triad. Now we know it could be something else too. But whatever it is, it triggers some specific need for them to kill their victims, and that specific need tends to lock them into their own particular MO."

"Okay," said the chief. "But why would a copycat cut off the victim's head and hands? The Slasher hasn't ever done that, has he?"

Rhodes shook his head. "No," he conceded. "But remember, we haven't released details about the bodies the Slasher's dumped. We've said that the victims were naked and found in Kapiʻolani Park. A copycat killer would have to guess what else to copy."

"Noriko Yoshida doesn't think the Slasher did it either," Kawika added. "And as you know, there's that note on my desk, supposedly the Slasher saying the headless victim wasn't his."

Kyu Sakamoto shook his head. "I don't think we can put much weight on that note, Chief. People send us stuff every day, pretending to be the Slasher. It's sick. Not helpful either."

Jerry Rhodes disagreed. "I think we can put a good deal of weight on that note," he said. "We didn't get it in the mail. It was on Major Wong's desk. What if you'd found it on your desk, Chief? You wouldn't consider it the same as stuff that comes through the mail, would you? Anyone can send us a letter. But managing to get a message to Major Wong's desk? That's pretty unusual. Someone clever who thinks his message is important. My guess is it's the Slasher."

No one spoke for a moment. Then the chief raised her eyebrows, followed by a quick nod. "All right," she said. "Let's leave it there. For now, we'll assume the headless vic probably isn't the Slasher's. And that the Slasher is smart as hell. But we knew that already."

The detectives started to stand, but she motioned for them to stay seated. "I've got something to tell you," she said. "As you know, I've announced my retirement and promised to step down as soon as the mayor names my successor." She looked at Kawika, a small smile deepening the wrinkles at the corners of her eyes. "That search is about over. But I visited the mayor yesterday about timing. I told her I do *not* want to quit with the Slasher case unsolved. I don't want a repeat of the Strangler case. I'm determined to see this bastard caught on my watch. You're the ones who'll do it. And until you do, I'll keep sitting right here, at least within reason. I'll get you whatever you need. But you get *me* this killer."

The chief stood, and the detectives did too. “Kyu and Jerry, thank you very much for coming. Go catch him! Kawika, I’d like another minute. Yvonne, you’re welcome to stay.”

“Actually,” Chief Fremont admitted, once the door had closed, “it’s Yvonne I want to speak with. I just wanted to do it in a smaller group. It’s good for you to hear this too, Kawika.”

The chief emerged from behind her desk and stood in front of Yvonne, nearly toe-to-toe. “Detective Ivanovna,” she said, “don’t be fooled by the fact that Honolulu’s chief of police is a woman. We’ve got a chief of police who’s a woman because we’ve got a mayor who’s a woman. We’ve got a mayor who’s a woman because of the voters, not because of the men in this department. It’s a tough department. You’ll have to be a tough cop. And good. Very, very good. It’s hard work. Harder than for a man.”

Kawika noticed Yvonne pale slightly. She thanked Chief Fremont and shook her hand.

“One more thing, Yvonne,” the chief added, holding the door. “I recommend you rethink your hairstyle. Go for the shortest hair you’re comfortable with, or if you want to keep it long, try a braid or twist or a bun.” The chief turned her head so Yvonne could see her own twist. “But whatever you do, if you want these men to take you seriously, get your hair off your face. I’m not saying it’s fair. I’m just telling you the way it is. And you’ll look more professional, too, when you’re wearing your hat or cap.”

As Kawika stepped through the doorway, the chief poked his chest with an admonitory finger. “Don’t you dare let those SOBs eat her up, Major.”

“I won’t,” he assured her.

“I’m counting on you, in more ways than one,” Mighty Mo Fremont reminded him, removing her finger from Kawika’s chest and pointing it toward her desk. She held the pose long enough to give him a knowing wink.

6

Honolulu

After more time in her newspaper's morgue, Zoë Akona called Terry Tanaka in Hilo to ask about Cushing's claim that the real killer of Ralph Fortunato had avoided arrest and escaped justice. She wasn't going to tell him right away that Sammy Kāʻai, a Hawaiʻi County homicide detective and Tanaka's direct report, had just endorsed that claim. She wanted to surprise him. Sometimes surprise could be a reporter's best tool for eliciting candor, she'd learned in Elle's journalism class. Even if—perhaps especially if—the interviewee hadn't intended to be candid.

With a sigh of exasperation, Tanaka told Zoë, "Look, you should've called me first. I'll tell you now what you could have printed then. Michael Cushing is a convicted murderer. He confessed to that crime. He hired a California contract killer named Rocco Preston to murder Fortunato, not just Melanie Munu. And to kill Kawika Wong too—which failed, fortunately."

"Yes, that *was* fortunate," she agreed, hoping to encourage him.

"Rocco the hit man dictated and signed a confession," Tanaka continued. "He said Cushing hired him to kill Fortunato with a spear, and Fortunato *was* killed with a spear—a spear that Cushing admitted he owned. There was other evidence from Cushing's house on Fortunato's body, special objects to make it look like Hawaiians killed Fortunato. Cushing was trying to frame them. Not only did Cushing admit hiring Rocco to kill Fortunato, he pleaded guilty to it in court, in front of a judge and the media. So the Fortunato case was open-and-shut. And still is."

"Then why after all this time would Cushing deny just that one killing?" she asked. "Right when he's getting out of prison?"

"No idea."

"Really? Cushing told me he had no choice; it was part of the plea bargain."

"Well, he accepted the plea bargain, didn't he? He could have rejected it, but he didn't. Could he explain the things from his house on Fortunato's body? No. Could he explain why, when we searched his home, we found handcuffs that had left distinctive marks on Fortunato's wrists? No. He hired a hit man to kill Fortunato and make it look like some Hawaiians did it. That's why he's in Walla Walla; he wouldn't have survived in a Hawaiian prison. He might have gotten away with the murder too, if his hit man hadn't confessed. Moral of the story? If you want to kill someone, don't hire a hit man. Do it yourself."

Zoë had one last question about Cushing. "You're the man who put him away. What do you think about him getting out after only twelve years?"

"No comment," Tanaka replied. His tone was harsh. That pleased her. She'd write it as *"No comment," Major Tanaka replied harshly when asked . . .* Her editor might remove the adverb, but it was worth a try.

"Okay, then let's switch topics," she resumed. "What about D. K. Parkes, the haole victim at Shark Cliff? Sammy Kā'ai says you and Kawika Wong know more about this D. K. Parkes than you said at the time—which was nothing, far as I can tell from the archives."

"Sammy Kā'ai?" Tanaka asked in surprise. "You talked with Sammy?"

"Yeah," she replied. "About Cushing's claim and about D. K. Parkes too. Sammy's a family friend, basically 'ohana. I was in Hilo, so I stopped by to see him." She didn't volunteer that she'd gone to Hilo for the sole purpose of seeing him.

"And Sammy talked about those cases?"

"Yup, he did. He agrees with Cushing, by the way."

Tanaka was silent for a moment. She guessed he was fuming. But then, with a snort, he answered, "Okay. D. K. Parkes? I'd forgotten all about that poor guy. Shark Cliff had nothing to do with the Fortunato murder, Ms. Akona. And there's nothing I can tell you about D. K. Parkes. That case was a dead end. Wait—poor choice of words. Say instead, 'We never established anything in that case.' Exact opposite of the Fortunato case. We established everything in that one."

"Okay, Major," she said. "Thank you for speaking on the record," she added, just to remind him she'd quote him directly.

Afterward, Zoë walked down the hall and up the stairs to Bernard Scully's corner office. "Got a minute?" she asked.

* * *

"Yeah, Bernie," Kawika said, taking Scully's call. "Nothing new on the Slasher today, I'm afraid."

"Not calling about the Slasher," Scully replied. "Something out of the past, back when I first met you. Back on the Big Island: the Fortunato case. I'm helping a young colleague with a story."

Caught off guard, Kawika said, "What? The story that already ran?"

"No, a follow-up she's writing. She interviewed Sammy Kā'ai and Terry Tanaka and got more material from them." Scully repeated what Sammy and Tanaka had told Zoë, then waited during a silence on Kawika's end. "I'm sure you can tell me more," Scully prodded. "She's got your colleagues on the record, and she's going with what they said. You were the lead detective. Given what Kā'ai and Tanaka told her, the story will probably be front page."

"That case is more than ten years old," Kawika finally replied. "I left the Big Island pretty much right after that, and I've been in Honolulu ever since, as you know. Sammy didn't work on the Fortunato case, as I recall. If she's talked with Terry Tanaka, there's probably nothing I can add, Bernie. Nowadays I remember my wife's novel that's loosely based on the Fortunato case better than the investigation itself. I'm sorry, I really don't think I can help here."

Before Kawika could hang up, Scully quickly asked, "Then how about a D. K. Parkes? You know, the haole who got tossed off Shark Cliff?"

Scully had to wait for a reply. "That wasn't even my case, Shark Cliff," Kawika finally responded. "That was Sammy's, and she's already talked with Sammy, you say? So, same answer. I can't help, I'm afraid."

Yeah, Scully thought. *Maybe you actually are afraid. Or beginning to be.*

He turned to Zoë, who faced him across his desk, impatient to hear what he'd learned.

"I think you may be onto something," Scully said.

* * *

Zoë felt very grateful to Scully. He'd helped her in two important ways. By calling Kawika, he'd spared her the discomfort of confronting Elle da Silva's husband herself. He'd also offered to add his byline to hers when the article ran, thereby elevating her status at the paper and the prominence of the story. Scully had even insisted her name should go first. "It's really your story," he said. "Not mine."

But Zoë wanted additional material to make the story more substantial. She decided to call Sammy Kā'ai to see if he could help again.

"Sammy," she began, "Tanaka gave me the standard 'We did everything right' line about Fortunato. Kawika Wong wouldn't give us anything at all about Fortunato or D. K. Parkes. I had our top crime reporter call him, a guy who covered the Fortunato case. Who else can I talk with? You and I are off the record this time, by the way. I just need some suggestions."

Sammy took a moment to think. "Kawika's sidekick on the Fortunato case was Tommy Kekoa, a detective up in Waimea," he replied. "Tommy's still there. Probably won't talk if Kawika won't."

"Tommy Kekoa," she repeated, writing it down.

"But like I said, he won't talk if Kawika won't. Now, there was a woman too—Patience Quinn, from San Francisco. A journalist like you. Had a condo at the Mauna Lani. She's the one who reported Fortunato's body. Kawika ended up banging her. Sorry, shoulda said she and Kawika '*had a relationship*.'" Zoë could imagine Sammy gesturing with his beer bottle in one hand and putting air quotes around that phrase.

"She was a key witness," he continued, "so *sleeping* with her"—Zoë imagined more air quotes—"was really unprofessional. Don't know if she still goes by the name Quinn. Anyway, Kawika might have told her a lot—pillow talk, you know. I mentioned her to that tax lady from Honolulu. Thought the Quinn woman might be able to give the tax lady a lead on D. K. Parkes, since she and Kawika were tight at the time."

"Wait a minute—where's this Quinn woman now?"

"No idea," Sammy said. "Just know she was from San Francisco back then, a journalist, like I said, and Kawika spent a lot of nights with her. When he'd show up at the station, which wasn't that often, he looked like she'd worn him out."

"An unusual name," Zoë mused aloud, ignoring Sammy's last remark. "If she's still using it, I gotta believe your Honolulu tax lady would've found her."

"No doubt," Sammy said. "That tax lady was on a mission to find those Parkes kids. If there *are* any Parkes kids. Who knows?"

7

Honolulu

Kawika slapped the *Star-Advertiser* down on his desk in disgust. "Christ," he said aloud. He ran his hand through his graying hair. *Getting grayer by the minute*, he thought. Then he dialed Terry Tanaka in Hilo.

"You seen the *Star-Advertiser* today, Terry?" he asked.

"No. Hasn't shown up here yet. What's in it?"

"Zoë Akona's interview with Sammy Kāʻai," Kawika answered. "Plus what you gave her and what I told Bernie Scully, a reporter who's helping her. No idea why she decided to interview Sammy. Or why Sammy talked to her about Fortunato. He hardly worked on that case."

"What'd she print?"

"She wrote that Sammy agrees with Cushing, backs up Cushing's story. That someone besides Cushing's hit man probably killed Fortunato. Also, that Sammy suggested she ask you and me about D. K. Parkes."

"Ugh," Tanaka grunted. "Sammy's taking early retirement, thank goodness. It's time he left. No judgment anymore. He's drinking a lot, letting himself go all to heck." *All to heck*, Kawika noted, *not all to hell. Typical Tanaka.*

"Sammy's bitter—bitter at me, still carrying a grudge about you," Tanaka added. "His retirement party's at Aunty Sally's Luau House next week. With the amount he drinks these days, I hope the department can handle the bill. Anyway, I can't discipline him at this point. Not for this. Not just for shooting his mouth off."

"Well, this reporter, she's a bloodhound on a scent," Kawika said. "Big trip to Walla Walla, then to Hilo to talk with Sammy in person, then interviewing the two of us. She mentioned Elle's book in the article—she was actually Elle's student at UH Mānoa. Elle gave her an A, so she's well trained. And she's not done, it sounds like. She should be writing about the Slasher like everyone else, but instead she's basically reopening the whole Fortunato case. Shark Cliff too, with D. K. Parkes. It's bad."

"Very bad," Tanaka agreed.

"It's also terrible timing. You know I'm bucking for chief over here, Terry. There's a nationwide search, but it's the mayor's decision, and the mayor likes me. Chief Fremont is helping too. I think I've got the inside track, if I don't blow the Slasher case. I'm ready to move up, Terry. I've spent enough years around dead bodies. But if this Zoë Akona reopens the whole Fortunato thing—and Shark Cliff too—if she goes really deep, I can't defend everything we did."

"Everything *I* did, you mean," Tanaka said.

"No, *we*, Terry. There's stuff I never told you."

"Stuff you spared me, more like it. You warned me the facts didn't fit, at least on Fortunato. You told me not to worry about D. K. Parkes, that he'd been an accomplice to some unsolved old murder, but you said his own killer was already dead, so we couldn't arrest the killer. I was happy to let that one go; probably shouldn't have been. But, Kawika, we *did* have Cushing cold for your shooting and for Melanie Munu's murder."

"Yeah, Terry, we did. And Cushing's not disputing that. Sammy isn't either. But now Sammy and Cushing have both said publicly that someone else killed Fortunato. And that you and I know more than we made public about D. K. Parkes."

"Damn," said Tanaka, using his strongest epithet. "There'll be an investigation now for sure."

"Right," Kawika agreed, thinking what he couldn't say to Tanaka: *a big-ass investigation.* He looked around his office at the pictures on his walls and bookshelves. Among others, there were photos of him with Tanaka in uniform, both smiling. Photos of him with Ana Carvalho, also in uniform and smiling broadly.

He cursed under his breath. He realized he wouldn't see smiles on those two faces again anytime soon. All because of a cub reporter who wasn't quitting, who was determined to drag that unsettling corpse of the Fortunato investigation from its long-sealed crypt and force everyone to look at it again—this time in the unsparing Hawaiian sunlight.

8

Honolulu

After their session with Chief Fremont, Kawika convened a meeting with Kyu Sakamoto, Jerry Rhodes, and other top members of the Slasher Task Force. He again invited Yvonne to accompany him.

The task force had become stressed and discouraged. In recent meetings, some members had grown uncharacteristically snappish and short answered. Despite repeatedly reexamining the scant evidence and every halfway credible—even barely credible—tip on the task force hotline, they had almost nothing to go on.

"So we're pretty sure Robespierre isn't a victim of the Slasher," Kawika began, picking up where they'd left off with the chief. "Which leaves the number of the Slasher's victims at five. He seems to have paused. Does anyone believe he's stopped?"

"Serial killers don't stop," Jerry Rhodes said glumly. "I imagine he paused because Robespierre getting dumped in Kapiʻolani Park surprised and, uh, what's the word?"

"Disconcerted?" Kawika suggested. He'd rediscovered *disconcerted* in reading one of Elle's books. It seemed apt quite often.

"Yeah, disconcerted him," Rhodes confirmed with a nod to Kawika. "Threw him off for a bit. But no reason to think he's stopped."

Kyu Sakamoto frowned. "The Strangler stopped," he offered. "He stopped at five. So it does happen."

"Well," Rhodes replied, "let's assume the Slasher's not going to be satisfied with tying the record. He'll want to break it. We've got to assume he'll kill again, at least one time. Probably more. Going for the gold, you might say."

"Okay," Kawika said. "I'm willing to assume that. Now, how do we stop him? What exactly do we know?"

"We know," Rhodes said, "that he's almost certainly a white male, for starters. Serial killers just are. We also know there're about a hundred and fifty thousand white males in Hawai'i. We can probably exclude guys older than sixty-five and younger than fifteen. So maybe ninety thousand eligibles. We can figure he's on O'ahu, not the other islands. That makes, what? A pool of at least fifty or sixty thousand guys."

Sakamoto spoke up again. "We can guess he's tall and right-handed, based on how the first victim's throat was cut. That narrows the field a bit, but not much. We can also guess he's heterosexual, since his first victim was a woman. That's a pretty reliable indicator, according to the FBI's profiling data."

"And that takes us down to about thirty to forty thousand possibles, instead of fifty to sixty," Rhodes remarked. "It doesn't narrow things much further to say he dumps the bodies at night, or dumps them naked, or dumps them in a park."

Kawika asked if the task force had any theories about the killer's motivation.

"It doesn't seem sexual," Rhodes said. "Apparently he's just a killer, not a sex pervert." Kawika noted how the task force deferred to Rhodes, the one member with serial killer experience, although Kyu Sakamoto was senior in service at HPD, and the detective Kawika had thought would be the task force's natural leader.

"He just enjoys killing people?" Kawika asked. It wasn't a new question. They'd gone over this before. They kept going over it because the Slasher, with his random selection of victims and his great care with physical evidence, methodically denied them real clues.

No one responded. Kawika decided to bring Yvonne into the conversation. "Yvonne actually had the benefit of the FBI's course on serial killers, didn't you?"

Yvonne seemed a bit flustered by this invitation to speak. "It was just a summer course when I was studying criminology in college," she began. "I don't think it's likely to be of much use here."

"None at all?" Kawika asked.

"Well, maybe one thing," she conceded. "They kept drilling into us that profiling a serial killer is a very inexact science. It wouldn't help us narrow down a field of thirty thousand possibles. What they emphasized, over and over, is that you should never let your profiling efforts distract you from your main focus: catching the killer."

"Very true," Rhodes responded, clapping his hands a few times, then giving her a thumbs-up. Yvonne's face reddened.

"But we're not just doing profiling," Rhodes continued.

He cataloged the more basic police work in which the task force was engaged. Continuing to look for anything that might link the victims; it still seemed that nothing did. Determining from family members and coworkers when and where each victim had last been seen alive. Establishing that the victims had all been taken while on foot, with their cars and bicycles parked exactly where they should have been. Guessing that the Slasher must have a day job, since two of the victims had disappeared on weekdays after normal working hours, two on weekends, and one at lunchtime. Trying to establish from those facts and the distribution of the victims' disappearances where the Slasher must be centered in Honolulu, where he could work or live or handle the bodies. Looking for a pattern the Slasher might have revealed accidentally.

"Looking for a pattern," Rhodes repeated. "But not finding one."

Kawika turned next to Sakamoto, who added that they continued to use every means available to find matches for whatever bits of stray DNA the medical examiner had found on any of the bodies. There was no DNA on any victim, however, that was on any other victim; there was no common DNA anywhere. The only DNA for which they'd found matches came from family members of the victims, mere traces on the victims' hands or cheeks. There was nothing under the victims' fingernails that suggested defensive wounds or yielded the DNA of any stranger.

After listening to these discouraging accounts, Kawika said, "Unfortunately, I think we've probably got to catch him in the act of dumping a body. That means at least one more victim. But he's going to go back to Kapi'olani Park, right?" No one in the room dissented.

"I wish we could *disconcert* him again"—Kawika smiled at Jerry Rhodes—"by dropping another decapitated body in Kapi'olani Park; maybe he'd be outraged enough to cough up another clue. But I can't think of any ethical way to do that." He smiled for the entire group to signal that they shouldn't take him seriously.

"So, Kyu," Kawika said, wanting to bring Sakamoto back into the discussion. "What would you do to catch him at Kapi'olani Park?"

"Well," Sakamoto replied, "I've been thinking we could ring the park with police cruisers. Say, one every two hundred yards or so. Maybe ten or fifteen cars. Some could be empty. But some could have officers sitting there, ready to move. We start doing that, the Slasher's not going to know at first that some of the cruisers are empty. He'll probably think the officers from those cars are patrolling the park, flashlights off, ready to pounce. But it's a game for him; otherwise he wouldn't be dumping them all in Kapi'olani Park to begin with, right? So he may rise to the challenge. We might get him that way."

"Or we might just drive him to use another park," observed Rhodes.

Kawika shrugged. "Even if he moves to another park," he said, "at least we'll throw him off his routine. He'll have to start over, to some extent at least. If he believes he's invulnerable, he may make a mistake. So it's worth a try. We've certainly got enough cruisers. Whether we have enough cops for all that extra night duty is another matter. Anyway, Kyu, why don't you draw up a plan, including staffing and shifts. I'll go over it with you and we'll see what happens. I wish we could stop the next killing, though."

Rhodes shook his head sadly. "I'm afraid we can't, boss," he said. "The Slasher will keep killing unless we catch him. Until we catch him, I mean. Or unless he just stops for reasons of his own."

After the meeting, Kawika walked down the hall with Yvonne. She suggested an added thought. "Killers want to avoid getting caught," she said. "Most of them, anyway. But that's not their motivation for killing—it's not *why* they kill people. This guy might be different, though, if it's not some sexual thing. His motivation might simply be to prove that he *can't* be caught. That he's smarter than the cops. He's a genius and we're fools. Killing people and not getting caught might be his way of drawing attention to his own brilliance. You know, a narcissist."

Kawika pondered that all the way to his office. When he got there, his assistant had a message for him.

"The EMTs say a dozen body bags are missing from their stockroom," she said. "They reported it to procurement so they could get replacements. Procurement thought it was something worth passing along to us here in homicide."

"Great," Kawika responded wearily. "So now in addition to the Slasher, we're going to have a bunch of murders by the Honolulu Body Bagger?"

9

Mauna Kea Beach Resort

Pursuing her lead from Sammy Kā'ai and focused now on D. K. Parkes as well as Fortunato, Zoë Akona did a little online research and easily located Patience Quinn, a San Francisco freelance journalist. She also found that Patience owned a second home at the Mauna Kea Beach Resort and, with a phone call, that Patience happened to be visiting. Zoë made an appointment—"journalist to journalist," she assured Patience—and took a quick flight to the Big Island to interview her.

Zoë rented a subcompact car at the Kailua-Kona airport and took her chances driving thirty miles north on Route 19, the Queen Ka'ahumanu Highway, known locally as the Queen K, reputedly the deadliest in the United States for head-on collisions. No highway divider, lots of highway drunks and drugged-up drivers. She wished she were driving a Hummer.

The guard at the Mauna Kea gatehouse was expecting her and told Zoë how to find Patience's house on the Fairways South. A sign at the driveway said *Hale Kea*—Hawaiian for "White House." The single-story structure was faced entirely with white stucco, with cobalt-blue tiles for a roof. It wasn't new or grand, not even Hawaiian looking, but it was surrounded by coco palms and flowering Hawaiian trees—white plumeria, bluish Hong Kong orchid, flaming-red-orange royal poinciana—and a profusion of bougainvillea in all colors. Zoë parked her tiny car and walked across the polished-lava flagstones to the koa front door. She removed her slippahs as soon as Patience invited her in.

"You want me to confirm that I knew Kawika Wong back in 2002?" Patience repeated, after seating Zoë on the *lanai* and handing her some iced tea. "Yes, I did know Kawika Wong back then. I haven't seen him since. You can print that if you want. Otherwise, we're off the record, 'journalist to journalist,' as we agreed."

Zoë affirmed this with a nod. Though she was inquiring about events from many years earlier, Zoë could see that Patience—a strikingly good-looking, diminutive blonde with flawless skin—wasn't old, or even conventionally middle-aged in appearance. She'd taken good care of herself, it seemed, and had well-defined arm and leg muscles. Low body fat, obviously. Tennis? Zoë wondered. Time in the gym? Zoë was athletic herself, and she knew others considered her an attractive young Hawaiian woman. But Patience, she recognized, was a rare beauty.

Zoë hadn't seen any family photos in the house as they'd walked out to the lanai, just numerous bold Pegge Hopper prints—signed originals—of massive Hawaiian women, idle and expressionless, wearing solid-colored muumuus and bright flowers in their jet-black hair. There was nothing on shelves or the walls to indicate Patience had kids or a family. Zoë had also noticed Patience wasn't wearing a wedding ring. Divorced? Widowed? Never married? Zoë knew only that Patience had once been a lover of Kawika Wong, according to Sammy Kāʻai. That was why Sammy had suggested she might know something about D. K. Parkes.

"And journalist to journalist," Patience continued, "I have to ask: Did you interview Major Wong before you ran your Michael Cushing story?"

Zoë was tongue-tied momentarily, then replied. "Uh, you really mean, *shouldn't* I have interviewed Major Wong first? I've asked myself that too. But I was over in Walla Walla, I had to catch a flight, I already had the prosecutors as sources, and I was on deadline. Later I did interview Major Tanaka, and a colleague of mine who knows Major Wong interviewed him. We quoted them in my second piece, after I interviewed Sammy Kāʻai, another detective from Hilo. You saw that story?"

Patience nodded, but Zoë still sensed her disapproval.

"I'm not going to talk about Major Wong," Patience said crisply. "If you want to know more about him, call him yourself. Or read his wife's novel. She hasn't fictionalized him or the Fortunato case too much, even though she made her detective a woman."

"Of course, of course!" Zoë replied. "I've read her book—who hasn't? And I was her journalism student at UH Mānoa. But I'm not here to ask about Major Wong or his wife. Honestly. I want to ask about something different."

"And what would that be?"

"I'm wondering," the reporter said, "whether someone—a tax lady from Honolulu, maybe—contacted you recently about a man named D. K. Parkes?"

"A tax lady?" Patience replied, shaking her head and looking confused. "No, not a tax lady. And not from Honolulu. A woman from Kahului, on Maui, calling from a life insurance company. Something about her company not having paid what they should have on a policy when D. K. Parkes died. She said he'd been murdered, and the policy was supposed to have paid more because of that. She was looking for his children, asking me if he had any. Why are people asking me about D. K. Parkes all of a sudden? I've never heard of him, much less his children."

"He was murdered here on the Big Island," Zoë informed her. "The police nicknamed him the Handcuffed Haole before they identified him. Killed at Shark Cliff, the Waipiʻo Valley Lookout, back in 2002, if you remember that case."

"Vaguely. I don't remember anything about a handcuffed haole, though. Or any haole at all, for that matter."

"Okay," said Zoë, pressing on. "The Shark Cliff murders were happening at Waipiʻo at the same time Ralph Fortunato was killed. You found Fortunato's body, yeah?"

"Yes," Patience answered cautiously. "I found his body here—well, at the Mauna Lani, not here at the Mauna Kea. I had a place there then. But Waipiʻo is on the other side of the island. All I know about Shark Cliff is what I got from the news at the time. Nothing to do with the Fortunato case, was it?"

"That's what I'm trying to figure out," said Zoë. "Whether this murder of D. K. Parkes relates to the Fortunato case somehow."

"Why would it?"

"It may not. But that Hilo detective I quoted in my second story, Sammy Kāʻai, believes it might. He thinks the murders are linked because they occurred at almost the same time, both victims were haoles, and both had handcuff marks—and the handcuffs were missing. No other victims at Shark Cliff were haoles, much less handcuffed."

Patience frowned, considering this. *It really is new to her*, Zoë realized.

"And you think Major Wong knows about that possible connection?" Patience asked. She seemed genuinely puzzled.

"That's what his former colleague Sammy Kāʻai suspects. Major Wong, plus Major Tanaka, who was Detective Wong's boss in Hilo at the time.

Sammy thinks they covered up what they knew in both cases. It's just his guess, but a pretty well-informed one."

Patience stiffened visibly. Then she stood up suddenly, signaling an end to the interview. "I've never met Major Tanaka in person," she said coolly, as she motioned a startled Zoë from the lanai toward the front door. "And I don't remember Detective Wong ever mentioning this Shark Cliff case at all, much less anyone who got murdered there. Sorry I can't help you. And I'm sorry you came all this way just to see me."

"No problem," replied Zoë, standing now. "My parents live in Hilo. I'll go see them now, if my little rental car can make it over the Saddle Road. And besides, you did help me."

"I did? How?"

"You told me there's an insurance lady," Zoë said. "Until today I just knew about a tax lady. Now there are two, a tax lady in Honolulu and an insurance lady on Maui. Both looking at the same time for children of D. K. Parkes, who's been dead for years. Curious, don't you think?"

"Maybe he left something behind," Patience suggested. "It happens." Then she closed the door, even before Zoë had her feet back in her slippahs.

10

Honolulu

"Kawika, thanks for taking my call," said Ana Carvalho, the relatively new chief of police for Hawai'i County.

Kawika knew her well. They'd worked together at Honolulu PD for more than a decade, first as detective partners for years until they'd both been promoted, she to deputy chief and he to head of homicide. He looked again at the photo on his office shelf of the two them together, smiling. A nice color photo in a koa frame, taken less than a year earlier.

"Hope you understand," she began. "There has to be a review of the Fortunato case. I've got one of my detectives, Sammy Kā'ai, saying publicly that you and Terry Tanaka covered up the truth about a major homicide. Plus a killer recanting his confession after twelve years in prison. The state's biggest newspaper is on it. A review can't be avoided. I wish it could be, but it can't."

"I understand," Kawika replied cautiously.

"But I'm not turning this over to a commission," the chief continued. "This all happened when Haia Kalākalani was chief and I was still in Honolulu. So I'm going to conduct this myself. Personally."

"Very good," said Kawika, silently exhaling a deep breath and feeling a bit reassured.

"And I'm not going to call it an investigation," she went on. "I'm calling it an 'official review.' I'm not putting anyone under oath. I don't want to interrupt your work or Terry's, or have people start hiring lawyers. And no matter what I find, I'm definitely not thinking of hanging you or Terry out to dry."

"Good to know," he said gratefully. "Thank you."

"Look, Kawika, I worked with you in Honolulu longer than anyone did here in Hilo," she continued. "I'm friends with you and with Elle. We Portuguesas, we stick together, yeah?"

"Yeah," Kawika said. "Elle says that too."

"I like both of you a lot," Ana said. "And you're a good cop. I know you're in line to become chief in Honolulu—a much bigger job than mine here. I don't want this review to derail that."

"We always thought you'd get the Honolulu job yourself," Kawika said diplomatically. "You were the deputy, after all. Lot shorter jump to chief than it is from homicide."

"I would've tried for it," she responded, with a small laugh. "But the mayor was never going to pick me. I haven't ever told you this, and don't tell anyone else. But years ago, back when you were still in Hilo, I arrested her daughter. The kid was eighteen, a senior at Punahou—pretty privileged, yeah? But she was turning tricks to get drugs. Oral sex for *pakalōlō*—weed—and more for other stuff. The mayor was still a state senator back then. She asked me to let the kid go, don't ruin her life, and so forth. She could've been charged as an adult. Keep the whole thing quiet, her mom begged me. Which I did. But as a result, I knew she'd never trust me once she became mayor. Not fully. She'd worry I'd become J. Ana Hoover and use it against her somehow." Ana laughed a second time, this time ruefully. "And don't you use it against her either, now that I've told you," she admonished.

"Of course I won't," Kawika promised. "I never knew any of that. What a crappy situation. I'm sure I would've done the same thing you did."

"Anyway," Ana continued, "much as I don't want to harm your prospects—or Terry, of course, my top detective—I've got to be objective. Unbiased. I can't write the conclusion in advance. But I'll say this right now: I know Sammy Kā'ai was once a fine detective—in certain respects, at least. I also know he's a troublemaker. I'm glad he's retiring. He's become slovenly, unreliable. All sorts of crap in his head. Got a chip on his shoulder about Terry. And from the newspaper, I'm guessing he doesn't care much for you."

"No," Kawika agreed. "Sammy thought I was a rival somehow, although I never was. He was way senior to me. Terry gave me the Fortunato case. The crime scene was in South Kohala, and the division chief in Waimea asked for me by name. Shark Cliff seemed much more important at the time. We had a lot of bodies there, not just one. Terry needed Sammy to lead it. He was a lot tougher than me back then."

"Maybe back then," she observed. "But not today. I've seen you both in action. Good basis for comparison. Sammy has really let himself go."

"I don't know about that," Kawika said. "I haven't seen Sammy in years. Anyway, in the end, the Fortunato case turned out to be the bigger one."

"Yet you didn't solve it, if I understand correctly," the chief said. "The hit man's confession solved it instead, yeah? Whereas Sammy did solve the Shark Cliff case."

"Yes and no," Kawika replied, suddenly alert and snapping out of the light conversation they'd slipped into.

"Yes and no?" she inquired. "Which part is yes, and which part is no?"

Kawika paused. "Ana," he said at last. "Your 'official review' just started, didn't it?"

The chief laughed one last time. "I guess so," she acknowledged. "Okay, I'd better call Terry in here, let him know. Then I'll start by grilling Sammy Kā'ai. After that, my predecessor, Haia Kalākalani. *That* should be fun."

11

Honolulu

Kawika woke early and couldn't get back to sleep. It was still dark, too early for work, and he didn't want to wake Elle. So he made a cup of instant coffee and quietly slipped out the sliding glass door and onto the deck of the condo. Despite the traffic noise, muffled indoors by double-pane glass, Kawika savored the outdoor air at dawn and watching the first rays of sunlight strike the palms and the distant surf beyond the park. This morning he had many things to think about—and not just murder cases. A single cup of coffee wouldn't be enough.

One big thing: Kawika was about to become a father. A few months earlier, he and Elle had decided to have a baby. "Let's leave the timing to Lono," Elle had suggested, invoking the Hawaiian god of fertility. She was thirty-six now, he was forty-one, and both were established professionally, she at UH Mānoa as an associate professor of journalism, a field that never ran out of students even though jobs in journalism kept disappearing.

The university and HPD offered generous parental leave. Elle and Kawika could afford a child, and no one could be sure Elle would conceive if they waited longer, or what the risks might be. They'd frozen some of Elle's eggs when she was thirty-one, not knowing what the future might hold. But now they felt they'd waited long enough.

So Elle had gone off the pill. Still, it had surprised them both when Elle bolted from the breakfast table, ran to the bathroom, and began throwing up. Kawika followed, knelt beside her, stroked her shoulder gently, and held her hair back. Soon, after she'd washed her mouth not just twice but three times, then brushed her teeth and washed her whole face, he held her lightly—as if suddenly she'd become delicate—and kissed her.

"You think this is it?" he asked.

"Yup, I think this is it. And we've got the kit right here. So stand back and let me pee."

Kawika stood back. He turned around, giving her some privacy, until he heard her flush. Then he joined her to watch as the test strip changed color—more quickly than he'd expected.

"Guess we won't need your frozen eggs," Kawika said cheerfully, giving her a kiss. "Not this time anyway."

"Tell you what," Elle replied, grinning. "The first person I'll tell will be Ana Carvalho. I'll say that if it's a girl, we're naming it after her."

"Clever. And tell her if it's a boy, we're naming him Terry Tanaka Wong."

"Terry *Carvalho* Wong," Elle had amended. "Might as well make our one chance with Ana count."

* * *

His recollection of that moment reminded Kawika that Elle and Ana Carvalho had been friends before he and Elle met—which led him to reminisce, pleasantly, about that first meeting. He'd been a guest speaker for a criminology class at the university. Elle had attended as a faculty member, doing research for her own detective fiction. She'd found herself fascinated by his talk and stayed afterward to ask questions, which led to coffee, which eventually led to all the rest.

Before meeting Kawika, she'd published two lighthearted Hawaiian murder mysteries featuring her fictional young hapa haole Hawaiian detective, Malia Maikalani, the surname meaning "from heaven" in Hawaiian. But as Elle had learned more of the realities of homicide from Kawika, her work had darkened. Detective Malia Maikalani kept growing and becoming more battle hardened, just like Kawika. And just as the real-life analog had done for Kawika, *Murder at the Mauna Lani* had wrought a jump shift in the fictional detective's perspectives and maturity.

By the time Elle wrote that book, her third and most successful, she'd tired of frothy beach fare as Hawaiian detective fiction. Her next two books included gritty fragments of bleak Hawaiian reality that beach books omitted—poverty, drug addiction, welfare, obesity, homelessness, the breakdown of Hawaiian families, the turning away from education, and the displacement and hopelessness of so many unemployed or underemployed young people, Hawaiians in particular.

With that, and with the grimness of Kawika's homicide cases from which her literary ones evolved, Elle in her continuing series had started a darker and intentionally hard-boiled school of Hawaiian detective fiction—what reviewers called "Hawaiian noir." Rejecting the *noir* appellation, she called it "Hawaiian realism" herself.

Kawika felt proud of Elle's books and gratified to help with material; at least something good came from his cases, whether horrific or squalidly mundane. But the more detective fiction she wrote, the less he read, apart from hers. This was a change. Murder mysteries had been his passion since boyhood. The realities of homicide, especially the Fortunato case, had contributed to his waning interest in the genre. After that case, fictional homicide investigations struck him as too unrealistic; he couldn't suspend disbelief long enough to enjoy them.

But the Fortunato case had produced one great gift for him, which the racially diverse Honolulu PD had solidified: he no longer agonized about his hapa haole identity. He'd worried enough about it—Hawaiian or Mainlander, Native or haole, the conundrum of a Hawaiian father and a haole mother who raised him in Seattle after she and his father had divorced. The racial part of his identity meant almost nothing to him now. The most important strand of his identity, he'd decided, and not just his job description, was law enforcement professional. A leader of homicide detectives today, perhaps chief of police tomorrow. That was the identity he felt sure of—a career police officer, comfortable in his own mixed-race skin. Focused on catching a killer. Actually, two killers, it now seemed. And thanks to Zoë Akona, forced to think about a third, long-dead one too.

* * *

This morning Kawika also had his father on his mind. That required the second cup of coffee. For ten years after Kawika had moved to Honolulu from the Big Island, his dad, the outsize Jarvis Wong, had lived at Puakō, still managing the groundskeeping crew at the Mauna Kea resort. Honolulu to Kona was a quick flight, but Kawika never got away as often as his father would've liked. Fortunately, Jarvis and Elle had formed a special bond—"He's the father I never had," she'd told Kawika—so she often went to visit Jarvis's seaside bungalow even when Kawika could not.

Then, a decade after Kawika came to Honolulu and five years after he'd married Elle, Jarvis had suffered a devastating and particularly cruel stroke. It left him unable to walk, feed himself, or write. Most distressingly, it left him unable to speak intelligibly, to nod, or to communicate in other ways, even by moving his head or his eyes. He still blinked, but involuntarily; it wasn't something he could control. He couldn't recognize letters on an alphabet board, so that tool was useless in Jarvis's case. "Both sides of his brain," the doctor explained. Jarvis had become trapped inside his massive body, immobile and silent except for enigmatic grunts and efforts to sound a single consonant. Fortunately, the strangled consonants he could produce included *yuh-yuh-yuh* for yes and *nuh-nuh-nuh* for no.

"Thank God for small favors," Kawika said to his wife. It was one of his mother's sayings. That his father could still indicate yes and no struck him as a small favor indeed, but a favor nonetheless.

What made the favor even smaller was that almost no one other than Kawika and Elle could elicit from Jarvis even *yuh-yuh-yuh* and *nuh-nuh-nuh*—a major inconvenience to his caregivers. And Jarvis's disabilities meant he required full-time care. He had no wife or other children to attend him, and no one else on the Big Island except his best friend Terry Tanaka and his niece Ku'ulei. But they both lived in Hilo, on the other side of the island, and were chained to their work as thoroughly as Kawika. All they could do when they visited was smile, talk to him, hold his unresponsive hand, drive his motorized wheelchair. That was tough duty, not easy to undertake too often.

Kawika and Elle had found Jarvis the best facility on the Big Island, a well-run and sunlit advanced-care nursing home in Waikoloa Village, the Queen Ka'ahumanu Long-Term Care Center. Jarvis's employer, the Mauna Kea resort, had a generous disability provision in its employee health insurance plan that covered most of the cost initially. Jarvis's retirement plan and various forms of government assistance helped too.

Finally, rather than sell Jarvis's seaside bungalow in Puakō, Kawika and Elle had decided to put a mortgage on it—the value was almost entirely in the waterfront land—and use the funds for Jarvis's care. So it didn't cost Kawika and Elle more than the mortgage payments to assure the quality of Jarvis's care as long as necessary, and to have funds available to fix up Jarvis's house so they could use it when they came to visit him. The two of them—although often Elle alone—visited more frequently than before Jarvis was stricken; she claimed she didn't find it too depressing, and she enjoyed fixing up the house.

Tanaka and Jarvis's niece Ku'ulei visited too, though not as often. Jarvis always showed his pleasure in the limited way he could, a sort of gurgle that visitors took for a smile. Jarvis's estranged sister down in Puna, who was a drug addict, never visited, which her daughter Ku'ulei and nephew Kawika considered just as well.

Of course, Jarvis wasn't merely immobilized and rendered incapable of speech. Although his cognitive abilities, trapped in the rubble, still seemed active, like any victim of such devastation, Jarvis was actually dying. Not quickly—he was somehow too tough for that—but dying nonetheless. Jarvis's doctor had called Kawika the day before. "It won't be long now," she told him. "Within the year, I expect."

Will he get to see his grandchild? Kawika wondered. It would mean a lot to Elle, he knew. Heck, it would mean a lot to Kawika and Jarvis too.

* * *

Thinking about his father's mortality led Kawika, still out on his deck, to contemplate other changes—big ones. For Kawika, the distance between Fortunato's murder and the Slasher case twelve years later couldn't be measured just in time or miles or symbolized by the vast stretches of blue water between the Big Island and O'ahu.

He knew he'd aged, of course, and become somewhat less idealistic. Not surprisingly for a longtime homicide detective, he'd also grown more weary and violence-numbed. He'd knelt beside too many corpses, seen too much wanton cruelty, especially to women, and a lot of craziness by men and women alike, but mostly men. He and his teams had caught plenty of killers—also mainly men. He'd pitied some of them, but most simply disgusted him. He knew the Slasher would be one who disgusted him.

The Fortunato case had left Kawika feeling torn and damaged, and now he was forced to think about it again. It had put him directly at odds with his superior Terry Tanaka. Tanaka had been Kawika's professional mentor and protective guardian before the Fortunato case. Though they'd both tried to repair the relationship afterward, that hadn't been easy. They couldn't talk about the investigation after it ended, and although they retained affection for each other, they couldn't completely reestablish trust. Kawika's joining the Honolulu PD, a career move Tanaka had long expected and advocated, offered a graceful way out—a way for Kawika and Tanaka to remain friends without working together. Kawika valued that friendship and knew Tanaka did too. But what would happen to it now, with Ana Carvalho investigating how they'd handled the Fortunato case—and D. K. Parkes's death as well?

* * *

As he finished his coffee and got ready for work, and after he'd given the awakening Elle a morning kiss, Kawika felt more energized. He had a team of professionals downtown, all working for him and needing his supervision and direction. And he had a shot at becoming chief. He wanted the job, which meant he needed to keep politicking and socializing with municipal officials, the mayor most of all. Plus he needed the Slasher case solved—quickly.

Aware of his professional stakes, not just the likelihood of additional victims, Kawika had assigned his best detectives to the Slasher case. Even now, after so many victims, he felt confident they'd catch the killer; he wouldn't escape, as the Honolulu Strangler had done. But what sort of body count would he create first? Did the body bags missing from the EMT storeroom portend yet another serial killer? And what about this new killer, the possible copycat, the one who'd cut off his victim's head and hands? Was he getting started on a spree of his own?

As Kawika finished dressing, those questions diverted his thoughts to Robespierre, the decapitated and still-unidentified male victim. Showing initiative Kawika admired, Yvonne Ivanovna had volunteered to see if Robespierre might be identified via his genital piercing—not necessarily a hopeless task, she told Kawika, if the piercing had been performed in Honolulu. Or if it might be recognized in "certain local circles, straight or gay," she pointed out delicately.

"We really don't know anything else about him," Yvonne had said, "but someone in Honolulu is surely familiar with that piercing." She'd suggested it might be enough just to begin showing a high-resolution photograph to piercing parlors and select other people. "An eight-by-ten penis picture ought to get their attention," Yvonne had pointed out. He'd let her run with it, glad she seemed undaunted despite the police academy course on human genitals she'd found repellent.

As he grabbed his keys and left the condo, he felt grateful for having such an able trainee. Initially, he'd simply intended to help her. But she was proving surprisingly helpful herself.

PART TWO

2014

By no premeditated contrivance of our own, by the cooperation of a series of events which, however dependent step by step upon human action, were not intended to prepare the present crisis, [we are] compelled to answer a question—to make a decision . . . For let it not be overlooked that, whether we wish or no, we *must* answer the question, we *must* make the decision. The issue cannot be dodged.

—Alfred Thayer Mahan,
"Hawaii and Our Future Sea-Power," *The Forum* 15 (1893)

12

Honolulu

When Terry Tanaka next called, it wasn't about Ana Carvalho's review of the Fortunato case, as Kawika might have expected. The call came while Kawika was standing over another corpse.

"What a coincidence," Kawika said. "I'm out in a park again with my trainee and another victim. Not Kapi'olani Park, though—Ala Moana Beach Park this time. Practically in Elle's and my front yard."

Of course he meant "temporary front yard," because he and Elle were just house-sitting in the condo. But a body had shown up directly across the boulevard from their building, and Kawika knew it would unsettle Elle. Writing murder mysteries was one thing; an actual murder victim just across the street was another.

"Ugh, sorry to interrupt you in the field again," Tanaka said. "I'll be quick: here's another coincidence. A missing-person report up in Waimea. They brought it to me straightaway because of the name. Keoni Parkes."

"Parkes?"

"Yup. Same spelling as D. K. Parkes, from Shark Cliff."

Kawika was stunned. "Keoni Parkes?" he repeated. "From Waimea?" He didn't need to add *Waimea is where D. K. Parkes lived.*

"Yeah," Tanaka replied. "Keoni Parkes from Waimea. Hasn't shown up at work or been home all week. His boss, a Dr. Emma Phillips, called it in. She's with the TMT project—you know, the Thirty Meter Telescope they're trying to build on Mauna Kea. Big controversy over here. I'm going up to Waimea to see her. Handling this one myself."

"You going alone?"

"No, I asked Tommy to meet me."

Kawika required no explanation. Tommy Kekoa, a detective around his own age from the Waimea station, had helped Kawika in the Fortunato investigation and become his best Big Island friend after Tanaka. They'd even been a shore-fishing team for a few years before Kawika left for Honolulu. Kawika understood Tanaka's reasoning: any possible connection of the newly missing Keoni Parkes to D. K. Parkes might seriously complicate Chief Carvalho's inquiry, which would include the D. K. Parkes case. Tommy would understand at once.

"I'm also taking Ku'ulei," Tanaka added.

A year earlier, Ku'ulei Wong, Kawika's much-younger cousin, fresh from the police academy, had become Tanaka's detective trainee in Hilo, just as Yvonne Ivanovna had recently become Kawika's in Honolulu. Kawika could never forget Ku'ulei as a coltish preteen, the brave girl who'd been with him when he'd been shot and wounded in the Queen Lili'uokalani Gardens. But he recognized her now as a formidable young woman and aspiring police professional, physically very strong yet always carrying her sidearm and taser on her service belt, unlike Kawika. "You forget," she told Kawika when he teased her about that. "I'm a woman." That was one of two things she was helping him understand better; being Hawaiian was the other.

"Yeah, Ku'ulei," Tanaka repeated. "Good experience for her. This missing Keoni Parkes is Hawaiian. She can help if that turns out to matter. Plus Ku'ulei grew up in Puakō, your dad raising her there and all that, and she went to school in Waimea. So this whole thing is more her territory than mine."

"True," Kawika allowed.

"And Kawika, if Keoni Parkes is related to D. K. Parkes—which I bet he is—I'll need someone I trust by my side in Hilo. Not just Tommy up in Waimea."

"Also true," Kawika agreed reluctantly. "Things go wrong, Tommy could get dragged into Ana's review." He didn't need to elaborate, given Tommy's former role as Kawika's partner in the Fortunato murder case and at the time of D. K. Parke's murder. "That can't happen to Ku'ulei."

"Right. That's what I'm thinking."

"Ku'ulei is very sharp. She's also loyal, Terry. You explain the situation, she won't let you down."

"Won't let *us* down," Tanaka corrected.

"Yup," Kawika agreed. "Us."

Kawika tried with only partial success to turn his attention back to Yvonne Ivanovna and the naked body at their feet, throat slashed—just like the first of the Slasher's victims—but bloodless and otherwise intact. Despite being dumped in Ala Moana Beach Park, this one seemed like the too-familiar work of the Kapi'olani Park Slasher. And this time—a new touch—the victim's State of Hawaii driver's license rested conspicuously on the bare skin of his torso, right below the breastbone.

"Not trying to hide the victim's identity," Yvonne observed sardonically, as the crime scene team began their work. "He's making a statement."

"And the statement is . . . ?" Kawika gave her the chance to say it.

"How about this?" she began. "*That last victim at Kapi'olani Park, the one missing his head and hands, wasn't mine.*"

"*Iiko, iiko,*" Kawika said softly, less robustly than usual. He'd become a bit distracted. He kept thinking about the missing Keoni Parkes and the possible—probable?—link to D. K. Parkes of Shark Cliff. The murder victim Zoë Akona was asking people about. The victim whose killer Kawika alone knew.

Kawika and Elle, that is. Just like the murder of Ralph Fortunato, D. K. Parkes was a part of his past he couldn't have kept from her. But if Keoni Parkes was dead, not merely missing, and if D. K. Parkes and Keoni were related, then maybe the death of D. K. wasn't something entirely settled in the past. And for purposes of Ana Carvalho's review, that could mean *pilikia*, as Jarvis would have said. Trouble. Big trouble.

13

Waimea

When Tanaka and Ku'ulei arrived in Waimea, Dr. Emma Phillips, director of community relations and government affairs for the Thirty Meter Telescope Project, stood talking with Tommy Kekoa, the Waimea detective, on a grassy strip next to the TMT parking lot. Tanaka and Ku'ulei stepped out of the car into a wispy cloud of smoke fragrant with spit-roasted chicken and grilled pork wafting in from the barbecue stand across the street. Waimea bustled as usual with cars, pedestrians, food trucks, and kids jumping happily up and down or struggling with melting ice cream cones or shave ice, all against the background noise of the traffic and a few barking dogs. *Nothing out of the ordinary*, Tanaka thought. *Everyone just going about their lives, oblivious to one more missing person.*

Dr. Phillips appeared to Tanaka like someone approaching middle age or maybe already there, quite tall and very blonde, looking athletic rather than slender. She was dressed professionally in a sweater and skirt, wearing short heels and some inexpensive jewelry, and on this occasion very agitated, literally wringing her hands. After introductions, she led the detectives—she seemed surprised three had arrived—into the TMT's administration building and up some stairs to her spacious corner office, which afforded sweeping views of Mauna Kea to the southeast and Kohala Mountain rising almost from the building's backyard. In Waimea, they were halfway up its slope.

A neatly dressed young man, perhaps in his late twenties, waited in Dr. Phillips's office. She introduced him as Angel Delos Santos, her personal assistant or PA, pronouncing his first name *ahn-HELL*, the second syllable with a guttural *h*. Angel bowed slightly to acknowledge the introduction and shook hands. Unlike Dr. Phillips, Angel was dressed in Hawaiian garb: a crisp aloha shirt, nice cargo shorts, soft black shoes. A conspicuous gold cross, set with a bright-red gemstone, dangled from his neck.

"I'm really worried about Keoni," Dr. Phillips began, once everyone was seated. "This isn't like him at all."

"Doesn't skip work much?" Tanaka asked.

"No, never," she replied. "He's never gone without calling me. Now it's been almost a week. He hasn't shown up, hasn't called. He doesn't answer his phone. Doesn't return voice messages or texts or emails. Something is definitely wrong."

"Okay, let's start at the beginning," Tanaka said. "Tell us about him."

Dr. Phillips took a deep breath, puffed her cheeks as she exhaled, and calmed herself. Tanaka turned his head toward Ku'ulei, indicating she should take notes. Ku'ulei nodded and opened her spiral notebook. Unlike the Honolulu PD, the Hawai'i County PD didn't have iPads or similar devices yet, despite Ku'ulei's suggestions to Tanaka and the requests he'd run up the chain of command.

"His full name is Douglas Keoni Parkes," Dr. Phillips began, "but everyone just calls him Keoni. That's Hawaiian for John, you know."

Tanaka nodded; they knew, and they exchanged discreet smiles. A haole explaining Hawaiian things to local residents was so common it had its own name: "haole-splaining."

"He's the director of Hawaiian relations for TMT, reporting to me," Dr. Phillips continued. "It's the toughest job we have. So, okay, let's see. More details. He's thirty-four. Grew up here in Waimea, went to UH Hilo, did his junior year abroad—in Scotland, I think—then came home and graduated. Hapa haole, speaks Hawaiian, perfect for the position. Most TMT opponents—and most of us in Hawai'i, for that matter—are hapa haole too, of course, or hapa something else. So he's about as Hawaiian as anyone."

Ku'ulei and Tommy Kekoa, the two hapa haole Hawaiians in the room, surreptitiously exchanged amused glances. Like Tanaka, a silver-haired Japanese American, Dr. Phillips did not appear to be hapa anything, just haole. Tall blonde haole. Her assistant Angel Delos Santos, an apparent Filipino with no visible signs of hapa-ness, leaned forward and exhaled a nearly silent laugh, as if to defuse the awkwardness of her remark. The gold cross with the red gemstone swayed below his throat, the jewel glinting in the office's abundant sunlight.

"Where does this Keoni Parkes live?" Tanaka resumed.

"He's got a little house here in Waimea," Dr. Phillips answered. "I knocked on his door again yesterday and the day before. No answer. I peered in his windows and asked his neighbors. They haven't seen him." She wrote the address on a Post-it note and handed it to Tanaka, who gave it to Tommy Kekoa.

"I know the place," Tommy said after glancing at it. "Where it is, I mean. Nice neighborhood."

Tanaka turned back to Dr. Phillips. "Does Keoni ever go somewhere else—on weekends, maybe?" he asked.

Dr. Phillips nodded. "He keeps an apartment in Honolulu. I guess it's an apartment, anyway. He just calls it 'my place.' I've never seen it; could be another house, I suppose, though I'd be surprised if he can afford two. He usually flies to O'ahu on Friday after work. Not always, but most of the time. Flies back on Sunday night or Monday morning. Just a short hop, you know."

"You have a photo?" asked Tanaka. "We'll need one."

"Sure," she replied. "In his personnel file. I'll print it for you." She turned to her computer and began typing. "Three copies?"

Tanaka nodded. "Height? Weight?"

"Says here he's five nine, one hundred and sixty-five pounds," she answered. "He might be a bit shorter, actually. I'm a tall woman, as you've probably noticed. I've learned that five nine is the minimum declared height for men." She smiled softly. "And that one hundred and sixty-five seems a bit out of date; he's put on a little weight, wouldn't you say, Angel?" Angel Delos Santos nodded in confirmation; his necklace and little cross danced again.

"Keoni's not fat, just getting sort of stocky," Dr. Phillips continued. "Let's see, what else: black hair, brown eyes—naturally. Doesn't wear glasses. Could wear contacts, I suppose. Never noticed."

"Does his file list any relatives?" Tanaka asked.

"I'm not sure he has any," she said. "I know he's not married. He's gay, out and not closeted, but I don't think he has a partner on the Big Island. Maybe in Honolulu. Could be why he goes there on weekends." She turned to her computer again, clicked a few keys. Angel Delos Santos looked down, his face visibly flushed. Tanaka noticed. With a small tilt of his head, Tanaka indicated to Ku'ulei and Tommy that they should notice too.

"That's what I thought," Dr. Phillips said, turning back to Tanaka. "No relatives in his file. Both parents are deceased, I know. His dad was his haole parent, his mom the Hawaiian one. She passed away when Keoni was a child, he said. His dad was actually murdered—a long time ago. Keoni told me that just recently; he seems a little ashamed of it, for some reason. There was a story about it in the *Star-Advertiser* the other day, as you probably know. Unsolved case, evidently."

Angel rose and walked to the printer to retrieve the photos for the detectives.

Tanaka turned away to hide his reaction to what Dr. Phillips had said, hoping it appeared he wanted to consider her words while looking out at snowcapped Mauna Kea in the distance. But now Tanaka knew: the missing Keoni Parkes must be the son of D. K. Parkes, the haole thrown off Shark Cliff back in 2002. D. K. Parkes, the murder victim Zoë Akona was eager to learn more about. D. K. Parkes, the victim whose killer Kawika had discovered way back then, but whom Tanaka had deliberately chosen not to learn anything about, not even the killer's name. A choice he now regretted.

"No other relatives he might have mentioned, like siblings?" Tanaka resumed after clearing his throat, as Angel handed a photo of Keoni Parkes to each of them. Keoni was a handsome fellow, Tanaka noted. Clean-cut, no facial hair, with a friendly and open appearance in the photo. Smiling naturally for the TMT camera. Tanaka couldn't discern a resemblance to what he remembered of the dead D. K. Parkes, mostly because the thousand-foot drop from Shark Cliff had left D. K.'s face in shape to invite nightmares, not comparisons.

"No siblings," she replied, after Angel took his seat again. "At least, Keoni told me he's an only child."

Tanaka leaned forward, holding the photo, and rested his forearms on her desk. "Dr. Phillips," he said, "This is routine, but you understand we have to ask: Is there anyone who might want to harm him?"

She gave a rueful half laugh, half snort. "Ha! *Many* people might want to harm him," she said. "That's what worries me. I told you he has the toughest job at TMT. He's the one out on the front lines, the one dealing with Native Hawaiians and other TMT opponents every day. They're angry about this project. A few are *really* angry. And in truth, some people around here are angry with Keoni too."

"Around here?" Tanaka said. "At TMT, you mean?"

"Yes, definitely," she replied. "Here at TMT but also in the astronomy community more broadly. Keoni's been trying to find a middle way, a solution everyone can accept. A compromise to end this incredibly long, drawn-out dispute."

"A compromise?" Tommy asked in surprise. "On TMT? What's the compromise—build a fifteen-meter telescope instead of a thirty-meter one?"

"No," she responded with a shake of her head. "Not that. Thirty meters refers to the diameter of the telescopic array, not the height of the building. There's nothing remarkable about the building; what's remarkable are the amazing images that the light-gathering capacity and incredibly high resolution of a thirty-meter array make possible. TMT will also have the latest in adaptive optics—the things other telescopes are being retrofitted to include. These new optics can virtually eliminate any remaining effects of having to look through Earth's atmosphere." She paused for a sip of water from a glass on her desk.

"Recently Keoni's been working on the idea of TMT purchasing and then tearing down some older observatories at the summit of Mauna Kea," she continued. "You know, as partial mitigation for TMT being built up there. Build the TMT on the footprint of a demolished observatory, avoid any new intrusion on the sacred places of the Hawaiians at the summit. He's been floating the idea in public and with different stakeholder groups."

"And people might be angry with him about that?" Tanaka asked.

"Of course," she replied. "His idea doesn't appease Hawaiians who object to TMT the most. Just the opposite. They don't want TMT or any other new telescope up there under any circumstances. And it absolutely freaks out some people here—my boss, for one. Not to mention people who own or work for the observatories Keoni suggests tearing down. So Keoni's way out on a limb. All by himself, I'm afraid."

"You and your TMT colleagues don't support him?" Tanaka asked.

"Not in public," she said. "Though no one here is openly attacking him. We promised the community he'd be as independent as possible, sort of like a mediator or facilitator. Officially, we're keeping hands off. He's supposed to listen to all sides, maintain an open mind. Then try out new ideas, make new proposals. See if he can come up with something that satisfies as many factions as possible, at least grudgingly."

"Has he received threats?" Tanaka asked.

Dr. Phillips gave another rueful half laugh, then shook her head in disgust. "Major Tanaka," she answered, "we *all* receive threats. Keoni receives threats, I receive threats. Others at TMT receive threats too. I'll bet even Angel receives threats." She looked over in Angel's direction.

"A few," Angel confirmed. "Nothing serious in my case. People being nasty to me at the supermarket, that kind of thing. Keoni and Dr. Phillips are more in the line of fire."

Dr. Phillips resumed. "I'm sure the Hawaiians trying to stop TMT must get threats too, because a lot of locals support the project, including a lot of Hawaiians. Not every Hawaiian opposes it—not by a long shot. We've got Hawaiians mad at Hawaiians. We've got locals mad at Hawaiians—that makes three groups—and other locals supporting the Hawaiians who oppose TMT. So that's at least four groups, and the astronomy community makes five, but even we are divided. It's a mess. Keoni's right in the middle of it, and I've been particularly worried about him right now."

"Why right now? Some immediate crisis?"

"The situation's growing more tense," she replied. "Keoni's scheduled to explain his proposal in detail and make his case for it at a stakeholder meeting next week. He's reserved the Hōkūloa Church down in Puakō for the event. A neutral spot. Only principals invited, no press allowed. He's hoping to keep everyone civil, keep things from getting rowdy. The church is tiny, but even so, he may not fill it."

"Why?" Tanaka asked. He exchanged glances with Kuʻulei. Kuʻulei had grown up in Puakō, raised by her uncle, Jarvis Wong. Kuʻulei would know that little church.

Dr. Phillips sighed and shook her head. "Some Hawaiian groups say they'll boycott Keoni's meeting. They're refusing even to consider what he has to say. They don't want to hear anything about TMT getting built. And my bosses don't think we should attend either—they don't want TMT to be seen as advocating the demolition of other observatories. Then the other observatories, of course, their people are pretty upset with Keoni too, as you can imagine. They're suspicious he'll run them off the mountain before their time, just so our telescope can get built. And naturally, they assume we're behind the idea. So things are really fraught right now. But Keoni's determined to go ahead. He thinks enough people will show up and that he'll gain traction if he can make his case. And," she added with a small smile, waving her hand vaguely at the heavens, "if the stars align."

Tanaka noticed her wedding ring. "Are you and your family safe? Or you think you might be in danger too, if Keoni is?" he asked.

She smiled sadly, raising her left hand again and turning it over twice. "My husband died before I left the mainland," she said. "That's why I came here, took this job. Fresh start. No kids. I'm just not ready to be a merry widow yet." She looked down at the ring. "But yes, I feel reasonably safe. I'm not worried for myself. Are you, Angel?" She looked over at Angel, who frowned and shook his head.

"I'm just worried about Keoni," she emphasized. "*Really* worried." Angel nodded vigorously.

She twisted her ring, looking at Tanaka almost beseechingly, as if somehow he might end her distress. Tanaka doubted he could. From experience, intuition, and what little she'd told them, he guessed that Keoni Parkes was dead.

The detectives rose from their seats, shook hands, and let themselves out without offering what Tanaka thought likely to be false hope. Once they were back in the parking lot, standing by their cars in the thin plume of fragrant smoke from the barbecue across the street, Tanaka said, "The father was murdered. Maybe the son now too? Is this really about the TMT?"

"Not a coincidence, you're thinking?" Tommy asked.

"I don't believe in coincidences," Tanaka replied. "Do you?"

Tommy shrugged noncommittally and opened the door to his police cruiser. Tanaka took a few steps toward him. "Tommy," he said in a low voice, "I want you to interview Angel Delos Santos tonight, away from his office. Find an excuse. Take him out for pizza or something."

"Okay," Tommy said. "What're you thinking, Terry?"

"I'm thinking he has something to tell us—if his boss isn't listening."

* * *

Hours later, Tommy reached Tanaka at home. "Terry," he began, "sorry to call so late. But you were right. Angel says he and Keoni are lovers. Secretly. The secret isn't that they're gay—they've both been out for a long time."

"Why secret, then?"

"Because Dr. Phillips has a rule against her subordinates getting involved with one another, and they both work for her. Angel and Keoni don't want Dr. Phillips to know."

"Good going, Tommy. You think he'll give us more?"

"He already did," Tommy responded. "Angel says he and Keoni had a huge fight. Keoni doesn't believe in God, and Angel spends all day Sunday in mass and at services and Saturday performing good deeds for Catholic charities. Angel says that's why they spend weekends apart. He says Keoni finally told him their situation was impossible, and that's what caused the fight."

"When was this?"

"On Thursday," Tommy replied. "The day before Keoni flew to Honolulu and went missing."

14

Honolulu

"Hi, Cousin," Ku'ulei Wong began playfully, calling Kawika from Hilo. "Terry asked me to call you about our missing person, this Keoni Parkes, the guy who works at the Thirty Meter Telescope Project. He's been missing nearly a week. Full name Douglas Keoni Parkes. D. K. Parkes, in other words. But not D. K. Parkes Junior. His dad's middle name was Kenneth, apparently. Keoni was born in Waimea in 1980. His father was tossed off Shark Cliff back in 2002, which the *Star-Advertiser* just wrote about. Terry thought you should know."

"That seals it, I guess." Kawika sighed. "So Keoni Parkes is definitely the son of D. K. Parkes?" He'd hoped that somehow, miraculously, that conclusion could be avoided. Now he hoped Keoni Parkes was merely missing, not dead, his disappearance not tied in any way to the death of his father. *Let these two cases remain unrelated*, he silently pleaded.

"That's what Terry says. And he thinks the two cases may be linked. But Keoni's boss thinks Keoni's disappearance has something to do with the TMT. He has a tough job, out in public. A lot of people don't like him, it seems."

"Anything else I should know?"

"Lots, actually," she replied. "First, his boss says Keoni keeps a place in Honolulu. An apartment, she thinks. Apparently, he spends weekends there. He's gay, and he's got a partner here in Waimea—Angel Delos Santos. Spelled *angel* but pronounced *ahn-HELL*." She spoke the name as if softly clearing her throat.

"He works at TMT too, the personal assistant to Keoni's boss," Ku'ulei went on. "Terry thought Angel might have something to tell us. Tommy took him out after work, and Terry was right. Keoni's boss apparently doesn't know about the relationship. Angel and Keoni are keeping it secret because the boss doesn't want her people dating one another."

"Not keeping it secret because they're gay?"

"No, they've both been out a long time. But Terry's whiskers are twitching because of the secrecy—and because Keoni goes to Honolulu on weekends, whereas Angel says he doesn't go there himself. Terry wonders if Keoni might have another boyfriend in Honolulu, which could explain a lot. We've put out an alert for Keoni, but privately Terry's guessing he's dead. Terry's hoping you'll have HPD check out the apartment for us."

"To see if Keoni's there?"

"Yeah, well, and if he's not, to take a look inside."

"Get a warrant, or find an excuse?"

Ku'ulei laughed. "Up to you, Cuz. Whatever works."

"Okay. What else?"

"Terry wants you to check if there are missing-person reports on Keoni in Honolulu," she responded. "There might be, if he has a boyfriend on O'ahu."

"Makes sense. We'll check for you."

"Terry also says you two need to talk. In person, Kawika. About this Keoni Parkes and about Carvalho's investigation. Terry's hoping you'll pop over here."

"Yup," Kawika agreed. "We definitely need to talk about Carvalho's investigation. I'll get there soon—maybe this weekend. Elle might come if you can have dinner with us. Drop in and see Dad too? Put the airfare to good use."

"That brings up the last thing, Kawika. Terry thinks you should interview Keoni's boss while you're here—this Dr. Emma Phillips."

"Why? It's your case over there."

"Kawika, Terry's right. You want to do it yourself. She's a possible link to D. K. Parkes, through Keoni. Terry can't think of anyone else who might be, and he's guessing the cases of D. K. Parkes and his son Keoni Parkes might be linked. Otherwise, it's a coincidence, and you know what Terry thinks about coincidences. Terry's worried that if Keoni is dead and if his death relates to his dad's, then Carvalho will decide the D. K. Parkes murder is part of something that's still going on."

"Right," Kawika answered. That was his worry too. Objectively, he saw no reason to link Keoni's disappearance to his father's death. Even if Keoni was dead, there'd be a hundred more likely explanations. But against that Kawika had to weigh Tanaka's intuition, which Kawika respected.

"So, who is this Dr. Phillips exactly?" he asked.

"An astronomer in charge of public and government affairs for the TMT," Kuʻulei replied. "Apparently, she was famous once, among astronomers anyway—some sort of prodigy, I guess. Terry wanted me to ask around, and I did. She discovered something about twin stars, but I couldn't understand it; too technical. Anyway, that's why they picked her for TMT, I guess. She's just about your age. Good-looking, by the way. And she's a widow. A good-looking *blonde* widow, Kawika."

He laughed, knowing she was teasing him now. "Stop it, Kuʻulei. I'm a happily married man."

"Married to a good-looking blonde," she responded, laughing too. "I know you like 'em, that's all."

"Elle is *ash* blond, Cuz, not blonde-blonde."

"Well, I think Dr. Phillips would be too tall for you anyway."

"Ouch," said Kawika. "You're really mean, Cuz."

"Okay then," Kuʻulei concluded brightly. "I'll tell Terry you're coming. I'll tell your dad too—he'll be so pleased, Kawika. Especially if you bring Elle. And I'll set you up to interview Dr. Phillips."

"Stop it. I'm not going to interview your Dr. Phillips," Kawika insisted. "Keoni Parkes is your case over there on the Big Island. It's not my concern, unless Terry's right and this relates to his father's murder. That seems pretty unlikely at this stage. So I'll make sure the Honolulu stuff gets done. Otherwise, I'll just follow the investigation through you and Terry."

Kawika meant it. But he was forced to change his mind a day later, right before the weekend, when a city sanitation worker found a human head inside a plastic trash bag at Honolulu's main garbage transfer station. A man's head with a .22-caliber entry wound in the left temple, just as Dr. Noriko Yoshida had predicted.

It didn't take long to establish who the severed head belonged to. No DNA match was needed. A sobbing Dr. Emma Phillips identified it to Tanaka over the phone, once she'd seen the faxed photo Kawika had provided.

It was the head of Keoni Parkes.

* * *

"Well," Yvonne remarked, after Kawika had briefed the Honolulu detectives on this development in the Robespierre case—the last time they'd refer to the decapitated body that way; it was the Keoni Parkes case now. "At least we can focus our search."

"True," Kawika agreed. "We can be more selective, anyway."

"Right," she responded, seeming to think aloud. "We know our victim's name is Keoni Parkes, and we know he was gay. So unless the killing's random, the killer could be one of his gay acquaintances, don't you think? Might narrow the field, or at least give us a place to start. Maybe some weekend lover in Honolulu learns about Angel Delos Santos over on the Big Island, feels betrayed. Could happen to any cheater—gay or straight."

Occam's razor, Kawika thought. *She's feeling her way toward it, going for the simplest explanation first.* They hadn't discussed the concept, but she seemed about to discover it herself—if she didn't know it already. *Way too early to apply it here, though.* "Good thinking," he responded tactfully. "See if you can develop that idea some more. Still, Yvonne, don't fall in love with it. We just don't know enough yet."

Back at his desk, Kawika was surprised—only at first, because he realized he should have anticipated it—to find another envelope with another pencil-written note in block capitals: CHANGED TO ALA MOANA BEACH PARK BECAUSE OF THAT COPYCAT AT KAPIOLANI. KPS (NOW D/B/A AMBPS). He knew the last part meant *Now doing business as the Ala Moana Beach Park Slasher.*

Kawika found the sick humor revolting. *We really need to catch this guy,* Kawika said to himself. But the dead Keoni Parkes, apparently the victim of a different killer—copycat or not—was the victim most on his mind.

Kawika didn't rush the note to the lab. Instead, he called Yvonne to his desk. "Tell you what," he told her. "I want you to keep pursuing the betrayed-lover angle and spending a bit of time on Keoni Parkes. But otherwise, I'm going to assign you to the Slasher investigation. I'll get you started with the team right now. Our best detectives and forensics folks. You'll learn a lot. And I bet they'll learn some things from you."

Kawika called a meeting of the Slasher team in the homicide division's main conference room. Most were able to attend, and Kawika introduced Yvonne to the few who didn't already know her. When all were seated, Kawika explained that he still needed some of Yvonne's time for the Keoni Parkes case, but otherwise he wanted her immersed in the Slasher investigation, beginning at once. "She's new and she's young, but she's awfully sharp," he told the team. "You train her well, she'll become a star around HPD, not just on the Slasher case. And don't be surprised if she catches things you don't—like the killer. She's that good."

As the team dispersed, Jerry Rhodes looked at Yvonne the neophyte, as if thinking *How does she rate?* But he might have been thinking something different; Kawika let it pass. If anything, Rhodes's look seemed more surprised than inappropriate this time.

Despite Kawika's praise, Yvonne seemed perplexed by her new assignment, evidently not sure whether this was a promotion or the opposite. Kawika understood. "It's a promotion, Yvonne," he assured her. "Our most important case. We need it solved. I'd like to see you on it, and you deserve this."

But in truth, Kawika had a different notion in mind. He was thinking of where the Keoni Parkes investigation might lead, how it might affect Ana Carvalho's inquiry into the Fortunato and D. K. Parkes cases, and the peril it might pose for him and Tanaka, given that D. K. and Keoni were father and son and that the second death might relate to the first, as Tanaka suspected, thereby practically requiring that the first case—one he and Tanaka had covered up twelve years earlier—be reopened.

Kawika decided that for Tanaka's safety and his own, he needed to take charge of the Keoni Parkes case personally. That would mean ceding most of the direct responsibility for the Slasher investigation to the Two Jerrys, at least temporarily. He'd have to explain that unusual and professionally risky development to his team by emphasizing the Big Island locus of the two Parkes victims and his own past role in the earlier case.

Kawika didn't want anyone—especially not anyone as smart and inquisitive as Yvonne Ivanovna was proving to be—too close to his thinking on the Keoni Parkes matter right now. Not even Tanaka, to whom Kawika had never disclosed, in 2002 or since, everything he believed he understood about the death of D. K. Parkes. Kawika needed to learn a lot more about Keoni Parkes first.

15

Waikoloa Village

Kawika and Elle flew to the Big Island on Friday and spent the night in the Puakō cottage. They'd kept Jarvis's old car and fixed it up. So on Saturday morning, after dropping Kawika at the coffee shop where he would meet Tanaka, Elle drove the car—a big one, which Jarvis in his prime had required—to the nearby care center to visit her stroke-ravaged father-in-law. She opened the door to his private room to find another woman, blonde and petite, seated at his bedside and holding his hand. Elle stopped abruptly, her smile fading and her brows knitting in puzzlement. Then two things happened at once. Jarvis began making a plosive *puh-puh-puh* sound, and the other woman rose and extended her hand.

"Hi," she said. "I'm Patience Quinn. And you must be Elianna."

Jarvis uttered *luh-luh-luh*; he couldn't produce the sound of Elle's name itself, just the sound of the key consonant, which for Elle's name was just as good.

Elle stood, a bit stunned, then remembered to smile at Jarvis and nodded toward the other woman. "Patience Quinn, my goodness," Elle said, almost not believing it, taking Patience's proffered hand lightly. "Kawika has told me so much about you—all good, of course. Yes, I'm Elianna, but people just call me Elle. Excuse me a second."

Elle went to Jarvis's side, looked at him with a renewed warm smile, and bent down to kiss his cheek. Then she straightened up and looked at Patience. She tried her best to seem expressionless, not to show any feelings. She didn't actually know *what* she felt, other than surprise. And she'd already shown that.

"I've read three of your books," Patience offered, filling the brief silence, sounding respectful. "I even recognized a bit of myself in *Murder at the Mauna Lani*—although it seems you made me a man." Patience smiled, and Elle could see she was trying to defuse an awkward moment for them both.

Elle nodded and smiled back. "Well, my detective is a woman," she replied, adding a small laugh. "In that book, I felt her lover had to be a man—so *you* had to be a man. It wouldn't have worked any other way. Sorry about that!"

Patience responded with a small laugh too, along with a dismissive wave of her hand.

For a moment the two women stood in silence and regarded each other. Then Elle, always quick to make decisions, took action. "Jarvis," she said brightly to her father-in-law. "Patience and I are going to sit in the courtyard for a bit. I'll come back and see you after that, I promise. Maybe Patience will too. I'm sorry I interrupted her visit."

Jarvis produced a *yuh-yuh-yuh*. Yes.

Giving Jarvis another kiss and squeezing his hand one more time, she inclined her head toward the door and followed Patience out.

Walking behind the other woman, Elle couldn't help admiring her looks, her clothing, her sense of style—the impression she gave of money. *It's ridiculous to feel jealous*, Elle told herself. *I'm the one he married.* So Elle put jealousy aside. But she couldn't help thinking about, well, what she couldn't help thinking about. She guessed Patience might well wonder the same things about Kawika and Elle, having long ago shared intimacies with Kawika herself.

Once they'd seated themselves in the courtyard, surrounded by lush plantings of oleander and hibiscus and shaded by a sprawling Hong Kong orchid tree in full flower, Elle resumed their conversation. "I've always hoped we'd meet someday," she said. "Although I have to admit I didn't know you'd be so good-looking. It's a bit disconcerting, you know, for a wife to meet the gorgeous former girlfriend."

"Oh, please," Patience protested. "You're beautiful. It's disconcerting to *me* that Kawika found someone so lovely."

Elle recognized the flattery for what it was: mere politeness. In this instance, politeness as diplomacy. Elle knew she wasn't beautiful in the same sense as Patience. Elle was a good-looking woman, but mainly in a way no still photograph could fully capture. Her beauty lay in her liveliness, her vivacity, the natural delight and pleasure she so easily felt and cheerfully expressed.

She could see the effect in Kawika's gaze and that of others, not the mirror. And her pregnancy, although not showing yet, had added an attractive depth of color to her olive-skinned face.

"I've got nothing on you except a few extra years—which I try my best to conceal," Patience added graciously. "And you've still got your husband, whereas I lost mine. Both of them."

"Both of them?" Elle asked. "Kawika told me you were going through a divorce when he met you. Did you remarry?"

"Yes, I did—eventually. And that marriage ended in divorce too. Four years ago."

"Sorry to hear that. You still come to the Big Island, though? I mean, it must provide some comfort and continuity for you. It's so perfect here."

"Yes, it is perfect, and yes, I still do. Originally, I had a condo at the Mauna Lani, but I sold it after my divorce, and then—"

"That infamous condo," Elle interrupted teasingly, with a smile. "You probably recognized your condo, too, in *Murder at the Mauna Lani*. I took a look at it as part of my research for the book."

"Oh dear," Patience said in embarrassment, covering her face with both hands and looking down at her lap. "I was determined not to get all red-faced with you, yet here I am, blushing like the proverbial schoolgirl."

"I'm so sorry," Elle quickly reassured her, leaning forward and touching the other woman's arm. "Please don't worry. I knew everything about the two of you before I married him. It all happened years ago, before Kawika and I even met. Everything is fine now, Patience. Believe me. And I interrupted what you were about to say. Forgive me."

"No need to apologize," Patience responded, raising her head again. "I'm sure I'll interrupt you sometimes too. I do that a lot, I'm afraid."

"So do I, apparently," Elle said with a laugh. "But please go on. You sold the Mauna Lani condo, you were saying, and then . . . ?"

"*Then* I married husband two-point-oh," resumed Patience, "and talked him into buying a house at the Mauna Kea. We spent some happy times here, playing tennis and golfing, enjoying the beach, and so on. He was a good sport. About that, at least. Not so much about my work. Now I come here by myself."

"No children?"

Patience shook her head. "But at least until a few years ago, I got to see Jarvis," she said, "when he was still doing groundskeeping at the Mauna Kea. That's always been a pleasure, and at times in my life, a great comfort.

He'd come up to my lanai or I'd visit him in Puakō. We'd share a drink and talk story, as he liked to say. Once in a while I'd meet him after work and we'd hike the Ala Kahakai—you know, the ancient shoreline trail—from the Mauna Kea up to Kawaihae. We'd have a beer or two at the Dolphin, then one of Jarvis's buddies would drive us back to the resort. Everyone was Jarvis's buddy. It was all so different for him back then."

Patience paused, choking up a bit. But she soldiered on. "Anyway, I've known Jarvis since I was little. He nicknamed me Flea when I was about six—or *fuh-fuh-fuh* as he calls me now. I was surprised he was more formal today, trying to introduce me as Patience. You know, *puh-puh-puh*."

"I noticed that," Elle agreed with a nod. "When he sees Kawika nowadays, he says *kuh-kuh-kuh*. Same for Kawika's cousin Kuʻulei. With Terry Tanaka, he's *tuh-tuh-tuh*. Not stuttering, just trying to get that sound out."

"Poor guy," Patience said, with a shake of her head. "He's such a sweetie. Anyway, my family is longtime friends with Jarvis—you probably know that. My relationship with Jarvis isn't about Kawika, Elle. Didn't begin that way, hasn't ever been that way. I haven't seen Kawika for, what, a decade or more? So my visiting Jarvis has nothing to do with Kawika."

Elle waved a hand to dismiss the very thought. "I believe you," she quickly replied. "And I'm not worried, honestly, even though I was caught off guard today. And even though now I see you—plus having heard so much about you—well, naturally, I'm impressed. But mostly I'm just glad we've finally met. And really intrigued."

"That's kind of you," said Patience. "I'm intrigued too, of course. You're the lucky one. Congratulations, by the way. Sincerely. You got yourself a wonderful man."

Elle leaned forward and placed her hand on the other woman's arm again. "Let me tell you something," she confided. "Something I'm sure you already know. Kawika loved you, Patience. *Really* loved you. He's told me that more than once, and I've never doubted it. I think you're the one who taught him he *could* love someone, in fact. So what happened with you two had nothing to do with—"

"I never *knew* what happened," Patience quietly interrupted, as she'd said she might. To Elle's ear she sounded wistful, not bitter. "He just cut things off. Without a word."

"What happened," said Elle, resuming her explanation, "was something completely unexpected. Something he discovered in the Fortunato case, something he couldn't tell anyone—not you, not Terry Tanaka. Something that forced Kawika to deal with the case in a very unsatisfactory way. It left him isolated and, frankly, pretty tormented. He felt totally alone. He told *me* the whole story before we got married; I made him. But he and I still can't tell anyone. Not even you, who really deserves a better explanation. I'm sorry. I can only say that if none of that had happened, if he could have told you at the time, you'd probably be the one married to him—at least if he'd persuaded you, that is—and I'd probably be a spinster, writing fluffy beach fiction for tourists."

"Hardly a spinster!" Patience exclaimed. "And hardly fluffy beach fiction." But she averted her gaze, turning toward the bright flowers bordering the courtyard. Elle could see only one of Patience's eyes; it glistened and seemed ready to overflow.

"So, the official explanation of Fortunato's murder wasn't true?" Patience asked after a pause, wiping her eyes with the back of her hand. "That's basically what you just said, right? That's why you can never talk about it, because Kawika still has to protect Terry Tanaka? Maybe himself too? I always wondered about that official explanation. Kawika and I discovered so much, but then . . ." Her voice trailed off.

"Actually, you could help me understand something," Elle responded, glad to lead the conversation in a slightly new direction. "What you and Kawika discovered—did it include anything about a man named D. K. Parkes?"

Patience reacted with a grimace. "Why does everyone keep asking me about D. K. Parkes?" she asked.

* * *

Elle bit her lip and thought for a moment, looking at Patience searchingly. Then Elle decided to take Patience into her confidence.

"I can explain some things," Elle said. "But not everything. And almost none of this is public. But let's put our heads together. You may know things I don't."

They began with what Kawika believed: that two years before Parkes became a body thrown off Shark Cliff, he'd helped murder a man named Thomas Gray aboard Gray's fishing boat. Elle knew from Kawika that Patience had been the first to suggest Gray must've been murdered—by the resort developer Ralph Fortunato—and not drowned in a fishing accident. Gray had sold

Fortunato the land for his planned Big Island resort. The motive Patience and Kawika had ascribed to the killing was that Fortunato and Gray had colluded to defraud Fortunato's investors and Fortunato didn't want Gray available to testify against him if the feds came after him, which they'd done previously in Washington for a resort Fortunato had been developing there.

Elle pointed out that Kawika and Patience had parted long before the Handcuffed Haole was identified as D. K. Parkes. And only later, Elle explained, had Kawika guessed that Parkes had been Fortunato's accomplice in the Thomas Gray murder—a conclusion he'd mentioned to no one, not even Tanaka. No one until Elle, that is.

Yet neither of them could puzzle out why different women had telephoned recently to ask Patience and Sammy about Parkes so many years after his death, and why those women seemed interested solely in whether Parkes had children.

Impulsively taking a risk, and not at all sure Kawika would approve, Elle revealed to Patience the still-unreleased news that Parkes *did* have a child—Keoni. And that after those curious phone calls to Sammy and Patience, Keoni had turned up dead, a headless corpse in a Honolulu park.

It was easy to speculate that some connection might exist between the calls and Keoni's murder. But did the murder of Keoni relate to the fate of his father? Neither Elle nor Patience could guess. Elle didn't mention that Keoni had worked for the TMT. It seemed more important that Keoni was D. K.'s son and that both had been murdered—Keoni after two people had inquired about whether D. K. Parkes had children.

After pondering these mysteries inconclusively, Elle and Patience decided to return to Jarvis's bedside. "He must be wondering if we got into a catfight," Elle joked.

"A catfight! Not a term I thought a journalism professor would use these days," Patience teased. They left the flower-fragrant courtyard and stepped back into the antiseptic corridors of the care center. Jarvis awoke when they reentered his room.

"Sorry to leave you alone," Elle said. She took his hand and kissed him on the head. "But I hope you didn't worry. Patience and I got along just fine." To demonstrate this, Elle released his hand and gave Patience a hug. Although Patience seemed surprised, she hugged Elle back. Both women smiled in Jarvis's direction.

Then Elle handed Patience her phone. "Here," she said. "Why don't you give me your number?" Without hesitation, Patience took the phone and began typing. Elle hoped the gesture would further reassure her father-in-law. She felt moved that Patience had continued to be a friend to Jarvis through the years, especially with his immobility and near muteness.

"I just had an idea," Elle said as Patience handed back the phone. "Would you be willing to come to Oʻahu sometime and speak to my journalism class? If you talked about your career, about freelancing, about bouncing between Hawaiʻi and the mainland, it would be so valuable for the students, open their eyes to possibilities they might never imagine otherwise. For years my speakers have only been local reporters and editors. I'd be so grateful!"

Patience smiled. "Of course," she said. "I'm flattered you'd ask. I don't get to Oʻahu often enough, and that would be a great reason to go."

"Terrific!" Elle replied delightedly. "I'll call you and we'll set it up."

Then, with another kiss to Jarvis's head and another squeeze of his hand, Elle said she'd leave them to continue the conversation she'd interrupted. "But I'll see you soon, Jarvis," Elle promised. "Take you to the Saturday market in Waimea, yeah?"

Yuh-yuh-yuh, Jarvis replied. *Yuh-yuh-yuh.*

* * *

"So," Patience resumed when Elle had departed, taking the bedside chair again and holding Jarvis's hand. "Where was I? Oh yes—I was saying I'm going to write an article about the Thirty Meter Telescope Project. I'm learning from Hawaiians about Earth Mother, *Papa*, and Sky Father, *Wākea*, connecting to one another at the summit of Mauna Kea. And from astronomers about Chile and the Canary Islands and space telescopes and why they aren't substitutes for the TMT. Most people on the mainland know nothing about the TMT, I'm guessing. And anyone who's heard of it probably thinks it's a simple fight between Hawaiians and astronomers. But from what I can tell, it's more complicated."

She looked at Jarvis for a reaction, as if forgetting momentarily that he couldn't display one.

"What do *you* think about the TMT, Jarvis?" she asked, knowing he was a proud Hawaiian by ancestry and inclination, well schooled in Hawaiian culture and beliefs. "You opposed to it?"

Yuh-yuh-yuh, he said. *Yuh-yuh-yuh.* Patience felt gratified that Jarvis answered yes-or-no questions for her, his longtime friend, even if he couldn't or wouldn't for his caregivers and most others.

"I'm not surprised. But let me ask you something Elle reminded me of just now," she said, veering off the topic. "You knew Thomas Gray, right? When he was your neighbor in Puakō?"

Yuh-yuh-yuh.

"Kawika thinks Thomas Gray was murdered—murdered by Ralph Fortunato." She didn't add *and I think so too.* "Elle just told me Kawika believes Fortunato's accomplice was a man named D. K. Parkes. Did you know him too?"

Yuh-yuh-yuh.

"Oh, that's interesting. It seems his son Keoni Parkes was murdered in Honolulu recently. Did you know Keoni?"

This time she got a negative: *Nuh-nuh-nuh.*

"What about the children of Thomas Gray? I remember reading about them in his obituary. Both of them already adults back then. You knew them when they were growing up in Puakō?"

Yuh-yuh-yuh.

"Also interesting," Patience said. "I wonder what became of them?"

It wasn't a yes-or-no question. Jarvis couldn't help her with it. And he couldn't shrug.

Patience picked up her phone and made herself a note to check.

16

Waikoloa Village

Kawika had seen Tanaka looking ashen only once before. But he certainly looked ashen now. It was Saturday morning. Elle had gone off to visit Jarvis while Kawika and Tanaka met in a nearly empty Waikoloa Village coffee shop. A convenient spot, Kawika had thought in suggesting it: nice ambience, wood paneled, pleasant aromas. And they too could drop in and visit Jarvis once the two of them had talked.

As they settled themselves, it seemed to Kawika that apart from the drained and somber look on Terry's face, Tanaka hadn't aged much. His skin had wrinkles Kawika didn't remember, but Tanaka was still small and wiry and flexible. He sat with one heel on the seat of his chair, raising his knee to just below his chin, his other leg crossed under him—almost like a yoga position, Kawika thought. Yet today Tanaka also slumped where he sat, clearly morose. His normally dignified bearing had deserted him.

Kawika had often talked with Tanaka by phone—countless times, really—for more than a decade. But he'd seen him in person only rarely. The last time had been two years earlier, when Jarvis suffered his stroke. Kawika had rushed to the Big Island and found Tanaka at Jarvis's hospital bedside. Tanaka had looked drained and somber then too.

"Let's start with what we know," Kawika suggested. "Then we can consider how to handle Ana's investigation. It might take a while; more than one cup of coffee for me and a cup of tea for you. But we have to make a decision, Terry—together. So, maybe a full pot for you?" He smiled, trying to lighten the mood.

Tanaka nodded glumly. "We can go about this however you want, Kawika," he said, conceding the necessity of it. "But I know where it's going to end up. You and I are both going to be in the soup." Not *in deep shit*, Kawika noted. Even in crisis, Tanaka didn't use profanity.

"Maybe," Kawika replied. "But not if we both tell Ana the same story. That's the decision we have to make."

"How *can* we tell her the same story?" Tanaka asked with asperity. "You were right, I was wrong. It's all going to come out."

"Terry, don't assume that. Let's take this one step at a time. The two cases Ana's looking at, Fortunato and D. K. Parkes, are both from 2002. Now someone's murdered Keoni Parkes in Honolulu. And Keoni turns out to be the son of D. K. Parkes."

"Right."

"But we don't know Keoni's murder is linked to his father's, do we? Maybe it's linked to the TMT or to Keoni's personal life—or possibly even the Slasher, although I doubt it. The point is, unless we discover that Keoni's murder somehow relates to the murder of his father, you and I just need to decide what we're going to tell Ana about Fortunato and D. K. Parkes. And I have a suggestion for that."

Tanaka sighed. "Okay, Kawika. But there's something I have to tell you first. Something I need you to understand. When I gave my press conference after charging Cushing, I really did believe Cushing's hit man had killed Fortunato. But when you and I talked the next day, I understood what you were suggesting. You didn't come right out and say it, but you didn't have to." He looked at Kawika almost pitiably now, as if seeking forgiveness.

This was a completely different Tanaka from Kawika's experience, a Tanaka he'd never had a hint of. "Terry," Kawika reassured him. "If I'd reached you a day earlier, things might have been different. But I was *detained*, as you know—and it wasn't by Patience Quinn."

Tanaka looked surprised. "It wasn't?"

"No, it wasn't," Kawika declared. "I had to see you face-to-face, because there was evidence I couldn't tell you about by phone; our phones weren't secure. I couldn't even tell you *that* by phone."

"I finally guessed that, about our phones," Tanaka said with a nod. "But what I want to tell you, Kawika, the important thing, I still haven't said—"

"Terry, you don't have to—"

"But I do," Tanaka insisted. "I do. I was blinded by anger, Kawika. Anger at Cushing. Very unprofessional, getting angry at a suspect. But I was angry because he tried to have you killed. Could've killed Ku'ulei too."

"Yes," Kawika agreed. "I think about that almost every day. Ku'ulei was only eleven. She probably doesn't think about it quite so often now. But she sure did at the time!" He gave a small chuckle, trying to lighten things a bit.

But Tanaka seemed close to tears, wrenchingly for Kawika, who'd long recognized—a recognition that now hit him again, like a punch to the solar plexus—how much he owed and admired and even loved this older man, his mentor and former colleague, despite how they'd been separated and in part estranged by time, distance, and the Fortunato case, a painful and indigestible lump for them both.

"You came so close to being killed," Tanaka went on. "I just wanted to throw the book at Cushing. I wanted him sent away for a lot more than fifteen years."

Kawika laid a hand on Tanaka's arm. "I know you always looked out for me, Terry," he assured him. "You always protected me."

"But I—" Tanaka began.

Kawika stopped him. He wasn't Tanaka's protégé anymore, or even his junior colleague. He was his equal, if not more than that now, and in the matter of Carvalho's review, effectively his guidance counselor and coach.

"No, Terry, listen," he began. "You've confided in me now. And I hear you. But charging Cushing for Fortunato's murder was still perfectly reasonable, given the evidence. All of it pointed to Cushing."

Tanaka, unconvinced, shook his head.

"Terry," Kawika said firmly, "what matters now is this: we have to make a decision. We don't have a choice; we can't escape it. We *must* decide. This awful case coming to life again—it's not our doing, it's Cushing and Sammy talking to that reporter and Ana starting her investigation. We just have to agree on what to tell her. We have to get our stories straight."

Tanaka's eyes widened. Suddenly he looked more alert, but possibly more alarmed too, Kawika thought.

"Maybe it's time for another cup of coffee," Kawika said, rising and nodding toward the counter. "More tea for you?" A few people were in line. More time for Tanaka to collect himself, Kawika hoped. Kawika joined the line while Tanaka, already full of tea, visited the men's room.

With the single barista working at island speed, by the time they'd regained their seats with another round of hot drinks, almost ten minutes had passed. They'd chatted about other things once Tanaka joined Kawika waiting in line. Kawika saw that Tanaka had indeed collected himself—a bit.

"Now here's a key point, Terry," he said, leaning toward his mentor and picking up where he'd left off. "It's really important. *No one was harmed by your charging Cushing.* Fortunato was a killer who deserved what he got. So was Cushing."

Tanaka nodded to concede the point. "Not sure that's really relevant, though," he said. "I didn't do what I should have done."

"Doesn't matter," Kawika resumed, laying his hand on Tanaka's forearm again. "In the end, the Fortunato murder didn't add a single day to Cushing's sentence. Plus he's getting out early, for what that's worth."

Tanaka frowned, as if struggling to follow Kawika's logic. "So what are you saying?"

Kawika grasped Tanaka's arm again. "Just this, Terry. I'm saying we stick with your original story. The one you gave at your press conference after you arrested Cushing. We both tell Ana the same thing. That's our key decision. We tell her we checked all kinds of suspects in the Fortunato case, but none of those suspects did it. And then we got the hit man's confession, fingering Cushing—just like the physical evidence."

"But you knew the Fortunato part of the confession was false," Tanaka began. "Intentionally misleading, anyway."

"Yes, *I* knew. But no one else did. No one. You didn't know it yourself."

Tanaka shook his head again. "Not when I read it," he admitted. "Not before my press conference. But I knew it the next day, after you and I met and I read it again. Even then, I still let Cushing be prosecuted for that murder. That was more than a mistake, Kawika. It was probably a crime."

"But Terry, I never gave you another *name*," Kawika insisted. "There's nothing in the files about any suspect who remained plausible after our investigation, other than Cushing. There's no indication anywhere, except between you and me, that I ever disagreed with you about Fortunato's murderer. It's our *secret*, Terry. We have to keep it that way."

Kawika remained convinced, if only barely, that he'd done the right thing in 2002 by not calling out Tanaka's mistake when Tanaka charged Cushing for Fortunato's murder. Kawika had been very young. He hadn't been willing to contradict, much less expose, his mentor. He'd had other reasons too.

To come clean now would mean exposing Tanaka not just for having made a mistake but for failing to correct it. Kawika couldn't do that to him.

Moreover, Kawika had let the killer's accomplices go. Kawika had known who they were—three of them, at least. Tanaka did not. Kawika guessed they'd still be alive. To set the record straight now would mean having to expose and prosecute them all, because there was no statute of limitations for murder in Hawai'i.

Finally—and even he couldn't tell how much this affected his thinking—to admit being part of a twelve-year cover-up in one of Hawai'i's most notorious murder cases wouldn't help his chances of becoming chief of police in Honolulu. Not at all.

No, Kawika thought, he'd trapped himself long ago. What he needed now was to make sure the past remained the past, as dead as Fortunato himself. That meant Tanaka had to go along.

Tanaka looked searchingly into Kawika's eyes. But he seemed almost repelled, not relieved. Accusation shone from his gaze. "Kawika," he said, "I used to call you Mr. Clean. *What's happened to you* over there in Honolulu? You were never this kind of cop before."

Kawika felt as if he'd been slapped. But he had to keep going. He grasped both of Tanaka's arms, shaking them lightly to emphasize his point. "Terry, you protected me for years. Fiercely. You're my role model—my hero, really. Please let me return the favor. Let's just stick with the official story: Cushing's hit man killed Fortunato. Sammy can go pound sand on one of his retirement beaches. He's got nothing to show or tell Ana but his own suspicions. She won't believe him."

Tanaka's face shut down, went blank. "No, she won't believe him," he said in a flat tone. "And she won't believe us either, Kawika." He stood and began to return his teapot and cup to the counter.

Kawika didn't know what to do. He realized Tanaka didn't agree with him, couldn't be counted on to reaffirm what he'd said and done originally. Maybe he would think it over? Kawika hoped for that much, at least.

But then, turning to face him again, Tanaka added, "So, what lies shall we tell Ana about D. K. Parkes?"

17

Waimea

"If you're up to it, Dr. Phillips, we hope you'll tell us more about the fight over the TMT," Kawika began gently, once they were all seated at Dr. Phillips's Waimea home. "We need to interview members of the different groups, starting with their leaders."

"Why TMT?" she asked, sounding surprised but still subdued, still weary. "Someone killed Keoni in Honolulu—don't you think someone from his personal life did it? That's my only solace, that he didn't die because of TMT. I mean, what's the scene in Honolulu for single gay guys, for example? Could it have been a bad hookup or something?"

It was Saturday afternoon. Six of them—Kawika, Dr. Phillips, her assistant Angel Delos Santos, Tanaka, Tommy, and Ku'ulei—were seated in the sunken living room of the glass-walled midcentury modern house of the visibly saddened Dr. Phillips. Angel looked almost distraught. All of them had left their shoes at the door, Hawaiian-style. Dr. Phillips wore a tracksuit and house slippers. The others were in stocking feet. Her two-story home was perched high above the town, nestled amid lush flowering vegetation on the flank of Kohala Mountain. *A glorious spot*, Kawika thought, *on another occasion.*

When Elle had dropped Kawika off at the house, Dr. Phillips had been standing on the steps, greeting each new arrival solemnly. Elle had politely gotten out of the car to introduce herself, even though she didn't plan to stay. Dr. Phillips and Angel had both shaken Elle's hand lightly before turning to the other arrivals.

"I could use this woman in a book," Elle whispered to Kawika before getting back in the car. "She's an Amazon. Bet I could find a role for Angel too."

Kawika too had observed at once what Kuʻulei had told him: Dr. Phillips was tall, taller than Kawika. Imposing, even, though dressed casually on this Saturday afternoon. In her tracksuit and with her broad shoulders, she looked athletic, formidable, like the women's soccer coach at UH Mānoa. He wondered if, like the coach, she'd been an Olympian in some sport, maybe basketball or even discus or weight lifting; she might well have been, he thought. He saw no medals on her bookshelves, though, just photos of the widowed Dr. Phillips and her late and even-taller husband.

"We have detectives pursuing the Honolulu angles right now," Kawika said, acknowledging her point. "Some of our best people."

"When he first went missing, I worried it might relate to TMT," said Dr. Phillips. "That's what I told your colleagues." She tilted her head toward the three detectives she'd met originally. "But you found his body in Kapiʻolani Park. I mean, doesn't that . . . ?" She didn't complete the thought.

"You're probably right," Kawika replied, though he was far from sure. "Still, we have to check other possibilities. We don't have suspects yet. Not in Honolulu, not here."

Angel suddenly stood, bowed his head very quickly, and said tearfully, "I'm sorry, Emma. Sorry, all the rest of you. I just can't do this. Not yet." He nodded in their general direction and walked rapidly in his stocking feet to the door.

"Poor Angel," said Dr. Phillips when the door closed behind him. "He's taking this really hard. As we all are, but it's been particularly hard for him, it seems." The detectives exchanged surreptitious glances. All four of them knew Angel and Keoni had been lovers. Apparently, Dr. Phillips still didn't.

With a gesture, Tanaka indicated he'd like to begin the questioning. Kawika nodded assent, glad to see Tanaka assert himself despite their wrenching discussion at the coffee shop earlier. Although Keoni had died in Honolulu, they were on the Big Island now. The Big Island was Tanaka's territory, not Kawika's.

"Dr. Phillips," Tanaka began, "last time you said at least five groups are involved in the TMT conflict. Can you give us some details about them? It'll help us check all possibilities, like Major Wong mentioned."

Dr. Phillips agreed with evident reluctance. Kuʻulei prepared to take notes.

"Okay," the astronomer began. "There's background I have to explain first. Let's start with this: the summit of Mauna Kea is the best place in the world for astronomy. Absolutely the best."

Kawika exchanged discreet glances with his colleagues, who wore slightly amused expressions; once again Dr. Phillips was haole-splaining something they all knew, something everyone on the Big Island had long been told, namely that Mauna Kea was the world's best place for astronomy.

"Nothing else even comes close," she declared, "because of the high altitude and accessibility. Mauna Kea is almost exactly as tall as Mount Rainier, but you can't drive to the top of Mount Rainier. You can't build an observatory there." Kawika, who'd spent years in Seattle with glacier-encased Mount Rainier on the skyline, easily understood her point.

"Also," she went on, "there's the unpolluted air, the very limited light pollution, and in TMT's case, the ability to study the sky above the Northern Hemisphere and look directly into the heart of the Milky Way. The air at the summit is cold and dry, so the atmosphere is less turbulent than elsewhere, which allows us clearer vision into the depths of space. Do I need to explain about turbulence? No? Good."

Kawika nodded, not wanting to slow her down. He noted she'd begun to relax a bit, talking about astronomy instead of murder.

"Unfortunately," she continued, "the summit of Mauna Kea also lies within a tract of ceded Hawaiian lands."

"Ceded lands?" Tanaka asked. This was a term Kawika didn't recognize. But he noticed Ku'ulei nodding as Dr. Phillips continued.

"Yes, lands originally owned by the king but held for the benefit of the Hawaiian people—lands the federal government took over and then gave back to the state, supposedly still in trust for the Hawaiian people. Not the *people* of Hawai'i, you understand—the *Hawaiian* people. Native Hawaiians. The ceded lands are supposed to benefit Native Hawaiians. That's what the king wanted and all the subsequent governments have recognized. The king didn't say anything about benefiting astronomy. In addition, there are ancient sites at the summit—like a mystical body of water, Lake Waiau—sites some Hawaiians consider sacred."

"So there's a conflict," Tanaka said, encouraging her.

"Yes," she replied. "And several things make it worse. For decades, the University of Hawai'i has managed the ceded lands under a long-term lease from the Department of Land and Natural Resources—and most people, including a state court judge or two, believe the university has done a terrible job."

"For example?"

Dr. Phillips sighed. "For starters, the university allowed the first observatories to be built without permits. They said there'd be one observatory; now there are thirteen. They didn't take care to avoid sacred sites. For payment, they collected a dollar a year from each observatory—not much benefit to the Hawaiian people. And they did very little to protect the environment up there. Which, as you can understand, is pretty fragile at that altitude. There've been cases of dumping, construction waste, chemical spills, and so forth. All the observatories are on septic systems, so there's also discharge into the soil."

"Doesn't sound very good," Tanaka observed.

"No, and that's not our fault at the TMT!" she declared, with more animation than she'd shown so far. "But it is definitely part of our problem. A lot of opposition to a new telescope—any new telescope—reflects people getting fed up with the university's management. Hawaiians in particular, of course. Many people want a management change. And no new telescopes until that happens, or no new telescopes at all."

"Then why build the TMT at Mauna Kea?" Kawika asked, stepping in. "Isn't there a decent second-best site somewhere else? Is Mauna Kea really worth putting people like Keoni at risk?"

"You can build a thirty-meter telescope anywhere," she responded. "You just can't accomplish the same things with it. We need that thin, cold, dry air without turbulence to study what TMT is designed to study. We'll look deeper into space, see smaller and fainter and more distant stars and other objects than ever before. We could build TMT on a mountain in Chile, but then we couldn't see the night sky of the Northern Hemisphere. We could build it in the Canary Islands, but then we wouldn't have the clear cold air. No, we need the summit of Mauna Kea."

"Not even Mauna Loa would do?"

She looked at him with amusement. "No," she said. "Not quite high enough. Not to mention that Mauna Loa's pretty active. Constant tremors, swirling gases—even *molten lava*, you know." She chuckled a bit. She was haole-splaining again, but this time Kawika knew he deserved it.

Abashed, Kawika used the moment to look at his colleagues, effectively asking if they had questions. As it happened, Ku'ulei did.

"Why not a space telescope instead, then?" Ku'ulei asked. "That's what a lot of people seem to want."

Dr. Phillips turned to the young detective. "You mean like the James Webb Space Telescope?" she replied. "If it ever gets built. For one thing, its array is less than nine meters, whereas the TMT's will be thirty. Big difference in what we can detect out there. And if the TMT needs repairs or updated software, we can do that right here on the ground. Bring the new parts in a truck."

"But people have been able to fix the Hubble telescope, haven't they?" Ku'ulei asked, continuing to press. "And it's in orbit too."

The question elicited a sigh from Dr. Phillips; she'd obviously dealt with it before. "Hubble is in earth orbit, like a satellite," she explained. "We can send astronauts to fix it. In fact, we've already done that, just as you say. But the James Webb Space Telescope will orbit the sun, not the Earth. It'll be almost a million miles away, assuming it ever gets launched. We'd need an interplanetary mission to fix or upgrade it. Hugely expensive. A mission to repair it would cost more than the James Webb itself—which is saying something. Many billions of dollars. NASA doesn't even have contingency plans for such a mission. It'd be cheaper to build a new space telescope than try to fix the original."

At this point, Tanaka spoke again. "Okay, we see the basic problem. Let's talk about potential suspects now, if that's all right with you. Tell us about the various activist groups, like you mentioned when we met. You know, the Hawaiians and the others, the people on all sides. Who they are, who are their leaders, who we should talk to."

Dr. Phillips gave a dry, sardonic laugh.

"How much time do you have?" she asked.

18

Puakō

The interview with Dr. Phillips lasted a long time. In midafternoon she rose from her chair and busied herself in the kitchen with Tommy's help, returning with light refreshments. But by nightfall Dr. Phillips was visibly exhausted and everyone else was ready for dinner. Dr. Phillips seemed ready for a drink. The detectives thanked her, wrapped up the discussion, allocated their interview assignments from among the leads she'd provided, and dispersed to Hilo, Waimea, and Puakō.

Kawika and Elle dined alone at the Puakō house, carrying their food outdoors and sitting beneath the palms and the stars. They ate in a relaxed near silence, just listening to the breakers far offshore and the inshore flow of modest waves that crawled across the reef before spending themselves with a murmur along the sand.

Later, as they washed the dishes, they talked about the exciting yet daunting next chapter in their lives: parenthood and the many things they needed to do to get ready. Normally they would then have prepared for bed, but Elle surprised Kawika by asking, "Can we sit for a moment?"

"Sure," he replied, taking a seat beside her and resting an arm along the back of the couch. She tucked a bare foot under her opposite thigh and turned to face him.

"It's been a long day," she conceded. "But, Kawika, there's something I need to tell you before we go to sleep." He nodded for her to go ahead. "I met Patience today," she said matter-of-factly. "I was waiting for a good moment—alone—to tell you."

Kawika blinked in surprise. "Patience?" he repeated. "Patience Quinn?"

"Yes, Kawika—Patience Quinn. She was with Jarvis when I got to his room, by his bed and holding his hand. Don't worry, nothing bad happened. She was very nice, and I was nice too, honest." She placed a reassuring hand on his forearm. "Very polite, both of us, just a bit awkward at first. We sat down in the courtyard and had a pleasant talk."

"I didn't know she still visited Dad," Kawika said, feeling as awkward as he imagined his wife must have earlier. "Not since his stroke. I've never run into her at the care center—or anywhere else. She used to visit Dad when he was still working, I knew that. But I didn't know she still came to the Big Island at all, much less that she still sees my dad."

"She does—and that's nice for Jarvis. And she's read *Murder at the Mauna Lani* too. Even recognized herself as the lover, despite my making the lover a man. Recognized her condo too."

"Elle, I—"

She cut him off with a laugh, smiling, patting his forearm and then taking his hand from the top of the couch to hold in hers. "*Relax*, Kawika! It's all okay. Seriously. We both had premarital lives. I'm glad yours was mostly a happy one with beautiful women; mine sorta sucked. But Patience and I got along just fine. We exchanged phone numbers; I invited her to speak to my class. What I want to tell you, though, is about the *case*. Something she said about D. K. Parkes."

"D. K.? Did she say anything about Keoni?"

"No, his name never came up until I mentioned him. His identity's not public yet, is it?"

Kawika sighed. "Not tonight," he replied. "But it will be soon. Probably tomorrow, unless Zoë Akona takes weekends off."

Elle grimaced but pressed on. "Zoë is part of what Patience told me. We were talking about my book, so naturally we talked about the Fortunato case. She said the official explanation for Fortunato's murder never made sense to her, based on things you and she discovered back then."

"Okay," Kawika said. "About Fortunato, yes, she's right. But Patience and I had stopped seeing each other before I'd ever heard of D. K. Parkes."

Elle pumped his hand in hers for emphasis. "I know, and that's the point, Kawika. Patience said she'd never heard of Parkes. But she said everyone keeps asking her about him."

Kawika, startled, sat up sharply, quickly withdrawing his hand from hers. "*What*? Who's everyone? Zoë? Why would Zoë or anyone else ask *Patience* about D. K. Parkes?"

Elle took his hand again and began to explain. "Yes, Zoë found Patience and asked her about D. K. Parkes. But Patience also got a phone call from a woman on Maui, calling about a life insurance policy on Parkes. The woman asked Patience if she knew whether he'd had children."

Kawika, puzzled, frowned and furrowed his brow.

"I know, right?" Elle went on. "Calling about life insurance more than a decade after the man died? That's not all. When Patience asked why Zoë had come to interview her, Zoë said Sammy Kāʻai suggested it. He said you might have told Patience things about Parkes because Patience was your girlfriend at the time of Shark Cliff."

One of my girlfriends, Kawika thought, and felt his face flush. He hoped Elle didn't notice; fortunately, the light inside the cottage was low. His faithlessness to his actual girlfriend back then, Carolyn Kaʻaukai, his prolonged inability to choose between two lovers and the pain he'd caused, all inflicted by his indecision and caddishness as a young man, filled him with shame whenever he thought about it. Which he tried never to do.

"But guess what Sammy also told Zoë?" Elle continued. "He said a woman had called *him* recently, also asking about Parkes and whether he had children. And not a woman from Maui—a tax lady from Honolulu. Zoë relayed all this to Patience."

"Wait," Kawika said. "Two women called to ask about D. K.'s children? Just recently? One called Sammy and one called Patience?"

"Right, Kawika. Within the last month. Two phone calls out of the blue from two different women, one to Sammy and one to Patience, both asking if D. K. Parkes had children. Living children. Patience said she couldn't figure it out."

Kawika couldn't either. But an image of Patience—Patience as she lay across a bed with her laptop during the Fortunato case, trying to figure things out—had suddenly dropped him through a trapdoor into his past. He swallowed, knowing Elle was looking at him, knowing he should say something. Transfixed by that image, however, he couldn't speak.

* * *

Eventually, Kawika and Elle prepared for bed. It was then that Elle came to Kawika softly, barefoot in her robe. She asked that he hold her.

"What is it, babe?" he inquired, putting his arms around her.

"I felt a tiny bit insecure, meeting Patience," she answered, with her cheek against his chest. "Just for a moment. I knew I shouldn't; I'm your wife, after all. But Patience is so smart and articulate and obviously rich. And she's damn good-looking. You never really explained that part, Kawika. So beautiful and not a single figure fault. Even now, at her age."

"But Elle—"

Elle shushed him. "You don't need to reassure me, Kawika. I'm okay. Just let me finish. After my surprise at meeting her, I wasn't intimidated or jealous or any of those things. That faded pretty quickly. But sitting there, talking with her, I realized that if things had been slightly different—if you could've confided in her back then, told her the truth about Fortunato's murder—then you and I would never have met. Or never have gotten married, anyway. And that made me really sad."

Kawika didn't know quite how to respond. He wanted to reassure her, but she'd just said she didn't need reassurance. Perhaps he needed to tell her, once again, how glad he was that things had worked out as they had.

"Elle," he began, lifting her chin so she'd look at him. "Darling. You're perfect for me. You know that. Absolutely perfect. Even if I could've told Patience the truth back then, she and I never would've worked out. We were practically just kids. I was a confused Hawaiian cop, and she was a California journalist going through a divorce. It was just a passing thing. So you and I would still have met when we did, just the way we did. We would've gotten married, just like we did, and we'd still be married now, just like we are."

Elle looked at him questioningly. "You believe that? We were fated to meet?"

"I'm not saying that," he replied. "I'm just saying that nothing about Patience, about telling her the truth or not, would have made any difference in the end. Not for Patience and me. And not for you and me either. You and I would still be standing together in our own bathroom."

Kawika didn't know if he'd convinced his wife. He wasn't entirely convinced himself. He felt the unsettling sensation of being largely truthful when tact and complexity made complete truth impossible.

"I don't waste a minute thinking about how life might've been different," he continued. "*Occupy the life you've chosen*—that's what Dad always said, right? This is the life I've chosen, Elle. I chose you, life with you. I'm so glad I did."

Elle continued to regard him closely, as if evaluating his sincerity. But she didn't speak. Perhaps she needed him to say more, he thought. So he did.

"You're incredibly smart and articulate, Elle—you're a great teacher, your students love you, you write terrific books. Okay, we're not rich. But you keep me fascinated all the time, and you're such a cheerful person, always a delight and pleasure. You knew when we met how much I needed that. I really did. You've even taught me to speak and write much better than I did before. *Infinitely* better, see? And besides your being so *vivacious*"—he smiled, keeping alive the joke about his Elle-enhanced vocabulary—"to me you're the most beautiful woman I've ever met, even though you didn't need to be and still don't. Your beauty's a bonus. I appreciate it and feel lucky every day because of it."

He wasn't exaggerating. He loved her beauty, loved her body, never tired of either or took them for granted. He appreciated how she cared for herself. He always felt she deserved his doing more of that himself. He often swore silently, *No more junk food, no bacon, no cheese, definitely no bacon cheeseburgers, got to start running more, get to the gym.*

Elle pulled herself to him tightly and finally laughed, then pushed herself away to arm's length and shook her head. "Okay, smooth talker," she said. "How about you blink those big hazel eyes at me, like you did the first time, then take me to bed? I'd like that right now."

"All right. I'll blink three times for yes." Which he did, making her laugh again. She took his hand and led Kawika to the bedroom, where they made love tenderly, appreciatively.

"You know," she whispered as she began to fall asleep, "even after seven years of marriage, I'm still completely besotted with you, Kawika Wong."

"Besotted is a word?" he asked doubtfully.

"It is," she affirmed sleepily.

"Well then, Elianna Azevado da Silva," he whispered in return, "you besot me more."

Then he yawned and almost fell asleep himself. But a moment later he was suddenly fully awake again. Not thinking about Patience Quinn, not after making love with Elle. Thinking about Keoni Parkes. Who were the women who'd called to ask whether D. K. Parkes had children? Who'd then killed D. K.'s only child? Why?

Kawika remained awake a long time.

19

Kawaihae

Jeffrey Mokuli'i, leader of WMK—Warriors for Mauna Kea, the group Dr. Phillips had called the most radical of TMT opponents—had insisted on meeting Kawika and Ku'ulei near Kawaihae at the offering-strewn bare dirt ancient homesite of John 'Olohana Young, the favorite haole of Kamehameha the Great. Two centuries earlier Kamehameha had given this and more extensive tracts of land to John Young and allowed him to marry into Hawaiian royalty. Young had thereby become royalty by marriage and eventually the grandfather of the revered Queen Emma, who'd been born a hundred yards or so from John Young's homesite.

'Olohana was the nickname Kamehameha had bestowed on Young. An English sailor from Liverpool, Young had found himself captive in Kamehameha's court, involuntarily detained until his shipmates gave him up for lost and left Hawai'i without him. Considering his options, Young agreed to become admiral of the king's rustic fleet. He'd shouted, "All hands on deck!" to the Hawaiian crews he drilled. *All hands*, which probably sounded like *All Hans* in an eighteenth-century Liverpudlian accent, became *'Olohana* in Hawaiian.

Young trained Kamehameha's men to fire fusillades from muskets and small cannons in sea battles against the war canoes of the king's club- and spear-wielding enemies. Kamehameha's warriors loved 'Olohana Young not just for his amusing speech, but even more because the modern weapons he'd procured made sure that Kamehameha's enemies, not his own warriors, were the ones who got killed.

"It's a semi-sacred spot, John Young's place," Ku'ulei had explained to Kawika in setting up the Sunday morning meeting where Mokuli'i had demanded it. Kawika could tell Ku'ulei herself felt reverential as she sat there. He'd wanted to interview Mokuli'i in Waimea, but she'd persuaded him to accept Mokuli'i's terms. "He's surrounding himself with *mana*," Ku'ulei had said. "Power. We shouldn't object. He's agreed to come; we're not having to chase him."

And so Ku'ulei and Kawika sat on a lava rock wall in the gauzy shade of a kiawe tree. They were within the almost indiscernible outline of John Young's long-vanished house, their shoes on dusty and well-trodden red soil, awaiting Jeffrey Mokuli'i, who was late. Among the offerings at the site were flower leis of fragrant plumeria, so the wait was not entirely unpleasant.

"We have an 'Olohana Street in Waikīkī," Kawika remarked idly.

"Of course you do!" said Ku'ulei with feigned indignation—although not entirely feigned, Kawika could tell. "You O'ahu guys are cultural appropriators!" she joked.

Kawika noted, as often before, that Hawaiian history and culture were never far from her thoughts. Her studies represented an accomplishment he respected and envied; her police work would be better for it. He remembered times when his might have been too.

But he knew her passions for all things Hawaiian long preceded her joining the police force. He well remembered when she'd been a student at UH Mānoa and asked him to join her in Waikīkī one day. He'd assumed they'd swim or surf, but instead she just wanted to place a lei on sacred Kapaemahu, the so-called Wizard Stones, a set of boulders left centuries earlier by four mystical visitors from Tahiti who'd shared healing and soothsaying with the Hawaiians before departing. As Ku'ulei had reached over the guardrail to toss the lei lightly on the tallest stone, tourists had stopped momentarily to snap photos, then headed to the beach or the food stand or the shops. But once they'd turned away, Ku'ulei raised both hands, her thumbs touching her fingertips, and lifted her face to the sky as she murmured an ancient Hawaiian chant or prayer—Kawika couldn't tell which and, embarrassed, didn't ask.

"You've appropriated *all* our Big Island history," Ku'ulei resumed as they waited for Jeffrey Mokuli'i. "You've even got the splintered paddles on your police cruisers in Honolulu."

"The splintered paddles are yours?" Kawika asked, surprised. "I mean here, on the Big Island?"

"Of course!" she replied. "You know the story, don't you? No? Well, this island is where a fisherman beat Kamehameha over the head with a paddle until it broke. Kamehameha was going to sacrifice the fisherman, but eventually he forgave him, because the man had just been protecting his family. That's where the law of the splintered paddle comes from. It's part of what Kamehameha decreed after freeing the fisherman. Basically, *May everyone, from the old men and women to the children, be free to go forth and lie in the road without fear of harm.*"

"I know the law," Kawika assured her. "It's in the Hawai'i constitution. We had to learn it at HPD. They make us learn it because a lot of people take advantage of it. You've seen our homeless camps? Our parks? Even though Kamehameha never mentioned lying in parks, I bet."

"I haven't seen your parks recently. I live in Hilo these days, Kawika. In case you forgot."

He laughed, then continued. "Hawai'i must be the only state with a constitutional right to camp in city parks. You know what homeless people say in Honolulu as they thumb their noses at us? *Law of the splintered paddle.* You know what tourists say? *At least your homeless people are homeless with aloha.* Meaning, at least they keep to themselves and seem nice; they don't scare the visitors. A lot of them just hang out in their tents, drunk or drugged up on ice—crystal meth, that is."

"*Another* thing Honolulu appropriated from the Big Island!" she said sarcastically. "Ice, straight from the wilds of Puna."

"But nowadays even fentanyl is beginning to show up," Kawika added. "It's sad. Most of the users will end up dead."

"True on the Big Island too," Ku'ulei observed.

Kawika paused, lost for a moment in another memory: Ku'ulei at age eleven, innocent, sitting happily on his lap while he tried to eat, excitedly telling him about the pork and poi offerings wrapped in leaves of ti plants that she and her classmates were preparing for the god Lono during his four-month festival of Makahiki.

Wistfully, Kawika returned to the topic of the splintered paddles.

"Just so you know," he resumed, "I've got one of the cars with the redesigned HPD shield on the door. The paddles look like lollipops. So I guess you can have the splintered paddles back."

Ku'ulei snorted. "Probably HPD hired some graphic designer who knew absolutely zero about the splintered paddles," she said.

Just then Jeffrey Mokuli'i came into sight, striding up the ragged path and into the enclosure, raising a cloud of reddish dust. He sat down ostentatiously in the dirt, cross-legged, not waiting for the dust to settle, and smiled unpleasantly at the two detectives. His arrival put an end to the casual mood. His silver-streaked hair was oiled and secured in a bun with a carved stick. No shirt covered his light-skinned upper body, but he had lots of tattoos in traditional Polynesian patterns, telling stories unenlightened eyes couldn't read, and many rings and bracelets.

"Aloha," Mokuli'i deadpanned.

Mokuli'i's exotic appearance and insincere smile made a strong impression. But the strongest impression came from his necklace: dozens of woven strands bunched together into two thick black ropes supporting a carved pendant at their center. Like any other Hawaiian, Kawika could recognize the necklace as one that would belong to Hawaiian royalty or great chiefs in battle, the equivalent of a scepter or field marshal's baton. The pendant would be the ivory tooth of a sperm whale. Cut and polished, it resembled a tongue. Every island featured that necklace in statues and murals. It was absurdly grandiose and out of place for Mokuli'i to be wearing it now.

Momentarily nonplussed by the neckwear, Kawika hesitated. Ku'ulei stepped in. "You descended directly from kings yourself, Jeffrey? Or is that a fake *lei niho palaoa*?"

The sneering smile broadened. "No, it's not a *fake*," he replied. "It's a *replica*. No human hair, not a real whale tooth. But you don't have to be royalty to wear this lei anyway." He took the simulated tooth and rubbed it between his fingers. "If you've got an army of followers, you can wear it into battle. That's why I wear it. We're battling for Mauna Kea."

"And you have one great big army of followers?" Ku'ulei asked acidly, drawing out the words *one great big*, surprising Kawika by challenging Mokuli'i at the very start of the interview.

"Bigger than *your* group," he taunted her.

"Ha!" she exclaimed, disputing that claim.

Kawika intervened. "Your group?" he asked Ku'ulei.

"I'll explain later," she said. Mokuli'i's smile became a smirk.

Kawika didn't press her. "Good time to move on," he said, taking control. He began by telling Mokuli'i what Dr. Phillips had said about the hostility

Keoni had encountered on the front lines of the TMT controversy. Mokuli'i interrupted him.

"She tell you dat?" he snorted derisively, switching partly to pidgin. "Den she doan tell you da half. Not even da half." Instantly, Kawika knew what was going on: two Hawaiians—Mokuli'i and Ku'ulei, for example—would naturally speak pidgin to each other, and if Kawika spoke pidgin, he'd be included too. Mokuli'i was testing him: *Are you one of us or not?* Mokuli'i seemed to sense not, in which case he was speaking only to Ku'ulei, effectively ignoring Kawika.

Mokuli'i continued, with Ku'ulei translating the pidgin to make sure Kawika understood, saying that Keoni had "sold out his own people." Someone would get him for that, Mokuli'i insisted. "Maybe da *huaka'i pō*."

"The *what*?" Kawika understood the disrespect implicit in Mokuli'i using pidgin, but now he was mixing in Hawaiian too? Hundreds of thousands of Hawai'i residents spoke pidgin; very few spoke Hawaiian.

"The night marchers," explained Ku'ulei. "They're like ghosts, Kawika. Can be anything: dead priests, ancient warriors, even the gods. Could even be household gods, the *'aumakua*, like ours. You know, *pueo*—the owl—that's our family 'aumakua. The night marchers stream down from the top of Mauna Kea sometimes. They're deadly; they can kill you. You have to take off all your clothes and lie facedown, don't look at them."

Kawika hadn't known about the night marchers, or that the Wong family had a household god. But he liked that the family 'aumakua was the little native owl. He wondered whether Ku'ulei had gotten that from Jarvis, who'd raised her. He suspected she'd made pueo their 'aumakua herself.

"Dat's right," said Mokuli'i, smiling at Ku'ulei and extending a tattooed, ham-sized arm to pat her shoulder. She brushed it away immediately but kept translating for Kawika as Mokuli'i went on. "He says if you're in their way, the marchers, they're going to kill you. He says Keoni turned his back on the gods and his people, so they were going to kill him for sure."

They? Which 'they' would kill him? Kawika wondered. *The gods or his people?* But he didn't ask it aloud. Instead, he said to Mokuli'i, "You're laying it on a bit thick, aren't you?" Mokuli'i just grinned. Still not a nice grin.

"How about this, Kawika?" Ku'ulei replied smoothly. "Let me ask the questions to start. He's just mixing in some pidgin, aren't you, Jeffrey? He guessed you don't speak it." She didn't need to say *He's trying to piss you off.* This wasn't the first difficult witness he'd interviewed.

So Ku'ulei did the questioning, took notes, interpreted for her cousin. Kawika suggested topics and tried to follow along. He knew Jeffrey Mokuli'i could speak clear English. He led a well-publicized cultural group, and—Dr. Phillips had assured them—he was astute and media savvy. Even in Hawai'i the news media didn't go for too much pidgin.

Thus began the laborious process of trying to tease the truth from Jeffrey Mokuli'i, with Ku'ulei serving as translator of his pidgin, random Hawaiian, and occasional English. She first probed whether he or any of his followers had been in Honolulu the night Keoni Parkes died.

"Lotta us in Honolulu at da time," he replied. "Legislature dere, ya know. Dapartmen' too."

"The Department of Land and Natural Resources," Ku'ulei reminded Kawika. "Remember what Dr. Phillips said? The department leased the lands on Mauna Kea to the university."

The interview went slowly. Besides requiring translation of his pidgin to conventional English, Jeffrey Mokuli'i refused to jump ahead in time. He wanted to start with the moment when, in his words, telescopes began sprouting like weeds on the summit of Mauna Kea. Ku'ulei related his diatribe faithfully to her cousin. Not all of it was new; Dr. Phillips had explained much of it. But Mokuli'i told the tale rather differently.

Mokuli'i spoke of the university's treachery as landlord and lessor, promising one telescope and allowing thirteen. Covering the mountaintop with buildings and contamination, both chemical and spiritual, disturbing not only the beauty but the formation of clouds and the hydrology of the entire Big Island. Allowing astronomers to dig up or bury sacred sites and scar the skyline with massive structures, visible from everywhere, impossible to ignore. The astronomers got everything and did whatever they wanted. Hawaiians got nothing—nothing to speak of—in return for all the desecration, at least in Mokuli'i's telling of it.

"And *damn* Keoni," he now insisted in clearly enunciated English. "Hawaiian, yeah? But he tried to bring *another* telescope to Mauna Kea. Too many, man. No wonder he's gone." All stated in a manner suggesting almost anyone might have killed him, since so many people cared about the mountain and Keoni evidently didn't.

Mokuli'i concluded with a smile of self-satisfaction, locking his fingers and stretching his well-inked arms overhead before folding them across his equally well-inked chest.

"Okay," Kawika said, addressing the other man directly this time. "But how about the night Keoni Parkes was killed? Were you in Honolulu then? Yes or no."

"Whole lot of us were there at the time," Mokuliʻi replied. He grinned slyly. "We held a massive demonstration. *Massive*, I tell you. You didn't notice us? Oh well. Neither did the legislature."

"That was during the day, right? Where were you after that, on Friday evening and Friday night?"

After the demonstrators had dispersed, Mokuliʻi answered, some returned to the Big Island. Mokuliʻi said he and a smaller group ate dinner outdoors at Deck, a restaurant in the Queen Kapiʻolani Hotel on the south end of Waikīkī. Then after sunset they took a few beers and smoked some pakalōlō on the beach, where they met a group of young haole women from the mainland.

"We're the beach boys, yeah?" he said. "All those tourist *wahine*, they jus' *love* Waikīkī beach boys. Always have, always will."

"Sure," Kuʻulei replied skeptically. "Any of those women have names that you recall? Any of them able to confirm your story?"

One young woman would certainly remember him, Mokuliʻi boasted, given how they'd spent the evening together. But he never got her name.

"Where did you spend the night?" Kawika asked.

"In the park, man. Splintered paddle, you know."

"Kapiʻolani Park?"

"Yeah, that one, I guess."

"You slept on the ground?"

"Brought a bedroll. Big enough for two. Put it to good use with what's-her-name."

Mokuliʻi said he'd returned to the Big Island on Saturday at midday. They could check with the airline to confirm that, he offered, and Kawika assured him they would.

"We'll need the names of others of your group who were in Honolulu that Friday," Kawika said. "All of 'em."

"Oh, I'll get 'em for you, tomorrow morning, sure thing," Mokuliʻi promised sweetly, turning to Kuʻulei. "Some of 'em, anyway. Can't remember all of 'em, of course."

"Of *course*," Kuʻulei replied in disgust.

Kawika stood up and ended the interview, but without shaking hands. "*Mahalo* for the *kōkua*," he said—basically "thanks for the compliance," a stock phrase found on every sign asking pedestrians not to litter. Like the signs in Kapi'olani Park. Kawika felt pretty sure Mokuli'i would interpret it as a slight. Just as Kawika intended.

* * *

Kawika and his young cousin walked to their car, leaving Jeffrey Mokuli'i and the ruins of John Young's house behind. "*Hō'oio*," Ku'ulei spat out. "Show-off," she added, for Kawika's benefit.

"You'll follow up with him tomorrow?" Kawika asked.

"First thing," she promised. "Then we'll get 'em all interviewed. There's really just a handful of WMK people. But you know the only names he'll give us are for people who can't be the killer. He won't mention the rest."

Kawika nodded. "But maybe one of the others will slip up and we'll find more suspects that way," he said. "They won't all be as clever as he is. And incidentally, I heard him say *hydrology*. No good word for that in pidgin, I guess?"

"If there is, I don't know it," Ku'ulei affirmed, still sounding irritated with Mokuli'i. "I'm not sure we have a good word for *hydrology* even in Hawaiian, and I bet I know more Hawaiian than he does. He's such a . . . hō'oio, like I said. I'm trying to be polite, you understand."

"So, what did you think of him, besides 'show-off'?" Kawika asked, in part to advance her training, just as he would've with Yvonne Ivanovna. But he also found Jeffrey Mokuli'i puzzling. He wanted Ku'ulei's assessment of him.

"Arrogant? Conceited? Boaster? *Hō'oio* covers them all. He's just a terrible spokesman for the cause," she replied. "More important, he could be the killer, Kawika—or one of them. He was using that ridiculous chiefly appearance and his bragging, his pidgin, the night marchers and so on, to distract us. He had motive and opportunity. Keoni would have opened the door to him if he'd shown up in Honolulu. He's got no real alibi either."

"I agree," Kawika said. He was beginning to suspect that Keoni's killer or killers might indeed be found among Mokoli'i and his adherents.

"But don't judge the cause by that jerk," Ku'ulei advised. "Remember, Dr. Phillips said he leads the most *radical* group, not the *largest* group—that's the

Mea Pale ʻAhu, the MPA. The ʻDefenders,' basically. A *mea pale ʻahu* is a mat you spread over a canoe to protect it, Kawika. In this case, spread over Mauna Kea to protect the mountain. The MPA is a lot larger, and they're *not* jerks."

"You know them, these Defenders?"

"Sure," she replied, lips tight with seriousness. "I'm one of them, Kawika. That's what Jeffrey meant by ʻyour group.' I've been with MPA ever since college. We believe the things Jeffrey was saying—not about Keoni, of course, but about the mountain. We just don't like *him* saying them, because he hurts the cause. Too extreme, too deceitful, that guy. He's on a power trip. But he doesn't have many followers. A few dozen at most, I bet. That's a lot to interview, but compared to MPA, it's a tiny group. He's alienated a hundred times more people than he's persuaded. A thousand times more, maybe."

Her answer had become heated. She stopped suddenly. Kawika thought she'd finished. Yet she added another thought, this time more calmly. "But those things he was talking about at the summit, Kawika? They're important. There are *wahi pana* up there—sacred places. The entire summit is wahi pana. The entire *mountain* is wahi pana."

Kawika took his eyes off the road briefly and regarded her with a mix of admiration and surprise. "You oppose the TMT yourself, Kuʻulei?" he asked. "I didn't realize that."

"You know Jarvis does too?" she replied defensively. "Your dad was one of us; he joined MPA right before his stroke. He doesn't want another telescope up there. He can't say it anymore. But you ask him a yes-or-no question, he'll tell you."

Kawika considered how best to respond. "Good for Dad," he finally said. "And good for you too, Cuz. I had no idea."

"Most people don't. That's the problem, Cuz. And if you don't mind my saying so," Kuʻulei added, "for a Hawaiian born on the Big Island, you're a bit late to the party."

20

Hilo

While Kawika and Ku'ulei dealt with Jeffrey Mokuli'i in Kawaihae, Tanaka and Tommy met in Hilo to interview Jonathan Kalākalani, the leader of Big Island 'Ohana, the strongest group of local TMT supporters. Jonathan Kalākalani was the forty-year-old nephew of Haia Kalākalani, the former chief of police—Ana Carvalho's immediate predecessor—under whom Tanaka, Tommy, and Kawika had all served. Jonathan had been educated on the mainland before returning to Hilo, where he now worked as a public school administrator. Tanaka had known him since Jonathan's boyhood, and Jonathan called Tanaka "Uncle" in the familiar Hawaiian fashion for addressing an elder in one's extended family.

They met at Jonathan's home on Hilo's outskirts, a modest house with a spectacular ocean view, dominated just then by a dark rainstorm approaching ominously from the east.

"Of *course* someone killed Keoni because of TMT," Jonathan declared flatly to Tanaka and Tommy. "But it wasn't us. We weren't *that* angry with him, just frustrated. Keoni was willing to scrap a bunch of other telescopes to get TMT built. We weren't. Didn't need to pay that high a price. Didn't need to compromise at all, really—just promise to be really careful when building something on the summit, which TMT will be anyway. So Keoni was going too far, you know? Lost his nerve with people shouting and calling him a traitor to his ancestors, to his race.

"People call me a traitor to my race too," Jonathan continued defensively. "But you know what I tell 'em? I'm not a traitor to my race; I'm a traitor to the *tyranny* of race. Keoni should've said that too, but he didn't. You know the expression 'converted by the natives'? Well, Keoni got converted by the natives—the Native Hawaiians."

Tommy, taking notes by hand, bristled at that. Tanaka noticed, but Jonathan apparently didn't. "Uncle," he resumed, addressing Tanaka, "some conflicts can be solved by compromise, right? But not a civil war. In a civil war, one side has to win and one side has to lose. That's what Keoni never understood. He was trying to compromise a civil war. He should have tried to win it. Winning this one is important."

Jonathan kept going but changed tack. "Uncle, you know I'm as Hawaiian as the next guy, okay? Our Kalākalani family 'aumakua is the shark, and I swam with them as a boy. My dad made me; it was magical." He sounded wistful, and paused for a moment before resuming. "But sometimes we get too romantic and sentimental about ourselves as Hawaiians. When we do that, we become selective. We want certain things to be sacred from Kamehameha's time, from before the overthrow of the old religion. But in those days our religion had human sacrifice at its center. We don't want to bring that back, do we? The king and the chiefs and the priests had the absolute right of *kapu* over everyone. They could condemn people to death on the spot whenever they chose. The men didn't eat with women back then, and women couldn't eat pork or bananas. What everyone did eat was dogs. We want to return to all that? Of course not."

Tanaka could tell Jonathan was in the mood to talk. "Okay," he said. "Go ahead, Jonathan. Tell us what you want us to know. Then we'll go from there."

Jonathan seemed to welcome the opportunity. He explained that as far back as the end of World War II, putting telescopes on Mauna Kea had been chosen as a key way to boost the Big Island economy, which in those days depended on sugarcane.

"The sugar's long gone," Jonathan said. "So apart from the telescopes, what do we have? Mostly tourism—that and a little coffee, a few macadamia nuts. The tourism's mainly a Kona and Kohala thing, not much anywhere else on the island. And for the whole Big Island, we've got what by way of tourists? Half what Maui has. Half, Uncle! Maybe twenty percent of O'ahu's. Even Kaua'i has nearly as many as we do. We don't have Senator Inouye anymore to bring us highway work and hospitals and those kinds of construction jobs. Without the telescopes, Uncle, unemployment on this side of the island would be at Great Depression levels. Although if we lost the telescopes, I suppose we'd still have the meth labs."

Then he turned serious again and began rattling off talking points, counting on his fingers as he spoke. "TMT is worth one and a half billion dollars," he said. "Think of that. A billion and a half dollars in new investment. And overall, the observatories already bring the Big Island a hundred million dollars a year. TMT will add a lot to that, not even counting the tax benefits. Also, TMT's already begun paying for more education on the Big Island. They're bringing in scientists and other professionals who care about better schools for their kids. All before they've even broken ground."

"But breaking ground is exactly the problem, isn't it?" Tanaka asked. "I mean, that's why there's opposition, right?"

Jonathan released a big sigh. "Okay, but let's be honest," he said. "After fifty years and thirteen telescopes, the summit of Mauna Kea's not exactly pristine. Sure, TMT will be eighteen stories high, but we aren't talking about building the first observatory on virgin soil. We can't turn back the clock, Uncle. Which is why it was stupid for Keoni to propose tearing down observatories to make way for a new one. There'd be no point! You'd still have the reality: *there's a telescope industrial complex up there*, just like TMT's opponents complain. And they're right. That's what they call it, Uncle, the telescope industrial complex."

Jonathan paused and pointed to a wall plaque hanging behind his desk. "This is what we teach our Hilo schoolkids," he said.

> *Everyone you love, everyone you know, everyone you ever heard of, every human being who ever was, lived out their lives on a mote of dust suspended in a sunbeam.*
>
> —*Carl Sagan*

After the detectives had read it, Jonathan turned toward them and said, "We Hawaiians talk about Earth Mother and Sky Father—Papa and Wākea—being physically joined at the summit of Mauna Kea. Mating, in effect. Personally, I think the telescopes join Papa and Wākea together more deeply. More intimately, you might say. The telescopes extend Earth up into the heavens; they bring the heavens down to Earth. And anyway, the stars are beyond the sky—beyond Earth's atmosphere, that is, beyond what's blue. The universe is beyond our sky; the cosmos is beyond our sky. In cosmic terms, we're just tiny specks on this mote of dust."

Tanaka cleared his throat and turned the discussion to smaller concepts. "There are still sacred sites at the top of the mountain, right?" he asked. "That lake, for example? Some Hawaiians and other local tiny specks seem to care a lot about them."

Jonathan would concede nothing. He responded hotly, his voice rising in exasperation. "You know what else was sacred to the old Hawaiians, Uncle? Way above Lake Waiau and other stuff at the summit? Stars, Uncle. Stars were sacred to the old Hawaiians. How do you think they navigated their big canoes, traveling all over Polynesia? They paid more attention to stars and knew more about them than almost anyone in the world, before or since. Their lives depended on knowing all about the stars. You really think the old Hawaiians wouldn't want us to learn as much as we possibly can about *stars*? It's ridiculous—completely crazy!"

He paused, but when he spoke again, he did so even more heatedly. "Uncle, there are *thousands* of sacred sites throughout Polynesia. Hundreds on this island alone. But there is only one place in the entire world that is the absolute best for astronomy, and that's the summit of Mauna Kea. We need more telescopes up there, not fewer, and Keoni was proposing to tear a bunch down, trying to appease people who can't be appeased. He just didn't understand. He was harming the cause, not helping it. He was actually in the way, slowing things down, not speeding them up. It was *madness*!"

With that last declaration, nearly a shout, Jonathan banged his palm hard on the desk—so hard that a framed photo of his wife fell over with a clatter.

Tanaka froze and regarded Jonathan closely for a moment. Jonathan, face reddened, said nothing as he restored his wife's picture to an upright position. Then Tanaka nodded to Tommy, indicating he should take over.

"Mr. Kalākalani," Tommy began. "I worked for your actual uncle, Haia Kalākalani, when he was our chief. He always stayed calm, far as I could tell. But you sound really angry. And that makes me wonder: You *sure* no one in your group was angry enough to kill Keoni for what he was proposing?"

Tommy paused, allowing Jonathan a moment to think. Then he continued, looking at Jonathan Kalākalani with discernible menace. "Maybe it's time you give me and your uncle Terry here some names and addresses, Mr. Kalākalani. And tell us where you were yourself the night Keoni died."

An hour later, walking to their cruiser, with the rain having arrived, Tommy remarked to Tanaka, "Keoni converted by the Native Hawaiians? Keoni *was* Native Hawaiian. So's Jonathan Kalākalani. We Hawaiians are on every side of the TMT issue. What a stupid thing for him to say."

"Maybe it runs in the family," Tanaka remarked. "Haia was a good guy and a decent boss. But he was always one pig short of a luau."

* * *

Tanaka didn't say anything more, but despite what they'd just heard, he remained unpersuaded that Keoni's role at TMT explained his murder. He had hardly even allowed himself to hope that it might. From the moment he'd first heard Keoni's name, first learned that Keoni lived in Waimea—where D. K. Parkes had lived years before—Tanaka had intuitively felt that Keoni was D. K.'s son, that Keoni was dead, and that the investigation of Keoni's killing wouldn't prove to be a new case but the continuation of the earlier one. He'd effectively said as much to Tommy on the very first day, standing in the TMT parking lot, after learning from their initial interview with Dr. Phillips that Keoni was indeed D. K.'s son.

Intuitive leaps were familiar to Tanaka, but feeling spooked was not. And this case had him spooked. He tried to figure out why. First, he knew the rate of homicides in Hawai'i—half that of the United States as a whole—was simply too minuscule for the killings of father and son, separated by time as these were, to be any sort of reasonable coincidence. Tanaka tried to estimate the odds of these being completely independent events: roughly one in a million, he guessed. Possible, but not likely.

In addition, never having known the explanation for D. K. Parkes's death deepened Tanaka's unease now. Back in 2002, Kawika had let Tanaka know he'd figured out the case. But he hadn't said much more than that, and Tanaka hadn't asked. He'd excused himself from learning more—he hadn't *wanted* to learn more—once Kawika told him D. K. Parkes's killer was already dead and couldn't be brought to justice.

Tanaka knew why he'd let the matter drop: he hadn't wanted to reopen the Fortunato case and had in fact abhorred that possibility. Back then, the cautious way Kawika had imparted to Tanaka even a few scant facts about D. K. had effectively signaled to Tanaka, *Dig very far into the death of D. K. Parkes, and we'll be forced to exhume the case of Ralph Fortunato.* Neither Kawika nor Tanaka had been willing to do that.

Now, even with Keoni dead too, Kawika had made clear he still wasn't willing to do it, at least if they could avoid it. And that was the difference: Kawika hoped to avoid it; Tanaka didn't think they could.

What spooked Tanaka was an additional thought. If the murders were linked, as Tanaka believed they were, then whoever had killed Keoni had also known Keoni's father. Who could that be? More than a decade ago Kawika had told Tanaka—*assured* him—that D. K.'s killer was already dead.

21

Hawaiian Home Lands, Kawaihae

Kawika's and Ku'ulei's next interview was with Grace 'Ōpūnui, the leader of the Mea Pale 'Ahu—MPA, the Defenders. She lived in Kawaihae just a few miles from the dilapidated remains of John Young's homesite.

"You're about to see one of the grossest sights on the Big Island," Ku'ulei advised her cousin as they drove. To Kawika's amusement she'd assumed the role of tour guide, though he was hardly a stranger to the Big Island. But he was happy to indulge her.

"A big ol' real estate development right next to the Hawaiian Home Lands," said Ku'ulei. "Practically side by side. It's disgusting."

"Disgusting how?"

"Look," she said, as the Home Lands came into view. She gestured up the slope of Kohala Mountain. "This first part is inspiring, actually. All these new houses, just for Hawaiians. See 'em?"

The few dozen houses, each very modest—many the size and shape of a single-wide mobile home, and devoid of palms or other large vegetation—stood splayed out against the barren lower flanks of Kohala Mountain. From a distance these dwellings resembled temporary quarters for construction workers. That's what Kawika would have taken them for had Ku'ulei not explained.

"Now you can see the real estate development," she said, as they rounded a bend in the shoreline road. "Kohala Ranch. You remember Kohala Ranch?"

"Barely," he said. "I don't remember driving this road when I lived in Hilo. No surfing up here," he added with a smile. "Elle and I don't drive it if we go to Hāwī or Pololū. We always take the Mountain Road. You can see Kohala Ranch from there, but not much of it, because of the trees." He was referring to the ironwood trees lining both sides of Kohala Mountain Road, planted in the 1930s as a windbreak for cattle.

"Take a good look now," Kuʻulei suggested. "Notice any difference from the Home Lands?"

The contrast could hardly have been more stark. Like the Home Lands, Kohala Ranch stretched up the slope of Kohala Mountain but much farther, all the way to the Mountain Road. The two properties were parallel on the mountainside, a fence demarcating the boundary between the dozens of sprawling homes of Kohala Ranch and the rest of the Big Island. Kohala Ranch shone brightly in the sunlight, grassy and adorned with palms and innumerable flowering trees and shrubs. In white-fenced enclosures, horses grazed in lush pastures, just as they might on Kentucky bluegrass farms. A riding trail encircled a portion of the property.

"That's what's disgusting," Kuʻulei remarked, waving her hand toward Kohala Ranch. "It's one thing to see this type of house—this type of money—all up and down the South Kohala coast. It's something else to see it alongside the houses Hawaiians live in—little houses, houses they are *lucky* to live in. Houses they've got a long old waiting list to live in."

"You're right," Kawika acknowledged. By now he'd turned into the entrance to the Home Lands. "I see your point, Cuz." He looked at her briefly and nodded. "And here we are, almost at Grace's house. So let's switch to solving this murder, okay?" He smiled and reached over to squeeze her shoulder.

But Kawika realized he was now in a very Hawaiian part of Hawaiʻi, a place where he knew things might not move in a straightforward manner or at the pace a Honolulu detective would prefer.

Grace ʻŌpūnui greeted Kuʻulei heartily as she and Kawika stepped out of the car. As Jarvis used to do with Kawika—and he felt the pang of it now—the enormous silver-haired Grace enfolded Kuʻulei in her arms, engulfing her in flesh. Kuʻulei clearly loved it, making no effort to escape. "Aloha, Auntie," she said, before introducing Kawika.

Grace took Kawika's hand in both of hers. "Aloha, Kawika," she said in a deep, melodic voice. "You're Kuʻulei's cousin. She's one of our best. And you're Jarvis's son. He was among our first supporters, a man everyone loves. So you're doubly welcome here. And you may call me Auntie too."

"Mahalo," he said, glancing at Ku'ulei, who was beaming at Grace. "Thank you for agreeing to meet us." He didn't call her Auntie yet. They'd just met, and he was here on police business.

"Have you been in the Hawaiian Home Lands before?" Grace asked pleasantly, leading her visitors to the *makai* side of the house, the side facing the sea. Kawika noticed that the house, although just a one-story manufactured home, was neatly landscaped with healthy shrubs and tropical plantings of ginger, anthurium, and low-growing bougainvillea.

"Well," he replied as he followed her. "We have Home Lands in Hilo too. I visited them when I worked there." He didn't mention why. For Hilo cops, a visit to the local Home Lands was often a sad and sometimes a dangerous part of the job. They were not the most prosperous places on the other side of the island. "But the Home Lands in Hilo are just part of the city, not a separate settlement like this," he added.

Once they reached the makai side of the house, they heard Hawaiian slack-key guitar music accompanying a man's soft voice in song. "Do you know who that is, Cuz?" Ku'ulei asked him.

"Sorry," he said. "I don't."

Ku'ulei laughed. "It's Dennis Kamakahi," she informed him. "Our greatest songwriter since Queen Lili'uokalani." To Grace, she explained, "Kawika only *looks* Hawaiian and *is* Hawaiian. He just can't be bothered to *be* Hawaiian."

"Ouch," he said, treating it as just a witticism. Still, he was surprised Ku'ulei would say something so barbed in front of others. Ku'ulei must feel herself among family here, he realized. He guessed she'd probably been here many times as a Defender.

Grace chuckled good-naturedly, brushing Ku'ulei's jibe aside. "Come, then," she said, motioning for Kawika and Ku'ulei to take seats on the lanai, a narrow concrete pad. "My husband will bring us water. We'll tell Kawika a bit about the Home Lands, Ku'ulei, and enjoy this beautiful day and our view of the sea before we discuss poor Keoni and the TMT." She called for her husband, who emerged from indoors and stepped out onto the lanai.

"This is Gordon," Grace said. Then she swept her arm to indicate the visitors. "Gordon, you know Ku'ulei, of course. This is her cousin, Kawika Wong—Jarvis's son."

Gordon smiled brightly. "Aloha, Ku'u," he said, bending down and giving her a quick shoulder hug.

"Aloha, Uncle."

Kawika could see that Gordon, like his wife, was a Hawaiian in his late sixties, but the opposite of his wife in body type. She was hugely overweight; he was lean and visibly muscled. He looked like a quintessential Hawaiian man in old photographs and depicted in artwork predating the obesity epidemic afflicting Hawai'i since the 1960s and 1970s. Having lived with a father as overweight as Grace, Kawika recognized the complication: many Hawaiians had convinced themselves in recent decades to regard enormous body weight as something worthy of special respect, as if it had been a general attribute of their Hawaiian ancestors. Kawika knew that had never been true. It was a myth, save primarily for ancient queens like Ka'ahumanu, who was never allowed to walk and instead had been carried everywhere. Grace bore a striking similarity to Ka'ahumanu.

"And very glad to meet you, Kawika," said Gordon. "Your dad and I were good friends, back in the day. So sorry about his stroke."

"Thank you," Kawika acknowledged with a nod.

Grace, who was seated, looked up at Gordon and put an arm around his waist. "Kawika thinks he's going to come here, ask a few quick questions about Keoni Parkes, and then bid me *aloha 'oe*," she explained to her husband.

"Then you don't know Grace," he warned Kawika.

"Apparently not," Kawika conceded with a smile.

"Just be patient, Kawika. I will help you solve Keoni's murder," she said. "I will even give you names. But there are things I have to tell you first, things you have to understand."

"I better get one big pitcher," Gordon said, laughing. "Maybe malasadas too, yeah? Isn't that what folks give police, malasadas? Well, you're in luck. I made 'em this morning. Had a hunch you might be coming." He winked at Ku'ulei and disappeared back into the house.

* * *

"Now, Kawika," Grace said, after Gordon had rejoined them and as they began enjoying his sugar-coated malasadas, a Portuguese fried-dough specialty. They were very good, and Kawika smiled to himself, thinking how Elle insisted Hawaiians produced only an inferior imitation of the real thing. "You know who Prince Jonah Kūhiō was?"

"Actually, no, I'm sorry to say," Kawika replied apologetically, wondering how long this was going to take. "I didn't really grow up in Hawai'i, Grace.

Mostly I just came for summers and stayed with Dad. Ku'ulei's the one with a Hawaiian education—as she likes to remind me."

Grace continued to smile pleasantly. "That's all right, Kawika. I understand." She reached over and patted his forearm. "Prince Jonah Kūhiō Kalaniana'ole is one of our great heroes. He was educated on the continent—he introduced surfing to California, by the way. He was of royal blood, of course, so when the Kingdom was overthrown in 1893, he joined the revolutionaries. For that, he was imprisoned as a traitor. They let him out when Queen Lili'uokalani renounced her claim to the throne so that her followers could go free. He was mad at the queen for that, for giving up. He married a chiefess, and they went into voluntary exile. But before long our people called him back. We needed him. He became Hawai'i's territorial delegate in Congress, where he served for twenty years, until his death nearly a hundred years ago."

Grace paused to take a leisurely bite of her malasada and a sip of her water, then continued. "Even though he didn't have a vote in Congress, he got a lot of things done. On this island alone, he got the national park for the volcanoes and he got the big breakwater built in Hilo. He introduced the first bill for Hawai'i statehood, forty years before we got it. But his most important accomplishment, Kawika, was creating these Hawaiian Home Lands. He told Congress that Native Hawaiians were a dying race—those are the words he used, *a dying race*—and that the only way to rehabilitate our dying race was to return us to the soil, to the land. And that's how we got the land we're sitting on right now. It's part of two hundred thousand acres of Home Lands on all the islands.

"Now," she went on, "the law says that to qualify for a home on these lands, you've got to be at least fifty percent Hawaiian by blood. No one can change that except Congress. They'd have to amend the Hawaiian Home Lands Commission Act of 1920. Almost a century old, that law, Kawika."

"Ah," Kawika said, feeling he should respond somehow. "So Dad would be eligible, since he's three-quarters Hawaiian. But I wouldn't be, because my mom is white." Kawika would not use the word *haole*, with its suggestion of slight contempt, to describe his own family members. "But Ku'ulei's dad wasn't white, so she'd qualify."

"Wasn't white as far as we know," Ku'ulei ruefully corrected him. "Mom never did keep good records."

"So," Grace continued, evidently having heard that before, "even with this very restrictive eligibility requirement, you know what? We've still got a waiting list of nearly thirty thousand families. Think of it, Kawika—not a lot of Hawaiians these days are fifty percent Hawaiian by blood; the 1920s are more than four generations ago. A lot of mixing since then. And many who *are* fifty percent or more, like your dad, never needed to live in the Home Lands. But even so, nearly thirty thousand families who can prove they're fifty percent Hawaiian are still waiting for homes on these lands. The program is barely funded at all.

"That's the plight of the Hawaiian people in a nutshell," she concluded. "Almost a century after Prince Jonah Kūhiō got these lands set aside for us, because we were a dying race. A dying race that one hundred years later still can't get homes on our own lands."

Then she revealed her point. "So, Kawika, you can see why we Hawaiians might be upset about yet another telescope being built on *other* lands that are also supposed to be for our benefit, lands that are actually sacred to us."

Kawika nodded. "I do understand," he said. "Thank you for the instruction. Does this mean we can talk about the murder of Keoni Parkes now? You indicated you were going to give me some names." He signaled to Ku'ulei, who brushed malasada sugar from her fingertips and reached into her bag for her pad so she could begin taking notes.

"We can talk about Keoni," Grace said. "Of course, and we will, Kawika. But first I have to explain to you about Papa and Wākea and the summit of Mauna Kea. The same way I explained it to Keoni."

* * *

"We Hawaiians believe Mauna Kea was born from the union of Papa and Wākea," Grace began. "Mauna Kea was the very first child of that pairing, born before the oceans and the stars and everything we know as nature. Born even before the oldest events described in the earliest creation chants. Before time, in fact.

"We Hawaiians know this," she said, "first because Mauna Kea is the highest point in Oceania, with precedence over every other mountain on Earth—thirty-six thousand feet from the sea floor to the summit, which is where Papa and Wākea actually touch and connect."

She raised her fleshy right arm, pointing one thick finger upward as if connecting Papa and Wākea through her own body. She held her hand there for several moments and looked Kawika firmly in the eye.

"And second," she resumed, dropping her hand, "we know this because of Mauna Kea's physical presence. It's what maintains our Big Island hydrology"—there was that word again, Kawika noted—"our winds, the transport of moisture. It creates the clouds that hold the water that feeds the island and lets people and animals and plants live here. It's so important in our daily lives. That's another reason we defend it, not just because it's sacred. The mountain is what made it possible for us to live here, to live here as a race and as a people, the way it made it possible for our ancestors to live here long before Captain Cook arrived.

"Now, Keoni," she said, becoming less lyrical, "he was hapa haole like you, Kawika. He didn't have fifty percent Hawaiian blood. His mom would've needed to be pure Hawaiian for that, and there's only a handful of pure Hawaiians left in the world. But you don't need fifty percent Hawaiian blood to consider yourself Hawaiian. After all, most Hawaiians don't come close to that. It's the felt connection to our Hawaiian ancestors that makes us Hawaiian, Kawika. *The felt connection to our ancestors.*"

She paused again, her eyes fixing on his. "Maybe you don't feel that connection much, Kawika. Yet your father, he feels it. Your cousin, she feels it. But Keoni? He didn't feel it at all. He separated himself from his race, from his ancestors. Unlike you, *his* father wasn't Hawaiian; that was his mother. She died when he was a little boy. She never had a chance to teach him."

Grace went on to describe Keoni as someone who didn't want to talk about the past or even think about it. He always just focused on solving a problem instead of understanding what lay behind it, she said. His job was to get the TMT built by mollifying Hawaiians who objected to it, not to tell TMT's top management that they should listen to those objections and build the telescope elsewhere. "He never said that to anyone," Grace emphasized. "He never said, 'Gee, maybe we should take the TMT somewhere else.'

"So did Keoni get killed because of his work for the TMT?" Grace asked, before answering her own question. "Yes, I expect he did. I think the TMT got Keoni killed. But was he killed by a Hawaiian? That's harder to say. He might have been, though not by a member of Mea Pale 'Ahu. Maybe by Jeffrey Mokuli'i or one of his hotheads; as I promised, I will give you some names."

Almost there, Kawika thought, with relief.

"But he wasn't killed by one of us," Grace insisted, not yet ready to name names. "We don't have hotheads. Don't allow 'em. We'll resort to civil disobedience if we must, like Gandhi or Martin Luther King. In fact, just watch us, if this thing goes on much longer. We are *not* going to let TMT happen. But we are a very peaceful movement. Our whole point is aloha—aloha and *hōʻihi*, respect. Aloha and hōʻihi that Hawaiians have not been shown.

"I should say, aloha and hōʻihi and *ʻāina*—land. Just like this Home Land right here is for our benefit, Kawika, for the benefit of our race, *so is the land on top of Mauna Kea.*" She emphasized each word slowly, jabbing a finger at him insistently with each syllable. "Even if Mauna Kea were not sacred to us—which it is—that land is supposed to be held for our benefit. And how have we benefited from the observatories? How has the purpose of those lands been fulfilled? A purpose our king solemnly declared in giving us the land—land he could have kept for his own family. A purpose our governments—the territorial government, the federal government, and finally the state—each solemnly promised to fulfill when they accepted stewardship of that land. Has that promise been kept? What do you think Prince Jonah Kūhiō would say, Kawika?"

She dropped her hands to her lap and looked at Kawika sadly, waiting for his answer. He realized she really did want an answer; her questions weren't just rhetorical. And he needed to slow down and answer her.

"Auntie—you said I could call you Auntie?" he began. She nodded, and even smiled.

"Once upon a time," he continued, "long ago, that is, I thought that one day I might become chief of police in Honolulu, and then maybe mayor of Honolulu, and maybe one day after that, even governor. That's what my boss in Hilo always predicted, and that's what he told my father, who's his best friend. So naturally that's what Dad expected of me, and sometimes I even dreamed those things myself. I was very ambitious. And if I'd gone into government, well, maybe I could help fix these indignities of which you speak. But I'm just a cop, Auntie. Kuʻulei is better than me that way. She's more than a cop, and I'm proud of her for that. But I can't fix the affronts to our people. So, although I appreciate the lesson you've given me—I do; I will read about Prince Jonah Kūhiō now and think about what you've taught me—I am still here for only one reason, Auntie. I am here to solve a murder. And I'd like your help. I'd like those names."

Grace listened to Kawika patiently, as he had to her. Then she looked at Kuʻulei before responding—Kuʻulei who had yet to take a note. "All right, Kawika," Grace agreed, though she seemed to say it somewhat slyly. "I will try to help you. I did love poor Keoni, I really did. He was a decent soul, even though he was misguided. It's terrible that he's dead, and that TMT killed him. And I've talked about Papa and Wākea enough recently anyway. Just last week, in fact, I told your former girlfriend all about them."

"Wait, what?" Ku'ulei sounded intrigued. "His former *girlfriend*?" She turned toward Kawika.

"Yes, Ku'ulei," answered Grace. "A haole named Patience Quinn. She's going to write an article about the TMT, about us, about our Hawaiian history and our struggle. She'll get it published on the continent, draw national attention to our efforts."

"Wow," Ku'ulei murmured.

"She's doing it for Jarvis," Grace added.

She smiled. Then, true to her word, she gave Kawika names—pointing her finger straight at her despised rivals, Jeffrey Mokuli'i and half a dozen of his Warriors.

22

Puakō

The four detectives reassembled, as agreed, at the Puakō house. The others chatted while Kawika called Honolulu for an update on the Slasher investigation from the Two Jerrys. Frustratingly, they had little to tell him. "No new bodies, at least," Kyu Sakamoto said. No new victims, but nothing new to go on either, apart from useless calls on the tip line: someone's neighbor had been observed coming and going mysteriously in the night; another caller had seen a young man at Kapiʻolani Park carrying a straight razor in his back pocket; and so on. Kawika thanked the pair, rang off, and rejoined the guests.

"I really like how you've fixed up the place," Tanaka remarked to Elle, who beamed her appreciation. "Jarvis would've loved it."

"He does love it, I think," she said. "I bring him when the weather's right—not too hot, not too windy. That's why Kawika and I had the ramp built. Jarvis likes to sit on the porch under the coco palms and look out at the surf and sea. At least that's what he signals: *yuh-yuh-yuh*."

Kawika hugged her with one arm and gave her a quick kiss. "That's not a great title for your next book, Elle," he said. "But with a small change, it could be. Instead of *yuh-yuh-yuh*, how about something more easily understood, like *Three Blinks for Yes*?" Kawika smiled at Elle, hoping she'd catch their private joke from the night before. But he did often think about how much easier things would be if Jarvis hadn't lost the ability to blink.

Elle laughed, then said, "Okay, I'll bring you guys stuff to eat while you talk. I'll just eavesdrop so I can get material for my next bestseller, *Three Blinks for Yes*. Jarvis will be the key character, the guru who answers the yes-or-no questions that allow Detective Malia Maikalani to solve the awful crime."

Ku'ulei and the men chortled, then seated themselves in a circle in the small living room while Elle stepped into the kitchen. "Beer and quesadillas," she called over her shoulder. "Fresh fruit too. Coming right up." Within minutes the dwelling filled with the pleasant aromas of cooking.

Looking at his colleagues—Tanaka, Tommy, and Ku'ulei—Kawika said, "We've got a lot of Big Island names now for your teams to interview. I'll get back to Honolulu and see how many people we've got to interview there. A lot, probably."

He paused, took a deep breath, then looked at each of them in turn. "But meanwhile," he resumed reluctantly, "because Terry doesn't believe in coincidences, I should tell you what I know—or what I suspect—about D. K. Parkes, Keoni's father, in case that helps us solve Keoni's murder. I don't think Keoni's murder relates to his father's. It seems more likely Keoni got killed because of the TMT or, as Dr. Phillips believes, for some personal reason in Honolulu. But Terry's hunches are often right." Tanaka acknowledged this with a snort. "So just in case there's a connection, I'll tell you what I've already told Elle about D. K.'s murder."

"Listen carefully!" Elle called cheerfully from the kitchen. "I'm going to work this into a novel somehow."

Kawika smiled at that. Then, as his colleagues regarded him closely—and while they ate Elle's quesadillas and drank beer—Kawika began to lay out the entire tale.

"Before Ralph Fortunato got murdered, he was a murderer himself," Kawika began. "On the mainland first. But not just on the mainland."

"On the *continent*, Cuz," Ku'ulei corrected him. "You gotta say *continent* if you want to sound up-to-date. Remember Grace 'Ōpūnui?"

"It's a Big Island thing," Tommy told Kawika. "You'll be saying it in Honolulu soon. *Mainland* makes *islands* sound inferior, less important."

Kawika smiled in surprise. "Okay," he continued. "Correction, then: on the *continent*. Fortunato was the prime suspect in two murders there, but he never got arrested."

"They tried, the feds," Tanaka added for the others. He knew this much of the story.

Kawika resumed with a nod. "The thing is, one of Fortunato's victims, Bruce Harding, was the guy who sold Fortunato the land for a resort

Fortunato was trying to develop. Fortunato paid Harding a ridiculously high price for the land, way above market value, and got a big kickback from Harding. So Fortunato was defrauding his investors, and Harding could've been a witness in a fraud case the FBI and federal prosecutors were trying to build against Fortunato. But then Harding drowned while fishing in a lake, right before he was supposed to testify to the grand jury."

"And the connection to D. K. Parkes?" Tanaka asked.

Now Kawika was in territory he'd never explained to Tanaka. "Once he came to Hawai'i, Fortunato almost certainly murdered another victim, a man named Thomas Gray, who lived down the street right here in Puakō. Gray was the guy who sold Fortunato the land for Kohala Kea Loa, the resort Fortunato was trying to develop here. And like Bruce Harding, who'd sold Fortunato the land for his mainland resort—his resort on the *continent,* I mean—Thomas Gray supposedly fell off his boat and drowned while fishing. His boat was found way out in the Maui Channel."

"Wait, why was Fortunato murdering people who sold him land?" Ku'ulei asked.

"Simple," Kawika answered. "He was using his investors' money to buy huge tracts of land. He'd pay way above fair market value—telling his investors the land was really special, really unique—and then, by getting a kickback, he'd split the overpayment with the guy who'd sold him the land. Bruce Harding became a risk to Fortunato once the feds took an interest in his real estate fraud on the *continent.*" Kawika smiled. "My guess is Fortunato wasn't going to let Gray become a risk too."

Kawika handed them photocopies of an obituary from the *Puako Post,* dated June 30, 2000. He didn't mention that Patience Quinn had come across it in 2002, when Kawika was trying to catch the killer of Ralph Fortunato.

Instead he said, "This obituary, and the fact that Bruce Harding drowned while fishing in Washington, were the only clues I had to link Fortunato to both murders. It's relevant to what I have to tell you about D. K. Parkes. So why don't you all read it while I eat a bit of my quesadilla?" His colleagues had finished theirs and were starting on the sliced fruit that Elle had prepared—pineapple, mango, papaya, banana. They dried their hands and began reading.

Kawika took his first bite of the quesadilla. "Delicious," he said to Elle, who'd pulled up a chair next to Ku'ulei. Both women began reading the obituary for the first time.

OBITUARY

Thomas ("Tom-Tom") Gray, Loved to Fish

PUAKO—Services were held Sunday, June 25, at Hōkūloa United Church of Christ for kama'aina Thomas ("Tom-Tom") Gray, 58, a well-known fisherman of the Kona Coast missing and presumed drowned after his 35-foot sportfisher, the *Mahi Mia*, was found adrift near the midchannel buoy between Maui and Hawaii on Thursday, May 25.

Gray was born in Hilo on April 8, 1942, the son of William Gray, a Parker Ranch supervisor, and Leslie Mercer Gray, a homemaker. He was educated at Waimea schools and West Point, an appointee of former U.S. Senator Hiram Fong (R-HI). He served in the Mekong Delta of Vietnam as a first lieutenant and won promotion to captain in the U.S. Army. In 1965 he was decorated for bravery in combat. He received the Purple Heart in 1966.

After Vietnam, Gray returned home and started his Puako-based realty firm. In 1999, on behalf of the Gray Family Trust, he sold the land for Kohala Kea Loa to NOH, a Japanese consortium. He retired and realized a lifelong dream by buying the *Mahi Mia*, on which he set forth almost daily from Kawaihae Harbor in pursuit of his own "grander," or thousand-pound marlin.

Gray never caught his grander, but he came close with a 904-pound monster in December 1999. He was well-known for sharing catches with neighbors in Puako and Kawaihae. Friends nicknamed him "Tom-Tom" in reference to his frequent boast that he was one-quarter Cherokee.

Authorities believe Gray fell overboard while fighting a fish or attempting to retrieve a fishing rod or other object.

Gray's children, son Kamehameha "Kam" Gray and daughter Emma Gray, returned from the mainland for the service. They remembered their father with stories of warm aloha. Gray's wife, Leilani, preceded him in death in 1988. The family suggests donations to Kohala Kats, a feline rescue organization Thomas Gray founded in 1989.

Ku'ulei was the first to speak. "Okay, we see the pattern. Fortunato murdered the guys who sold him land and made it look like they drowned. But where does D. K. Parkes fit in?"

Tommy suggested one possible answer. "To get back from the middle of the Maui Channel, Fortunato would've needed someone with a second boat to pick him up, right? That was D. K. Parkes?"

"Fortunato definitely needed help to get to shore," Kawika agreed. "Parkes was a captain for hire, a guy who skippered boats for owners like Thomas Gray who wanted to concentrate on fishing. Before Fortunato's widow left the Big Island, I showed her a photo of Parkes. She recognized him. She said he used to skipper Gray's boat when Fortunato and Gray went fishing together."

Ku'ulei brightened. "So you're thinking Fortunato and Parkes were both on Gray's boat and killed him together? They just needed another boat to pick them up, out in the Maui Channel, like Tommy says?"

"It might have happened that way," Kawika agreed. "I do believe Parkes helped Fortunato kill Gray on the boat."

"But then who killed Parkes?" Tommy asked. "Who threw him off Shark Cliff?"

Kawika and Tanaka exchanged wary glances. Elle looked steadily at Kawika, her expression unchanging. She didn't look at Tanaka.

"Gray had two adult children—Kam and Emma," Tommy began, as if trying to answer his own questions. "It says so right in this obituary." He waved the paper in the air. "They would've had a motive for killing both Parkes *and* Fortunato, if Parkes and Fortunato murdered their father. Is that what you're telling us, Kawika? That Gray's kids killed them both? That we got the Fortunato murder investigation all wrong, that Cushing's innocent? Innocent of killing Fortunato, at least?"

That awful possibility hung in the air and silenced everyone.

No one responded to Tommy's questions.

Tanaka interrupted instead. "Just a minute, Tommy," he said, and turned quickly to Kawika with questions of his own—questions he hadn't asked twelve years earlier. "Then who picked them up out in the Channel, Kawika? Fortunato and Parkes, I mean. Who came to get them? Who drove the getaway boat?"

But just then Kawika's cell phone rang. "Oof," he said, looking at the screen. "It's a reporter. Bernie Scully from the *Star-Advertiser*."

Everyone exchanged glances.

Kawika decided to answer. "Aloha, Bernie, what's up?" he said into the phone. He listened as his wife and colleagues waited inquisitively. Finally, Kawika said into the phone, "We've released no information on that case yet, Bernie. So I can't comment." He listened again briefly. "Sorry," he said. "Again, no comment. Yeah, that's right. No, nothing new on the Slasher either. So, ah, good-bye."

Then he turned to the others, a look of consternation on his face. "He and Zoë know the headless victim we found in Kapiʻolani Park is named Keoni Parkes. He says they know Keoni was the son of D. K. Parkes and that he worked for the TMT. No idea how they got that information. But here's what's weird: he says Zoë has a source here on the Big Island who told her Keoni was killed because of his work for the TMT. Told her that for a fact, Bernie said. 'Definitely killed because of TMT,' according to Zoë's source. Bernie wanted me to confirm it."

"Where'd she get that?" Tanaka asked angrily.

"No idea," Kawika replied. "But we know she's got Sammy Kāʻai's phone number."

"Sammy," Tanaka said in disgust. "I bet that's it. Shooting his mouth off again."

Kuʻulei had an entirely different reaction. "Just a minute," she said. "If that's right—if the reporters *know* Keoni was killed because of the TMT—then we don't need your moldy old fishing boat story, do we, Kawika? The only reason you were telling us about the *Mahi Mia* was in case it could help solve Keoni's murder, right?"

"If Bernie's right," Kawika replied, "and Keoni really did die because of the TMT, then true, you don't need my moldy old fishing boat story, as you call it. What happened on the *Mahi Mia* wouldn't matter." Kawika looked at the others, but no one spoke. He was glad to drop the topic, although he knew he might be dropping it too quickly. But after Scully's call, he wanted time to think.

Tanaka grunted. "*If* the reporters are right," he added, casting a skeptical look at Kawika. "We'll probably know soon enough if they're not." He rose from his chair, signaling the end of the evening—he was the boss of the other Big Island detectives in the room—and leaving Tommy's questions unanswered. Kawika caught Tanaka's eye, thankful Tanaka had cut the discussion short. But Tanaka looked away.

Kuʻulei apparently didn't want more edification either. She folded the obituary, put it in her shirt pocket, said her good-byes, and followed Tanaka to the door. She thanked Elle but said nothing to her cousin. Kawika knew that Kuʻulei, like Tanaka, resented his having kept important things from them—and that they both further resented having had to be the ones to end the discussion in order to allow Kawika to preserve secrets they evidently could tell he'd prefer not to disclose.

Tommy, however, had something to say before leaving. "You never told me, Kawika. We worked the Fortunato case together from day one. We became best friends, we talked about that case a hundred times—we even shore-fished all night long, more than once. Yet you never told me. You've let me believe for twelve years—*twelve years*, Kawika—that Cushing's hit man killed Fortunato. You never told me anything about who killed D. K. Parkes—not even one word—much less that the same person might've killed them both. And as soon as some *reporter* tells you Keoni got killed because of the TMT, you cut off the whole discussion."

"Tommy—"

"Stop, Kawika, just stop." Tommy held up his hand to fend Kawika off. He backed away, moving toward the door. His voice broke with emotion. "If you didn't tell me back then, didn't tell your best friend and your partner on the case, don't bother telling me now. I'll wait and read about it when Ana Carvalho finishes her report. I'm sure there'll be a big article in the paper—one that will make all of us who worked on the Fortunato case look bad."

After Tommy left, Kawika turned to Elle. "My God," he said in distress. "Tommy's right. I could've told him the truth back then. He would've kept the secret. He would've protected Terry and me. But Elle—I never even considered that. How good a friend was I?"

Elle grimaced. "Now it's even worse, in a way," she said.

"Worse?"

"Yeah, Kawika. You let him leave here believing Thomas Gray's children killed Fortunato."

"Oh shit. I did, didn't I?"

PART THREE

[The botanist David] Douglas, on a fact-gathering expedition on the rugged slopes of Mauna Kea, never returned. His body was found at the bottom of a deep pit that was used at the time to catch feral cattle. Douglas had spent the previous night at a cabin occupied by an Australian who had been a convict. Many suspected that the Australian had murdered Douglas in a robbery attempt and thrown his body into the pit to hide the deed.

—J. D. Bisignani,
Big Island of Hawaii Handbook (1998)

23

On the Saddle Road

Early Monday morning Kawika and Elle prepared to close up the house in Puakō. Because soon all they'd hear would be Honolulu traffic, they took their coffee out to the still-sandy front lawn and paused for a few last moments to listen to the surf crash rhythmically and then roll across the Puakō reef. Foamy spent waves slowed before retreating softly a few yards from the little lava rock wall protecting the yard.

After a minute or so, Kawika put down his cup and reached to take Elle's hand. "I've been thinking about the responsibilities of fatherhood," he said. "Maybe because my parents divorced when I was eight, or maybe because your dad left when you were little. Whatever the reason, I'm remembering something I read that really resonates with me now."

"Which is?"

"Which is that the greatest gift any man can give his child is to love the child's mother. And I do really love you, Elle."

Elle nodded slowly, lips pursed. Then she spoke—a bit irritably, to his surprise. "Yes, Kawika, I've heard that one. I imagine most fathers have heard it too. But you know what? The greatest gift you can give *our* child is even simpler: don't get killed. That's it, Kawika. Just don't get killed. You've been shot once already. Once is enough." She tossed her remaining coffee on the lawn and turned to take her cup back toward the kitchen.

Kawika drove Elle to Kona so she could catch her flight to Honolulu. They traveled most of the thirty miles in silence. Kawika had thought of things to say, but when he stopped at the airport curbside, Elle spoke first. "I'm sorry for losing it back there, Kawika. Careening hormones, I think. I'm not used to being pregnant; I'm still a bit befuddled by it. I apologize."

"And I apologize for getting shot," he replied, trying to lighten her mood. "I won't let it happen again."

"Stabbed?"

"Nope."

"Strangled?"

"Never."

"Drowned? Poisoned? Thrown off a cliff?" Elle was starting to smile now.

"No, Elle, I won't get killed. No matter what. Not even to help the plot of *Three Blinks for Yes*."

"Promise?"

"Promise. Well, unless Ana crucifies me at the station in Hilo today, of course."

They shared protracted good-bye kisses. "Okay, I'm not befuddled anymore," she assured him, opening the car door to get out.

"So now you're fuddled?"

She laughed and kissed him again. "Yeah, now I'm fuddled."

"Good," he said. "But I hope you're not sotted."

"You goofball!" she teased, shaking her head. "Yes, I'm still besotted. Now get out of here." So Kawika drove away, heading up the long slope of Hualālai toward the Māmalahoa Highway and its junction with the Saddle Road. It was the shortest route to Hilo and a journey Kawika was compelled to take.

Chief Ana Carvalho had asked Kawika to come to Hilo, the county seat and center of Big Island law enforcement, so that she could interview him, her former HPD colleague, for her official review of the Fortunato and D. K. Parkes murder investigations. For Kawika, there was no avoiding it.

The chief had said she assumed the two cases—Fortunato and Parkes—were unrelated, apart from Sammy Kā'ai having suggested that Kawika and Tanaka had committed improprieties in handling both. That was a relief. But Kawika knew the cases weren't entirely unrelated. And he'd now told his three colleagues, all of whom worked for Ana Carvalho, that the cases were not unrelated, at least as he saw them. He knew all three were unhappy with him; he'd kept secrets from them too long, having confided only in Elle.

Driving over the Saddle Road, which had been a twisting two-lane ribbon of blacktop when he'd lived in Hilo and a gravel track only a few years before,

Kawika had intended to concentrate on what to tell Ana. He hoped to keep the Fortunato and Parkes cases separate and his story and Tanaka's straight. But he found himself distracted by how the Saddle Road had changed.

The road's undulating and impossibly sharp curves, treacherous in the fog that often blanketed the route, were in the process of being flattened, widened, gently banked, and transformed into a major highway. A sign said the highway would be named for the state's recently deceased U.S. Senator, Daniel K. Inouye, like practically everything else in Hawai'i that had been named or renamed since Inouye's death. *He probably found the funds for his own memorial,* Kawika thought. "No more naming highways for Kamehameha's wives," he muttered aloud, thinking of the Queen Ka'ahumanu Highway linking Kona with Kohala—the Queen K, a road he traveled every time he visited the Big Island.

Driving the Saddle Road, unrecognizable now, made Kawika reflect that he hadn't returned to Hilo in more than a decade, via the Saddle Road or otherwise. As he mused, his cell phone rang. Yvonne Ivanovna.

"You driving, boss?" she asked.

"Yup. What's up?"

"You'll want to pull over for this. Trust me."

So Kawika pulled over. He'd just reached the dry desert of the Humu'ula Saddle, high on the point of convergence between the two great volcanoes, Mauna Kea and Mauna Loa, at nearly seven thousand feet. He rolled down his window. The air was surprisingly cold, and he enjoyed the unusual sensation. He could look up and see snow on the observatory-festooned summit of Mauna Kea.

"Okay," he said. "I'm parked and all ears."

"We found Keoni Parkes's place in Honolulu," Yvonne said without preliminaries. "It's a small bungalow on Catherine Street in the Kaimukī neighborhood. And it's definitely the murder scene. Looks like something out of a horror movie."

Yvonne explained that the Honolulu police had redoubled their efforts to locate the O'ahu residence of someone named Keoni Parkes. They'd even checked the Honolulu suburbs and nearby towns. Finally, someone reminded the others that the Hawaiian name Keoni meant John. Then, when Yvonne had stepped away from the Slasher investigation for a few hours, intending to check in with the Keoni Parkes team just briefly, she'd been the one to suggest—when no John or Jack Parkes turned up—that maybe they should try Parker instead of Parkes. And sure enough: in Honolulu, it seemed, Keoni Parkes had called himself John Parker. He'd rented the Catherine Street house under that name.

Once they had his name, the police discovered they also had a week-old missing-person report for John Parker. A man named Jay Goddard had filed it the previous Saturday, when John Parker hadn't shown up in Honolulu as Goddard had expected on Friday night.

"As you might expect, Jay Goddard is young and gay and handsome like Keoni," Yvonne related. "He's an IT manager for a tech firm. He describes himself as John Parker's partner. Not live-in partner, but more than just a boyfriend. When Parker didn't show up that Friday night, Jay went over the next morning to check. He couldn't get in, but he saw John's car was gone. He filed the missing-person report but worried that maybe John had just dumped him unceremoniously and run off with someone else. So he didn't do anything to find him after that."

"He thought his partner might just leave him," Kawika asked, "without saying a word?"

"Yeah, according to him. And his fingerprints are all over the house, so I think they probably are partners of some sort. He says he and Parker normally spend Friday night at Catherine Street and stroll down to Leonard's on Saturday morning for a malasada. He says they're quiet, stay-at-home types. Don't go out much or party. Jay claims they spend most weekends puttering in the garden and with the houseplants, watch a lot of movies, and Sunday mornings sometimes go to church—not Catholic ones. Right now Jay's downtown in tears, basically stunned and uncomprehending. He's being interviewed by the team."

"Sensitively, I hope? No third degree?"

"Yeah, I think so," Yvonne said. "He seems too broken by it all to be a suspect. He's sobbing away, having trouble responding to questioning. Genuine tears, I think."

Yvonne added that Jay claimed he had no idea his partner had worked for the TMT. He said John Parker had told him he managed cargo for the Port of Hilo. Jay never went to visit because John—Keoni, that is—said he couldn't bear staying on the Big Island for the weekend.

"We're looking for the car Jay says Keoni kept at the bungalow," Yvonne continued. "Jay has an apartment in Kaka'ako and a car of his own. We're having both searched. Anyway, I got assigned to bring you up-to-date."

"Thank you," Kawika said. "I appreciate it." *So Keoni was leading a double life*, Kawika thought. He recalled his father's observation: *A double life will make you miserable.* And his own response: *It can also make you dead.*

"Tell me about the house and the murder scene," Kawika asked.

Yvonne detailed it for him succinctly, like the skilled professional she was fast becoming. House a small bungalow, with no sign of forced entry. One bedroom, not recently slept in. Another room combining kitchen and dining area. Tiny adjacent living room for about four people. All well-kept, indoors and out. Nicely landscaped with tropical trees and plants. Small backyard with a cascading water feature. Interior decoration mostly very retro—1950s stuff—but also eclectic, with Tiffany lamps. Framed posters of stylized scenes from Palm Springs. Bakelite phones; he had a landline. Succulents for houseplants, all in tasteful vintage pots. Vintage record player, too, with lots of old Hawaiian vinyl—Linda Dela Cruz and Lena Machado—and other women singers, some old, some more recent. Nice aloha shirts and slacks in the closet. Flip-flops and Birkenstocks for slippahs. Well-equipped kitchen, and again, lots of vintage stuff—Mixmaster, percolator, Formica counters. Gardening tools hanging neatly by the back door.

"And then there's the bathroom?" Kawika guessed.

"Yeah. And then there's the bathroom." Kawika imagined he could hear Yvonne shudder. She explained that Keoni had evidently been shot while bound to a chair in the kitchen. The police had found a gag and black plastic zip ties. The .22-caliber pistol, bought on Oʻahu recently and registered to Keoni Parkes, not John Parker—a fake name wouldn't work for a firearms purchase in Hawaiʻi—missing only one bullet from the clip. Pistol lying on the kitchen counter by the sink; ballistics folks had taken it and were checking it now.

After shooting Keoni, she said, the killer had taken his body to the bathroom and dumped it in the tub. "That's where he cut him up. Right in the tub. As I said, it's like a scene from a movie. I even wonder if that's how our killer—an amateur, remember Dr. Yoshida said—got his idea of what to do, from TV and movies. Dr. Yoshida was right about the pruning saw too. It's lying on the bathroom floor, right next to the tub."

"Prints?" Kawika asked.

"At first we thought there weren't any, apart from Keoni's and Jay's," Yvonne responded. She explained that the killer must have worn gloves the whole time, maybe used several pairs during the dismemberment. A careful killer, not needing to wipe many things because apparently he'd touched almost nothing inside the house without gloves.

"But?"

"But I had an idea," Yvonne said. "There was a box of plastic garbage bags in the bathroom. The killer probably brought them for the body parts—you know, the head and hands."

"Right."

"And I figured he wouldn't have worn gloves when he bought those bags. Not in a grocery or hardware store. And maybe he forgot to wipe the box later. It was just a hunch, but it turned out there are good prints on the box. Almost all one person's, and not Keoni's or Jay's, the fingerprint folks say."

"Any match?"

"No, unfortunately, no match yet. But if we find a suspect, those prints will come in handy, right?"

"Right."

"One more thing, Major Wong."

"You can start calling me Kawika now, Yvonne."

"All right, I will. Thank you. One more thing, Kawika: Keoni had a laptop there—a personal one. It's smashed to bits. Right in the kitchen. And it's missing the hard drive. Forensics folks are trying to see if they can locate its contents in the cloud, but without the IP address, they don't have much to go on."

"And for the IP address, they need the missing hard drive?"

"Basically, yeah, since right now they don't know anything about this laptop otherwise."

"Can't they get it from emails Jay has, ones Keoni sent him?"

"We thought of that, but Jay says he and Keoni—John, as Jay knew him—always communicated with text messages and phone calls, never emails. The forensics team says they've got other possible ways of getting the IP address, but it could take a while."

Kawika pondered all this. He could draw the obvious conclusions but decided to see what Yvonne thought first. "So from all that, we're thinking . . . what, exactly?" he asked.

She listed her tentative conclusions. Keoni had probably known his killer—an amateur, as Dr. Yoshida had said, and with no criminal record, since there was no record for the prints on the garbage bag box. The killing had been premeditated—the garbage bags, the gloves. Keoni probably opened the door to his killer shortly after arriving in Honolulu, because Jay Goddard had expected to see him that night and the bed in the bungalow hadn't been slept in. The killer probably knew Keoni owned a pistol, because Keoni wouldn't have left it out in plain sight. Maybe the killer already knew where Keoni kept it, or maybe he'd extracted that information while Keoni was bound to the kitchen chair.

Further, Yvonne said, the killer was interested in something on Keoni's laptop—maybe that was even the motive. He could've just taken the laptop instead of smashing it to get the hard drive, but perhaps he had his hands full with a body, a severed head in a bag, and Keoni's two hands, probably in an as-yet-undiscovered bag of their own, all of which the killer disposed of separately, presumably to delay identification of the body. Same reason the body was naked and the clothes were left in the bloody bathroom, unless the killer actually was imitating the Slasher.

The killer was probably in a rush, Yvonne speculated. He had to dump the body while it was still dark, and cutting up the corpse must have taken a good deal of time. The killer might have turned Keoni's car to his own purposes that night, just as he'd done with Keoni's pistol and the pruning saw, since the car and all of Keoni's keys were missing, along with his cell phone.

Finally, she concluded, maybe the killer wasn't trying to imitate the Slasher when he dumped the body in Kapi'olani Park. Maybe he picked Kapi'olani Park because it was convenient. "It's only a few blocks from Catherine Street," Yvonne pointed out. "If the killer was short of time, Kapi'olani Park would be a logical spot to dump it."

"On the other hand," Kawika mused, "as Jerry said when we met with Chief Fremont, we've released so few details on the Slasher's victims that maybe all a copycat killer knew was that the Slasher left his victims naked in Kapi'olani Park."

"Could be," she said. "But if the killer came from the Big Island, maybe he just doesn't know Honolulu very well. He might've been flustered, in a rush, and just dumped the body in the nearest place he could be unobserved in the night."

"*Iiko, iiko*," Kawika told her, and he meant it. "But one more thing: Did the killer toss the place? You know, looking for something besides what Keoni had on his laptop?"

"No sign of that," Yvonne said. "No indication the killer looked for other things. Maybe he didn't care about anything else."

"Or maybe he didn't have time," Kawika responded. "Do me a favor, Yvonne. Take another detective and go toss the place yourself."

"Literally?"

"No, not literally. Just look through it very carefully. See what you can find."

"You have a hunch?"

"More like a hope."

* * *

Before resuming his drive to Hilo, Kawika called ahead to talk with Tanaka. He reached him between interviews of Jeffrey Mokuliʻi and members of the Warriors, including those Grace ʻŌpūnui had suggested. Kawika related what Yvonne had just told him.

Tanaka received the information quietly, with a few questions. He didn't seem in a talkative mood, or maybe he was just rushed—although he didn't sound rushed. Working with his former protégé hadn't produced much pleasure for Tanaka, Kawika thought, probably because of Ana Carvalho's looming investigation and Tanaka's discomfort with the course Kawika had suggested.

Nonetheless, Tanaka updated Kawika crisply in turn. He'd sent a team to look through Keoni's house in Waimea. Didn't expect as dramatic a scene as in Honolulu, of course. He had Tommy Kekoa and another detective interviewing Angel Delos Santos at the Waimea station. "Angel's nearly hysterical," Tanaka said. "Swears he didn't go to Honolulu that weekend. We're checking with the airlines just the same."

Tanaka also advised Kawika to look at the *Star-Advertiser*'s online edition. Tanaka said the paper had named Keoni as the decapitated victim found a week earlier in Kapiʻolani Park, just as Scully had told Kawika they would.

Kawika hung up and used his cell phone to find the story on the internet. Zoë and Scully had written about Keoni's role at TMT and done a decent job summarizing the heated controversy at whose center his job had placed him. At least one Big Island source had confirmed, they wrote, that police believed Keoni's death was TMT related.

There it is again, Kawika thought.

The article drew a distinction—the first in public—between Keoni's murder and the work of the Slasher, even though Keoni's corpse had been found in Kapiʻolani Park. *Good*, Kawika thought, willing to give credit for getting that right. The article also stated, correctly, that Honolulu police believed the newest victim—the one found with his driver's license on his bare torso—was the Slasher's record-setting sixth, despite being deposited in Ala Moana Beach Park.

So Zoë and Scully were continuing to collaborate on the story. But if Sammy Kā'ai, a cop on the Big Island, was Zoë's source for the TMT link to Keoni's murder, then who, Kawika wondered, was the source for what Honolulu police believed about the Slasher?

24
Hilo

Although Kawika hadn't seen it in years, the Hilo police station seemed completely familiar to him. The building hadn't changed much, inside or out. Not even the venetian blinds seemed new, he noted, although they'd been dusted. The office decor had been pleasant in his day, but now the art and minimal upholstery and wall photos had all faded from the sun. The station looked worn and tired. Kawika guessed that Ana Carvalho would not have been pleased by that when she'd arrived from Honolulu to take up her new post.

A young sergeant met Kawika at reception. She told him Tanaka and Ku'ulei were still out interviewing members of the Warriors. She offered him coffee and ushered him to a large room to await Chief Carvalho. Along the way, Kawika noted that except for the title on Tanaka's frosted glass door, which stood wide open, Tanaka's office hadn't changed either, despite Tanaka's promotion to major. Kawika spotted the photo of him with Tanaka on one of Tanaka's shelves. *Good*, he thought. *At least Terry isn't hiding that.*

The sergeant hadn't needed to show him the way. It was the same room in which Kawika had so often discussed murders with Tanaka—including murders he was about to discuss with Ana Carvalho. He awaited her for quite a long time. When at last she strode into the room, she wasn't smiling. Kawika rose awkwardly, but instead of shaking hands, she motioned curtly for him to resume his seat. She took a chair across from him. With a thud, she dropped a stack of files on the table along with a yellow legal pad, on which she seemed to have taken many notes.

"Thank you for coming, Major," she began formally. No preliminaries. No, *Aloha, Kawika.* No *How's Elle?* Nothing about the pregnancy—maybe Elle hadn't told her yet, despite joking about it. Whatever the explanation, Ana's lack of warmth worried Kawika. He even wondered if she'd chosen to record their session without telling him. He decided not to ask.

"I had a crappy weekend," the chief said. "It started with Zoë Akona, that reporter, calling me at home Friday night. How she got my number, she wouldn't say. She wanted to know—she *demanded* to know—what steps I'd taken to investigate the allegations of Michael Cushing and our dear departing colleague Sammy Kāʻai. I told her I wasn't going to talk with her from home on a Friday night, so she should call me on Monday afternoon—this afternoon—at work."

"You mean, after you've talked with me?"

"Exactly. So in order to prepare, I spent the entire weekend reading these files," the chief said, thumping them twice with her knuckles as if knocking on a door. "A lot of the case notes are on paper. A lot were never even written up, it seems. Almost no investigatory documents at all in the computer archives."

"It was a long time ago," Kawika explained. "We didn't have laptops or iPads here then."

"We still don't," she replied. "They didn't warn me about that before I came. They didn't warn me about what's in these files either. And neither did you." She stabbed her finger on the top file and regarded him coldly.

Kawika cleared his throat. "I never thought there was anything to warn you about," he said. "The Fortunato investigation and the Shark Cliff case had been closed for years."

The chief shook her head slowly and waggled a finger at him. "D. K. Parkes was thrown off Shark Cliff in 2002, and that case was never closed," she corrected him. "Sammy finally identified the body, and the Victim Assistance Unit notified his next of kin. You know who that was? It was Keoni Parkes, your headless vic over in Honolulu. Keoni was twenty-two then, just out of college. Doesn't look like any of you ever talked with him, apart from Victim Assistance."

Kawika shrugged apologetically. "Not my case," he offered, turning his hands palm upward on the table. "I never knew Keoni existed." Just the same, he was surprised to learn that Keoni's relationship to D. K. Parkes had been buried in Hilo's case files all along.

"Sammy ruled out the Hawaiian kids who killed the others at Shark Cliff," Ana continued, ignoring Kawika's response. "But what other follow-up did any of you do about D. K.? There's nothing in the files. Not one scrap of paper. No suspect ever identified."

She paused, allowing Kawika an opportunity to speak. He decided not to take it. This was going fast and not at all as he'd expected; he'd thought they'd discuss Fortunato first, not D. K. Parkes. He waited for the chief to resume. At last she did, with no solicitude in her voice.

"Sammy claims you and Terry knew more about the Parkes murder than you let on. Did you?"

Kawika had known she'd ask the question, although he hadn't expected it so soon. Calmly, he said again that D. K. Parkes had been Sammy's case, not his. He added that he'd pursued the matter himself only a bit at the time, on a hunch and out of curiosity, once Sammy established that Parkes had worked as a for-hire captain of local sportfishing boats.

"I didn't *know* anything about his murder," Kawika said. "I had a guess, that's all."

"Explain," she demanded. She began tapping the eraser end of a pencil slowly against her lips and regarded him intently.

"Remember, I wasn't working on Shark Cliff," he began. "I'd been in charge of the Fortunato case. I knew Fortunato had bought the land for his planned resort from a local guy named Thomas Gray. Gray used part of the money to buy a big sportfishing boat, the *Mahi Mia*. Then one day in 2000—so, two years before the Fortunato murder and two years before Shark Cliff—Thomas Gray drowned. Fell overboard while fishing alone, everyone thought at the time. The Coast Guard found the *Mahi Mia* drifting out in the Maui Channel."

"And Parkes?" the chief asked.

Kawika had practiced this. "I came along two years later, in 2002, trying to find Fortunato's killer. And in the course of that, I guessed—and this was just a guess—that Thomas Gray hadn't drowned accidentally. I also guessed that Parkes had been involved."

"Why? I thought the Fortunato and Parkes murders were unrelated."

"Yes and no," he responded. "They were and they weren't."

"Explain," she said again, pencil still tapping her lips.

"If there's a relationship, it centers on the murder of Thomas Gray. My dad knew Gray, and he'd talked with Gray's kids at the memorial service.

They'd come over from the mainland. They doubted their dad fell overboard. He never took the boat out alone, they said—it was a thirty-five-footer and he was a complete novice at boating. Even an expert can't drive a boat that big and fish at the same time. Especially if you hook a marlin, which is what Gray fished for. He had his heart set on catching a marlin weighing more than a thousand pounds. Marlin fishing is high-speed trolling; one guy runs the boat while others fish. If someone hooks a marlin, the guy with the fishing rod needs someone else at the controls."

"I've been marlin fishing, thank you," the chief said coolly.

"Okay, good. So I asked around. I learned that Gray used to hire Parkes to skipper the *Mahi Mia* when Gray and his guests went fishing. So Parkes was connected to Gray, and Gray was connected to Fortunato."

Ana Carvalho continued to regard Kawika with evident wariness. "So you guessed Gray'd been murdered?" she ventured. "With Parkes involved? And then what? One of Gray's kids murdered Parkes in revenge? Quite a few leaps there, wouldn't you say? For one thing, how would Parkes have gotten back to shore? Parkes and whoever else was involved, I mean."

Kawika rubbed his temples with his fingertips. "Bear with me," he asked. "I did guess Gray had been murdered—yes. By Ralph Fortunato."

"*Fortunato*?" she asked, sounding astonished. Her eyebrows rose. It was clear she hadn't expected that.

Kawika reminded her that during the Fortunato investigation, he himself had been wounded by a shooter and evacuated to Washington state for his safety. While there he'd visited the Methow Valley, where Fortunato had tried to develop a resort before moving to Hawai'i.

"And there I learned that Fortunato had evidently murdered the guy who'd sold him the land for *that* resort, in order to keep him from testifying before a federal grand jury investigating Fortunato for real estate fraud. And in that case, Fortunato had made it look like the victim had fallen out of his boat and drowned while fishing in a small lake."

Chief Carvalho gave a slight nod. "So you figured—" she began.

"So I figured Fortunato might have murdered Thomas Gray too. Maybe for the same reason Fortunato murdered the fellow back in Washington, just as a precaution, in case there was a fraud investigation here. Because Fortunato had paid Gray what we learned was a wildly excessive price for the land in South Kohala. Fortunato probably got a kickback from Gray. That's where the fraud came in: Fortunato was defrauding his investors. Gray represented a potential risk to Fortunato if the feds came after him in Hawai'i as they had in Washington."

"And Parkes?" the chief asked impatiently. "Where's he fit?"

"Yes, well, Parkes. If someone killed Gray out at midchannel and left the *Mahi Mia* there, then somehow the killer needed to get back to shore, just as you suggested. To leave the *Mahi Mia* out in the Maui Channel, he needed an accomplice."

Again Chief Carvalho nodded, though Kawika could tell her impatience was growing. "But still, D. K. Parkes?" she asked. "How'd you figure him as the accomplice?"

"I didn't," Kawika said. "Not at first. But on a hunch, I showed Parkes's picture to Fortunato's widow. And she identified Parkes as someone who'd skippered the *Mahi Mia* whenever her husband had gone fishing with Gray."

"Ah, three guys on the boat. And two of them needed to get back to shore, right? Sort of a cannibals-and-missionaries problem."

"Yes, there had to be another boat," he agreed.

Chief Carvalho continued tapping the pencil against her lips while she thought. "Fascinating, I agree. Yet you didn't report any of this. Why, Major Wong?" she asked at last.

Kawika turned both palms upward again. "It was all just conjecture on my part. Pure speculation. I didn't have any proof. No evidence at all. All three were already dead: Gray, Fortunato, Parkes. There were no leads. Gray was a widower whose children were on the mainland—the *continent*, I'm told we should say nowadays—when their dad drowned. Corazon Fortunato had told me everything she could. No one knew who else had actually been on *Mahi Mia* that day with Gray. You say Victim Assistance talked with Keoni Parkes, but I didn't know he existed; D. K. Parkes and Shark Cliff weren't mine, they were Sammy's. Did Keoni say anything that could've been useful? You've reviewed the files and I haven't."

The chief shook her head. "Not a scrap in the files about what Keoni may have said," she answered. "So why didn't you tell Terry Tanaka? He was your supervisor."

Kawika sighed. "I did mention it to Terry," he began. "Just in passing, though. I didn't tell him enough. I said I *guessed* Parkes had been an accomplice in what I *guessed* had been a homicide, one that was already two years old. But I said I couldn't prove it, and I told Terry the guy I suspected as Parkes's killer was already dead. I didn't mention Gray's name to Terry, or that I suspected Fortunato of having killed him. At the time it seemed pointless. Fortunato was dead, Gray was dead, Parkes was dead, and I had no proof anyway. Sammy didn't have any leads in the Parkes case. I was only twenty-nine. If I had it to do all over again, I'd tell Terry what I suspected, even though we'd never prove it."

"Maybe you'd look for Parkes's killer too?" she suggested acidly. She didn't disguise her disapproval. "Not quit trying, just because his killer *might* already be dead? I mean, you were just guessing about Parkes's killer, you said. So what if it was a bad guess? Then someone *else* killed D. K. Parkes, and that killer might still have been alive. Might still be alive today, for that matter."

Kawika nodded. "I probably should've done that." But Kawika knew who'd killed Parkes. He'd known back then too. And he knew the killer was long dead.

Chief Carvalho regarded Kawika for a long time. "Okay," she finally said. "Let me reframe my question, just so we're clear: You don't know who killed Parkes?"

Kawika looked down and shook his head.

"But you have a guess?"

"I *had* a guess," he responded. "I hadn't found any evidence."

Chief Carvalho pinned him with a very hard look. "That's your final answer?" she asked. "You guessed who killed Parkes back in 2002 or so, but even now you're not going to tell me? Why not? Are you protecting the killer, Kawika?"

Kawika looked up and met her eyes. "No, I'm definitely not protecting the killer," he insisted. *Not now, at any rate*, he thought to himself. *The killer's been dead for more than a decade.*

The chief waited, now tapping her pencil on her lips more rapidly, then finally spoke. "Here's *my* guess," she said. "My guess is that you don't have to speculate—you *know* who killed Parkes. And I suspect you're not telling me who did it because you know the person who killed Parkes also killed Ralph Fortunato—and it wasn't Michael Cushing or his hit man Rocco, was it?"

This put Kawika in an immediate quandary. He hadn't expected Carvalho to connect the two murders and hadn't prepared anything to deflect her.

"Think of it this way," she went on. "What if I assume you and Terry *did* cover up who killed Fortunato? Suppose Terry charging the wrong person wasn't a mistake; that he knew he'd charged the wrong person. Now, *why* would you cover that up, Kawika? Either you'd be protecting Terry or you'd be protecting the killer. And Kawika, I know you. You'd protect Terry out of loyalty, just like you'd have protected me when we were partners in Honolulu. It's one of your admirable traits. But I don't think you'd protect the killer. You with me so far?"

Kawika nodded glumly. He knew what she'd say next.

"Okay. You've *also* told me that Fortunato and Parkes, working together, killed Thomas Gray. So it's not too big a leap to guess that whoever killed Parkes killed Fortunato too. Killed them in the same year and on the same island as revenge for murdering Thomas Gray. And if *that's* correct, then it explains why you won't tell me who killed Parkes—because you'd be telling me who killed Fortunato." She paused, as if for effect, before continuing. "And we both know neither Michael Cushing nor his hit man Rocco killed *Parkes*. Parkes isn't even mentioned in the hit man's confession, and I can't imagine any reason Cushing would want Parkes dead, if he even knew who Parkes was. Can you?"

Kawika shook his head.

"So, if the same person killed Fortunato and Parkes, *and* if Cushing's hit man didn't kill Parkes, then by definition we'd know that Cushing's hit man didn't kill Fortunato either, wouldn't we? Which, of course, is precisely what Cushing and Sammy Kāʻai assert and what Zoë Akona is trying to prove."

Kawika tried to look disbelieving, but he could tell it wasn't working. He swallowed hard and started to speak. "I—" he stammered.

"Save it," she said roughly, raising her hand to stop him. "I won't believe anything you tell me now, so don't even try."

She stood and collected the files and her legal pad. "You're lying to me, Kawika. I worked with you for years at HPD; I never would've thought you'd tell lies. Not about something this important. Not to me—your friend, your wife's friend, your former partner. And not to a chief of police. Any chief of police. What's happened to you, Kawika? For God's sake, Kawika, *what has happened to you?*"

It was the second time he'd faced the accusing question in forty-eight hours, first from Tanaka and now from Carvalho. The second time two old colleagues, steadfast in their loyalty and friendship until now, had expressed utter disappointment in him, even repugnance.

The chief started to walk from the room but turned as she reached the door. "Since you're lying to me about Parkes, I won't even ask you about

Fortunato yet. I'll start with Terry. I can trust Terry. He'll tell me whether my hypothetical is correct. He'll tell me the truth, even if it means confessing."

Kawika realized, all of a sudden, that she was right: Tanaka *would* tell her the truth, despite everything Kawika had urged. Tanaka would confess he'd charged the wrong man, that there'd been a cover-up, and that the cover-up had continued ever since.

Things were coming apart.

25

Honolulu

After that worrisome Monday morning, it seemed fitting to Kawika upon his return to O'ahu that the week began with four days of low black clouds and cold, unrelenting rain. In Honolulu the streets flooded and the Ala Wai Canal overflowed, carrying trash into the harbor and onto the beaches of Waikīkī and Ala Moana Beach Park. On Maui a mudslide destroyed dozens of cars in the garage of a condo building, cracking several supports and causing the structure itself to be condemned. In Hilo, the nation's most rainy city, it seemed people almost didn't notice, and if they did, a lot of them laughed. But in Kona and on the normally arid Kohala Coast, several imperfectly engineered roads washed out, inconveniencing residents and tourists. On all the islands, tides and surf ran high. The sea overflowed low walls and deposited reef fish and sand in front yards and parking lots.

"I should go back and check the Puakō house," a concerned Elle told Kawika. "I can fly over on Friday after class."

"I wish I could join you," he said. "But I can't—these two cases. Too much on my plate."

"Of course," she said. "I get it."

Kawika actually had four cases to worry about, but he forced himself to put Keoni Parkes and Slasher ahead of Fortunato and D. K. It was the professional thing to do, and focusing on the current investigations also kept him from obsessing about the long shadow of the old ones. He reminded himself of what his mother Lily often advised: *Sufficient unto the day is the evil thereof.* He knew the words came from the Bible, but it helped to think of them as Lily's.

Each day possessed ample amounts of evil, or at least difficult tasks. The Slasher seemed to have taken some time off—maybe because of the rain, the Two Jerrys suggested when Kawika asked for an update. But there'd been no progress in the investigation; the Task Force just kept going over the same meager evidence and useless hotline tips again and again. The Keoni Parkes investigation, now Kawika's primary concern, required laborious interviews and reinterviews all week long: Angel Delos Santos and Jay Goddard, a score of Warriors, Defenders, and members of Jonathan Kalākalani's Big Island ʻOhana, and a long list of more remote possibles, both in Honolulu and on the Big Island.

Tanaka had also sent Ku'ulei to interview astronomers and employees at the various observatory headquarters in Hilo and Waimea. "It's frustrating," she reported to Kawika. "Like I told Terry, these people all know about Keoni, but basically, they won't answer my questions. They just want to talk about astronomy, the importance of the TMT. A lot of them are freaked out by the opposition to it. Some are really angry, like, 'How can myths be more important than science?' Ridiculous, they say. They're all, 'Who owns science? Who gets to block scientific discovery?' Very indignant, and they look at me suspiciously, like they can tell I'm not on their side. I guess discovering a killer isn't scientific enough for them."

"Well, it's scientific enough for us," Kawika said in sympathy.

In the other two cases—those of Ralph Fortunato and D. K. Parkes—there'd been more activity than Kawika would have liked and too much of what he'd feared. Zoë Akona had written a snide article in the *Star-Advertiser*—with Scully's added byline—reviewing "the controversy," as the article called it, over Tanaka's possible malfeasance in the Fortunato and D. K. Parkes murder cases. Kawika's name wasn't mentioned.

The article insinuated that Chief Ana Carvalho either didn't take the matter seriously or intended to keep her official review from the press, despite what the article described as "the risk that the public will see the new chief as perpetuating an alleged cover-up that Teruo Tanaka initiated." *But who'd created that risk?* No one would have given a thought to Michael Cushing or Ralph Fortunato without the articles Zoë had written.

The article troubled Kawika. And why had the article named only Tanaka and not Kawika himself, especially since Scully's byline was on the story and Scully had interviewed him?

Much worse, Tanaka had called Kawika to tell him, coldly and as a courtesy, that he'd just confessed everything to Ana Carvalho. Confessed it freely and thoroughly, Tanaka said. He sounded only a bit apologetic. *He's relieved*, Kawika recognized.

It was Chief Carvalho who told Kawika where matters stood. "Terry admits he let Cushing be prosecuted for Fortunato's murder, knowing Cushing's hired hit man Rocco hadn't committed the crime," the chief began. "He says when he arrested Cushing, he believed the hit man actually had killed Fortunato, having read the hit man's confession. I can see how he got there, especially given the physical evidence; the confession is cleverly worded. But Terry admits that once you quizzed him the day after his press conference, he realized the Fortunato part of the confession was wrong and the evidence was planted. Yet he still let Cushing be prosecuted for Fortunato's murder."

Kawika could think of nothing to say. He wasn't sure where she was headed. But he knew it would get worse.

"You still there, Major? Good. Terry says you never told him the name of the individual you suspected for Fortunato—"

"I didn't."

"But he figured it out from what you'd said, then he double-checked it himself to confirm what you'd said, and *still* he didn't act on that information. You can understand that this was a gross dereliction of duty, Major Wong. And the false prosecution of Cushing may well have been a crime."

"Though it added nothing to Cushing's sentence," Kawika offered.

"That's immaterial. You don't let someone be prosecuted for a crime you know someone else committed. And just as important, you don't let the real killer go. Terry did both."

Kawika swallowed hard, then admitted, "A lot of the responsibility is mine. I could have done more."

"Yes, that's very true. But you were twenty-nine and still learning. You followed the chain of command. Terry was your superior. Maybe more important, you're at HPD now, and I can't discipline you. But I can discipline Terry, and I don't have a choice."

"Ana, there were extenuating circumstances—"

"Don't call me Ana right now, okay? And let me finish. Terry admits that you explained to him that D. K. Parkes had been an accomplice in another murder, yet Terry didn't ask you which one. He says you told him the person who killed D. K. was already dead—"

"By the time I guessed who it was, that was true."

"And he didn't ask you about that either, what you knew and how you knew. He just ignored the information." She paused briefly. "So here's what I'm going to do," she concluded. "I'll wrap up my investigation—my official review—as soon as possible. I've got a few more people to interview, including Tommy Kekoa and you again. This time you're going to tell me the truth, or I *will* blow up your chances of becoming chief in Honolulu. You understand?"

"Yes, I understand."

"And even though it's a cold case, a *very* cold case, after you guys catch Keoni's killer, we're going to try to find out who killed D. K. Parkes. And you're going to cooperate with me on that, right?"

"Right, Chief. Of course."

"In the Fortunato matter, I realize Terry acted out of loyalty to you, to avenge Cushing's hit man shooting you, and you acted—or failed to act—out of loyalty to Terry," she continued. "That's admirable on a personal level, and I know it's just who you are. But professionally, it can't excuse what either of you did or the cover-up you've perpetuated ever since. You're not twenty-nine anymore, Major."

She paused with that reproof, but only briefly. "I'm not going to fire Terry and I'm not going to say anything publicly that's more than mildly critical of either of you," she resumed. "I'll find some way to paper this over, make a statement about how things always look clearer in retrospect, we all have twenty-twenty hindsight and so on. It's distasteful to do that, and I'll have to talk with the county's lawyers first. But I'm not going to throw raw meat to that odious reporter. Zoë's all over me about this review. In the end, I'll find some justification for not taking official action."

For the first time on the call, Kawika began to feel a bit of relief.

"But," the chief continued quickly, "I've told Terry that once you guys solve the Keoni Parkes case, he's going to announce his retirement. He accepts that. He's old enough, and solving that case will be a fitting end to his distinguished career. We'll throw a big party for him."

She waited a moment, then said, "That's all," and hung up.

Kawika almost never cried; he hadn't cried since Jarvis's stroke. But sometimes he threw up. He felt ready to do so now.

26

Honolulu

Frustratingly, the action of the Kapi'olani Park Slasher in depositing his latest victim in Ala Moana Beach Park—the corpse that came with its own driver's license—after someone else had dumped Keoni's body in Kapi'olani Park forced the Task Force to rethink the deployment of cops and cruisers to catch the Slasher. The anxiety level throughout the city had risen dramatically, along with the font size in the headlines of the *Star-Advertiser*'s Slasher stories—stories all written by Bernard Scully. The entire HPD felt the pressure.

The task force assembled this time without Kawika; his assistant said he was on the phone with Chief Carvalho in Hilo but encouraged them to go ahead.

Jerry Rhodes, who'd predicted the Slasher might change his dumping ground once he spotted police cars ringing Kapi'olani Park, was gracious to Sakamoto and didn't say *I told you so.*

"Kyu," Rhodes consoled his partner, "I had the same type of problem with the Griffith Park guy in LA. It's a move in a chess game, his changing his MO. The killer is going to react to our moves, like staking out Kapi'olani Park. We've just got to anticipate his."

Of course, that was easier said than done. What would the killer do next? Keep using Ala Moana Beach Park to dump bodies? If they ringed Ala Moana with officers and cars as they'd done at Kapi'olani, would the Slasher just go back to using his original park? The department didn't have enough officers to cordon the perimeters of both parks that thoroughly. And the Slasher had scores of other parks to choose from; if they ringed two, he'd just pick a third. Who said he needed to confine himself to parks anyway? It was maddening.

One task force member suggested hopefully that perhaps the Slasher would stop killing, now that he'd broken the record and the media had blared that news to the world. Others shrugged or glumly shook their heads. "Doesn't seem likely," Sakamoto replied gently. "In any event, we can't count on it. We can't let up."

After several suggestions had been considered and rejected, Rhodes offered one that seemed as good as any. "How about we add a *few* cops and cruisers—like, one or two, not more—at Ala Moana Beach Park? And reduce the number at Kapiʻolani by maybe six or ten? So now we're offering the Slasher a lightly defended perimeter at one park and a perimeter at the other that's less heavily defended than before. See which way he jumps. I'm guessing he'll rise to the challenge and try Kapiʻolani Park next time."

Hearing this, Yvonne shuddered visibly. "What are you thinking, Detective?" Sakamoto asked her. "You don't like Jerry's idea?"

"No, it's not that," she replied. "It's just that we're trying to catch him in the act. So we're still planning on him killing someone else. If we're going to do that, can't we at least put some night vision cameras around the two parks? Make this next victim his last one, if he kills again?"

Rhodes nodded. "We could do that, Yvonne," he responded supportively. "It's not a bad idea. But how many cameras would we need? Like, fifty or more for each park? And we couldn't hide what we'd be doing when we installed them. We have to assume the Slasher is watching us, watching what we do in those parks. So it's the same old problem: we armor the defenses of two parks and probably just drive him to a third. I mean, we could put up klieg lights, but the problem would be the same, right? I think we have to play to his ego instead, his sense of superiority, his belief that he can't get caught. Reduce the armor a bit and tempt him to try one of the two parks again, preferably Kapiʻolani."

Sakamoto reluctantly agreed. Going to the whiteboard, he wrote bullet points for a revised plan: a single police car circling Ala Moana Beach Park, stopping at unpredictable intervals, with the officer getting out occasionally and doing some reconnaissance on foot. The Slasher might figure he could outsmart one cop if he chose his moment carefully. So Ala Moana Beach Park would be very lightly guarded, especially given its size. And maybe the Slasher would keep using it. Maybe they could catch him in the act. At the very least, it would tell them something. Then they could devise a plan to fool him into thinking he'd still be safe the next time.

For Kapi'olani Park, Sakamoto decided to increase the distance between parked cruisers to about four hundred yards—some were empty cars, as before, for lack of sufficient officers—with two cars circling the park, stopping unpredictably, like the single car at Ala Moana. Even if they didn't catch him this time, they could figure out how to make it a lot riskier for the Slasher going forward, depending on which park he chose. If he chose either.

"We can't expect anything the first night," Rhodes cautioned. "He'll probably take some time to watch us and make sure he's figured out the pattern. Listen to us on his police scanner. He might even wait a week or two, lulling us into thinking he's quit, waiting to see how we reduce our coverage. He'll know he can wait us out if he pauses for a while."

It was another glum thought, reminding everyone of the task force's basic helplessness, the desperation of this unpromising and only semi-sensible plan that none of them believed would really work. Yet all they really had to go on was that the Slasher still deposited his victims in one particular park, and now a second one nearby. His selection of victims might be random, but his selection of dumping grounds was not.

Sakamoto ended the meeting crisply by telling the team he'd have their assignments worked out later in the day. "Keep checking," he told them.

"Yvonne should ride with me," Rhodes suggested. "As Major Wong says, it'd be good experience for her." He looked at Yvonne and smiled.

"Nope," Sakamoto said firmly. "We don't have enough people to double up. Yvonne will have her own car and radio. Use the radio if you see anything."

"Of course, Kyu, but I'm also firearms trained and certified," Yvonne protested.

"Yes, and I'm sure you're an excellent shot," he replied. "You just don't have enough field experience yet for this case. Experience, judgment—that takes a while. Don't rush it."

* * *

An older detective, Nani Palakiko, had become Yvonne's best friend on the task force. Nani sought out Yvonne as the meeting adjourned.

"Jerry sure was nice to you today," Nani said as they walked toward their desks. "I think he's sweet on you."

"Sweet on me? Nani, he's *hitting* on me. He does it all the time. I can't get him to stop."

Nani halted and grabbed Yvonne's arm. "Really?" she responded. "Have you *told* him to stop?"

Yvonne turned to her friend, face lowered. "Not in so many words," she admitted quietly, as others passed in the hallway. "I told him I'm not going to date anyone in the department. But it doesn't stop him. He says, 'Dinner to talk about work isn't really a date,' 'You could benefit from my experience,' and things like that. Or even 'Well, where else are you going to meet someone? At a traffic stop?' He says he's not harassing me, 'just trying to get to know me better.' It's constant. Every time there's no one around."

Nani tightened her grip on Yvonne's arm. "Yvonne, you have to tell him to stop. Seriously. You have to say you'll report him if he doesn't."

Yvonne lightly shook her head. "I'm afraid of him, Nani. If you could see his eyes, his face, when he says things like that. And he's always holding on to me when he says them."

"Holding on to you!" Nani quickly released her grip. "You're afraid he's going to hurt you?"

"No, but I'm afraid he'll hurt my chances around here. If I'm more direct with him, I know he'll get angry and start picking on me, or freezing me out on task force matters, or working behind the scenes to block other good assignments, once he understands there's absolutely no chance I'm ever going to get involved with him."

"If he does that, you'll just have to report him. It's textbook harassment."

Yvonne shook her head more firmly. "Nani, the only time I'd claim harassment would be if he got me fired. As long as I'm working here, I'm not going to file a harassment claim against a senior man in the department. It'd be a career-killing move. You know that."

Nani grimaced. "Yeah," she conceded, and gave Yvonne a quick hug. "I guess I do know that. *Damn.* But there has to be a solution."

27

Honolulu

During the week of record rainfall, Kawika stayed informed about the interviews of potential suspects as the Keoni Parkes murder investigation moved ahead. The Big Island detectives interviewing Angel Delos Santos had made a quick job of their part. They could imagine Angel having a motive, and—at a stretch—the means, namely, Keoni's pistol and pruning saw, if Angel had gone to Honolulu.

Yet it seemed Angel had remained firmly on the wrong island. He had no alibi that anyone could confirm for that particular Friday night, but the airlines found no record of his having flown to O'ahu in over a year. No plausible alternative presented itself, especially because early that Saturday morning Angel had shown up as usual at Catholic Community Services in Hilo, where he volunteered teaching English as a second language and conducting civics lessons for immigrants facing citizenship exams.

"We don't think he did it," a Waimea detective told Kawika by phone. "Unless he used a paddleboard, Hilo to Honolulu roundtrip."

In Honolulu, Jay Goddard's situation was more complex. Because of what Yvonne had reported about Jay's overwhelmed reaction to the death of his partner, combined with his shock at learning of John Parker's perfidy and double life, Kawika didn't consider Jay a promising suspect—although he wished Jay were, since a lover having killed Keoni would be far better for Kawika and Tanaka than if Keoni's death was linked to that of his father, given that Chief Ana Carvalho's investigation included a fresh look at the D. K. Parkes case.

The first detectives who interviewed Jay also concluded he couldn't be the killer, and told Kawika so. They accepted what Kawika had long counseled, namely, that guilty people couldn't act—meaning they couldn't convincingly act innocent. It was a point on which Kawika and Tanaka had agreed back in Kawika's Big Island days.

Nothing Kawika had seen since coming to Honolulu altered his view on that. But his Honolulu homicide detectives included plenty of experienced veterans, not all of whom were quite so sure. On their own initiative, two of them had decided to question Jay again downtown, at the Alapa'i police headquarters.

The detectives had gotten on the wrong track initially, because of Jay claiming he'd made phone calls to his lover that Friday night. The police had the records of Keoni's phone calls and texts, and there were none—zero—on that night. It took time to find out that Keoni had *two* cell phones, the second one in the name of John Parker.

When the detectives got the records for that second phone, they saw Jay Goddard had been telling the truth. He'd kept calling until eleven PM. But Jay couldn't otherwise account for his Friday evening and couldn't name anyone who'd seen him after he'd left work that afternoon. The detectives found this suspicious.

Kawika read Jay's interview transcript on his office computer. The two detectives had pressed their suspect on what he'd done after he couldn't reach the man he knew as John:

> *SUSPECT: I'd been awake all night, trying to think what could possibly have happened. Maybe he'd been in a car accident. Maybe he was in a hospital somewhere. I was going crazy, losing my mind with worry and anger and sleeplessness. I went over to his house as soon as it was daylight, and his car was gone, no lights were on, no one answered when I knocked and pushed the doorbell.*

All of it rang true to Kawika. After reading the transcript, Kawika summoned the two detectives who'd honed in on Jay Goddard as their prime suspect. He listened carefully and looked at their materials. He yearned for Goddard to be the killer, just as he yearned for Keoni's death to be TMT related; either way, the disconnect between Keoni's death and that of his father would be complete. Keoni's murder would be entirely unrelated to how

Kawika had handled D. K. Parkes's murder years earlier, not evidence proving to Ana Carvalho that he'd mishandled it completely and that the death of D. K. had been part of a series rather than the one-off that Kawika had assumed.

But the detectives simply hadn't made a case against Jay Goddard—there wasn't any real evidence against him. Kawika believed the earlier detectives had been right: Goddard wasn't the killer.

"Sorry, guys," Kawika said sympathetically. "But you're doing good work. I mean it. So keep at it, okay?"

28

Waimea

By Friday afternoon the rains had stopped. Elle reached the Puakō house just before sunset—a spectacular one, painting with vibrant colors the towering clouds of the tropical Pacific. Between thumb and forefinger, she lifted a dozen dead and discolored reef fish one by one from the front lawn, stepped over the low lava rock wall, and threw the fish back into a now-placid sea ablaze like the clouds with the hues of the sunset. She couldn't do anything about the sand, which covered the lawn unevenly, inches deep in places. It might harm the lawn for a while, but she hoped the torrential rains had washed away most of the salt.

She'd stopped at the Puakō General Store to pick up some groceries. While preparing dinner, she called Kawika. "I've got a nice meal here—pickles and ice cream," she joked. "No, seriously, I'm fine. No weird food cravings yet. And the house is fine too. One little leak in the back room, no damage, easy to fix, I think. But the lawn is trashed, Kawika, just covered in sand. Maybe I should have left the dead fish for fertilizer!"

Kawika expressed relief about the house. "So what'll you do now?" he asked.

She said she'd collect Kawika's dad in the morning and take him to the Saturday market in Waimea. "He loves doing that. He's got friends up there who're always so glad to see him. After that I'll drive over to Hilo and have dinner with Kuʻulei. Maybe I can take her an orchid from the market. If Ana agrees to meet for coffee or brunch on Sunday in Hilo, I'll spend the night with Kuʻulei. Otherwise I'll drive back here tomorrow night. I should be home Sunday afternoon."

"Can't wait," Kawika said. "Thank you for doing all this, Elle. I wish I were doing it with you. Except for seeing Ana again, that is."

On Saturday morning, after a simple breakfast, Elle drove up to the care center in Waikoloa Village. She kissed Jarvis on the cheek and reminded him about the outing she'd planned. "*Yuh-yuh-yuh*," he said, indicating his pleasure at the prospect.

The caregivers shifted Jarvis into his motorized wheelchair, drove him outdoors—the morning was cool and fresh after the recent rains—and loaded him into the center's van with the wheelchair lift. They snapped shut various buckles and fasteners to hold the wheelchair securely. "Locked and loaded," Elle told Jarvis with a smile as she climbed into the seat facing him. The driver, Keanu Fuchida, was a huge and jovial Hawaiian. He told Elle he was looking forward to visiting the Saturday market again himself.

After arriving in Waimea, Fuchida opened the sliding door, unsnapped the restraints, rolled the wheelchair to the lift, and gently lowered Jarvis and his chair to the ground. Elle took her place behind him, driving the wheelchair using the hand controls, allowing Fuchida to stroll the market on his own. From many prior trips with Jarvis, Elle knew the controls well. She enjoyed being Jarvis's ground-level chauffeur and lightheartedly chattered away to him.

In general appearance the Waimea market resembled farmers' markets throughout the world, but the sights and smells were distinctively Hawaiian. All sorts of colorful tropical plants and fruits and vegetables for sale. Malasadas and lumpia frying in hot oil. Flower leis hanging from stalls in colorful profusion. Local goat cheese and dried ahi. Short lengths of sugarcane—all that remained of the Big Island's once-dominant industry—for sale as treats. Shave ice for the *keiki*, local ice cream for other keiki and their parents.

As Elle had anticipated, many vendors called out, "Aloha, Jarvis!" as the wheelchair passed. Some stepped from their stalls to take his hand and say a few encouraging words. *Huh-huh-huh*, Jarvis responded each time. Elle knew he was trying to suggest *hello* rather than *aloha*; he could voice consonants more easily than vowels.

Such a pity, Elle thought. *He must be the best-loved man in Kohala. How he'd enjoy being able to shake hands, embrace these friends, laugh, and exchange slaps on the back.*

The affectionate displays for Jarvis made Elle think, with a pang, how much Jarvis would've enjoyed seeing Terry Tanaka, his longtime best friend, when Tanaka had visited the Puakō house recently. She knew Jarvis had often entertained Tanaka there before his stroke. The two might have seemed an unlikely pair to others, Jarvis the deep-voiced outsized Hawaiian and Tanaka the small *Sansei*, or third-generation Japanese American. The highly specialized sport of shore fishing for hundred-pound giant trevally, known as *ulua* in Hawai'i, supposedly explained their bond, but Elle guessed fishing had merely deepened it.

The real bond, as Elle with her novelist's sensibility imagined it, was the unspoken sadness of their long bachelorhoods, Jarvis's from his youthful divorce but Tanaka's from even more painful circumstances. Before his stroke, Jarvis had explained to Elle that during World War II Tanaka's father, a second-generation Japanese American, or *Nisei,* had volunteered with other Nisei for the 100th Infantry Battalion of the U.S. Army and left his wife and infant son Terry behind in the Manzanar War Relocation Center. He'd been killed fighting Germans in Italy. His widow's bitterness at America—for her husband's death, for her years in Manzanar, for her son growing up with no father—had never abated, even after her postwar move to Hawai'i's large and Japanese American community.

Tanaka's mother had insisted her son marry no one but a Japanese woman from the family's original prefecture, Niigata, and Tanaka had dutifully acceded to her wishes. By the time a suitable woman had been found, Tanaka was nearly thirty and his bride-to-be was working for an international aid agency in India. After meeting Tanaka just once, in Hilo, she flew back to resign her post so they could marry. She died with eighty-one others when her Japan Airlines flight crashed short of the runway in New Delhi. And that, for Tanaka, had been that. He'd never married and, except to Jarvis, never spoken of it.

Elle's thoughts returned to the present as she arrived with Jarvis's wheelchair at a stall displaying all sorts and colors of orchids. She hoped to find one to take to Ku'ulei in Hilo. Another customer turned to look at Elle and Jarvis, and Elle recognized her as Emma Phillips. Elle smiled with pleasure, but quickly muted her expression when Dr. Phillips didn't respond in kind. *Too soon,* Elle reasoned. *She's still grieving for Keoni.* Elle extended Dr. Phillips a gentle hand and an "Aloha."

"Let me introduce my father-in-law," Elle said. "Jarvis, this is Dr. Phillips. She's a famous astronomer, part of the TMT project. And Dr. Phillips, this is Jarvis Wong."

Dr. Phillips smiled politely and nodded at Jarvis. "I'm pleased to meet you, Mr. Wong. You have a lovely daughter-in-law. I recently met your son Kawika as well."

Jarvis responded unexpectedly, voicing *muh-muh-muh* repeatedly. "I'm sorry," Elle explained. "He's had a serious stroke, sadly. He can't speak anymore. As you can tell, he'd like to if he could."

Muh-muh-muh, Jarvis repeated. *Muh-muh-muh.*

Dr. Phillips smiled again and excused herself. With a small wave to Elle, she set off strolling casually in the opposite direction, pausing briefly at other stalls as she went.

Muh-muh-muh, Jarvis intoned, much more loudly than usual. *Muh-muh-muh, muh-muh-muh.* Over and over again.

Elle had never seen Jarvis this animated in the years since his stroke. Animated or agitated? she wondered. She didn't know whether to be concerned. She decided to get him back to the care center, where medical staff could attend to him. She spotted Keanu Fuchida, the van driver, at the malasada booth and signaled him to come quickly. Within minutes they'd loaded Jarvis in the van and were headed toward Waikoloa Village.

It wasn't a short ride. Elle had time to elicit more from Jarvis if she could. She leaned forward and began to quiz him. "You're saying M, right?"

Yuh-yuh-yuh.

"And you're referring to Dr. Phillips?"

Yuh-yuh-yuh.

"Well, her first name *is* Emma."

Yuh-yuh-yuh.

"Is that what you're trying to tell me? That her first name is Emma?"

Nuh-nuh-nuh.

By the time they'd settled Jarvis in his room at the care center, Elle still hadn't discerned what he was trying to convey. She held his hand and tried to think of questions he could answer with yes or no. As so often before, she felt frustration—and sympathy—that he couldn't nod or shake his head or recognize letters pointed out to him so that he could spell. But Jarvis didn't wait to be questioned further. *Guh-guh-guh*, he volunteered. *Guh-guh-guh.*

"You're saying G now, Jarvis?"

Yuh-yuh-yuh.

"Referring to Dr. Phillips?"

Jarvis responded with another cluster of sounds for yes. Through trial and error, Elle grasped that Jarvis was telling her a second name for Emma Phillips—a name other than Phillips.

"Okay, so the second name begins with a G, correct?" she asked.

Jarvis indicated yes.

"What's the next letter?"

Ruh-ruh-ruh.

"So it's R," Elle said. "What's comes after that?"

Uh-uh-uh.

Elle knew Jarvis's *uh-uh-uh* meant a vowel, but it might be any vowel. He could give reliable utterance only to consonants. Fortunately, there weren't many vowels; Elle could try them one by one. She succeeded on the first attempt. When she proposed *a*, Jarvis immediately responded with *yuh-yuh-yuh.*

"G-R-A," Elle said. She tried to think of what letter might come next. So many seemed possible. She almost began with *b.*

Yuh-yuh-YUH, Jarvis suddenly stressed, without waiting. Not quite the way he usually made the sound for yes.

"Y?" she asked him, guessing. "The letter Y?"

Yuh-yuh-yuh. Yuh-yuh-yuh.

"Gray? Emma Gray?"

Another *yuh-yuh-yuh* from Jarvis indicated she'd gotten it right. *Yuh-yuh-yuh*, he repeated.

Elle sat back in her chair, puzzled. "Thank you, Jarvis," she said at last. "I should go now. There's something I need to check." She kissed him on the top of his head and squeezed his hand, though whether he could feel the squeeze or the kiss, she didn't know.

She walked to her car, the one that had once been his. Then she drove down to Puakō.

What she wanted to check was a piece of paper she'd left in the cottage the weekend before—the photocopy of Thomas Gray's obituary. The one that named the adult children who'd survived him: Kam, named after Kamehameha, and daughter Emma.

Emma Gray. The same Emma Gray? Now Emma Gray Phillips? An Emma whom Jarvis had recognized at once, but who'd acted as if she were meeting him for the first time. Yet that couldn't be right. Jarvis had known the two Gray children when they were growing up, Kawika had told Elle and his colleagues at the Puakō cottage just the other night, adding that as adults, Gray's children had expressed doubt to Jarvis about Thomas Gray having drowned accidentally.

So did Emma pretend not to know Jarvis at the Saturday market? Elle wondered. He'd lost weight since his stroke, but he was still a very large man, still recognizable as Jarvis Wong. And Elle had even introduced him to Emma by name. *Why hadn't she said to Jarvis, "You probably remember me as Emma Gray, Tom Gray's daughter"?*

When reading the *Puako Post* obituary the first time, Elle had unconsciously assumed that Thomas Gray's children would be hapa haole Hawaiians, because the obituary gave their mother's name as Leilani. But that assumption could be wrong, Elle now realized; a mother named Leilani needn't imply anything about the race of her children. After all, Emma was a popular name throughout Hawai'i, thanks to a favorite Hawaiian queen.

"So did she pretend or just forget?" Elle asked herself aloud. She wondered about that as she began preparing her lunch. Then the phone rang.

"Hello?" Elle answered.

"Aloha," came a woman's voice. "Is this Elle?"

"Yes—who's this?"

"Oh, good. Elle, this is Dr. Phillips. Emma Phillips. I found your mobile number online, in the UH Mānoa faculty directory. I hope you don't mind my calling? I just wanted to check on your father-in-law. I worry I disturbed him at the market this morning. Is he okay?"

"Yes, thanks, he's fine now," Elle assured her. "Very thoughtful of you to ask. He was just trying to say he recognized you as Emma Gray—a big effort for him." Elle wondered what Emma would say to that. Would she explain herself?

The other woman laughed. "That's right!" she confirmed. "I *am* Emma Gray. Or I was, anyway. I feel like such an idiot. Jarvis's memory is way better than mine, it seems. I completely spaced on knowing him myself. When I grew up in Puakō, he was our neighbor. I haven't seen him in years—not since my dad's memorial service, I think, and that was back in 2000. Long before his stroke, I guess."

"Right. His stroke was just a couple of years ago."

"Still, I should've recognized him! I just wasn't thinking. In the years I've been back, he's actually the first person to remember me as Emma Gray. I should've put it together when I met your husband. But Kawika arrived from Honolulu, so I didn't think of it. And as you know, I had Keoni's murder on my mind that day. I was still dazed. Preoccupied, anyway. And I'd never actually met Kawika before."

"Probably because Kawika grew up mostly in Seattle with his mom," Elle said. "He was in Puakō with Jarvis only in the summers."

"That must be it," Emma said. "I was *never* here in summer. My mom died, and my dad worked full-time. So he always sent my brother and me to California to be with Mom's relatives as soon as school let out."

Elle smiled; evidentally Emma just hadn't recognized Jarvis. Elle thought about what to say next. To end the conversation on that note seemed too abrupt. "Kawika was actually talking about your father recently," she decided to reply.

"Why was that?" Emma sounded surprised.

"Because of your father's death," Elle replied. "About which I'm very sorry, by the way."

"Thank you," said Emma. "But that happened so long ago. What made your husband think of it?"

Belatedly, Elle realized she probably shouldn't have said anything about Thomas Gray. She didn't want to mention D. K. Parkes or Ralph Fortunato or reveal anything that wasn't public. "Oh, Kawika just mentioned in passing that you and your brother didn't believe your dad died accidentally," she answered. "Kawika doesn't have evidence about that himself. Just a hunch, he said. But I think he agrees with you."

Emma gasped. "He *does*? Oh my goodness," she said. "I can't tell you what a relief that is to hear. Someone agreeing with my brother and me, after all these years. And a detective too! You can't believe how frustrating it's been for us. Is your husband thinking about reopening the case, I hope?"

"Oh, no, not at all. I didn't mean to suggest that—my apologies. Kawika was talking about another old case, and your dad's happened to come up. Old cases were on Kawika's mind, I guess."

"Along with Keoni's," said Emma. "I sure hope that's on his mind too."

"Definitely," Elle said. "Kawika and the others are hard at work on that one. I'm sure they'll solve it, Emma. They almost always do."

"Good," said Emma. She paused, then added a different thought. "By the way, I'm heading down to Puakō this afternoon. Would you like to join me for a swim?"

"Oh, thanks, I'd love to, but I have to leave soon. I'm meeting Kawika's cousin—you remember her, Detective Ku'ulei Wong?—for dinner in Hilo."

"Even better!" Emma exclaimed. "Let's meet at my place in Waimea, then. You remember where it is? We can share a cup of coffee before you head to Hilo. I'm right on your way, if you take the Belt Road."

Elle thought for a moment. "I'd like that," she said.

29

Honolulu

With Elle out of town, Kawika tried to catch up on the Slasher investigation, despite his primary focus on the murder of Keoni Parkes; his personal stakes seemed high in both cases. He met with the Two Jerrys about the Slasher, but once again there were no new victims and, maddeningly, no new leads, at least if one discounted the anonymous tip line report of little green men dropping the Slasher's victims into Kapi'olani Park from a hovering UFO. Kawika could never decide whether people who left such messages were crazy or just complete jerks.

Yvonne, too, had been working with the Slasher Task Force as Kawika had directed, but she could only shake her head and shrug when he asked if she had fresh insights.

It was about Keoni's case that Yvonne asked to meet Kawika for lunch at Nico's on Saturday. "Well, mostly Keoni's case," she said. "There's a lot to discuss." Impressed as always with her initiative in dealing with him as her superior, Kawika readily agreed. Besides, Nico's was a great choice for seafood in the open air. For a relative newcomer, Yvonne was learning her way around Honolulu.

Once they'd collected their food and found a table facing the harbor, with its bright-colored fishing boats moored along the pier, they began their discussion with the discovery of Keoni's hands. They'd been encased in a black plastic bag, the same kind as those in the box at the murder scene. The bag had been found at the confluence of Makiki Stream and the Ala Wai Canal. The killer had presumably dumped the bag elsewhere in the canal, but the days of unrelieved downpour that had swelled the canal could have rolled the bag along toward the harbor while the canal was running like a river. As the waters receded, the bag had fetched up on a sandbar.

The bag contained two human hands—the confirmatory DNA tests were underway—tied to the hole in the handle of a brightly enameled cast-iron saucepan that matched the rest of Keoni's cookware. Resourceful fish had managed to wriggle into the bag through various torn places; several had been found inside. The hands were in ragged condition, with strips of discolored flesh clinging to the bones. The DNA testing, not fingerprints, had to be relied on for identification.

"So, what do you make of it?" Kawika asked.

"Well," began Yvonne, "logistically it probably made a bit of sense to dump the hands in the canal. Especially tied to a heavy saucepan."

Like Kawika, Yvonne had opted for Nico's fish and chips—swordfish, on this occasion—and she took a moment to wipe her hands with a paper napkin and dab the corner of her mouth.

"Just a *bit* of sense?" Kawika asked.

"It wasn't an ideal choice," she replied. "I mean, obviously. The canal's not hugely deep." In reality, the Ala Wai Canal wasn't a canal at all—it was a massive Depression-era drainage ditch, one that had allowed Waikīkī to be built on reclaimed swampland and rice paddies.

"So the bag might've eventually been found, as it was," Yvonne continued, "although not when or where the killer might've expected."

"What if the killer wasn't very familiar with Honolulu?" Kawika asked. "Wasn't that your suggestion at first? Maybe he didn't know the canal could turn into a river after a major rainstorm."

"Good point. Still, I'd guess the killer was simply in a hurry. Maybe it was getting light by the time the killer had cut up the body, gotten it in the car, and found a place to dump it in the park without being spotted. That could have taken a while; even at night there might be passing traffic, joggers, people walking their dogs. So maybe the killer just chose what seemed a good place to dump the hands, not the very best place."

"Yet Keoni's head turned up in the transfer station," observed Kawika. "The killer could have dealt with the hands the same way."

Yvonne frowned. "Yeah, but a head would be harder to tie to a saucepot than a pair of hands. The killer probably thought it made sense to keep the hands separate and drop the head in a dumpster. That's how the head ended up at the transfer station, right?"

Kawika smiled. He liked the way this young woman thought.

"Now there's another thing about the hands," Yvonne added. "This is a wild guess, low probability of being correct and all that. Just something to consider. So promise not to laugh."

"I won't laugh."

"The hands being tied to a saucepot made me wonder," she began, "for the first time, whether the killer could be a woman."

"A woman?" Kawika asked in surprise, although once she'd mentioned it, he couldn't think of any immediate reason to rule out the possibility.

"I mean, would a man think of using a saucepot to weigh down the bag?" Yvonne asked. "How many men, without someone suggesting it, would realize a saucepan has a hole in the handle? *Some* men would know it. But a much higher percentage of women, I bet."

"Let me buy you another beer," Kawika said.

* * *

With lunch concluded and another beer in their hands, Kawika and Yvonne moved to a sunnier table closer to the harbor and gazed out at the seabirds and the towering Central Pacific clouds.

"Here's the next thing," Yvonne said. "Topic number two. Two out of three. I brought you something I found when I went back to the Catherine Street bungalow yesterday. My third trip. This is just a photocopy; the original's in evidence now. It's a notebook, Kawika. A fancy leather-bound one. It was under a stack of shorts in a drawer. We never noticed it before; the pile just looks like his other neatly stored clothes, and we didn't actually toss the place, we just searched it. I guess that's where he kept it, under those shorts, although it might've been a one-time thing. Maybe he hid it when someone came to visit. Maybe he just didn't want Jay to see it, because it's partly filled with TMT things, and Jay thought he worked for the Port of Hilo. It also contains things about Jay himself, and about Angel Delos Santos, although just their initials."

Yvonne unzipped her backpack and handed Kawika a slender brown envelope. "This is a photocopy of the pages," she explained. "They made me use two-sided copying, of course. Sorry about that. What he wrote is in two sections. One's personal stuff. The other has notes he made for the TMT presentation you said he was supposed to give in Puakō."

"Just notes, not an actual speech?"

"No, just notes. He probably used his laptop to compose the actual speech or slide deck or whatever he was going to speak from. Whatever it was, it's gone with the hard drive."

Kawika started to open the envelope, but Yvonne dissuaded him. "It'll take time for you to read this. There aren't many pages, but they're double-sided and he had small handwriting. He had a lot he wanted to say, it seems. It begins with a draft of his TMT proposal—his 'Fourteen Points,' he called them. The rest of the TMT material is inspirational stuff, the sales pitch for his idea. But I don't think TMT's the interesting stuff."

"Then what's the interesting stuff?" asked Kawika.

"The personal section," Yvonne answered. "It's about some internal struggle he's having. Dealing with guilt. Guilt and expiation, sin and forgiveness—that sort of thing. Guilt for what, he doesn't say specifically. But something was weighing on him. Maybe that's why he and Jay kept trying churches on Sunday. Although you'd think Keoni would try Catholic churches too, if he was looking for absolution."

The possibility of Keoni wrestling with guilt struck Kawika as potentially important. "Guilt about Angel and Jay, you think?" he asked. "About two-timing them?"

Yvonne shrugged. "I don't think so," she replied. "It seems more serious than that. Much more serious, in fact. You'll see."

* * *

"And topic number three?" Kawika asked. He was guessing she'd saved the most important for last.

Yvonne sighed deeply. "This is the tough one," she began. "This is why I wanted to meet in person. I'm really grateful you added me to the Slasher team, Kawika. It's been an honor, I know; a sign of your confidence in me. As I say, I really thank you for that. But now I'd like to request that you take me off the case. Let me focus on Keoni Parkes, or other cases as they come up. I just need to be reassigned from the Slasher investigation."

"Wow. Really? I'm surprised."

"Yeah, I know. But it's what I need, I think."

"Tell me why," he requested gently.

"Okay," she replied. "It's messy, and you won't like to hear it. But the problem is Jerry Rhodes. He won't leave me alone. At first he was just hitting on me, basically trying to get me into bed, then trying to feel me up when no one was looking, as if that would persuade me. But when he finally got the message that I wasn't interested, that I was getting angry, that I might report him, he began criticizing my ideas and my work harshly in front of the whole team—harshly and unfairly. Humiliating me. Sakamoto sticks up for me sometimes. More often the guys just roll their eyes or shrug, or say *tsk-tsk*, or walk away. And when no one's looking, when he knows I'm going to rebuff him, he'll taunt me. He'll say things like 'What's a girl with a chest like yours doing in a place like this anyway?' Only he doesn't use the word *chest*. Gross stuff like that."

Yvonne's revelation upset Kawika immediately. "You're right, I don't like hearing this," he said angrily. "Not because of you, of course—because of Jerry. I'm shocked, honestly—or I would be, if I hadn't seen this sort of thing from other cops before. Appalled, not shocked, I guess I should say. I'm really mad at Jerry, behaving that way. It's inexcusable. I had much higher hopes for him, especially because he's a good detective and the only one here with serial killer experience. I'm really sorry and angry that you've been subjected to this."

"Thank you," she said, sounding grateful.

"In the old days," Kawika continued, his anger showing in his voice, "I'd act on this directly myself. Right away, this afternoon. Come down on him like a ton of bricks, suspend him, send him to training. Whatever. But nowadays I can't do any of that—the conduct didn't take place before my eyes, except for one inappropriate remark that was much milder than what you've described. There has to be a formal complaint these days, Yvonne—a complaint from you or someone who's observed the behavior directly. Then there's a review process. The department and the union contract created rules—"

"I understand," she interrupted. "That's why I just want to be taken off the case."

"But you have to report that behavior, Yvonne. You can't simply jump ship."

Yvonne shook her head. "Reporting would make it worse, Kawika. Worse for me, worse for him, worse for the department. A pushy young woman in her first year at HPD complaining about a famous cop? All the other cops would clam up. No one on the team would support me. Word would get around. Pretty soon everyone on the force would avoid me, treat me as a troublemaker. I'd be a pariah. They wouldn't want to work with me. They'd say I'm too delicate, that I can't take the rough-and-tumble of police work. That I'm sure to wash out."

"Oh, I don't think it would be quite that bad—"

"It would be *worse*, Kawika! I can tell you right now that Jerry would retaliate. And then I'd have to complain about *that*. I'd end up spending my days in review proceedings, not working on cases, not in the field. My police career—at least at HPD—would come to an end pretty quickly. I *would* wash out. Which would just confirm what everyone expected anyway."

To dispute her assertions at this point, Kawika knew, would be useless. Besides, her reasoning did strike him as sound, unfortunately. "Okay," he finally said, "but even without a formal complaint, it's still my job to support you. So tell me your alternative. Spell it out for me."

Yvonne took another sip of beer. "I *have* done a good job on the Keoni Parkes case so far, haven't I?"

Kawika nodded. "Yes," he said. "Definitely."

"Couldn't you simply announce that you need more of my time on that investigation? The Parkes team is small. Everyone would welcome more eyes and ears, more fingers on the keyboard. You wouldn't have to say anything to Jerry. In fact, I hope you won't. Don't even tell Kyu Sakamoto, because he'd tell Jerry for sure, and that would just make Jerry retaliate."

Deep in thought, Kawika looked out at the fishing boats and the harbor, the seabirds wheeling acrobatically overhead. He took a deep breath, then a sip of beer.

"Thank you for telling me this, Yvonne," he finally said. "It's very troubling. I'll think about your request and let you know. Maybe deal with Jerry later, I don't know; that behavior can't go on, whether there's a formal complaint or not. So, anything else right now?"

"Yes," she replied. "One more thing. Even though you don't, I'd like to carry a sidearm all the time—just the department's standard Smith & Wesson. I'm trained on it."

"Why do you want a gun all the time?"

"Because if you transfer me, like I hope, I'm worried Jerry Rhodes might start stalking me."

30

Honolulu

After three beers and the luncheon platter of fish and chips, Kawika drove home carefully and very full. Then he took a nap. Around three thirty he got up, donned running clothes, and jogged twice around Ala Moana Beach Park, including out to the point of Magic Island with its view of Waikīkī and Diamond Head. As usual, a bride and groom were having photos taken against that picturesque backdrop, not far from where the Slasher's sixth victim had been found. The four-mile run made Kawika feel alert again. He resolved to limit himself to two beers next time.

Showered and dressed, he decided on dinner at Jade Dynasty in the Ala Moana mall, where he often ate when alone. The servers found a table large enough for him to read Keoni's photocopied journal while eating. He had the weekend to himself and time to review the entire document.

The journal's first page set forth Keoni's proposal for resolving the TMT controversy. It began with the heading "Fourteen Points." Keoni had added a parenthetical note: "(Mention Woodrow Wilson's peace plan)." *College boy*, Kawika thought. Then Keoni had listed the fourteen points of his own peace plan.

Kawika found many points familiar, given the preview Dr. Phillips had provided. The removal of a "significant" number of existing telescopes was point number one. Keoni had outlined a process for deciding which ones to demolish. Factors included each facility's relative obsolescence; whether its scientific work could be accomplished by other telescopes; whether it stood on particularly sacred ground ("recognizing that the whole mountain is sacred, but also that some telescopes will remain"); whether its waste treatment and chemicals handling systems had been upgraded to state-of-the-art; and so on. Legal issues might matter in the end, Keoni had noted, but they should be considered separately from determining the best solution without them.

Point number two: Keoni proposed a "Hui of Stakeholders" to carry out the evaluation process—a group with representatives from all relevant parties, including activists and state and county government. The *Hui* should have professional staff, he suggested, and be chaired by a respected scholar of Hawaiian history and culture.

The points continued: reparations for environmental damage; frequent repermitting for existing facilities; restoration of the summit's sacred places; new astronomy-related education and job opportunities, with preference for Native Hawaiians—"to the extent legal," Keoni had added.

A key point: The international astronomy community should create an endowed Mauna Kea Protection Fund, the costs to be allocated among their corporate and university sponsors. The fund should cover the expenses of the Hui and any other items for which the Fourteen Points made the astronomy community responsible.

Two points in particular caught Kawika's attention: The state should revoke the university's stewardship of Mauna Kea's ceded lands and vest that responsibility in the Hui or an entity the Hui recommended. Keoni also proposed that new objects in the heavens, ones whose discovery the TMT made possible, should be given Hawaiian names, not those of the astronomers who discovered them ("requires a change in current practice and protocols," Keoni conceded), and that the TMT itself should be given a Hawaiian name.

Finally, the fourteenth point: When the other conditions had been met or agreed to in enforceable form, the TMT should be built on the least offensive site among those of the demolished telescopes—that site to be selected by the Hui.

Keoni had also begun writing notes for the talk he planned for gaining acceptance, or at least consideration, of his peace plan. It appeared he intended to argue that the TMT dispute was about values, not race or ancestry. Keoni had written:

> *Let me begin with a quote from Ancient Hawaiian Civilization, the 1933 book of lectures for Hawaiian students at the Kamehameha Schools:*
>
> > *This feeling of aloha is one of the things we consider Hawaiian. Any such attitude belongs to anyone who feels it, whether he has Hawaiian blood or not. It belongs to the Japanese—if they feel it. It*

> *belongs to the Chinese—if they feel it. It belongs to the Portuguese or to the Filipinos—if they feel it.*

And to the haoles—if they feel it. These words were written by men and women who'd known the Hawaiian kings and queens personally. Yet they didn't claim aloha exclusively for people of Hawaiian blood.

Consider also these words of Titus Coan, a mid-19th-century missionary:

> *I have seen Mauna Kea veiled with the mantle of night, and casting its gigantic shadow of darkness upon us. Again I have seen it when the first rays of the rising sun began to gild its summit. Watching it for a little while, the light poured down its rocky sides, chasing the night before it, until the mighty pile stood out clothed in burnished gold, and shining like a monarch arrayed in robes of glory.*

Titus Coan had not a drop of Hawaiian blood. It shouldn't be difficult for all of us to revere Mauna Kea the same way he did. Reverence won't resolve the TMT issue, but in this sacred little church, we should consider it as pew rent, something the mountain is due.

The remaining notes didn't appear to be part of the presentation Keoni intended. Instead they continued, almost rifflike, on matters of ancestry and race:

As Grace ʻŌpūnui reminds us, what makes us Hawaiian is our felt connection to our ancestors—or if they are not our actual ancestors, our felt connection to the people who came here from Tahiti and the Marquesas and elsewhere in Polynesia and established a relationship with the land and the ocean and the mountains that we can still respect.

This might please Grace, Kawika thought, although extending that felt connection to ancient Hawaiians and other Polynesians even if "they are not our actual ancestors" probably stretched Grace's exhortation further than she would've liked.

Keoni's notes continued:

For most of us, the vast majority of our ancestors are non-Hawaiians who weren't here before Captain Cook. And that's our blood mixture, if we go by blood. That's why it's our felt connection, not our blood quantum, that actually makes us Hawaiian.

We don't have to believe the same things to celebrate the same things. Think of Christmas. Mele Kalikimaka! We haven't confined Christmas to churchgoing Christians.

So we can all celebrate this magnificent mountain. We can all celebrate the mysterious stars. The old Hawaiians celebrated both; that celebration should be part of our felt connection to them.

Kawika finished this portion of Keoni's notebook wistfully. It seemed a pity Keoni would never give his speech, whatever it might have been—that missing hard drive! His proposals struck Kawika as idealistic but not naïve.

He didn't waste his education, Kawika thought.

Kawika put down the document, paid his bill, and stepped outside to call his wife as he walked home. He wanted to share the mood Keoni's notes had prompted—he was feeling more Hawaiian than usual—and to learn about her day. He'd expected she would've called after her Saturday market outing with Jarvis; maybe he'd missed her then. He tried her cell phone, but the call went straight to voice mail.

* * *

Back at the condo, Kawika read the next section of the notebook, which Keoni had labeled "Personal." It was shorter but more intriguing to Kawika as a detective. Here Keoni had written only fragments, but the fragments were revealing.

If you've committed a great sin, can you make it disappear? Have it vanish entirely?

Your options:

Confession (doesn't extinguish guilt; creates consequences)
Atonement, penance, contrition (they don't extinguish guilt, just make you pay a fine)
Expiation (removal of the sin, in theory, but how is it actually achieved?)
Reparation, amends, recompense (not applicable in my case)
Tashlich (cast off one's sins in water—Jewish ritual)
Absolution (Catholic ritual—yes, but . . .)

What about without *religion? Can you erase a sin by a lifetime of good works? Expunge it? The religions and scholars say no. It feels that way too. "All the perfumes of Arabia, etc."—the impossibility of eliminating one's sins, Macbeth and Lady Macbeth. What's done cannot be undone.*

You can't get clean through good works, only through faith. What if you have no faith? Are there any good excuses?

"Honor thy father." I did that. Dad paid with his life for his part in it. But that didn't eliminate my sin. I've tried to pay with good works. Service to others. Kindness. Community. Science. Doesn't erase the sin. Doesn't wash me clean.

"I was young." But not a boy. Already in college. Hid out in a Scottish university afterwards. Junior year abroad from sin. I knew what was going on before I turned the key in the ignition. I was reluctant and I was scared but I went ahead and did it.

Need to confide in someone. Confide privately without confessing to cops. Haven't found that someone:

Can't confide in ADS. Way too Catholic. I'd get the same as from a priest: confess thy sin, throw thyself on God's mercy, do penance, be absolved. Hocus-pocus.

JG's too sweet and unimaginative. Likes to putter and bake and garden. Such a gentle soul. My confiding would destroy him.

I'm unfaithful in searching for a confidant. Making it worse.

I could be faithful to someone if I could confide in him. I don't know such a man.

I could be faithful to someone if I didn't need to confide, because I'd done it already.

Need to find someone else to confide in. Who?

Kawika read back over the words—and saw what he'd never even considered before. The last piece of the puzzle fell into place with such force it nearly clanged aloud: *Keoni had driven the getaway boat.* He'd motored out to the *Mahi Mia* to pick up his father and Fortunato after they'd murdered Thomas Gray. He "knew what was going on" before he turned the key in the boat's ignition, just as he'd written. He'd spent fourteen years agonizing over his guilt, trying to make it go away, hoping that confiding in someone would produce some sort of getaway boat from sin.

Holy shit, Kawika thought.

It was Saturday night. Who should he call? Tanaka? He should be told. Yvonne? She was working on Keoni's case, but she hadn't put the pieces together from the journal, knowing little if anything about D. K. Parkes or Thomas Gray or even Fortunato. Should he call Ana Carvalho and supplement the fateful interview he'd had with her on Monday? To what end, though? How would she react to learning that Keoni, not just his father and Fortunato, had helped murder Thomas Gray?

Kawika decided to call Tanaka. But as he started to act, Kawika remembered he hadn't reached Elle. He wanted to speak with her first of all; he needed her just then. Again, however, he got Elle's voice mailbox instead of Elle.

So Kawika dialed Kuʻulei. "Hey, Cuz, did Elle forget to turn her phone on after dinner?" he asked when she answered.

"Kawika," Kuʻulei responded, worry in her voice, "We were supposed to meet at the restaurant. Elle never showed up. I kept calling, but I couldn't reach her. So I came back to my place, in case for some reason she came straight here instead. But she's not here, Kawika. I called Auntie Kailani in Puakō and asked her to go next door and check; she says Elle's not there and neither is the car. I was just about to call you. Do you know if she went someplace else? Or maybe got stuck with Jarvis for some reason—I know she took him to the Saturday market. But she was going to spend the night here with me if Ana Carvalho agreed to see her tomorrow."

Kawika tried the location tracking feature of Elle's cell phone, without result. He called Jarvis's care center in Waikoloa Village, but the staff told him Elle had left after her morning outing with his father. He called Ana Carvalho next, much as he hated to, but she hadn't heard from Elle either. He could tell that Ana immediately began to share his concern.

He couldn't think of any other Big Island friend Elle might have visited—surely not her new acquaintance Patience? He didn't want to call Patience, didn't even know how to reach her, but he called the gatehouse at the Mauna Kea Beach Resort and learned that Patience had already locked up her house and returned to the mainland two days earlier. The guard told him Elle hadn't passed that way either.

Kawika's perplexity gave way to worry. This wasn't like Elle. Something was definitely wrong.

Finally, Kawika called Tanaka, reaching him at home. "Elle's missing," he blurted out, and explained the situation, trying to control his voice and his rising alarm.

Tanaka was silent for a long moment, as if trying to solve the puzzle. "Let me call Ana," he then said, taking charge. "I'll call you back right after I talk to her. We'll turn the island upside down if we have to, Kawika. Starting right now, tonight. We'll find her. Don't worry."

Yet Kawika could hardly avoid worrying. And it was too late to get to the Big Island. The last flights to Hilo and to Kona had already left.

* * *

Tanaka called Kawika back within minutes. "Let's make this quick," Tanaka said. "I need to get everyone out in the field. Just tell me anyplace on the Big Island you think she might possibly be. Anyplace she might have gone on her way to Hilo. Apart from the highways themselves, that is—we'll check the Saddle Road, the Queen K, the Belt Road. Waimea and Hilo too. But what about other destinations, stopping points, favorite places she liked? She might've gotten out of the car, taken a walk, maybe fallen, Kawika. Sprained an ankle or broken her leg or something. Lost her phone over a ledge. If we find the parked car, we'll find Elle."

Kawika struggled to think where Elle might have stopped en route to Hilo. The South Kohala resorts. Laupahoehoe, a spiritual place of solemn remembrance and reflection where a teacher and twenty-five students had been lost to a tidal wave. The major waterfalls—Rainbow, Kahūnā, Kulaniapia. The botanical gardens or the bioreserve. Tanaka wrote them all down.

"Okay," Tanaka said, before ringing off. "We'll check those. Call me if you think of more. Catch the first flight in the morning, okay? And Kawika—get some sleep if you can. Could be a long day tomorrow." *If we don't find her tonight* didn't need to be spoken.

Kawika moaned at the thought of sleep; there'd be no sleep for him this night. But he couldn't sit still either. He needed to get outdoors, to walk; to think of any other place on the Big Island that Elle might be. It was inexplicable, her being missing; completely baffling.

Kawika left the condo, crossed the street, and found himself walking through Ala Moana Beach Park toward Waikīkī. He strode purposefully, not aimlessly, yet without consciously realizing where he was headed. He crossed the bridge over the Ala Wai Canal and began making his way through the nighttime tourists crowding the sidewalks of Waikīkī, sometimes bumping into people in his distraction. The garish lights and raucous noise of Waikīkī made him wince. But he kept walking, aware of his destination only once he'd reached it.

Kawika had come to Kapaemahu—the Wizard Stones. He hadn't seen them in years, never even noticed them while driving through Waikīkī in his police cruiser. He'd visited them only once, with Ku'ulei, back when she was studying Hawaiian history and culture at UH Mānoa. The incongruity of these ancient sacred boulders, separated physically from the mass of tourists by an iron guardrail but culturally by a gulf of Hawaiian understanding and belief impossible to cross, struck Kawika all at once. Suddenly he felt the Hawaiian part of himself—or at least a yearning to feel it. Not quite the same thing.

He bought a fragrant lei of plumeria blossoms from a nearby street vendor. Ignoring the tourists, most of whom ignored him too, Kawika leaned across the guardrail and gently tossed the lei like a quoit onto the tallest stone, just as Ku'ulei had done so long ago. Then, just as Ku'ulei had also done, Kawika raised his hands, thumbs pressed to fingers, tilted his face to the heavens, and earnestly offered a soundless prayer for Elle's safety. But Ku'ulei, with her prayer, had been looking up into a clear blue sky on a sunny day. Kawika was staring into a moonless night, and the glare of Waikīkī obscured the very stars.

PART FOUR

Women often accompanied their husbands, carrying water and food to refresh them and attending to their wounds. Some bore weapons and fought side by side with their men. When their husbands were killed they were almost certain to be killed also.

—E. Smith et al.
Ancient Hawaiian Civilization (1933)

31

Hilo

Elle's disappearance prompted an abrupt change in the disposition of the Big Island's police resources: Major Tanaka, at the command of Chief Ana Carvalho, immediately threw every cop and other potentially useful county employee into the effort to find Elle da Silva. Ana agreed with Tanaka that the situation just seemed wrong, and ominously so. "This takes priority over everything else," she ordered without hesitation, momentarily putting aside her anger with Tanaka and Kawika. "I want you to run it personally, Terry." The search mattered more right now—much more.

Tanaka called in everyone who could possibly help, including Ku'ulei and Tommy Kekoa and his colleagues in Waimea. The quest began Saturday evening, immediately after Kawika's call to Tanaka. Tommy was the first to reach the Puakō house, confirming what the neighbor had told Ku'ulei earlier: the house was empty and the car was gone.

The police knew every moment might count, but apart from Kawika's list, they had almost nothing to go on. They could only put out bulletins and advisories and conduct routine search procedures, albeit rapidly and en masse—"Flood the zone," Tanaka instructed them. There was no pretense that this was a routine police response to a missing-person report.

Somehow Elle had disappeared between Waikoloa Village, where she'd left Jarvis after the Saturday market, and Hilo, where she'd intended to join Ku'ulei for dinner. The police could find no trace of her car, not at any logical place she might have stopped and not along the Saddle Road or on any other route. They actually hoped she might have had an accident and now be trapped, still alive, in some sort of roadside wreck down an embankment obscured by vegetation. It was a long shot, and not a pleasant one. But everything else was a long shot too. They would recheck all those roads carefully in daylight.

Tanaka tried at once to extract Elle's phone records from her carrier. But despite the urgency, the phone company rebuffed him. It was the weekend, they explained. He'd need a warrant, they said, and since her particular phone company was based on the mainland, he'd need to get the warrant from a court over there. And once he got the warrant, which would take time, that piece of paper would join a stack of others the company was doing its best to work through.

"So how long before we get the records?" Tanaka demanded.

"Two, maybe three weeks," the company representative said. "Could be a month."

"That's ridiculous. Can't you speed it up?"

"Only if it's a murder case," came the unruffled reply. "Or a missing child, maybe."

"Well, this could be a murder case."

"*Could be* isn't good enough, I'm afraid. Every missing-person case *could be* a murder case, and there are thousands of missing-person cases. You need a corpse."

"Let me emphasize," Tanaka insisted, trying to control his temper. "We're not asking for the phone records of a suspect. We're looking for a victim."

"Sorry. Our customers need to know we'll protect their privacy no matter what."

"You're not protecting your customer right now," Tanaka said. "You're protecting someone who may have murdered your customer."

"That's always the risk, isn't it?" came the reply. "With privacy and confidentiality, I mean."

Tanaka hung up in disgust, then sent a text message to the county's lawyers. He included all the necessary information about Elle's phone, and added, "Please do everything possible to get Ms. da Silva's call and text records ASAP."

Midnight approached, yet Tanaka's phone rang. "Found anything?" Ana Carvalho asked.

"Nothing," Tanaka replied. "Not a trace."

* * *

Having slept little, Kawika rose in the night and caught the 5:45 AM flight from Honolulu. He landed in Kona at six thirty, just as the sun appeared over Hualālai. He'd reserved a rental car at the airport and drove straight to the house in Puakō, certain he'd find some clue to Elle's whereabouts that others had missed. But there was nothing: nothing unusual, nothing out of place. Had she packed an overnight bag for her trip to Hilo? Kawika couldn't tell whether any of her Puakō clothes or cosmetics were missing, but she might have packed a bag for the weekend before leaving Honolulu. He found nothing in the cottage to suggest Elle had departed in any unusual way or for any unusual purpose.

Kawika made a cup of instant coffee, then sat down to think. He knew Tanaka's teams would search every spot Kawika had suggested she might logically stop, and every logical highway route. But what about illogical routes, illogical stops?

Elle must have had time on her hands between returning Jarvis to his care center and her dinner date with Kuʻulei in Hilo. She could get to Hilo in ninety minutes, so she might have had six or even eight hours to fill. What might she have done in that time? They'd all just assumed that after leaving Jarvis, she would have returned to Puakō and busied herself there or in the neighborhood before setting off for Hilo. But what if she hadn't?

It occurred to Kawika that in the years he and Elle had visited the Big Island together, they'd never driven farther south than Kailua on that side of the island, and even then only for a single trip when they'd been refurbishing the Puakō house. He'd often told her his own inflexible rule: Never drive south of the Kailua-Kona airport. The traffic, the stoplights, the congestion of tourists and tourism, the sprawling development, the strip malls and plastic and neon lights, all of which he accepted in Honolulu, contrasted too painfully with South Kohala's austere beauty and majestic views. "We have the illusion of paradise up here," he'd said. "You drive to Kailua, you shatter it."

But Kawika knew there was a lot of the Big Island worth seeing south of Kailua. And now he wondered whether Elle might have decided to do that, driving the long way around the island to reach Hilo. He checked his watch: seven thirty AM. Not too early to call Tanaka on the morning of a search.

"Terry," he asked, "do you have anyone looking in Kona or Kaʻū, or at the volcanoes or in Puna?"

"No," Tanaka answered. "We figured she'd go through Waimea on the Belt Road or take Waikoloa Village Road to get to the Saddle Road. So we're not searching south of that. You thinking she might have taken the long way?"

"That just occurred to me," Kawika answered. "She might've gone that way; she had a lot of time between the Saturday market and dinner in Hilo. You have enough people to search down there?"

"Gosh, Kawika, we hardly have enough people to search this end of the island. You know what I always say: the Big Island is a big island. Bigger than all the others combined. We're focusing on everything between Puakō and Hilo, the normal routes. That's a lot of territory."

"I'll drive the other way, then," Kawika said. "Just in case I spot her car somewhere in Kailua or at a sightseeing spot. I'll see you in Hilo when I get there. Call me if you learn anything first."

"You too," Tanaka replied.

Kawika drove south and checked first in Kailua, until he got discouraged. It was pointless; he couldn't drive down every street. There were too many, and all were stoppered with traffic. He checked the likely places he could think of, then got back on the highway and continued south.

He stopped next at the trailhead for the Captain Cook memorial at Kealakekua Bay, in case she'd decided to hike out to visit the white obelisk marking the spot of Cook's death at the hands of Hawaiians in 1779. It was a sort of pilgrimage that writers and historians sometimes took. Elle, who strove for verisimilitude in her writing, might have wanted to see it, to stand on the beach where Cook had died, get the feel of the place as a locale for one of her books. But Elle's car wasn't at the trailhead.

He drove next to City of Refuge, the restored ceremonial complex where ancient Hawaiians who'd broken the kapu and been condemned to death could, if they could reach it in time, be absolved by a powerful *kahuna*, or priest, and allowed to go forth freely. Keoni, in his quest for absolution, might have come here himself, Kawika thought. Yet Kawika knew that Elle, who'd never been south of Kailua, had never visited this sacred place in the past. Might she have chosen this time to do so? He was desperate to find her here, or somewhere, and quickly. But in the crowded parking lot beyond the entry sign—displaying *Puʻuhonua o Hōnaunau* in large raised letters, Hawaiian for "Refuge of Hōnaunau"—Kawika couldn't find Elle's car. He slammed his hand against the steering wheel and headed back to the highway.

Now Kawika was beginning to panic. He tried to calm himself, knowing he should and must. But by now Elle hadn't been seen or heard from in twenty-four hours. Even if she'd suffered a mishap, tumbled off a trail and broken a leg as Tanaka had suggested—even if she'd lost her phone when she fell and couldn't regain it—she'd been out in the elements for a day and a night. She could be dying of thirst or exposure.

Worse, what if she'd been abducted? If he or Tanaka's team found her car but not Elle herself, abduction would be a frightening possibility. But what if she'd been abducted *in* her car? Then their chances of finding her would plummet even further; she and the car and her abductors could be anywhere. *The Big Island is a big island*: Kawika couldn't help dwelling on Tanaka's oft-repeated saying.

Thinking hard now, he tried to imagine any other place on this route—short of the rim of Kīlauea Volcano itself—where Elle might have parked, gotten out to explore or take a selfie, and possibly tumbled from a trail or a ledge and injured herself badly enough to be unable to attract help or get back to her car. Only one place came to mind: Ka Lae, known as South Point, the desolate tip of the island, the southernmost point in the United States and a tourist stop for that reason.

Kawika had been there only once, as a boy, on a summertime trip with his dad. Jarvis had stood behind him, hands on Kawika's shoulders, and explained that Ka Lae—"the point" in Hawaiian—was where the ancient Polynesians had first landed in Hawai'i; told him the nearest land if you sailed east was the mainland, five thousand miles away, or if you sailed south, Antarctica. "Lucky for the Old Ones, they didn't miss Ka Lae, yeah?" Jarvis had said.

South Point was more than an hour from Pu'uhonua o Hōnaunau, the City of Refuge. Kawika drove as fast as he could, but that wasn't very fast. Traffic crawled through a succession of small towns, past coffee plantations and macadamia nut farms, and slowed again for each roadside stand selling tourist trinkets or orchids, pineapples imported from Ecuador, cheap ukeleles or boogie boards or beach towels. Probably marijuana—pakalōlō, or "numbing tobacco" in Hawaiian—if you knew how to ask. He hated this junky aspect of Hawai'i and knew it was spreading relentlessly. Everything he'd seen since driving south of the airport only confirmed why he never drove south of the airport.

He took the turnoff for South Point and started down the narrow twelve-mile road, which soon became a one-lane track through vast grasslands and the sad wreckage of an old wind power project. A newer wind project appeared further along, gleaming white blades turning vigorously in the South Point breeze.

Kawika remembered the platform on South Point's cliff top, a high place from which adventurous visitors leapt into the ocean thirty or forty feet below, just to say they'd done it. *It's the sort of thing Elle would have dared when she was younger,* he realized. She'd bungee-jumped in a mainland canyon on her twenty-fifth birthday, she'd told him. Gone skydiving with her friend Ana Carvalho right before she'd met him. Ridden a bike down from the summit of Haleakalā during an academic conference on Maui. Zip-lined—without him; he'd adamantly refused—on a trip to the Big Island a few years earlier.

If she'd thought of South Point as a stop on her way to Hilo, he realized, Elle might even have brought a swimsuit. *But would she jump here by herself?* Kawika asked, unable to believe it. *While pregnant?* She was impulsive and bold, but not foolhardy—far from it, he reassured himself. Yet if she'd come to South Point only for the view, just to sightsee, and not been heard from since . . . He didn't want to consider that possibility. Jaw set, he kept driving south, eyes fixedly ahead.

When he finally arrived, he found only two cars at the end of South Point Road. Neither was Elle's. Kawika felt relieved yet bitterly frustrated at the same time. *Where the hell are you, Elle?*

Exhausted now—he hadn't eaten since Jade Dynasty in Honolulu, and his lack of sleep had begun to muddy his thinking—he realized he could never check every parking lot at every place of attraction between South Point and Hilo. He felt a powerful desire to turn around and go back to Puakō, irrationally certain he'd find Elle there, laughing, safe, calming him with some simple explanation for her disappearance.

Grimly, he resolved to undertake the two-hour drive to Hilo, stopping only at Hawai'i Volcanoes National Park to check the parking lots there. He could get back to Puakō from Hilo by nightfall and complete his circuit of the island, if he didn't squander his time. He knew Elle might also have chosen to visit the Ka'ū Forest Reserve, since the reserve had played a part in *Murder at the Mauna Lani.* She'd never actually seen the reserve, Kawika knew. But there were too many trailheads to consider there, and no trail he could think of, nothing precipitous enough, where she might have broken a leg. A sprained ankle, yes, but that wouldn't have been enough to keep Elle from retrieving a dropped phone or getting back to her car.

At Volcanoes National Park, after fruitlessly checking the jammed parking lot from which Elle might have begun a hike to view Halemaʻumaʻu, the active pit crater volcano in Kīlauea's summit, Kawika finally paused for a meal at Volcano House. Breakfast? Lunch? Fatigue and hunger combined to disorient him.

To his surprise, he ate ravenously. Then he called Tanaka.

"Any news?"

"No. None on your end either?"

"Nope," Kawika replied. "No ransom demands or anything, Terry?"

"No, sorry. We've got nothing, Kawika."

Kawika didn't need Tanaka to say more. He understood what the tone of Tanaka's voice suggested, as clearly as if Tanaka had said it aloud: *Things don't look good.* Kawika began to despair.

It took Kawika less than an hour to drive to Hilo after he'd eaten. When he arrived, Tanaka and Kuʻulei were out in the field, and Ana Carvalho met him at the station. Worry etched her face—worry and fear, he realized. She embraced him, and he clung to her briefly. Then he composed himself and said good-bye, without looking her in the eye.

Kawika managed to drive the additional distance to Puakō, constantly examining the sides of the Saddle Road for some sign his wife had veered off it.

Elle wasn't at the cottage when he arrived. Ignoring the sunset, Kawika flopped fully clothed onto the bed where she should have been, burying his nose in the fragrance of her pillow until sleep finally overcame him.

32

Hilo

On Monday morning Tanaka, with growing foreboding, still had almost the entire Big Island police force continuing to search everywhere for Elle. Tanaka felt he couldn't do less than this for Kawika, for Elle. But he was struggling to decide how and when to begin pulling people back to work on other things. He could think of nothing Kawika could do to help the search either, yet he knew Kawika needed to do something. "Why not search the north end of the island?" Tanaka suggested. "All the places that aren't on the way to Hilo. Sights she might have detoured to see?"

Kawika could think of a few. So, for the second time in ten days, he drove the coast road through Kawaihae, passing the Hawaiian Home Lands and the gatehouse for Kohala Ranch. He checked the parking lot at Lapakahi State Historical Park, with its ruins of an ancient Hawaiian settlement—nothing there—and proceeded up the stormy shoreline to the turnoff for the rutted and nearly impassable road to Moʻokini Heiau. Nothing there either. He couldn't imagine Elle visiting that particular *heiau* anyway. The ghosts of thousands of ancient Hawaiians sacrificed there—as many as forty thousand by some estimates—made it a haunted and dismal place.

He drove on through Hāwī, then through Kapaʻau with Elle's favorite ice cream store, and past the larger-than-life statue of Kamehameha the Great, draped today with a dozen flower leis. The statue had been cast in Europe in the nineteenth century, lost at sea en route to Hawaiʻi, then mysteriously salvaged and transported to the Falkland Islands. Yet it had eventually made its way to Kohala. Looking at it, Kawika tried to will Elle to make her way back too.

At the Pololū lookout, with its sweeping views of the coastline of towering cliffs, he had to stop and walk down the long line of parked cars that constricted the dead-end narrow road. He desperately hoped to find Elle's among them; she might have hiked down into the pristine Pololū Valley, as the two of them had often done before. But there was nothing there, just the end of the road.

The end of the road, Kawika said to himself. Tears of frustration filled his eyes. Distraught—as distraught as he could be, even still clinging to shreds of hope—he walked back to his car and drove home slowly via the Kohala Mountain Road. He didn't expect to find her car there. It was simply a beautiful drive he knew she'd loved.

* * *

A little before noon on the same day, the 911 dispatcher in Hilo received a call from Miriam "Mimi" Charles, a prominent local citizen whom the police themselves used to help discover secrets hidden in human remains. Mimi was a forensic anthropologist who'd semi-retired to Hilo after a professional career solving crimes and archaeological puzzles on the mainland and internationally. She was sufficiently well-known that writers of detective fiction often sought her opinion on matters of crime scene forensics and postmortem examinations.

Mimi owned a dog she was training to become a human remains detection dog, a label Mimi preferred to "cadaver dog." Given the animal's designation as an HRD dog, she'd named him Harold and hoped for his future. Harold was the type of mixed-breed mongrel Hawaiians call a *poi* dog, the sort you got from an animal shelter, where Mimi had indeed gotten Harold, not an actual poi dog like those of the ancient Hawaiians. Those had been a distinct and homely breed fed largely on poi—fermented taro root, baked and pounded into a purplish paste—and raised primarily to be eaten. They'd been extinct for a century.

Harold the contemporary poi dog had grown to be much larger than typical. He had a yellowish coat and somewhat resembled a Labrador retriever. As he'd grown, he'd begun to display a sophisticated sense of smell. That had boosted Mimi's confidence about being able to train him.

Harold had never detected human remains himself. The best way to train a dog to detect human remains was to train him on cadavers, and Mimi didn't have those. So she'd taught Harold to detect the chemicals that dead bodies begin to emit almost immediately, namely, cadaverine and putrescine. And when she had a limb or other fragment of a corpse the police had asked her to analyze in the small lab she'd added to her house, she let Harold sniff those too.

Today Mimi had arranged to have brunch with a friend at the Hilo Yacht Club. Harold didn't like being left home when she went out. She could tie him up in the shade at the Yacht Club with a big pan of water and he'd be fine, but it would be prudent to take him for a walk first, before the day got too hot. So she drove to the Yacht Club early and began walking Harold back toward the main road. She decided to turn onto the little-used stub of Keaukaha Road, a back route to Kealoha Beach Park. She noticed the asphalt sported dozens of black tire tracks, the result of locals using the road to race or lay rubber. This short segment of road was lightly trafficked otherwise.

As usual, Harold kept his nose to the ground, sniffing the road surface and weaving left and right as he tugged his leash in his forward rush. Suddenly he stopped and looked back at Mimi for a mere second. Then he plunged into the thick vegetation that lined the road and began pulling her into the brush in earnest, emitting excited sounds she'd never heard from him before. Mimi tried to protect herself from branches and sharp leaves and lianas and other vines, but she could feel herself getting scratched and her hair disarranged. She stumbled and nearly fell twice. Her blouse and linen pants snagged and tore. "Slow down, boy!" she pleaded. But Harold couldn't be distracted from his mission.

No more than thirty feet into the unkempt jungle, Harold used his front paws to frantically clear away some loose plant cuttings before burying his nose in freshly turned earth that the cuttings had hidden. Mimi immediately recognized the mounded rectangle of dirt for what it was: a grave. But without Harold, neither she nor anyone else would ever have seen it. No one would have entered this impenetrable stand of overgrown vegetation without being dragged there by an unstoppable dog.

Mimi jerked Harold back from his excavation efforts; he'd already begun throwing fresh dirt all over her shoes and pant legs. She had difficulty restraining him as he stood on his hind legs and threw his body weight against the resistance of the leash. He began barking and whimpering loudly.

Somehow Mimi managed to get out her cell phone and dial 911. Harold almost pulled her over as she did so. "I need to report a fresh grave by the side of Keaukaha Road in Hilo," she told the operator over Harold's frantic background noise. "There's a body in it." Pause. "Yes, I'm sure of that." Pause. "No, I haven't seen the body. It's buried." Pause. "No, I did *not* put the body there myself. Please send police to Keaukaha Road, the jungly part, not the beach part. I'll be standing there with my cadaver dog." Mimi said *cadaver dog* because she judged it would make an impression on the dispatcher.

Two police officers drove up quickly, having apparently been nearby when the call came. They found Mimi, her face scratched and bleeding, her clothes and hair a mess, and Harold jumping up and down as she tried to restrain him. Struggling with the dog, she pointed the officers into the roadside jungle. They regarded her skeptically. But they soon took her seriously. Slowly and carefully, swearing aloud as the growth ensnared them, they worked their way back through the vegetation in the direction she'd pointed them.

A minute later both officers emerged, looking grim. "I think you're right," one told her. "We need to get a whole other team here. We'll need a statement from you, of course." He took her driver's license so he could record her name and address. "But would you like to get cleaned up first? Put away the dog?"

As Mimi considered this offer, the other policeman dialed his phone. "Major Tanaka," he said into the phone. "A woman named Miriam Charles"—he was looking over his partner's shoulder at Mimi's driver's license—"found what sure looks like a fresh grave while she was walking her dog on Keaukaha Road. You'll want to get over here if you can. Keep Kawika away though, yeah? This could be Elle da Silva."

"*Elle da Silva?*" Mimi exclaimed. "Why Elle da Silva? Is she missing? I *know* Elle da Silva! She's a friend! I've helped her with her books!"

"Then you won't want to be here when we open this grave," the first officer said grimly. "Elle da Silva's been missing since Saturday."

"Oh, wait a minute," said the officer on the phone with Terry Tanaka. "Ma'am, Major Tanaka would like to speak with you." He handed Mimi the phone.

"Terry—" she began. Her face had drained of color.

"Mimi," he interrupted. "I'm sorry this may turn out to be your friend. If it's Elle, I know you've worked with her. She's my friend too. But Mimi, we're not going to move a teaspoon of dirt without you there. The case is too important. Sorry, it has to be you; just can't be helped. Now please hand the phone back to Officer Hekekia."

Officer Hekekia exchanged a few more words with Tanaka, then hung up. "Ma'am, the major says you've got to stay here," he reported. "But if you like, we can take your dog home for you and feed him once Major Tanaka arrives."

The other officer patted Harold and nodded appreciatively. "It's amazing," he said, "your dog being able to sniff a corpse this fresh. I mean, this body is probably less than two days old—if it belongs to Elle da Silva, that is. Of course, it could be someone else."

Mimi handed Harold's leash to Officer Hekekia and sat down on the pavement. With her head in her hands, she muttered, "Oh no, oh no," over and over.

Yet when Tanaka arrived with the forensics team, Mimi sniffled briefly and pulled herself together, working carefully and professionally with the others to exhume the body. Fully encased in protective clothing, she knelt by the shallow grave and began removing soil. Her face shield caught the few tears she couldn't entirely prevent. Otherwise, they would have fallen directly onto the pale, cyanotic face of her friend.

33

The Big Island

Kawika's devastation was total. He who rarely cried now could not stop. He who sometimes threw up now vomited his way through his stomach contents and then through residual saliva and mucus until finally he was reduced to dry retching that produced nothing but intense esophageal pain. He wasn't coherent to his four police colleagues—Tanaka, Kuʻulei, Tommy, and Ana Carvalho—who tried helplessly to comfort him in the dingy reception area of the morgue in the old Memorial Hospital, holding his arms when he tried to stand, easing him down when he tried to sit. He wanted to see Elle's body right away, but he couldn't, not until Dr. Elaine Ko, the medical examiner for Hilo, had spent time with the body herself.

Tanaka and Dr. Ko had a side conversation. "The rest of us can all identify Elle's body for you," he proposed. "We don't need Kawika for that. Then you can do your work. I'll have Tommy stay with him until it's time to bring him back."

"Good," she said. "It won't take me long. When I'm done, I can clean her face, get the dirt off it. That's all I'm going to show him, her face. He can kiss her and stroke her hair. In this case, since it appears she was strangled, I won't even show him her neck. I'll have to open it up, check the hyoid bone for fractures, and so on."

Dr. Ko also had a sedative she was prepared to dispense, if everyone agreed not to mention it. "He probably hasn't slept since she went missing," she told Tanaka. "He needs to sleep now. Make sure he takes this. It's mild, but I won't be ready for him until tomorrow morning, and he can sleep until then. I'll give him extra pills in case he can't get back to sleep in the night."

It would have made sense for Kawika to stay in Hilo overnight. But he insisted on returning to Puakō, somehow sure that he'd find Elle waiting for him there. He swallowed the sedative, and Tommy pocketed the additional doses. Then Kawika and Tommy set out for Puakō, with Tommy at the wheel.

Once Kawika had left, Dr. Ko allowed the other officers to see the body. Although pale in death, Elle's face displayed a bluish pallor. Dr. Ko told them Elle had been strangled, probably with a tightly wound scarf or similar piece of fabric.

"Basically garroted, it appears," Dr. Ko said. "But not with a rope or wire, based on the abrasions. She's fully dressed, including undergarments. Her hands and feet were bound with duct tape at some point, and there was duct tape across her mouth. The tape was removed before she was buried—probably to eliminate any chance of it being traced. Although she's still covered with dirt, there's no sign of stabbing or a bullet wound, and no blood. She urinated and defecated, presumably as she was being strangled. As you know, her handbag was buried with her, and your crime scene guys say the only obvious thing missing is her car key. That's all for now. I'll know more later; I have to open her up—those are the rules. You've ID'd her now, so I can get to work."

As the three officers moved to depart, Dr. Ko added mournfully, "So sorry for your loss. Truly." Tanaka was the only one who knew Dr. Ko well—well enough to recognize her words as heartfelt, not obligatory.

Back in the hallway, Tanaka, Ku'ulei, and Ana collapsed into a tearful embrace. Then they hugged one another in pairs. Finally, they returned to the waiting area, sat down, and tried to compose themselves. Ku'ulei was still crying softly and shaking her head.

"Let's go back to the station," Tanaka suggested.

By now it was early Monday evening. At the station, Ana wanted to discuss who they'd need to inform of Elle's death. Ku'ulei said she'd call Kawika's mother, Lily, in Seattle. "She'll want to fly out here with Kawika's stepdad, Pat. I can work with them on that." Ku'ulei also volunteered to tell Jarvis Wong, Kawika's dad—her uncle and the man who'd raised her.

"I'll go with you to see Jarvis," Tanaka added. "He's my best friend."

Ana said she'd call Mo Fremont, the chief of police in Honolulu. "We're friends, and chief-to-chief is the right way to handle this," she said. "She'll have to tell Kawika's detectives what's happened and figure out how to manage their cases. Kawika won't be able to do it."

"No," Tanaka agreed, "he really won't."

Ana also said she'd call Elle's mother. "I'm dreading that. Her mom's in Lāhainā. Elle's dad moved away when sugar was failing on Maui, and that's the last the family heard of him. So, no way to reach him."

Then there were the general public and the news media to contend with. "I can't see any point in delaying that past tomorrow, can you?" Ana asked Tanaka. "I mean, they know we've been trying to find her—we've been asking their help. Let Kawika see Elle tomorrow, then sequester him in Puakō for the time being. The press probably doesn't know he has a place there, and anyway, it'll be harder for them to descend on him. We'll issue a release from here in Hilo, maybe at midday tomorrow."

"You should do a press conference, not just a release," Tanaka said. "This case justifies it. We want people's help. We need to describe Elle's car, what she was wearing, when and where she was last seen. A press conference will get us the widest exposure for that."

Ana nodded, accepting his suggestion.

"We'll help you, Chief," said Tanaka. "But Kuʻulei and I need to go visit Jarvis now. Then we'll join our folks in the field. Let's get our calls done and go catch this killer. We'll mourn later."

Tanaka and Kuʻulei set off over the Saddle Road, figuring that telling Jarvis, difficult as it would be, shouldn't wait until the next day.

They both had calls to make while they drove. Kuʻulei had to break the awful news to Kawika's mother and stepfather.

Pat answered the phone in Seattle. Struggling to keep her composure, Kuʻulei asked him to put Lily on the phone too. Pat and Lily had never given up their landline and had phones in several rooms of the house. Somehow Kuʻulei managed to convey the grim news, getting a decent start before struggling in response to Lily's gasps and Pat's exclamations of disbelief. They both wanted to know who could have done this terrible thing, where Kawika was, *how* he was, whether they could talk to him. Kuʻulei didn't know how to make Kawika's condition sound less awful than it was, or even whether to try. Lily and Pat, listening in different rooms, were speaking over each other, Lily amid lamentations and Pat urgently asking questions that Kuʻulei tried to make out. Within a few minutes Pat said he needed to go to Lily; he said they'd call back later.

Kuʻulei turned to Tanaka at the wheel and dissolved into tears. "That's *terrible*," she sobbed, "giving parents news like that." Tanaka tried to console her just as his own phone rang. It was Dr. Elaine Ko calling from the morgue.

"I've basically just gotten started, and maybe you already knew this," Dr. Ko said, "but if not, I thought you'd want to know right away. Elle was about two or three months pregnant. She was far enough along that I'm fairly sure she would've told her husband. So Kawika probably knows."

Tanaka, stunned, thanked her and hung up. Ku'ulei hadn't overheard, so Tanaka grimly conveyed the news.

"Oh God," was all Ku'ulei could say, both hands covering her face. "Oh God."

"Let's not tell Jarvis that part," Tanaka suggested. "Elle will be all he can handle right now—if that."

"Let's not tell Chief Carvalho yet either," Ku'ulei added shakily. "She's Elle's really good friend. She should get through the next day first."

Tanaka's phone rang again. It was Tommy, calling from Puakō. "Terry," he began, "I got Kawika here all right. He's asleep now—that sedative definitely worked. But as I was getting him into bed, he grabbed my arm and said I had to tell you something. He made me repeat it to make sure I got it right."

"What is it?"

"He said to tell you, 'Keoni Parkes drove the getaway boat.'"

34

Waikoloa Village

Jarvis was asleep when Tanaka and Ku'ulei arrived at the Queen Ka'ahumanu Long-Term Care Center. Ku'ulei thought they should wake him, but Tanaka had a different idea.

"Bad news can wait a bit," he said. "Let's see if we can find whoever took Jarvis and Elle to the market on Saturday. Maybe we can learn something."

At first they seemed in luck. The attendant who'd driven Elle and Jarvis to Waimea, Keanu Fuchida, was still on duty, scrolling through his text messages when they found him in the staff lunchroom. Keanu was a large young man, almost as large as Jarvis had once been. Tanaka figured him to be about twenty-five years old, another Hawaiian among the legions named for Keanu Reeves.

Keanu Fuchida hauled himself from his chair when the detectives approached. Brown skinned, he was dressed and tattooed in the manner of others who counted themselves Hawaiian. He also wore a cowrie-shell necklace, and his black hair was oiled and gathered in a bun. At first he seemed relaxed and happy to help.

"Yeah, I drove Jarvis and Ms. da Silva—Elle, I call her—to the Saturday market," he confirmed in answer to Tanaka's first question. "I drive 'em all the time—like to Waimea, to Puakō, sometimes to Pu'ukoholā Heiau. Jarvis, he likes visiting that heiau a lot," Keanu continued expansively. It seemed apparent he didn't know Elle was dead.

"Did anything special happen at the market? Anything out of the ordinary?"

"No, don't think so, man. I mean Elle, like, cut the visit short. *That* was unusual, I guess. But otherwise, no, same as other times. People came out to say hello to Jarvis; Elle wheeled him around—you know? She lets me do my own thing when we're there. I got some ice cream. Also malasadas."

"She cut the visit short how, exactly?"

"Well, I was eating an ice cream and, like, buying malasadas. She waved at me across a few stalls. So I, like, paid for my malasadas and met 'em at the van, got Jarvis all loaded up and ready to go."

"Did Elle say anything?"

"Nothing I remember, before we got in the van. Jarvis was saying a lot, though."

"Saying what?"

"He was, like, making a *muh-muh-muh* sound, you know? He was saying that over and over."

"And Elle wasn't saying anything?"

"Not until I started driving, I don't think." Keanu began to look concerned. "Is something wrong, man? Like, why're you asking me all this?"

"Just answer my questions, please," Tanaka replied, courteously but firmly. "Elle wasn't saying anything?"

"Well, once we started driving, she, like, started talking to Jarvis, yeah? She always does that. Sometimes asking him about folks they met at the market, old friends, you know."

"Did she mention any names?"

"Man, I didn't hear much. I was driving, maybe I had the radio on a bit. She was talking to Jarvis a lot. I don't really listen when she's back there with him."

"So you didn't hear anything?"

"Well, yeah, one thing. When I stopped at the light—you know, the one by the Parker Ranch Center?—I heard Elle say, 'Emma Phillips?' Like she was asking him a question. And Jarvis, he said *nuh-nuh-nuh* the way he does, man. You know, *nuh-nuh-nuh* for no."

"Wait a minute," Ku'ulei interjected. "Let me get this straight. She asked about Emma Phillips, and Jarvis said no? You sure?"

"That's right, yeah. That's who she, like, asked about, and Jarvis, he said no."

"Keanu, do you know who Emma Phillips is?" Ku'ulei asked. "Would you recognize her?"

"Yeah, of course. Everyone knows Dr. Phillips. But I didn't, like, see her at the market," he replied. Then added cautiously, "Doesn't mean she wasn't there. It was crowded. It's always crowded."

Tanaka and Kuʻulei exchanged glances. "We could ask her," Kuʻulei suggested.

Tanaka nodded and changed tack. "Where were you, Keanu, after you got Jarvis and Elle back here to the center?"

"I was here. I, like, got Jarvis into his bed and left Elle there with him. She took off a few minutes later."

"And did you follow her?" Tanaka asked, watching for the young man's reaction.

"What? No, of course not! I was still on duty. On duty, like, all weekend. Tuesday and Wednesday are my days off." Now he looked scared.

"Are there people here who can confirm that you didn't leave after Elle did?"

"Of course, of course! Yeah, of course. I've got, like, supervisors and other folks I work with. Hey, what's this all about?"

"Something happened to Elle," Kuʻulei told him. "After she left here. Major Tanaka has to find out if you have an alibi."

Keanu staggered back a few steps and sat down heavily in a plastic lunchroom chair, sending it screeching backward. "Oh, man," he said. "I would never hurt Elle. She's one fine lady, yeah? We're, like, *friends.* Is she okay?"

"No," Tanaka replied tiredly. "Unfortunately, Elle is not okay." He thanked Keanu for his cooperation. Then Tanaka and Kuʻulei walked away, down the hall toward Jarvis's room, leaving Keanu obviously confused and frightened.

"It's time we woke Jarvis," Tanaka said reluctantly. "No point in putting it off longer."

Seeing Kuʻulei's eyes suddenly glisten, Tanaka put a hand on her arm.

"I'll tell him," he said. "You just hold him and kiss him and cry right along with him. I'm his best friend. You're his family."

In the tears that followed, and with the anguished *nuh-nuh-nuh* of Jarvis's denial repeated endlessly, there was no way they could question him about his conversation with Elle. And had they attempted it, in that terrible moment there would've been no way he could have answered.

35

Hilo

Having seen dozens of dead people on the job didn't prepare Kawika for seeing his wife in the morgue. He'd known it wouldn't; he'd too often been present at scenes like the one he was about to be part of. He was still in shock, unable to make sense of something that made no sense, something so sudden and jarring in its awful finality, its totality.

A world without Elle in it? He felt himself almost sleepwalking through the morgue with Tommy holding his arm, walking not only to Elle's body but also, he sensed, to his own death, perhaps a self-given one, a prospect to which he felt numb and indifferent. He had no thought of recovering from this. He actively did not want to recover from it; it would seem disloyal to Elle if he *could* recover or if he even tried. He could not imagine anything following this, or any next steps. Before him all he could envision was nothing, nothingness, a void.

Dr. Ko had known Kawika in his days as a Hilo cop, and she expressed brief condolences as she led him and Tommy to the dreaded room. She had the body waiting for him, covered in a clean white sheet with only Elle's face revealed. It was unbruised, and Dr. Ko had cleaned it carefully but not applied any makeup nor done much with Elle's hair. Elle looked pale and peaceful and blue and dead. There was no mistaking her for someone sleeping. There never is, Kawika knew.

Kawika made no effort to see more of her, even to uncover her neck. Dr. Ko stood by to prevent that, but it wasn't necessary. Kawika just gently put his cheek next to Elle's cold and bluish one and with equal gentleness encircled her head in his arms. At first he was not in tears, more in disbelief, still just numb. But after he'd kissed Elle's cold, unresponsive lips—it did not feel at all like kissing Elle—he put his head by her other cheek and began to weep. No loud lamentation, no wracking sobs. Just soft tears.

Dr. Ko waited silently, not rushing him. Tommy, on the other hand, began to lose his composure. Saying nothing, with a motion of his head he indicated to Dr. Ko that he needed to leave the room. He did so silently and out of Kawika's sight, because Kawika's eyes were buried in Elle's ash-blonde hair.

* * *

Across town, Chief Ana Carvalho stepped to the microphone in the overflowing conference room of a Hilo hotel. The police station had no room large enough for this event.

"As you know from our alerts and announcements," she told the assembled media representatives, "on Saturday a young woman named Elianna Azevado da Silva, nicknamed Elle, went missing. Yesterday morning her body was found in a shallow grave on Keaukaha Road. Today we are asking the public and the media to help find her killer. In particular, we want to know if anyone saw her after eleven on Saturday morning, and if so, where. We also need anyone who was on Keaukaha Road between that time and ten thirty yesterday morning to come forward so we can determine whether you saw anything that could aid us in our investigation. We need to know if anyone has seen Ms. da Silva's car, and if so, when and where. If anyone has this or any other information that might be relevant to the case, we urgently ask you to contact us without delay."

The chief then described Elle, the clothes she'd been wearing, the car she'd driven, the handbag she'd carried, where she'd last been seen, and so on. All this information was compiled in a one-page flyer bearing Elle's photo, which the police handed to the assembled media representatives. The flyer also described Elle as a journalism professor at UH Mānoa, a well-known novelist, and the wife of Major Kawika Wong of the Honolulu Police Department.

The chief then ventured further in unscripted remarks. "Elle da Silva was my close personal friend of many years, a fellow Portuguesa, as we liked to joke. So this case is special for me. I really hope members of the public will respond to our plea today. Please help us catch this killer. Please help us put this murderer away."

Chief Carvalho then took questions from the press. Many were irrelevant for investigatory purposes, but a few focused on details of the crime. Then came the questioner who brought the press conference to a halt—Zoë Akona of the *Star-Advertiser.*

"Chief Carvalho," Zoë began, raising her voice in order to be heard. "Since Elle da Silva was your close friend, a fellow Portuguesa, as you say, and since she was also married to Major Kawika Wong, formerly a homicide detective for Hawai'i County and now a presumably grieving widower whose friends like you must all be feeling enormous sympathy for him, how can you personally conduct an unbiased investigation of Major Wong's and Major Teruo Tanaka's apparent cover-up of the real murderers in the Ralph Fortunato and D. K. Parkes cases from 2002? Don't you need to appoint an independent commission to run that investigation now?"

The anger this prompted showed all too clearly in Ana Carvalho's flared nostrils, and it was photos of her face at that moment, she foresaw clearly, that would end up in the *Star-Advertiser* and other print and video news outlets across the state and nation. It didn't matter to her. She could not have controlled her ire in any event.

"Ms. Akona," she responded icily. "We are here today to ask the public's help, urgently, in catching the brutal murderer of a brilliant young woman, Professor Elianna Azevado da Silva. Professor da Silva was widely beloved throughout the state, not just by me, and beloved in particular by her students—of which, she told me, you were one yourself, correct? I believe she also helped you get your current job, did she not?" At this, Chief Carvalho glared at the young journalist; a lot of photographers' flashes captured that expression too.

But the chief wasn't done with Zoë yet. "We are not here to talk about ancient cases that happened long before my time," she continued, "and about which there is no urgency—zero urgency, Ms. Akona—at this particular moment. Your personal agenda about the distant past may seem more important to you than our catching a killer who is now at large, but the rest of us don't share that view. So please show respect for Professor da Silva, your one-time teacher and benefactor, and for our purpose here today. Don't distract others with matters unrelated to her death. Everything in its time and place. This isn't the time or place for your issue. Show a little decency, please."

With that, the chief thanked the media for attending, and particularly for their anticipated help in the hunt for Elle's killer. Then she strode from the lectern and exited the room through a side door.

"Argh," she said to one of her lieutenants as she stepped into her car. "I can't stand that young woman."

* * *

The chief's rebuff of Zoë's questions didn't shame Zoë into declining an interview with a Hilo radio reporter who'd attended the news conference. On the contrary, the humiliation inflamed her.

"I got all that on tape," the radio reporter said. "Are you going to let Chief Carvalho have the last word, or would you like to respond?" Against her better judgment, a still-incensed Zoë decided that she did want to respond. She did so with heated words for everyone on the Big Island and beyond to hear. Then she retreated to her parents' home, cooling off only a bit, and pounded out an unpleasant article, filled with innuendo, for the next day's *Star-Advertiser.*

When the next day came, the chief read Zoë's article coolly and thoughtfully. "Notice that Bernie Scully's missing from the byline now," she said to Tanaka, showing him the paper. "I bet he's not pleased with her tirade on the radio yesterday, or this article. She's gone too far for him this time; crossed a line. She's dragged Kawika's name into her accusation of a cover-up, not just your name and mine. Maybe she doesn't realize Scully was a good friend of Elle's, and that he's worked with Kawika all year on the Slasher story. He's not going to blow his access to that. Which gives me an idea—one you're going to like, Terry. But you go catch this killer first. Then I'll teach Ms. Zoë Akona a lesson."

36

South Kohala

Tanaka arranged for a policeman to meet Kawika's mother, Lily, and stepfather, Pat, at the airport and bring them to the Hapuna Prince hotel. Once they'd checked in, the policeman drove them to the nearby house in Puakō, where Kawika had returned after his wrenching morning in Hilo. Following tearful embraces, the three spent the afternoon gathered closely at the cottage that had been Jarvis's but then effectively become Elle's once she'd renovated and added her own touches to it.

Kawika remained almost nonresponsive in Lily and Pat's presence. He knew this added to their distress, but he felt powerless to do or say more. They just sat together quietly on the lawn, holding hands some of the time, facing the hypnotic surf and the painfully beautiful sea. Kawika thought clearly enough to provide sunscreen and remind them to use it, although how such matters came to him while he tumbled endlessly in abyssal grief he did not know. Eventually the driver, who'd stood by patiently, returned Lily and Pat to the hotel so they could rest before dinner, leaving Kawika to do the same.

Dinner at the hotel, overlooking Hapuna Beach and the ocean, brought little relief. They all picked at their meals in near silence. No one had an appetite. Kawika could see that Lily and Pat were exhausted from the long flight, the long day, and the emotion of their reunion and the terrible circumstances of Elle's death. It made sense for them to retire early, Hawai'i time, as they were still on Seattle time, three hours later. After more embraces, all of them trying not to dissolve again, Lily and Pat went to their room, and Kawika dutifully drove his rental car up the hill to see his father.

As he drove, a thought slowly began to form, rousing him from his nearly catatonic state: Jarvis had spent Saturday morning with Elle. They'd visited the market together. Apart from her killer, Jarvis might have been the last person to see her alive. *And Jarvis could answer questions*—at least if Kawika or Elle asked them. Kawika began to drive faster.

"Mom's here on the island with Pat," Kawika told his father, even before sitting down and taking Jarvis's hand. "They're at the Hapuna Prince. She'll come see you tomorrow, Dad—she and Pat. Meanwhile, can I ask you a few questions?"

Jarvis responded with a *yuh-yuh-yuh*.

"Okay, then: Did anything unusual happen when you and Elle were at the Saturday market? Something Elle paid special attention to?"

Yuh-yuh-yuh.

"Something she bought?"

Negative response.

"Did you and Elle meet someone there?"

Yuh-yuh-yuh.

"Someone you knew?"

Affirmative response from Jarvis.

"Can you give me a hint?"

Muh-muh-muh.

"M?"

Affirmative.

"The letter M?"

Nuh-nuh-nuh.

"The sound?

Affirmative.

"Can you tell me the next sound then?"

Uh-uh-uh.

This could mean any vowel, Kawika knew, but it could also be the sound Kawika had asked for. He decided to try the sound first. "Em-uh?"

Affirmative.

"Emma? The name Emma? You and Elle met someone named Emma at the market?"

Affirmative.

"Emma Phillips? The woman from the TMT?" She was the only Emma he could suggest. He didn't know any other Emmas on the Big Island, though he realized there must be hundreds, with Queen Emma as a common namesake.

"Emma Phillips?" he repeated.

Yuh-yuh-yuh.

This puzzled Kawika. Why would seeing Emma Phillips at a popular market in the town where she lived seem unusual? But then Jarvis unexpectedly added *nuh-nuh-nuh.*

"No? Yes and no? Is that what you mean?"

Affirmative.

Perplexed, Kawika tried to think what to ask. But Jarvis didn't wait. *Guh-guh-guh,* he voiced.

"G? The letter G?"

Affirmative.

Ruh-ruh-ruh.

"G-R? Spelling something?"

Uh-uh-uh, Jarvis uttered, not answering the question, just plunging ahead.

"Vowel?"

Affirmative.

"A?"

Yuh-yuh-yuh.

"G-R-A?"

Affirmative.

Kawika stopped. A chill ran down his neck, and his arms sprouted goose bumps. "Emma *Gray*?" he asked. "You met Emma Phillips at the market, and you think Emma Phillips is Emma Gray? The daughter of Tom-Tom Gray?"

Yuh-yuh-yuh, Jarvis replied. *Yuh-yuh-YUH.*

"Oh my God," Kawika said aloud. "Did Elle ask you about this? Did she know you recognized Emma Gray? That Dr. Emma Phillips and Emma Gray are the same person? Think, Dad—this is really important."

YUH-YUH-YUH.

* * *

All the way back to Puakō and then while he lay in bed, long after he'd expected to fall asleep, Kawika obsessively pondered the significance of Dr. Emma Phillips being Emma Gray. And of Keoni Parkes driving the getaway boat for her father's killers. Elle had apparently extracted the Emma Gray part from Jarvis. Had she acted on it? But she hadn't known about Keoni driving the getaway boat, and Kawika could think of no way she might have discovered it. Tanaka, on the other hand, knew Keoni had driven the getaway boat—at least if Tommy had relayed Kawika's message. But Tanaka didn't know Emma Phillips was also Emma Gray. Only Kawika knew both pieces of the puzzle.

Kawika also knew, as Tanaka did not, that Keoni had agonized over someone to confide in. Someone other than his boyfriends Angel Delos Santos and Jay Goddard. *Got to find someone else to confide in. Who?* Had Keoni found that someone, and made a fatal mistake by confiding in Emma without realizing—until too late—that his boss was the daughter of the man he'd helped kill? Kawika's mind raced.

Did he really want to share this with Tanaka right now? After a moment, he decided he'd rather act on it himself. After all, it was his wife who'd been murdered and his unborn child who'd been lost. Kawika realized his grief confused his thinking—and now his anger did too. He tried to take account of that, of his adrenaline beginning to surge. But his need to confront Dr. Phillips was too strong to resist.

So, after a fitful night, Kawika called the hotel and told his mother he really needed to be alone one more day. Of course, she understood perfectly, Lily assured him. She and Pat could use a day to rest too. Kawika suggested she visit Jarvis at his care facility; in fact, he said, he'd told Jarvis to expect her. Kawika also said he'd ask Tanaka to join her and Pat for lunch, or coffee at least. It would be good for them to meet in person at last.

"Terry," he began, when he reached Tanaka, "I really don't feel like seeing anyone today. Just one more day. But is there any way you could get free to have lunch with my mom and Pat at the hotel? Or coffee? Just for an hour or so?"

"Of course," Tanaka replied. "I'll bring Ku'ulei too. Your mom's her aunt, right?"

"Yeah, from when Mom was married to Jarvis."

"Good. Consider it done."

Next, Kawika called Dr. Phillips in Waimea. Her secretary said Dr. Phillips was at the top of Mauna Kea all week, working in the retired Szkody-Brownlee Observatory, which was being decommissioned. "She's seeing if anything can be salvaged for the TMT. I can connect you to her up there, though, if you'd like?"

"Mahalo," Kawika said.

After a few clicks and buzzes, Dr. Phillips picked up the line. "Major Wong," she began. "I'm surprised to hear from you. I'm so, so sorry for your loss. I met your wife only briefly. But I've read two of her books, and she seemed like such an intelligent and vibrant young woman, not to mention a talented writer and very beautiful."

"Thank you. She was all that and more."

"I lost my husband too," Dr. Phillips went on. "Of course, he wasn't murdered—how dreadful, murder. He died in a climbing accident. Still, he was about your wife's age when it happened, far too young, and of course it was sudden and shocking, completely unexpected. One day he was there, the next day he wasn't. I was totally unprepared. So I sympathize, if that's not too presumptuous. But how are you back at work already? So soon? I could never have done that."

"Time off made things worse, I guess," Kawika said. "I sit here in Puakō, in our house she remodeled, and I can move around all right—I don't bump into things. But it's as if I'm moving through familiar rooms in the dark. As if the lights are all out and they're never coming back on."

"Dear me," she responded. "That's a good way of saying it. I remember feeling that way exactly."

"So," he continued, "I'm still here on the Big Island because, well, you know, I have to stay a while longer. But I've done all I can to help the investigation into my wife's death; it's in other hands, and I just have to wait. So I'm trying to work. Right now I'm picking up some threads in the Keoni Parkes case."

"Oh, good," she said. "I'm glad you're still on it."

"The good news, if you can call it that," Kawika went on, "is that you were probably right: the killer's someone in Honolulu, almost for certain. We've got a suspect, someone he shared his place with there. I thought you'd be glad to hear that." Suspect or not, Jay Goddard could be turned to use at the moment.

"Definitely glad to hear it," Dr. Phillips replied, "though it's overshadowed by Keoni's death itself—and by your wife's, of course."

"I understand. Meanwhile, I'm following up on a few TMT possibilities you alerted us to. We interviewed Grace 'Ōpūnui and Jonathan Kalākalani and lots of their followers, as you suggested, but the ones who were in Honolulu that night have solid alibis. So there's not much more to pursue with those two groups."

"Just as well you're focused on a Honolulu suspect, then?"

"Correct. But Detective Ku'ulei Wong—you remember her, my young cousin? She and I met with Jeffrey Mokuli'i, also as you suggested. And that's a different story. He and *his* followers—about all the ones he's got, I guess—were in Honolulu that day, and some stayed over. We've followed up with those we can find. Some of them raise suspicions."

"Oh?"

"It's just something we've got to do, you understand. Routine. Cross the *t*'s and all that. We've got photos of the guys who interest us. Mostly mug shots—they've been in trouble before. Their names probably won't mean anything, but their faces might, if you've seen them at work or in a crowd of demonstrators. We suspect Keoni knew them by sight. If they'd come to his door in Honolulu, he probably would've opened it. So any of them could be the killer. We doubt they are, but still, we have to check 'em out. I'd like to show you the photos, see if you recognize anyone."

"Happy to help," she replied. "But I'm up on the mountain all week. I'm going through the old Szkody-Brownlee Observatory to figure out if anything could be useful for the TMT. Not the telescope, of course. Just the mechanical stuff. Right now I'm looking at a cabinet full of pipe wrenches." She laughed. "I could meet you in Waimea next week, though."

"Darn," Kawika said. "I hope I'll be back in Honolulu next week. The Big Island's tough for me right now."

"Oh, of course—I understand."

"Could I maybe come see you on the mountain instead? Won't take more than a half hour of your time. And frankly, I could use the diversion."

Dr. Phillips chuckled. "You're very welcome up here, Major," she told him. "But you really want to come up for a half-hour meeting? Have you ever been here?"

"No, but I guess I'll try it," he said. "There has to be a first time for everyone, right?"

"Well, come ahead if you'd like. You'll need four-wheel drive to get beyond the visitor information station. That's at ninety-two hundred feet. They say to stop there for an hour to acclimate, but that's awfully brief. You should really allow two hours if you want to ask me coherent questions and understand the answers."

Kawika laughed lightly. "My questions aren't always coherent anyway," he said, "although my rental car does happen to be a four-wheel drive." That wasn't true. But he knew he could rent one—or commandeer it, if necessary—at the Mauna Kea hotel, less than a mile out of his way. "I'll start out now. I should be there in, what, about three hours?"

"I'll be waiting," she said. "Call when you're close. If your phone doesn't work up here, just follow the signs to Szkody-Brownlee and honk at the front door. I'll be right inside."

Kawika had no difficulty renting a four-wheel-drive SUV at the hotel, but his other prevarications hadn't been clever enough. When he arrived at the Szkody-Brownlee Observatory three hours later, Dr. Phillips was waiting and escorted him through the otherwise deserted, rather dark, and distinctly chilly building. He followed her into the former control room—the "inner sanctum," she called it. There, before he could even turn and ask her a question, she hit him hard across the temple with a pipe wrench as big as her forearm and knocked him out cold.

37

The Hapuna Prince Hotel

It made the most sense for Tanaka and Ku'ulei to meet Kawika's mother and stepfather for morning coffee at their hotel. Lily and Pat, still on mainland time, had eaten breakfast in the predawn hours, and Tanaka—although very willing to meet them, as Kawika had asked—didn't want to take the time for a sit-down lunch on a day of chasing Elle's killer.

Tanaka and Ku'ulei found Lily and Pat with a man they introduced as Professor David Hoff, the astronomer from the University of Hawai'i who'd loaned Kawika and Elle his Ala Moana condo while working on a project at the University of Washington. Although semi-retired, Lily was his active astronomer colleague on that project. Professor Hoff had volunteered to handle travel arrangements for Lily and Pat and join them on the trip. Time he paid a visit to Hawai'i anyway, he'd told Ku'ulei. Plus, he added, Lily and Pat were too shattered to handle the logistics.

So the five of them shared coffee—tea for Tanaka—in the open air at the Hapuna Prince. "This is so incongruous," Pat remarked, "to be here, *why* we're here, and be looking out at this." He swept his hand across the view—the morning-lit beach, the blue Pacific with its lazily rolling surf, and the many shades of green in the palms and kiawe trees and on the distant slopes of Hualālai, the well-forested volcano in the distance. Everyone at the table nodded sadly.

Lily began the real conversation. "Major Tanaka, both Pat and I want to thank you for the countless kindnesses you've shown Kawika for so long. Especially back when he got shot, but also for the years before that, when you trained him and looked after him. He absolutely reveres you—"

"Worships you," Pat interjected.

"—and we're both very grateful. He's so lucky to have you to help him through this horrible situation."

Tanaka demurred in part. "I've learned a lot from Kawika," he said. "And I've never again had such a great young colleague—well, except for Ku'ulei here, of course. Your niece is doing great, following in Kawika's footsteps. She may even surpass him in the end." He said this with a small smile and reached over to touch Ku'ulei lightly on the shoulder. She and the others smiled politely in turn.

"Now," Lily continued, "we'd like you to tell us what you can about Elle's death. You don't have to spare us the details. We want to know them."

Tanaka nodded. "Okay," he replied. "But none of this is easy."

"We know," said Pat. "We don't expect it to be easy. We just want to know whatever other people know, and especially what Kawika knows. We need that, as his parents."

So Tanaka explained the timing of Elle's disappearance and the discovery of her body. That she'd been strangled, probably with a scarf or other length of fabric, and that she'd been buried in her clothes and with her handbag; only her car key and the car itself were missing. It didn't appear she'd been sexually molested. And—Tanaka knew this would be hard—the autopsy revealed she'd been pregnant.

"Pregnant!" Lily exclaimed, her voice trembling. She fell sideways against her husband; Pat caught her as she began to sob. She leaned into him, burying her face in his chest and throwing an arm around his neck. Everyone waited awkwardly; the moment was excruciating. Tanaka and Ku'ulei were close to tears themselves. Tanaka knew Lily felt stabbed, losing a future grandchild—an added catastrophe for which she wasn't in the least prepared.

"I'm an old prosecutor," Pat ventured, still holding his wife but moving the conversation onto less fraught ground. "I'm curious about what Kawika was working on," he continued. "Just in case Elle's death relates to it somehow."

So Tanaka told them about the Kapi'olani Park Slasher, the case that had been Kawika's preoccupation since the serial killings began. Tanaka didn't know all the details, since he wasn't part of the police force in Honolulu. He simply explained that the Slasher had killed at least six people so far and that Kawika, as chief of homicide detectives in Honolulu, was naturally in charge.

"Kawika's in line to become chief of police in Honolulu," Tanaka added. "Maybe he told you that?" Lily looked up, but both she and Pat shook their heads. "This Slasher case could affect his chances. So he's been working hard on it for a long time. Now, of course . . ." Tanaka's voice trailed off.

"But then there's this *other* murder," Ku'ulei added. "A guy from the Big Island who spent weekends in Honolulu and got murdered there. That's what Kawika's been focused on lately."

"That's right," Tanaka confirmed. He decided those two cases were enough; no need to mention Chief Carvalho's ongoing official review. He knew Pat, as a prosecutor, would grasp the hazards to Kawika of such an investigation, even if Lily the astronomer might not. It would add to an already distressing situation.

"And this other case," Pat asked, "who was the victim? What was it about? Could it have anything to do with Elle's death, you think?"

Tanaka shook his head. "No," he said, "I don't think so. More likely it relates to a case Kawika and I worked on years ago, or else to a controversy here on the Big Island. The victim, Keoni Parkes, worked for the Thirty Meter Telescope Project. I expect you astronomers"—he nodded toward Lily and Professor Hoff—"know more about TMT than we do. Keoni had a very difficult position, the guy appointed to try to work out a compromise yet still allow the TMT to get built. Passions around TMT are almost out of control. Keoni was really exposed, partly because he was hapa haole and some Hawaiians considered him a traitor."

Lily had dried her tears and bravely regained her upright position. Now she looked at Tanaka with red-rimmed eyes. "The TMT," she said, turning to Professor Hoff. "That's where Emma Gray works."

"Emma Gray?" asked Tanaka.

"Yes," Lily replied. "She actually grew up in Puakō. I knew her family when she was a child, while Jarvis and I were still married. I remember her father, Tom, quite well. He doted on Emma and her brother—but especially Emma. Years later I heard he'd died in a boating accident. Emma went to school on the mainland and grew up to be a famous astronomer, very successful while still quite young. I remember the news when the TMT hired her."

"Emma Gray?" Tanaka asked again in consternation, teetering on the dizzying edge of comprehending every dreadful thing about so many murders—Elle's included—all at once.

Professor Hoff spoke up. "I think Lily's referring to Emma Phillips. Maybe Gray was her maiden name? But she's been Emma Phillips as long as I can remember—certainly years before she joined the TMT. Her husband,

Rodney, was a well-known astronomer in his own right. The two of them worked together on complex twin star astrophysics. They were famous for that—but also, I have to say, for elbowing aside professional colleagues. I wondered how her temperament would work for TMT. Anyway, Emma and Rodney had worked together a long time, twenty years or so, when he died in a climbing accident. In Yosemite, on El Capitan or Half Dome, I can't remember which. I think that's why she took a sabbatical from hard science and went into administration. That's what I recall from the publicity when she came here."

"Wait," Tanaka again insisted, still trying to grasp it, trying to be certain. "Are you saying that Dr. Emma Phillips of the TMT project is the same person as Emma Gray, the daughter of Thomas Gray?"

"Yes," Lily said. "I'd forgotten about her married name. David's right; it *is* Phillips. I just think of her as Emma Gray, from when she was a girl."

Tanaka turned to look at Ku'ulei, who stared back wide-eyed. Tanaka guessed she remembered what Keanu Fuchida had told them: Elle had suggested the name Emma Phillips to Jarvis, and he had responded *nuh-nuh-nuh*.

"I'm terribly sorry," Tanaka said abruptly, pushing back his chair. "Ku'ulei and I have to leave. That's important information you just gave us. I'll explain later. Right now we need to go see Kawika about this. Please excuse us."

Everyone stood and quickly shook hands—Ku'ulei shared a brief hug with her aunt—and then the detectives departed, leaving the others standing and nonplussed. Tanaka gave instructions to Ku'ulei as they hurried to the car.

"Call Kawika," he instructed her. "Tell him we're on our way to his place. I'll call Dr. Phillips and see where she is. If Kawika finds out she's Emma Gray, my guess is he'll confront her himself. We need to prevent that." Tanaka was thinking, *What if Elle discovered from Jarvis who Emma Phillips is? What might she have done?*

Ku'ulei couldn't reach Kawika. And Tanaka couldn't reach Dr. Phillips.

"She's at the summit this week, at the old Szkody-Brownlee telescope," her secretary told him. "I can connect you if you like. I connected Major Wong earlier. But then Dr. Phillips called me back and said she and Major Wong have agreed to meet in person Monday morning here at her office in Waimea. She'll be down from the mountain by then. Shall I make an appointment for you too?"

"No," Tanaka said, his voice growing tight. "Just connect me with her now. Please."

The connection worked, but there was no answer. No answer from Dr. Phillips. No answer from Kawika. Tanaka drew the worrisome conclusion. "Kawika is up at the summit, I bet," he told Ku'ulei, giving voice to an awful premonition. "He's going to get right in Emma Phillips's face, I just know it. And that darn guy refuses to carry a gun."

"Like you," she said. "But not like me." She touched her sidearm quickly, as if reassuring herself that she'd remembered to bring it.

"Call Tommy in Waimea," Tanaka instructed Ku'ulei hurriedly. "Tell him we'll pick him up in twenty minutes. We're going up the mountain. Ask him to bring warm jackets if he's got 'em. And enough oxygen kits from the EMTs so there's one for Kawika too. We're not stopping to acclimate. We don't have time. Just remind Tommy that Keoni drove the getaway boat, and tell him Emma Phillips is Emma Gray and she's up at the summit and we think Kawika's gone there to confront her. Tommy will understand right away."

Then Tanaka turned on his siren and flashing lights. He stood on the accelerator, his wiry body actually rising from the seat as he put all his weight into spurring the car to greater speed along the Queen K.

Moldy old fishing boat story, my ass, Tanaka thought. But even now he wouldn't say such a thing aloud. Not with Ku'ulei in the car.

38

On Mauna Kea

Kawika regained consciousness with cold water dripping off his face. He shook his head and tried to wipe his eyes but discovered his hands were bound with tape and bound in turn to his belt. His ankles were bound as well. He was in pain and felt terribly groggy from the blow and the altitude. He'd acclimated only partially at the visitor information station, not having paused for anything close to the two hours Dr. Phillips had recommended. He realized he was on his back in the telescope control room, his aching head propped up with a now-drenched cushion.

Dr. Phillips came into focus. She was pointing a gun at him. "Hello, Major Wong," she said. "Sorry to splash you; I thought it was time to wake you up."

"It's too late," Kawika said weakly, wasting no time. "You left your prints at Keoni's house."

Dr. Phillips laughed dismissively. "I believe the prints you're referring to belong to some random checkout person at some random retail store somewhere on either of two islands. If you choose dish towels first when shopping, Major Wong, you don't have to leave prints on anything else you put in your basket. The checkout folks will handle things from there."

Thinking as well as he could, yet still befogged, Kawika attempted a different approach, trying desperately to think logically and fast. "Major Tanaka knows Keoni drove the getaway boat," he said.

"Oh, good!" she replied. "I only learned that a few weeks ago myself, from Keoni. Maybe it'll help Major Tanaka solve my dad's murder at long last. But it won't help him solve Keoni's, will it? Not even if he discovers I'm Emma

Gray, as your wife did—and which he might not, unless he has reason and skill enough to elicit that information from Jarvis."

He might have skill enough, Kawika almost told her. *And so might Ku'ulei.* But Kawika realized, groggily, that suggesting they might possess that skill could get Jarvis killed, and maybe Tanaka and Ku'ulei too.

"Even if Major Tanaka discovers my maiden name, he won't suspect me of anything," Dr. Phillips asserted. "I'll be shocked, just *shocked*, to learn that Keoni took part in killing my father—what a weird coincidence, right? I mean, Daddy's death was supposedly an accident, right? Not a murder! Major Tanaka will just go on looking for Keoni's killer among his dozens of TMT-related enemies. And, of course, HPD will keep looking in Honolulu."

Kawika didn't want to say *Major Tanaka doesn't believe in coincidences*; that too might get Terry killed. He thought of saying, *If Major Tanaka learns you're Thomas Gray's daughter, he'll suspect you of killing Keoni in revenge, and if he suspects you, he'll find ways to nail you.* But he knew telling her that wouldn't save Terry or stop her from eliminating Kawika, the immediate threat lying at her feet.

So, with his adrenaline fighting the altitude and his throbbing head, Kawika finally grasped the obvious thing to say. "You wouldn't get away with it, Emma. I'm here. My rental car's here. We'd be found. We won't vanish."

"Oh, Major Wong," she said, shaking her head sadly. "I'm a scientist; don't sell me short. No one's found Keoni's car or your wife's car, have they? Yours is a nondescript rental, not a cop car. Not conspicuous up here; four-wheel-drive rental cars come and go all the time. No one will notice. No one will remember. No one will know what became of you."

"We haven't found their cars, but we did find their bodies," Kawika reminded her, hoping to make her pause.

Dr. Phillips smiled. "Not up on Mauna Kea, you didn't. It's an extremely large mountain, you know. There are still ancient cattle pits better hidden than the one David Douglas fell in. And the only reason anyone found *him* is because they had a good idea where to look. No one will know where to look for you. There's a one-in-a-billion chance anyone will find you. Billions are things astronomers understand, Major Wong."

"It'll never work," was all he could think to respond. Dr. Phillips smiled dismissively.

"I called my secretary," she said. "I told her you and I agreed to meet first thing Monday in my office. I'll be as astonished as everyone else when you don't show up. So unless you told someone or left a note—did you? I didn't think so—no one in the world knows you're up here."

She put down the gun and picked up the roll of duct tape, tearing off two strips. Then she stood, looming over him and seeming even taller than when they'd first met and he'd thought she looked like an Olympic athlete. "Now I need to keep you quiet, Major Wong. Not because anyone can hear you. No, just because there's a lot I have to tell you, and then a lot I'll have to do. I don't want this to take all day. You can blink if I ask you a question. Three blinks for yes, okay? Three slow blinks. That's my scientist's mind at work. No ambiguity about three slow blinks. Anything else is a no."

Three Blinks for Yes: Kawika felt the horror of the bizarre coincidence. Immediately, though, he focused on struggling as hard as he could, trying to evade Dr. Phillips by rolling violently away from her. He thrashed his head from side to side, yelling at her, and tried to bite her as she attempted to apply the tape. But she proved even stronger than she looked; she also had every other physical advantage. Eventually she subdued him, forced his mouth shut, and put both strips of duct tape across it, the shorter one diagonally across the longer for extra security. She wiped her hands on her thighs—she was dressed in a mechanic's blue coveralls—and stood up, regaining the swivel chair in which she'd sat earlier. She again trained the pistol on him.

"I had a chance to talk with your wife a bit," she began. "We discussed that scene in fiction where the bad guy holds the good guy at gunpoint and instead of just shooting him, the bad guy starts talking and boasting, expecting to be recognized for his criminal genius or whatever. And then—surprise!—out of the blue, Sergeant Preston of the Yukon or someone rides in to the rescue and the bad guy's thwarted. I told her I'd always considered that a hackneyed literary device, something to build suspense. It's only in fiction that Sergeant Preston shows up in time. Not much chance of that in real life. I could keep you here a week or a month or a year and Sergeant Preston still wouldn't show up. I won't do that to you, of course—don't worry. Or at least don't worry about *that*.

"I don't know what your wife thought about that scene, whether it's just a literary device for suspense or serves some other purpose," Dr. Phillips continued, with an apologetic smile. "She couldn't talk by then, for the same reason you can't now. She did do a lot of blinking, though. Anyway, I explained to her what I'd learned from Keoni: in real life, there's an altogether different reason the killer takes time to talk while holding a gun on the detective. *It's because the killer needs to confide in someone*, Major Wong—someone who can't turn that confidence into a confession."

She paused and let the point sink in. "Confiding gets the matter out in the open," she explained. "Off one's chest and off one's back at the same time, so to speak. Confiding brings you all the good things about confessing with none of the bad ones—as long as the person you confide in doesn't tell anyone, of course, or isn't in a position to. Confession has messy downsides, especially if you're confessing to murder. Keoni knew that, which is why he never confessed—he just *confided.* His impulse to confide was sound; his choice of confidants was unlucky. That wasn't his fault; he didn't know the person he'd helped murder was my father. He didn't know I was Emma Gray. You with me so far?"

Kawika responded with three blinks. Twice, in fact. Anything to slow this down.

"Good. Well, I executed Keoni because he was one of my father's killers. That's how I thought of it, and still do: execution. Simple justice, eye for an eye. That was as far as I ever expected this to go. I don't like killing people, Major Wong. I hope to God I never have to do it again. But as I told your wife, I wasn't about to sacrifice my entire career, my work at the TMT, my eminence in my field, the chance to assist an enormous leap in astronomy and human knowledge and complete some of the work my husband and I had started together—all of that has literal cosmic significance—just because I'd executed the last of Daddy's killers, the one you police allowed to escape, and just because your wife had come too close to figuring that out. As you've come too close yourself, Major Wong. But this will be the end of it, thank God, because no one else will ever come as close again."

Kawika remembered when Fortunato's killer had confided in him while holding him at gunpoint. But Fortunato's killer had silenced him with appeals to Kawika's sense of morality and justice, not a bullet. Kawika knew Emma Phillips intended the bullet.

She paused, then picked up a paper tablet from the countertop beside her. "After you called and I knew you were coming up here, I made notes of what I want to confide," she said. "The situation is more stressful for you than for me, I know, but it's plenty stressful for me too, believe me. I'm the one who has to talk and then pull the trigger. And the altitude still affects me a bit too. So forgive me for relying on notes."

She donned glasses to look over the notes, seeming to gird herself for a major effort. Kawika could see her hand trembling. He hoped her gun hand wouldn't tremble; he hoped she'd take her time. He was thinking as fast as he could—which wasn't very fast, the blow and the altitude still impeding him—trying to figure out how to avoid ending up undiscovered in an ancient cattle pit on the vast slopes of Mauna Kea.

Yet a little voice subversively suggested he consider just that. What would it be like to live without Elle and his unborn child? Why not join them? He remembered Tanaka advising him to pay attention to those little voices. This time he tried hard to ignore it, to stay focused on surviving. He could join Elle later.

"Okay," Dr. Phillips resumed, looking up from the notes. "You have to understand, I wasn't always this mad scientist, crazed with finding and executing my father's killers. I would've been fine with you police catching and convicting them, but you failed at that." She gave him an accusing look.

"Unlike the cops, though, I never believed my father drowned accidentally. Never. My brother and I told your dad that at the memorial service. It made no sense. Daddy wouldn't have taken the boat out by himself. I even confronted D. K. Parkes about it. I knew D. K. pretty well; we'd been out on the boat with him when Daddy first bought it. But D. K. swore Daddy had insisted he teach him all the controls, all the fishing stuff. He said Daddy wanted to be able to take *Mahi Mia* out alone, not have to pay D. K. each time. But I didn't believe that. Daddy could never run that boat, especially if he wanted to fish at the same time—and he would never have gone out except to fish. If he could afford the boat, he could certainly afford to pay D. K. whenever he went out."

At first, she explained, she'd thought D. K. or someone else must've killed her father on shore and sent *Mahi Mia* out to sea unmanned in order to mislead investigators. But the Coast Guard had found the boat with its ignition off and half a tank of fuel—enough for the boat to beach herself on Maui if someone had pointed her in that direction. Nothing had been programmed into the navigational equipment. The boat hadn't been on autopilot. Someone must've been aboard.

Emma said she'd spent time over the years trying to work out how D. K. Parkes might have killed her father alone, without help—and why. She couldn't see how one person could do it and get to shore. And she couldn't think of any motive for Parkes. But if Parkes worked with someone else, the logistics seemed feasible. And she knew someone who might've had a motive: Ralph Fortunato.

"I knew Daddy and Mr. Fortunato had engaged in *something* shady in the sale of that land," she said. "Before Mr. Fortunato came along, Daddy always said it was practically worthless. Then suddenly he sells it for a huge price, makes a bundle off it. He's instantly rich and promptly retires, spending a boatload of money—pardon the expression—to buy *Mahi Mia* and have her fitted out with top-of-the-line stuff. There was a lot of wink-wink, nod-nod about that real estate transaction.

"That's right," she admitted, "Daddy wasn't a saint. I don't think he was ever the same after Vietnam, whatever he was like before. He saw a lot of combat and got pretty badly wounded. But he was always tender with us. He could be very generous too—he founded that cat rescue organization, or whatever it is, and he loved sharing his catch, just like the obituary said. But he was also a risk-taker, a teller of tall tales, and a gambling addict. That boat itself was the only hard asset left when he died, and it turned out he'd even put a ship mortgage on it. I could easily imagine him doing something shady with Mr. Fortunato, who always struck me as a sleazebag.

"By the way," she added. "My father did not have any Native American blood. That Tom-Tom stuff was pure bullshit. But typical of him, to claim something like that. Still, for all his faults, my brother and I loved him dearly. He was such a caring father, always looking out for us. He raised us alone after Mom died. He put us through school on the mainland. He was our only parent. His killers had never been arrested, and if one of them remained at large, there was no way I was going to let that go."

When D. K. Parkes and Fortunato were murdered two years after her father's death, her first thought had been that her brother Kam had killed them without telling her, she said. But he denied it absolutely and had a solid alibi: he'd been on the mainland the entire year. Then Major Tanaka announced publicly that Michael Cushing's hit man had murdered Fortunato because of a business dispute. There'd been no explanation for the death of D. K. Parkes and no indication the police connected Fortunato or Parkes to the earlier death of Emma's father, which officially remained an unfortunate fishing mishap.

She'd pretty much given up on the whole thing and immersed herself in her work before she returned to the Big Island for the TMT job, she said. Keoni Parkes was already working for TMT when she arrived.

"It never occurred to me that Keoni might be related to D. K.," she told Kawika. "I know that sounds strange, but Keoni was Hawaiian and D. K. was as haole it gets. So it never crossed my mind. I liked Keoni a lot, and we had an excellent working relationship."

But then several thoughts began converging, she said. Being back at the scene of her father's death caused her to ponder again, after a long hiatus, how her father's killer or killers had gotten to shore. Of the possible scenarios, it seemed most likely her father had invited Fortunato to go fishing and asked D. K. Parkes to skipper. But then some third person must have taken the two aboard another vessel after the murder.

"That's when I became obsessed with finding that third person," she said. "The third person didn't have to be related to D. K. or Mr. Fortunato. I just became convinced a third person had been involved, and I was determined to discover that person—a bit consumed by the idea, I admit. I bet you think I should have gone to the police, right?"

Kawika blinked slowly three times. And another three times just to stall.

"I did consider it. But the case was more than a decade old, and Daddy's death had been ruled an accident. The Coast Guard report was uncontested—how could I contest it? D. K. and Mr. Fortunato had been dead for years. What would the police have done at that point? Nothing, of course. Who could you have interviewed? No one. The situation was maddening."

One day, though, it occurred to her that Keoni Parkes might be related to D. K. He might have a Hawaiian mother, after all, even though D. K. had been a haole. She could find nothing about his parents in his personnel file. She knew he lived in Waimea—most TMT employees lived there or in Hilo—but he said he'd been raised in Waimea too. That and the spelling of his last name seemed too much to be mere coincidence, she thought.

"But I didn't feel I could just come right out and ask him," she told Kawika. "After all, if his dad was D. K. Parkes, then his dad was a murderer and a murder victim too. Pretty sensitive topic. And even then, I still wasn't thinking of Keoni as an accomplice to Daddy's murder—he was such a nice guy. No, at that point I just wanted to know if he was a murderer's *son*—pure curiosity on my part. I couldn't find anything about D. K. Parkes on the internet, apart from his occupation and how he'd died. Couldn't locate anything about a Mrs. Parkes or about D. K.'s children, if any. So I started asking around."

Dr. Phillips gave a rueful laugh. "After your wife and I talked a bit, she asked whether I knew about an 'insurance lady from Maui' or a 'tax lady from Honolulu' who'd been asking people whether D. K. Parkes had children. Unfortunately, that pretty much tipped the balance about what I had to do with her. I mean, look what she already knew: She'd discovered I was Emma Gray. She knew from you that my father had been murdered and that D. K. Parkes was one of the killers. She knew Keoni was D. K.'s son. She'd guessed there'd been a getaway boat. Now she suspected I'd made those calls myself—I could just tell. So you see, Major Wong, your wife knew too much. She was getting too close. Ironically, the calls themselves were fruitless. But anyway, after I made them, something extraordinary happened."

The extraordinary thing, she explained, was that Keoni unexpectedly came to her office one day and said he needed to confide in someone about something—something that had been tormenting him for years, he said.

"I told him he could confide in me," she said. "I was flattered he'd consider me for that. I assured him we were good friends and excellent colleagues, which we were. I promised I'd keep his confidences. So what was bothering him? I asked. I honestly had no idea what he might reveal. It didn't occur to me that it might involve my father's murder. I didn't even know yet, not for sure, that Keoni was D. K.'s son, much less suspect him of killing Daddy."

What Keoni confided, she told Kawika, was that his father had been murdered and that the murder had never been solved.

"A perfect opening!" she exclaimed. "I told him my father had been murdered too, and that his murder had also never been solved. Keoni asked about the circumstances, but by then I had an inkling of where this was headed between Keoni and me. So I told him I found it too painful to talk about. I said that perhaps after he told me about his father, I might be able to tell him about mine.

"At that point he went further. He said his father had been involved in killing someone, and he believed that's why his father had been murdered. Worse, he said, he wasn't entirely innocent himself.

"It was a eureka moment for me, after so many years. And such an unexpected one. Keoni was starting to cry. At that point I told him, 'Look, this is just too dangerous to talk about here or anywhere in Waimea. People might wonder what's going on if they see us talking together and you—understandably—trying not to cry.' So I suggested meeting in Honolulu on the weekend. Start at a restaurant, and then, depending on where the conversation led, maybe continue at his place."

She paused and put down her notes. "You can guess where it went from there. You'd like to ask questions about the actual killing, I know. Or you would in different circumstances, anyway. Yes?"

Kawika blinked three times, then blinked three times again after a pause. Anything to keep her talking.

"Let's just say I intended to shoot him with this gun, the one I'm pointing at you. It's not traceable. My husband bought it years ago at some swap meet in Arizona—you know, a place where you pay cash and no one asks questions. He'd been saying we should keep a gun in the house for security, and there it was, an impulse purchase. But I didn't want to shoot Keoni while he was unconscious and tied to his kitchen chair. That would seem more like murder than execution. You don't execute someone who's unconscious. Now don't pretend to black out on me, Major Wong!"

She laughed, but it was a weak laugh, a tired one. Kawika felt sleepy, as if trying to think his way through balls of cotton; his adrenaline was running out. He could tell she was tiring too. Which was not a good sign.

"Anyway," she said, "I was looking for his laptop and anything that might suggest he intended to tell me, Emma Phillips, about his having helped murder someone—especially if he'd used the name Thomas Gray. I was surprised to find a gun in Keoni's nightstand. But I figured, what the heck, better than using this one. So when Keoni finally came to, I explained that the man he'd murdered had been my dad—only *helped* murder, he then began to beg me to understand, immediately after an hour of confiding that he felt as guilty as his father and Ralph Fortunato. Yeah, an hour earlier he'd told it all. He'd known exactly what D. K. and Mr. Fortunato intended. They'd shared their plan with him; his role as getaway driver was essential; they could never have carried out the killing if he hadn't agreed to bring the second boat; and so forth. But now, when he was crying and pleading for his life, suddenly he'd just been a naïve college kid who'd committed a misdemeanor at most."

She paused, but only briefly this time. Kawika could tell she was beginning to hurry.

"Then I shot him," she said, "and you know the rest. As I said in the beginning, I thought that would be the extent of it. Keoni's death would go unsolved—just like it will now—and we'd find someone else to take Keoni's place at the TMT, although I doubt we'll find anyone as good.

"And that's where it *would* have ended, if I hadn't run into Jarvis and your wife at the market, if he hadn't recognized me as Emma Gray. What bad luck that was. Apart from your dad, I haven't run into anyone since I got back here who ever knew me as Emma Gray. That didn't surprise me. I left Hawai'i as a girl, after all. I didn't really get my growth spurt until I was in college, by which point I was gone—for good, I thought at the time. That's also when I decided to become a blonde. And all that was years ago. But Jarvis did recognize me, and it was a no-win situation at that point.

"I pretended we hadn't met, because that seemed like the least bad choice in the moment. But Jarvis kept making noise, like he was protesting. That's what made your wife curious, once she'd somehow gotten my maiden name from Jarvis; I didn't know she'd be able to do that. She hadn't put it all together, though—she didn't know Keoni had anything to do with Daddy's murder, for example. She wasn't particularly suspicious, I don't think, just curious. But she was getting warm. And by the time she went home, the two of you would've figured it out together. So I had to act."

Even in his semi-foggy state, Kawika was screaming inwardly: *If only Elle had called! If only she'd told me Emma Phillips was Emma Gray!*

"By the way, before I taped her mouth and when she was begging for her life, she told me she was pregnant," Dr. Phillips added, in a tone suggesting she was nearly done. "I don't know if that was just a desperate ruse. But if it was true, I'm even more sorry about this. However, now I've confided in you fully. It's done. My confidences will be locked away with you forever—not with your body, not in that ancient cattle pit. I prefer to think of you carrying my confidences with you into a black hole in space. And who knows? Maybe you'll be reunited there with your wife. I mean it, though—I really am sorry." She paused. "Well, that's all, I guess. Can't think of anything else. So, good-bye, Major Wong."

She stood slowly and extended her arm, pointing the gun at Kawika as he lay at her feet. He began to roll desperately to avoid the shot.

At that moment, three figures wearing oxygen masks and enormous bulky jackets, looking like some species of alien, burst through the control room door. Seeing Dr. Phillips holding a gun on the tightly bound Kawika as he rolled on the floor, all three froze momentarily, then moved to surround Dr. Phillips on three sides.

"Dr. Phillips!" Tommy shouted, ripping off his oxygen mask and facing her. "Put down the gun, Dr. Phillips!" Tommy made downward gestures with his lowered hands, one empty and one holding the oxygen mask.

Tanaka followed Tommy's lead. From the opposite side, also having removed his mask, he offered calming words. "Dr. Phillips. You're a smart person. You can see the situation you're in. Shooting Kawika can't help. Drop the gun. We'll arrest you, you'll get a good lawyer, and who knows if we can convict you for the murders? You've covered your tracks pretty well, and your lawyer will know all about creating reasonable doubt for the jury. But if you shoot our colleague right before our eyes, we'll convict you of that for sure."

Dr. Phillips kept her gun trained firmly on Kawika. He hoped his colleagues wouldn't risk shooting her; her gun might still discharge if they did.

Then Ku'ulei spoke up, standing directly behind Dr. Phillips and aiming her service pistol right at her. "Dr. Phillips," Ku'ulei warned loudly, "you shoot my cousin and I'll blow your head off."

Emma Phillips, née Gray, seemed to weigh briefly what the three detectives had said. So did Kawika. He stopped rolling, riveted at the miraculous arrival of his colleagues, wondering like a spectator how all this would turn out.

Suddenly Emma reacted. She shot Kawika where he lay, sending him spinning in agony, then swiveled rapidly to her left and shot Tommy straight on, blowing him backward against a wall. She wheeled toward Ku'ulei and dropped into a crouch to fire again.

At that point, just as she'd warned, Ku'ulei squeezed the trigger.

39

North Hawai'i Community Hospital, Waimea

Dr. Terrence Smith, who through seniority had become the dean of the physician staff at North Hawai'i Community Hospital, no longer performed autopsies. After the Fortunato case, in which he'd performed several autopsies suspiciously, Dr. Smith had understood the police would never trust him again. Better to stay out of their way. But he'd gone right on performing surgeries.

"Oh no," Kawika mumbled as he looked up from the gurney into Dr. Smith's face, locking eyes with him for the first time in twelve years but unable to say anything more as the oxygen mask went on and the anesthesiologist began delivering a magic cocktail intravenously.

Dr. Smith laughed. "Don't worry, Major," he said. "I won't let you die." And he didn't. He didn't let Tommy die either.

Now, a few days later, Dr. Smith stood between the beds of Kawika and Tommy in one of the hospital's semi-private rooms. The doctor faced an attentive group: Kawika's mother and father, stepfather, cousin Ku'ulei, and Terry Tanaka. Tommy's family had visited earlier. Speaking in a soft voice to avoid waking the wounded men, Ku'ulei quizzed the doctor about their conditions and prognosis. A nurse divided her attention between the two patients, checking a measurement here, adjusting a sheet or blanket there.

"Good thing Dr. Phillips was a bad shot," Dr. Smith joked quietly, after assuring everyone the patients were out of danger. Kawika had been shot through the upper right chest while lying down, the bullet exiting higher on his back, shattering two ribs and his scapula and just missing his spine. Tommy had been shot through the diaphragm and stomach; several internal organs had been damaged. But again, although the bullet had pulverized some ribs, it missed the spine.

"And it's a good thing you weren't," Dr. Smith added softly, smiling at Ku'ulei. "A bad shot, I mean. You must be traumatized," he suggested, sounding sympathetic. "It's not a common experience. Most officers go their entire careers without firing their gun at anyone, don't they?"

"I'm not traumatized," Ku'ulei insisted, in a voice just above a whisper. "I'm mad I didn't figure it out the minute Elle went missing. Or even earlier. It seems so obvious now."

"It was *never* obvious," Tanaka assured her.

At that moment a diminutive blonde haole, well-groomed and modestly dressed, walked into the room carrying two small vases of flowers, the vases bearing satin ribbons. "Is it okay to visit Major Wong and Detective Kekoa?" she inquired softly. "If not, I can just leave the flowers."

"Oh, yes," the nurse assured her, making no apparent effort to speak quietly. "You come right in, sister. They're just restin'. All outa danger. Little crowded here, though. Kawika's papa's in that wheelchair, you got his mama and her husband over there, along with Miss Ku'u and Major Tanaka. Plus Doc Smith and me."

The room was large enough that despite the beds and the wheelchair, all ten people could just fit. Kawika and Tommy lay attached to various tubes, drips, and rhythmically beeping monitors, while oscilloscopes shone reassuringly with steadily advancing waves. Above their aloha-patterned coverlets, Kawika and Tommy both looked bruised and yellowed. They were resting, as the nurse had said. At the moment it seemed their rest consisted of deep sleep.

Five people had turned to regard the newcomer. Jarvis, the sixth, couldn't turn, but she walked over and lightly kissed his cheek. "Aloha, Jarvis," she said softly, before straightening up to face the others. "I'm Patience Quinn," she whispered.

Fuh-fuh-fuh, Jarvis intoned in his version of a whisper. *Fuh-fuh-fuh*.

Patience smiled. "*Normally* I'm Patience Quinn," she corrected herself quietly. "To Jarvis, I'm Flea." Then, after a pause, she said, "How are they doing? How are *you* all doing?"

Everyone stood speechless. Only Jarvis and the two unconscious patients had ever met Patience. But the others certainly knew about her, and she'd heard a lot about them. The room remained awkwardly silent except for electronic beeps from the monitors.

Lily spoke first, in a whisper too. "I'm Lily, Kawika's mom," she said, shaking Patience's hand. "I always hoped to meet you, Patience. We talked about you so much with Kawika, back in the day. He had such affection for you." Then Lily introduced the others.

"Major Tanaka, I'm glad to meet you at last," said Patience softly, shaking his hand in turn. "Although I'm very sad it's in these circumstances. Kawika spoke so highly of you when he was young. And Ku'ulei—I can hardly believe it, meeting you when you're already grown up and in uniform. Wow. You were just a girl when Kawika got shot. Got shot the first time, I mean. You were with him, right? How old were you then?"

"Almost twelve," Ku'ulei replied quietly, sounding a bit standoffish, as if she considered Patience an intruder in this family scene. "I'm twenty-four now. I work with Major Tanaka as a detective."

"Twenty-four!" Patience exclaimed softly, offering her hand, which Ku'ulei did not refuse. "And a detective working with Major Tanaka! Kawika must be so proud of you. And you saved his life too, as I understand it."

"And mine," Tanaka said in a low voice.

"And mine too," added Tommy weakly from his bed.

Patience turned to face the patient who'd awakened. "Hello, Tommy. It's been a long time." She walked to his bedside and started to extend a hand, but gently kissed his cheek instead, even though she'd met him only twice before, during the Fortunato case. "Kawika always spoke of you like a brother."

Kawika opened one eye slightly.

"P?" he asked uncertainly, his voice as weak as Tommy's.

Everyone turned, first toward him and then, looking puzzled, toward Patience.

"P?" he inquired again, more loudly this time.

But before she could step to Kawika's bedside, he'd fallen asleep again.

PART FIVE

2014

The high chief, or *mōʻī*, then pierced the mouth of the dead man with a ceremonial hook called the *mānaiakalani* [the legendary fishhook of the demigod Māui], and recited the following words:

"O Kū, O Lono
O Kāne and Kanaloa,
Give life to me until my old age;
Look at the rebel against the land
He who was seized for the sacrifice.
Finished . . ."

—Van James,
Ancient Sites of Hawaiʻi: Archaeological Places of Interest on the Big Island (1995)

Epilogue

There was no question of Kawika returning to active duty anytime soon, and hence no chance of his becoming chief of police in Honolulu, even if Ana Carvalho's investigation cleared him of past misconduct. The HPD placed him on indefinite medical leave, given the severity of his injuries, with a review scheduled after six months. As soon as he could board a plane, Kawika flew to O'ahu, aided by his mother and stepfather, and began recuperating in the Ala Moana condo he had shared with Elle. Professor Hoff urged Lily and Pat to stay there, too, for as long as they felt necessary during Kawika's recovery, which was slow.

Lily and Pat looked after Kawika lovingly and well. They encouraged and patiently helped him with his physical therapy. They also gave him time to be alone, recognizing he'd sustained damage not limited to his gunshot wound, to torn flesh and shattered bones. He seemed depressed, of course, but surprisingly resilient and also deeply concerned for Tommy, whose internal injuries threatened more serious long-term disabilities than Kawika's. He spoke to Tommy and Tommy's wife by phone almost daily. With Tommy's consent, he even discussed Tommy's case with Dr. Terrence Smith.

One day Ku'ulei flew over from the Big Island to visit him in Honolulu. "You up for a walk?" she asked. When he nodded, she said, "Let's go see Kapaemahu—the Wizard Stones."

And so they walked slowly, at Kawika's speed, through Ala Moana Beach Park, over the bridge to Waikīkī, and then in single file—Ku'ulei clearing the way for him—through the endless crush of tourists until they reached the sacred place, which the tourists ignored.

"These boulders came from the cliffs above the Kaimukī neighborhood," Ku'ulei told him, as Kawika held the guardrail to steady himself. "No one knows how they got all the way down from there." They'd bought two flower leis to cast on the stones. Kawika tried using his right arm, and it worked. This time neither of them offered a prayer. Instead, they embraced.

Neither Lily nor Pat knew when might be the right time to bring up with Kawika that he'd now been shot twice in just over ten years, something he certainly pondered himself. He still had a quarter century to go until retirement, and if the two shootings could be imagined to suggest a trend, that trend seemed ominous. How serious might the next shooting be? That it might be fatal didn't need to be spoken. His mother wanted him to find a new career while he was young enough to make a change.

"He's smart and well-educated," Lily insisted to Pat. "The world is chronically short of smart, well-educated people. There must be some other line of work—in Hawai'i or on the mainland—that he'd enjoy. One where he'd excel. One that would be safer."

"Yes," agreed Pat. "But it isn't that simple, is it? I mean, who *is* Kawika? An unfinished creation, of course, since he's only forty-one and a widower, someone who's naturally a bit adrift for now. But I wonder if his identity isn't already fixed, Lily. At his age I was a prosecutor, and that wasn't going to change. You were an astronomer and you still are, even in supposed retirement. I think Kawika is a detective. I don't think that's going to change. I think he's probably a cop forever."

After a month, Kawika moved alone to the house in Puakō. He encouraged Lily and Pat to come over when they wished. He often visited them in the Honolulu condo too. He didn't chafe in their presence; he knew he benefited from their solicitude, which at times even offered the simulated yet welcome coziness of his childhood. "What's next, Mom?" he teased her one evening as he gave her a hug. "Hot chocolate?"

But he felt he needed to begin becoming self-reliant again. And he needed to visit Jarvis, his father, as often as he could.

Jarvis had begun to fade alarmingly after the death of his beloved daughter-in-law and the serious injury of his son. He survived Kawika's shooting by only three months. Kawika was holding Jarvis when he died, kissing the top of his head and repeating to his father over and over, "So loved, so loved." Which was certainly true, and not limited to Jarvis's family.

* * *

Elle's memorial service had been postponed to some unspecified future date; no one, least of all Kawika, was in an emotional state to speak at it. With Jarvis it was the opposite: everyone Jarvis had ever known, it seemed, wanted a speaking part. Lily handled the arrangements and found she was good at it. She quickly discovered that the tiny Hōkūloa Church in Puakō, which Jarvis would undoubtedly have preferred for its charm and long history dating back to the first missionaries, could not possibly accommodate the expected number of attendees. It was the same church where Keoni was to have spoken about his TMT proposal, and which Dr. Phillips had said he'd have trouble filling.

Lily moved the service to Puakō's much larger Catholic church. Even so, when the day came, only a portion of the audience could squeeze inside. Lily made sure an outdoor speaker system was in place for the large number of others who stood or sat outdoors in as much shade as they could find. With a warm breeze blowing softly off the Pacific, the outdoor crowd listened intently, mourning and laughing in turn as the service and the eulogists remembered Jarvis in all his larger-than-life friendships and wisdom and aloha spirit.

Kawika and Lily, along with Jarvis's best friend, Tanaka, were among the speakers, most of whom were Jarvis's friends from the Mauna Kea resort and the local community. Even Grace ʻŌpūnui of the Mea Pale ʻAhu, the Defenders, spoke. But everyone agreed it was the twenty-four-year-old Kuʻulei whose remembrances of the man who'd raised her alternated between funniest and most moving.

After Elle's murder and the national publicity surrounding it, her books experienced a modest but sustained uptick in sales. Kawika even received a movie proposal from a Hollywood production company for *Murder at the Mauna Lani.* He reserved judgment on that but donated the royalties from her books to the University of Hawaiʻi, asking that the university create, if the funds proved sufficient, a lecture series in Elle's name for undergraduate journalism students at the Mānoa campus.

* * *

That Keoni Parkes's killer turned out to be his own boss, someone who'd grown up in South Kohala just a few years before Keoni himself—apparently without either of them realizing that coincidence—provided a strange conclusion to the murder investigation. Jay Goddard, the Honolulu boyfriend of Keoni, aka John Parker, was relieved the killer had been found. But the pain of his lover's loss and deceit left him struggling for a long time, just as it did for Angel Delos Santos. Angel also found himself grappling emotionally with having lost his lover to a killer who'd been his own boss too.

Jay and Angel learned a lot about each other from information the police imparted. Eventually they decided to meet. They found they liked each other, although neither could quite grasp what Keoni—or John—had seen in the other. There was no romantic spark between them, and they both moved on to other partners on their respective islands. But they found unexpected solace in their shared grief, and they formed a low-key but sincere friendship that comforted and gratified them both. "Hell of a way to meet, though," Jay remarked, and Angel agreed.

* * *

Although Kawika had to surrender leadership of the Kapi'olani Park Slasher investigation entirely—he chose Kyu Sakamoto to succeed him as interim chief of HPD homicide detectives—the investigation came to an abrupt conclusion almost immediately thereafter, thanks to Yvonne Ivanovna and a homeless woman living under a blue tarpaulin in Ala Moana Beach Park. One night at about one thirty AM, the woman used a pay phone in the park to dial 911 and report a man carrying over his shoulder what appeared to be a human body in a black bag.

"In case you're wondering," she told the 911 dispatcher, "yes, I am on meth, but I'm not blind and I wouldn't spend my coins for this call if I thought I was seeing things." The dispatcher thanked the caller and reminded her that the phone had not eaten her coins but instead had returned all of them. "Oh," replied the woman, as she searched the phone's coin return box. "There's more here than I put in. Maybe I should call again?"

As it happened, Yvonne was driving her police cruiser on Ala Moana Boulevard when the call came in, so she got the assignment to investigate. She hadn't worked homicide since the end of the Keoni Parkes case; she'd mostly done night patrol. Sakamoto hadn't considered it wise to put her back on the Slasher case, given her friction with Jerry Rhodes. There weren't many homicides in the city besides the Slasher's, and those few consisted mostly of open-and-shut domestic violence cases that officers more senior than Yvonne could handle. So the department had decided that Yvonne, as a trainee and someone relatively new to Honolulu, should take advantage of the lull to spend some time on night patrol in uniform and in a cruiser of her own.

When Yvonne got the call from the dispatcher about a man carrying an apparent body in Ala Moana Beach Park, she wisely—but also to avoid seeming overly dramatic—did not turn on her siren, just made a quick left onto the park's outer drive. She turned off her headlights and pulled over near the public phone the dispatcher had identified. Another police cruiser was parked fifty yards ahead of her, lights out. She guessed it belonged to a colleague Sakamoto had assigned to patrol the park in an effort to see where the Slasher might dump a body next. She parked her own cruiser and got out on foot, taking care not to slam the door.

Sure enough, in the near darkness, far from any streetlamp and dimly silhouetted against the distant lights of Waikīkī, she could just make out a man heading deeper into the park with something large draped over his shoulder.

She followed quickly and silently, with gun drawn, approaching at an angle from behind, avoiding her suspect's peripheral vision, just as she'd been taught. A homeless man poked his head out of a ragged tent, but Yvonne put a finger to her lips and he stayed quiet, retreating into his shelter like a startled animal. When she was less than twenty feet from the suspect, his face was suddenly illuminated by a burst of headlights from a stream of cars on the Boulevard. Even at an angle, Yvonne recognized him at once.

"Major Wong will be severely disappointed, Detective Rhodes," she said loudly. "Don't move, Jerry—I've got you in my sights."

He turned his head sharply but stopped walking. She kept her gun trained on him.

Rhodes started to move. "I told you, Jerry—don't move," she barked. "I've got you covered, and you know what? I'm a better shot than you."

He stopped and stared at her. Then suddenly he shed the body bag, almost hurling it at her, and in nearly the same motion he drew his own handgun and fired off two shots. But she sidestepped the tumbling bagged corpse, and both shots missed her. She took a shot while she was still moving, hoping to hit his torso, but caught him in the knee. He collapsed to the ground, cursing in pain, yet didn't let go of his gun. He lifted his arm, preparing to fire again, but she could see he was unsteady.

"For the last time, I'm telling you to drop it," she said, teeth gritted.

He didn't drop it. She shot him in the right shoulder, holding her pistol in both hands with arms extended. He screamed, and the gun fell to the grass as he grabbed his shoulder with his left hand. She could see he was wearing surgical gloves, clear ones. Blood oozed from between his fingers; she could tell the bullet hadn't hit a major artery.

"You're completely screwed now, Jerry," she said, looking down at him as he writhed on the ground in pain. "You realize that, don't you?"

Grimacing and cursing, he answered. "Yeah," he agreed, through nearly clenched teeth. "I'm screwed, you bitch."

So this man, the one who'd harassed her, her fellow officer, was the Kapi'olani Park Slasher, the one responsible for all these murders. It was almost too much to take in.

She waited briefly, considered what to do. "Shall I call the EMTs, try to get you an ambulance, before I call for backup?" After a moment, she added, "If you don't decide right now, then I've gotta apply a tourniquet and a compress and call the EMTs, Jerry. I can't just let you bleed out."

"Okay," he managed bitterly, seeming to accept the inevitable. "Go ahead."

But he'd let go of his shoulder and was reaching his left hand toward his dropped gun. Too late, she realized she should have kicked it away. "Shit, Jerry," she barked. "Touch it and I'll shoot."

He grabbed the gun and started to lift it, a look of bizarre glee on his face. Yvonne waited a second, hoping his grasp would fail, but he kept raising his arm.

She squeezed her trigger, hitting him in the chest.

The five gunshots—the first two from Rhodes, the next three from Yvonne—woke Lily and Pat in the nearby Ala Moana condo. "Oh dear," Lily exclaimed. "We should call 911." And she did. So did a lot of the neighbors.

Yvonne was there to greet the other cops when they arrived. Rhodes was dead. The victim in the body bag had earned him, posthumously, the new Hawai'i serial killer record of seven, breaking his own prior record of six.

The only person to whom Yvonne ever told the entire story, much later and tremulously, was Kawika. Like Keoni Parkes and Emma Phillips—and like Fortunato's killer years before—she needed to confide in someone after taking a life. Unlike Keoni, she made a sound choice of confidant, but just like Emma, she took her time confiding, replaying the awful night in her mind as she described it to Kawika.

Even before she told it all to Kawika, he and the whole department already knew the basics. Jerry had been using his police cruiser to transport the bodies. He drained them first, then carried them in body bags he'd stolen from the EMTs. He'd fitted his trunk with a plastic liner he would wash off if any remaining blood managed to leak from the body bags, but a careful inspection afterward suggested none ever did, or else he'd been very thorough in his cleaning. After dumping the corpses, he'd gotten rid of the body bags somehow. The used ones were never found, but the others eventually turned up in a storage locker he'd rented under a fake name.

Neither Kawika nor anyone else at HPD had a satisfactory answer for why Rhodes had killed his randomly selected victims. What had motivated him? It couldn't have been that he just enjoyed killing people; he had hundreds of square miles of forest and jungle and swamps in which he could have disposed of bodies and never been detected. Yet he chose major downtown parks. Kawika guessed that Yvonne's original speculation had been right: the killer had been taunting all of them, proving his brain power outmatched theirs, enjoying watching as the entire task force floundered. Jerry must have gotten added satisfaction, Kawika thought, from using his police cruiser as a secret hearse.

Kawika listened to Yvonne's account of the shooting without expression or comment, then gave her a long hug, not letting go while she wept from relief. He was still in a fragile emotional state himself, and her tearfulness nearly triggered his.

"I'm sorry for what you had to go through," he finally said. "I'm proud of you for solving the case—truly. Chance played a part; it almost always does. You were brave, and thank God you were a good shot. The Slasher was the biggest homicide case in city history, and you put an end to it. Plus you saved a lot of lives, Yvonne. He wouldn't have stopped killing, and who knows if we'd ever have caught him."

"Thank you, Kawika," she said, sniffling.

"But Yvonne," he cautioned. "Try not to let it happen again, okay? You don't ever want to shoot a second cop."

What Kawika didn't share with her—he wasn't ready—was the oppressive and inescapable personal responsibility he felt for the Slasher killings. It was he who'd brought Rhodes to Honolulu. He hadn't failed to quiz Rhodes about the shooting in Griffith Park; Rhodes's unsparing self-criticism had simply disarmed him.

"I really screwed up," Rhodes had told Kawika. "And it wasn't a small mistake—it was the worst kind of mistake. I'd never shot anyone, never fired my gun on the job. I could've tried for his legs. It might have taken a few shots; he was zigzagging and I was running too. Still, I could've stopped before I shot and probably brought him down without killing him. But there was a lot of brush, it was dark, and I was nervous and shaky and desperate not to let him get away. This was the Griffith Park killer! So me, the experienced homicide detective, the guy who always got top grades for marksmanship, in the heat of the moment I shot him in the torso—just one shot! And I killed him. I've kicked myself about it ever since."

"Well, we learn more from mistakes than from successes," Kawika had reassured him. "So welcome to Honolulu. I'm glad to have you."

Kawika had accepted Rhodes's account. He'd grabbed at the chance to add a celebrated homicide detective to the force. Now he tortured himself with questions, including whether his ambition to become chief, or some related inattention, might have added to his haste and sloppiness in recruiting this monster. He knew the self-doubt would never go away.

He also found he couldn't let the matter go. So weeks after Rhodes's death, Kawika called the head of homicide at LAPD again, the one who'd been Rhodes's boss and said nothing to warn Kawika off him when Kawika had first inquired.

"I'm sorry about that," Kawika's LAPD counterpart told him. "When someone leaves, our lawyers won't let us do more than confirm his or her rank and dates of employment, so we don't get sued. But now Rhodes is dead, I'll tell you this: we never completely believed him about that shooting in Griffith Park. His story sounded too neat. Yet when we looked into it, very quietly, we couldn't pin anything on him either. It was all murky. Still, some of us suspected Rhodes might have been the serial killer himself. I'm not saying he *was*. I'm just saying the killings stopped when Rhodes left. The guy he shot might just have been in the wrong place at the wrong time."

This disturbing information only served to agitate Kawika further. But he could think of nothing more to do, nothing that would offer him any peace of mind.

* * *

An HPD review established that Yvonne had fired in self-defense, since Rhodes had fired twice before the shot that killed him. The forensics team decided to overlook why Yvonne hadn't kicked Jerry's gun away once he'd dropped it from his right hand. Dr. Noriko Yoshida—"Three shots, Kyu? Two while he was lying on the ground?"—also required a forceful talking-to from Kyu Sakamoto. When she resisted, Sakamoto reminded Dr. Yoshida that HPD guessed it was she who'd been providing off-the-record information on Keoni Parkes and the Slasher case to Zoë Akona and Bernard Scully.

Yvonne received separate HPD and city commendations for her bravery, her marksmanship, and for bringing the notorious Kapiʻolani Park Slasher case to an end. But Sakamoto advised her privately that she should start thinking of moving on. "You shot and killed an HPD officer," he said. "Jerry was a bad guy, a serial killer, so you're in the clear. But people may think, given your marksmanship, that you could've wounded him again instead of killing him. In any event, Yvonne, you're now a cop killer. Everywhere you go, you'll be the cop who shot a cop."

Yvonne was despondent at Sakamoto's statement. *The cop who shot a cop.* So that's how she'd be known. Never mind that she had taken out a serial killer. To the public and local officials, she might be a hero. But within the department, she could become an outcast, a pariah. She believed that was what Sakamoto's words foretold. After thinking it over, carefully considering her options, she reluctantly decided she would probably have to quit the force. But then, over on the Big Island, her circumstances unexpectedly changed.

* * *

Chief Ana Carvalho held a press conference in Hilo. She had, she said, a number of important announcements. Terry Tanaka, hands clasped before him, stood beside her on the dais as she spoke. Both of them were in full uniform, even wearing their hats. Tanaka had what looked like several athletic medals hanging from his neck on aloha-patterned lanyards. Behind them on the dais, poster-sized photographic portraits of two smiling subjects rested on easels. One was Kawika, the other Elle. Elle's portrait was draped in black tapa cloth.

"What the fuck is this show?" Zoë Akona whispered to her seatmate. "Carvalho has something up her sleeve."

Once the audience had settled down, the chief announced that detectives from Hilo and Honolulu had determined that Dr. Emma Phillips, maiden name Emma Gray, had killed not only Keoni Parkes and Elianna Azevado da Silva, as previously announced, but also D. K. Parkes, Keoni's father, in 2002. The motive for the Parkes killings had been revenge in both cases. The father and son had murdered Emma's father, Thomas Gray of Puakō, back in 2000.

Thus, the chief said, the long-unresolved D. K. Parkes case could now be officially closed at last, and the accidental drowning of Thomas Gray would be reclassified as a homicide. But the sad tale also served as an object lesson, the chief added. Emma Gray Phillips, twisted and consumed by anger and hate, had assigned herself the roles of judge, jury, and executioner, the chief said, and in so doing Emma had destroyed a promising career, the gifts she might yet have brought to astronomy, the lives of three other human beings, and in the end, herself.

"Please," the chief said. "Let's learn from this. Always remember: leave law enforcement to the professionals, all right?"

Next, she announced that she'd conducted a top-to-bottom review of the 2002 Ralph Fortunato murder investigation. That investigation had been led by the then captain Teruo "Terry" Tanaka and the then Hawai'i County homicide detective Kawika Wong, now the chief of homicide detectives for HPD. And her official review had conclusively determined that the confessed and convicted murderer Michael Cushing, acting through his hired hit man Roger "Rocco" Preston, had indeed been responsible as charged for Fortunato's murder, despite suggestions to the contrary in the press and from ex-convict Cushing himself. The physical evidence against Cushing, in addition to his guilty plea in court, was overwhelming, she said, and nothing in the voluminous record of the investigation suggested any other individual was the killer.

It was unfortunate, Chief Carvalho remarked as an aside, that public resources had needed to be devoted to an internal review of a twelve-year-old case at a time when two high-profile murders, those of Keoni Parkes and Elle da Silva, demanded the attention of the county's detectives, including the highest-ranking one, Major Tanaka. Nonetheless, she said, a thorough investigation had been compelled by the accusations and warranted in order to assure public confidence in the county's police.

"I can't fucking believe this," gasped Zoë Akona to her seatmate. "She's covering up the cover-up! There's no way she can get away with this. No fucking way!"

Chief Carvalho continued. "Next," she told the audience, without pausing or inviting questions, "I spent the day yesterday in Honolulu with the mayor of that great city. She has authorized me to announce here today that beginning next month, I will become the new chief of police for the City and County of Honolulu, where I was deputy chief until I came here. Leaving the Big Island, which in a short time I've grown to love, is painful for me.

"But," she went on, raising her hand and one finger, "the mayor appealed directly to my sense of professional duty. She made clear that had Major Kawika Wong not been seriously wounded in a shooting, from which he is recovering slowly, and had he not also had to deal with the tragic death of his dear wife and my close friend Elle da Silva, whose beautiful photo you see here behind me, the mayor would've named Major Wong, pictured here in happier days, to become the new chief in Honolulu." She paused, turning to the two portraits and extending a hand toward them briefly, palm upward.

"Unfortunately," she continued, "as you know, Major Wong is now unavailable, and the position must be filled. I'm deeply grateful and honored by the mayor's trust in me, especially since I was not her first choice. I intend to make her proud, and to welcome Major Wong, my former longtime detective partner at the Honolulu Police Department, to join me again at HPD, this time as deputy chief, as soon as he's recovered."

At this news, the stirring of the audience and the flashes of the photographers intensified. The chief raised her voice in order to be heard. "Hold on," she implored. "I'm not done yet!" The crowd quieted a bit. "I also want to announce," she continued, still having to raise her voice a little, "that the mayor of our own County of Hawai'i, here in Hilo, has authorized me to announce that he has agreed with my recommendation and has chosen Major Tanaka to replace me as interim chief of police for Hawai'i County."

Chief Carvalho paused to look at Tanaka with a warm smile before turning back to the microphone. "Major Tanaka is our department's most senior serving officer," she went on, "and he is still just as smart and effective as ever. As you all know, by quick thinking he recently saved the life of Major Wong, with assistance from Detectives Tommy Kekoa and Ku'ulei Wong, an action for which all three have received well-deserved decorations from the governor, the county, and our department." She reached over and lifted the medals hanging down from the neck of Tanaka, who looked slightly embarrassed.

"Major Tanaka will be a superb leader of this department," the chief concluded. "I could not leave it in better hands until my permanent replacement is found." This time she shook hands with Tanaka and held the pose in a photo-worthy tableau. But she didn't ask him to speak. After they'd smiled for the cameras, the two left the dais without taking questions and walked down separate hallways to their respective offices.

Tanaka closed his office door and called Kawika, who was in Puakō recuperating. Kawika was astonished at the news.

"I can't believe this," he said. "I mean, the outcome seems great for you and me, better than we could have hoped. But why did she clear us?"

Tanaka chuckled. "Well," he said, "consider the position she found herself in after you were shot. Suddenly you were in no shape to take the job in Honolulu, and she decided she wanted it. I don't know what she did to get it, but she must've had some powerful leverage with the mayor, who's apparently known not to like Ana very much." Kawika let Tanaka continue, deciding not to reveal Ana's leverage over the mayor. *J. Ana Hoover after all*, he thought to himself.

"But even so," Tanaka explained, "she couldn't very well become chief in Honolulu if she trashed you and me in her report. We're both heroes at the moment—and you especially, over in Honolulu. You solved the notorious Keoni Parkes murder and nearly got killed for your trouble. And I led the posse that saved you."

"Sergeant Preston of the Yukon," Kawika murmured.

Tanaka didn't pause. "Plus, of course, everyone is still mourning Elle, so Ana would've run up against a lot of sympathy for you if she'd done anything else. But in order to clear us, Ana couldn't leave the D. K. Parkes matter hanging. Either you and I covered up for the killer or we didn't. That was Ana's problem. Pinning D. K.'s murder on Emma solved the problem. Fortunately for Ana, it turned out Emma actually was on the Big Island at the time of D. K.'s death, clearing up some matters of her father's estate.

"And Emma was a powerful woman—powerful physically. Remember what you said when you met her, that she looked like someone from the U.S. Olympic team? She dumped Keoni's body in Kapiʻolani Park, and she carried Elle's body into that jungle here in Hilo. So Carvalho had no trouble suggesting that Emma was certainly strong enough to throw D. K. off Shark Cliff. Emma had a habit of making her victims look like somebody else's, Ana decided to say. You know: *Emma copied the Shark Cliff killers with D. K., and she copied the Slasher with Keoni.* So Ana was able to tie up everything with a bow."

"Amazing," Kawika said.

"Plus, I have to tell you," Tanaka went on, "Ana really despises that reporter Zoë Akona. She told me, 'It's my investigation, and I'm not going to give that woman even one crumb.' Of course, Ana used a different word than *woman*."

Kawika was still disbelieving. "But she was so harsh about what you and I did."

Again Tanaka laughed, and then exclaimed, "Right! And I told her to her face, 'You realize, Ana, that what you're doing to Emma Phillips, pinning a murder on her that she didn't commit, is no better than what I did to Michael Cushing—an act you were going to fire me for, remember, years after the fact?' And you know what she said? She said, 'It's no better, but it's no worse either. Emma's not suffering any consequence, just like Cushing didn't. And just like Cushing, Emma actually was a murderer too.'"

"Wow," Kawika responded. "I don't know what else to say, Terry. I never expected any of this. It's still hard for me to comprehend."

But Tanaka *did* know what else to say. "Kawika," he began, "I know it's early still. But I've talked to our mayor here in Hilo, and even though Ana announced my post is just temporary, in fact the mayor's going to make me chief permanently, once Ana's off the island. Permanently, that is, until I retire, which is still about five years away."

"That's great, Terry. Really great. You deserve it, and there's no one who'd be better."

"Mahalo," Tanaka said, "but that's not why I'm telling you, Kawika. I know you might decide to hang it up, being a cop. And no one would blame you if you're sick of homicide. I also know what I can offer you is nothing compared with being chief of police in Honolulu, or even deputy. But I'd like you to come to Hilo and join me anyway. Join me and your cousin Kuʻulei. I'd like you to become chief of detectives for Hawaiʻi County, take the job I've got now. You don't have to decide right away. I'll keep the spot open as long as you like."

In his weakened emotional state, Kawika found something wet on his cheek. That had happened a lot since Elle's death, as if his eyes had a small leak. "Terry," he replied, with forced composure. "You don't have to make me chief of anything. Just let me come work for you again. I'd like to come back, Terry. I want to come home."

Days later, having thought about it, Kawika called Tanaka and added a condition: "I need to be able to bring my Honolulu trainee with me. I need Yvonne Ivanovna."

"Of course," Tanaka replied. "I'd be delighted. She and Ku'ulei can talk story about shooting bad guys, maybe teach us some things."

* * *

Kawika gave up the job and condo in Honolulu. He didn't give up being a detective, and he didn't give up homicide. He found a small apartment in Hilo and kept the Puakō house for weekends and occasions when work took him to the other side of the island.

He also spent a lot of time with his recovering colleague Tommy Kekoa up in Waimea. And one day Kawika sat down with Tommy and told him who'd killed Ralph Fortunato and D. K. Parkes, and why. It wasn't Thomas Gray's children, as Tommy had guessed that evening in Puakō. It wasn't even just one of them—the late Dr. Emma Gray Phillips—as Ana Carvalho had said publicly.

"I can't explain why I didn't tell you when I was twenty-nine," Kawika said. "You were my best friend and the one person in the world I could have told. God knows it was no fun carrying the secret around with me until Elle *made* me tell her. I apologize, Tommy. I'm so sorry. Truly."

Tommy appeared moved. "Kawika," he said, "I forgive you for having been young. You should forgive yourself too."

At the spot where Elle had lain in a shallow grave, Kawika built a small cairn with rocks he'd selected from the slopes of Mauna Kea and the beach at Puakō. He didn't know what else to do. He attached no sign to the cairn, leaving it with no indication to others of its significance, although he cut and maintained a narrow path through the jungle to reach it. He visited it whenever he was in Hilo, almost ritually and always alone.

Kawika finally staged Elle's memorial service in Honolulu, and was even able to join the many other speakers in celebrating her life. Afterward, he and Ku'ulei, sitting astride surfboards, scattered Elle's ashes at sea in a simple Hawaiian ceremony, casting flowers on the water and reciting the Lord's Prayer together in Hawaiian, Kawika intoning the soothing and sonorous words Ku'ulei had taught him in preparation for their somber little voyage. As Kawika paddled back to shore, he resolved to resume surfing again, just to be with Elle on waters now imbued with her spirit.

Shortly after he'd done all that, Kawika took a final step. He tracked down Sammy Kā'ai in retirement and suggested they go have a beer. "Time we made up, don't you think?" he asked Sammy. Overcome, Sammy collapsed against Kawika and clutched at him, startling Kawika by beginning to sob.

Tanaka, for his part, finally got the records from Elle's phone—about two weeks after Emma Gray Phillips was already dead. The only unexplained call had come from a pay phone outside the KTA grocery in Waimea on the afternoon Elle had disappeared. Tanaka could guess who'd placed it. He saw no point in trying to dust the phone for prints.

* * *

A month or so after Ana Carvalho's last press conference in Hilo, Zoë Akona was surprised to be offered, unsolicited and out of the blue, an eleven PM television news anchor job in Sacramento by a local network affiliate. Despite the dizzying salary and benefits the station proposed, even hinting they might listen if she asked for more, Zoë was undecided about leaving Hawai'i, about giving up her just-launched profession as a print journalist and particularly as a reporter—something she knew a TV news anchor job, especially the eleven PM slot, didn't offer in the modern era of talking heads.

Her indecision lasted until the TV station manager, in his effort to persuade her, told her she'd been suggested for the job by an old friend from his Honolulu TV days, the new chief of police, Ana Carvalho. Chief Carvalho had called him, he said, after watching the late-night news on his station when she happened to be passing through the city a few weeks earlier.

Hearing this, Zoë called Chief Carvalho and, to her surprise, readily got through to her. "Why did you tell a Sacramento TV station they should hire me?" she asked. "I mean, it's a remarkable opportunity, and I'm grateful. I'm just surprised you told them about me. You didn't even tell *me*."

"They need more racial diversity, Zoë," Ana replied evenly. "And the *Star-Advertiser* has plenty of Hawaiian reporters already. Plus, at the reception after my swearing-in, I had a nice chat with Bernie Scully. Bernie's an old friend, and it's great for him professionally, of course, that someone he knows personally is now chief. He was also a good friend of Elle da Silva's, like me. Spoke to Elle's journalism class and all that; maybe you first encountered him there? Anyway, Bernie and I talked about your career, and he suggested you need a little more experience. A few days later, he called to say that the managing editor's taking you off the police beat, maybe moving you to high school sports for a bit."

That was enough; Zoë understood everything she needed to know. "Ah," she said. "I just might take that job in Sacramento. Mahalo, Chief."

"Happy to help," the chief replied.

* * *

Out of consideration for Kawika's feelings, Patience Quinn left him alone. She did not forget about him. She sent him a brief note of condolence for Elle and a longer one for her old friend Jarvis. But otherwise, she decided that for once she should live up to her given name and wait.

She never stopped faulting herself for failing to follow up on the note she'd written to herself, while sitting with Jarvis, to find out what had become of Thomas Gray's children. Might Elle have been saved if she had? Patience often wondered about that, especially when she couldn't sleep, alone in her bed at her Mauna Kea house, watching as her ceiling fan turned slowly overhead.

She didn't know what the future might hold, and she didn't try to affect it. Not consciously, anyway. She finished her article on the TMT controversy and sold it to the *Washington Post*, where despite prominent placement in the Sunday edition, it attracted little attention or comment. That didn't trouble Patience much. By the time her TMT piece appeared, she had already immersed herself in researching and writing a respectful and ultimately highly regarded article for the *Atlantic* on the fascinating life and sad death of best-selling author Elianna Azevado da Silva. The article depicted Elle as a brilliant and beautiful young college professor, beloved by her students, and as a gifted writer who under the pen name Ellen Silver had pioneered the gritty detective fiction genre that others called Hawaiian noir but Elle herself had called Hawaiian realism.

The article's title, which the *Atlantic* editors and not Patience chose, was "A Shallow Grave in Hilo." She didn't like it, because her article focused on Elle's life, her books, and her teaching, not her murder. "Besides," Patience asked her editor, "how many people on the mainland—I mean, the *continent*—have ever heard of Hilo?"

Acknowledgments

My heartfelt thanks to:

My Big Island ʻohana—Carolyn Wong, Haia Auweloa, Kuʻulei Kaʻaukai, and Grace Auweloa—for inspiration, guidance, hōʻihi, aloha, and names for the Hawaiian characters.

Gail Mililani Makuakāne-Lundin, for reviewing the manuscript more than once and checking all matters of Hawaiian language, history, and culture; and for allowing me literary license on matters other than the language, to the Third Renaissance of which she and her colleagues at UH Hilo's Hawaiian Language program tirelessly devote themselves.

Noe Noe Wong-Wilson, a Hawaiian leader in the effort to protect Mauna Kea throughout the long-running TMT controversy, for teaching me some of what the protectors of Mauna Kea endeavor to teach Kawika in this book.

Todd Shumway, for reviewing drafts of the manuscript and helping me with matters of local Hawaiian and Big Island custom, parlance, idiom, and geography.

Jane Lasswell Hoff, a Hilo-based forensic anthropologist, author, and historian, for generously tutoring me on matters within and without her specialties.

Professor Em de Pilis, for her detective fiction set in Hawaiian universities and for providing the inspiration for Elle da Silva.

Barbara J. Anderson, who by dint of relentless urging persuaded me to write about Kawika Wong in the first place.

James Fallows, without whose assistance and support I would neither have become nor remained a writer of books.

Jonathan Moore, aka James Kestrel, my guide to Honolulu, for inspiring me with his superb *Five Decembers*, for his friendship, and for making me laugh.

Astronomers Paula Szkody and Donald Brownlee of the University of Washington, for friendship and suggestions, and for cheerfully allowing me to name a decommissioned Mauna Kea observatory for them.

Other astronomers in Hawai‘i and Washington who helped educate me about the TMT, but who asked not to be named.

Art Brodsky, for his thoughtful suggestions on an early version of the manuscript.

Emma Kellogg, for excellent research on matters related to the TMT.

K. M. Valentine, for *Hilo: Images of America*, containing the quotation from the Reverend Titus Coan.

Linda Campbell, for revising the maps from *Bones of Hilo* and for adding the map of Honolulu.

Sara J. Henry, my editor, for her *very* firm hand on the tiller, steering this tale to much smoother waters than the confused seas in which she first found it.

The wonderfully supportive and helpful people at Crooked Lane Books, Mikaela Bender, Dulce Botello, Rachel Keith, Matthew Martz, Rebecca Nelson, Thaisheemarie Fantauzzi Perez, Madeline Rathle, and Melissa Rechter.

Anne Depue, my literary agent, for finding patience where no ordinary mortal could, and for sticking with Kawika and me through plenty of pilikia.

Finally, to Heather Redman, Ian Redman, Graham Redman, and Jing Redman for putting up with me while I write, and for discerning when a hug or a wide berth may be the better thing to give me at any given moment.

If errors remain after all this generous assistance, they are mine alone.

—Eric Redman
Hilo, Kawaihae,
Honolulu & Seattle
2021–2023